1001 Dark Nights Compilation 26

1001 Dark Nights Compilation 26

Four Novellas
By
Larissa Ione
Susan Stoker
Joanna Wylde
and
Carly Phillips

1001 Dark Nights: Compilation 26
ISBN 978-1-951812-61-4

Published by Evil Eye Concepts, Incorporated

Table of Contents

One Thousand and One Dark Nights

Once upon a time, in the future…

I was a student fascinated with stories and learning. I studied philosophy, poetry, history, the occult, and the art and science of love and magic. I had a vast library at my father's home and collected thousands of volumes of fantastic tales.

I learned all about ancient races and bygone times. About myths and legends and dreams of all people through the millennium. And the more I read the stronger my imagination grew until I discovered that I was able to travel into the stories... to actually become part of them.

I wish I could say that I listened to my teacher and respected my gift, as I ought to have. If I had, I would not be telling you this tale now.
But I was foolhardy and confused, showing off with bravery.

One afternoon, curious about the myth of the Arabian Nights, I traveled back to ancient Persia to see for myself if it was true that every day Shahryar (Persian: شهریار*, "king") married a new virgin, and then sent yesterday's wife to be beheaded. It was written and I had read, that by the time he met Scheherazade, the vizier's daughter, he'd killed one thousand women.*

Something went wrong with my efforts. I arrived in the midst of the story and somehow exchanged places with Scheherazade – a phenomena that had never occurred before and that still to this day, I cannot explain.

Now I am trapped in that ancient past. I have taken on Scheherazade's life and the only way I can protect myself and stay alive is to do what she did to protect herself and stay alive.

Every night the King calls for me and listens as I spin tales. And when the evening ends and dawn breaks, I stop at a point that leaves him breathless and yearning for more. And so the King spares my life for one more day, so that he might hear the rest of my dark tale.

As soon as I finish a story... I begin a new one... like the one that you, dear reader, have before you now.

Cipher
A Demonica Underworld Novella
By Larissa Ione

1001
DARK
NIGHTS
CIPHER
A Demonica Underworld Novella
LARISSA
IONE
NEW YORK TIMES BESTSELLING AUTHOR

Acknowledgments from the Author

As always, I went to send out a huge thank you to everyone on the 1001 Dark Nights team. I'm blessed to be working with some of the smartest, savviest, and most supportive women in the business. Thank you, ladies!

Glossary

The Aegis—Society of human warriors dedicated to protecting the world from evil. Recent dissension among its ranks reduced its numbers and sent The Aegis in a new direction.

Fallen Angel—Believed to be evil by most humans, fallen angels can be grouped into two categories: True Fallen and Unfallen. Unfallen angels have been cast from Heaven and are earthbound, living a life in which they are neither truly good nor truly evil. In this state, they can, rarely, earn their way back into Heaven. Or they can choose to enter Sheoul, the demon realm, in order to complete their fall and become True Fallens.

Harrowgate—Vertical portals, invisible to humans, used to travel between locations on Earth and Sheoul. A very few beings can summon their own personal Harrowgates.

Inner Sanctum—A realm within Sheoul-gra that consists of five Rings, each housing the souls of demons categorized by their level of evil as defined by the Ufelskala. The Inner Sanctum is run by the fallen angel Hades and his staff of wardens, all fallen angels. Access to the Inner Sanctum is strictly limited, as the demons imprisoned within can take advantage of any outside object or living person in order to escape.

Memitim—Earthbound angels assigned to protect important humans called Primori. Memitim remain earthbound until they complete their duties, at which time they Ascend, earning their wings and entry into Heaven. Until recently, all Memitim were fathered by Azagoth and raised by humans, but they are now considered a class of angel that can be born and raised in Heaven.

Primori—Humans and demons whose lives are fated to affect the world in some crucial way.

Radiant—The most powerful class of Heavenly angel in existence. Unlike other angels, Radiants wield unlimited power in all known realms and can travel freely through much of Sheoul. The designation is awarded to only one angel at a time. Two can never exist simultaneously, and they cannot be destroyed except by God or Satan. The fallen angel equivalent is a Shadow Angel.

Shadow Angel—The most powerful class of fallen angel in existence, save Satan. Unlike other fallen angels, Shadow Angels can wield unlimited power in all known realms and they possess the ability to gain entrance into Heaven. The designation is awarded to only one angel at a time, and they can never exist without their Radiant equivalent. Shadow Angels cannot be destroyed except by God or Satan.

Sheoul—Demon realm some call Hell. Located on its own plane deep in the bowels of the Earth, accessible to most only by Harrowgates and hellmouths.

Sheoul-gra—A realm that exists independently of Sheoul, it is overseen by Azagoth, also known as the Grim Reaper. Within Sheoul-gra is the Inner Sanctum, where demon souls go to be kept in torturous limbo until they can be reborn.

Sheoulic—Universal demon language spoken by all, although many species also speak their own native language.

Ter'taceo— Demons who can pass as human, either because their species is naturally human in appearance, or because they can shapeshift into human form.

Ufelskala—A scoring system for demons, based on their degree of evil. All supernatural creatures and evil humans can be categorized into the five Tiers, with the Fifth Tier comprising the worst of the wicked.

Chapter One

Blood sport.

Seriously. What the hell?

Lyre watched the spectacle in the arena below, a death match between a fallen angel and a Nightlash demon, the outcome of which would normally be predictable. Fallen angels were a thousand times more powerful than any Nightlash.

But this fallen angel's wings—and source of his mystical powers—had been bound, limiting his abilities, and the Nightlash possessed an *aural*, one of the few reliably lethal weapons against an angel, fallen *or* Heavenly.

The whole thing was so...stupid. The point of this particular battle was to get the fallen angel to cooperate, which he wouldn't be able to do if he was dead.

She gripped the railing so hard her nails left dents in the wood as the Nightlash, his armor dented from Cipher's fists and feet, spun in a blur, slashing at Cipher's bare chest. Cipher fell back with a hiss, and the stench of burnt angel flesh carried to her nose.

"Dammit, Bael," she muttered. "He should have gotten armor too."

The cold air surrounding Bael stirred like the fog off dry ice. He didn't like his decisions being questioned. "Cipher should feel grateful that I allowed him to wear anything at all."

Sure, because jeans were great fighting gear. But they did look amazing on the guy, ripped and stained as they were. Months of captivity read like a horror novel on his pants, but the real story was told in the spark of resistance in Cipher's watchful blue eyes and the cocksure way he carried his lean, muscular body.

He hadn't broken yet, but he would. At least, he would if Bael didn't get him killed first.

Lyre glared at Bael, an ancient fallen angel whose impulsive cruelty and recklessness made him as stupid as it did dangerous. But his chaotic, bloodthirsty nature was exactly what had allowed him to excel as one of Satan's top generals.

"If Cipher dies, you lose your best shot at getting Azagoth's attention," she pointed out.

"Oh, I have The Grim Reaper's full attention." Next to her, Bael smiled coldly, his ebony gaze fixed on the battle below. "And Cipher isn't my only ace, my love."

She forced a smile of her own, but damn, she hated it when he called her, or any female, that. He knew nothing of love. All he knew was hate.

"I'm sure you do," she said, hoping he didn't notice the catch in her voice as Cipher dove to the blood-soaked ground to avoid a swing.

Cipher rolled and swept out his leg, catching the Nightlash behind the knees. Bael nodded in approval as the Nightlash hit the ground hard on his back. The five hundred or so demons in the stands booed. Demons always sided with demons over fallen angels.

Lyre generally didn't give a shit either way, but as Cipher wrenched the *aural* away from the Nightlash, she gave a mental sigh of relief.

Not that she gave a shit about Cipher, of course. She hadn't known Cipher when they'd been Heavenly angels, so she had no prior relationship with him, and while she hadn't been a fallen angel for much longer than he had, she already knew to never get attached to anyone. Sheoul, the demon realm humans called Hell, was a violent place, and no one could be trusted.

So while she couldn't afford to care about Cipher, she did like her job as his handler. She'd balked when Bael had first tasked her with what she'd viewed as a punishment. But it turned out that being assigned to gain Cipher's trust had been a welcome break from her usual duties as Bael's errand girl.

Errand girl.

So mundane. Such a waste of her talents. So not the reason she'd willingly submitted to one of Hell's most powerful warlords after losing her wings.

She wanted revenge on a lot of people, and if Bael played the board right he could make it happen.

But not if he kept sacrificing game pieces.

Cipher plunged the *aural* into the Nightlash's throat, and the crowd erupted in cheers as blood spewed from the demon's mouth. They might root for the demon during the fight, but they were happy to see anyone die.

"He's good," Bael grunted, a rare note of admiration in his hell-smoked voice. "But his hand-to-hand combat abilities are not the skills I need from him." He turned to her, his eyes glinting with black ice, his handsome face and mundane slicked-back chestnut hair concealing the monster that lived behind the mask. "I need what's in his head. I'm growing impatient."

"Impatient?" She snorted. "You once spent an entire century torturing someone for information."

His gaze turned inward, his full lips twisting into a cruel smile as he relived the incident she'd only read about in the history books of Heaven's Akashic Library.

"That was back when the idea of Armageddon was merely a dream," he said. "Now we know we have fewer than a thousand years to prepare for Satan's release from the prison that Revenant, that fucking traitor, put him in."

It was best to not let Bael focus on his hatred for Revenant, especially since, publicly, he professed support for the current ruler of Hell. If he realized he'd spoken aloud, he'd punish her for his own mistake.

The narcissistic asshole.

Quickly, she diverted his attention back to the victor of the fight and gestured to Cipher as he shoved to his feet in the arena below. He'd shown such remarkable resilience no matter what Bael threw at him—extra remarkable, given that with his wings bound, his body's natural ability to rapidly regenerate should have been reduced. But somehow, he healed quickly and maintained his wits.

"Time is short," she admitted. "But Cipher has been here only a few months. It could take decades, even centuries, to turn him. You knew that. It's that very quality, his loyalty to Azagoth, that you desire for yourself. If you want it, you'll have to break him slowly."

"It's not just his loyalty I desire. I need information." He reached out and dragged a finger along the length of her black braid.

She said nothing, gave no reaction as his knuckles brushed the exposed skin of her shoulder, leaving a stinging trail of welts everywhere he touched her. Today was not the day to have worn her favorite camo-print tank top. At least she'd gone for black tactical pants instead of shorts.

"Since you can't seem to get what I need from Cipher, I'm sending in Flail. Maybe she can seduce him into giving me what I want."

Lyre bit back a curse. Of course it would be Flail. That skank always seemed to find a way to screw her.

"She's welcome to *try* to get something from him," she said. "But he hates her for betraying him. If not for her, he'd still be comfy-cozy in Sheoul-gra with his friends and working for Azagoth. The only reason he'll lay his hands on her is to strangle her."

"If he'll give up the information I need, he's welcome to throttle her. Hell, I'd like to see that." He gestured to the guards below, signaling them to take Cipher back to his cell. "Tell him I'll make that deal."

Well, now. Wasn't that interesting? Sycophantic fallen angels like Flail didn't come a dime a dozen, so for Bael to be cool with her death in trade for intel, it meant he was either desperate or Cipher held some seriously important information. She wondered if Cipher would consider the offer. Even under torture, Cipher hadn't spilled anything of use against Azagoth, but he might just change his mind if he were allowed to kill the female who was responsible for every minute of his misery.

Lyre pondered that while she watched as he was escorted, limping, from the arena, blood streaming from dozens of wounds. His blond hair, shorn short when he'd first arrived, hung around his cheeks in limp, damp tangles. He shoved it out of his eyes and scanned the crowd, his gaze rapidly zeroing in and locking with Bael's.

The *fuck you, I'm not dead* message in Cipher's expression was unmistakable.

Lyre's lips twitched in amusement she hoped Bael didn't notice. But Cipher did.

His eyes shifted to her, and was it her imagination, or did he look...disappointed?

Her breath caught. If he was disappointed to see her at this spectacle, it must mean that he was softening toward her. Maybe she could finally get some useful information from him. Something that would earn her Bael's favor and help her get much desired revenge.

It was a small hope, but it was something.

Bael's hand clamped around the back of her neck, startling her so thoroughly she nearly yelped. "You need to step up your game, Lyre. I expected more from you."

Nettle pain stabbed into her skin like a million biting ants. He could turn it off if he desired, and it pissed her off that he chose not to. She'd served him faithfully for more than two years now, and she'd been patient as she waited for the day he fulfilled his promise to her. The day he would deliver pain to those who were responsible for her expulsion from Heaven and the death of the male she'd loved.

But Bael's promise was taking too long.

Snarling, she twisted out of his grip and nearly collided with one of Bael's Ramreel bodyguards. The odiferous, ram-headed beast stomped his hoof in irritation, but she ignored him.

It was a little harder to ignore his barnyard stench.

"Maybe if you allowed me to do what I'm good at," she snapped, "you'd get better results and I'd be closer to getting justice."

"I don't give a hellrat's ass what you're good at." A three-eyed raven landed on the railing, and Bael reached out to stroke his pet's shimmering feathers. "What do I need an expert in demonic history for? *I* lived it. *You* learned it from books written by angels."

She'd explained this to him a million times, so hey, what was one more? "At the Academy of Angels I also studied the various political factions in Sheoul," she reminded him. "Later, I was one of the intelligence department's top analysts. It's why I came to you after I fell. I can help you build alliances with other warlords as we move toward a confrontation with Heaven. I know who supports Revenant and who plots a coup against him to seat themselves or to re-seat Satan—"

Pain went off like a bomb in her head, a sudden crack of agony that made her empathize with broken eggs. But instead of yolk, warm, sticky blood oozed from her nose and ears.

Bael's voice scrambled her brain inside her shattered skull. "You do not speak of such things in the open, stupid whore!"

"I'm sorry, my lord," she rasped, dropping to her knees as the misery wrapped around her entire body and burrowed deep into her bones. She hated submitting to him, hated being so weak and vulnerable, but she'd lived like that in Heaven too. She'd had a lot of practice. "I—I'll do better."

"Yes," he growled, "you will."

He grasped the top of her head and forced her to look up at him as he laughed, his fangs visibly throbbing as he got off on her pain.

And this, she knew all too well, was merely the foreplay.

Chapter Two

Cipher's nightmares had teeth.

Lots of them. Hell, even the dreams in which he was living in a Heavenly palace of crystal featured gaping maws lined with rows of razor sharp fangs. The only difference was that in those dreams, the teeth were beautiful instead of dripping with saliva, blood, and bits of flesh.

And the only thing worse than the nightmares was waking up.

Cipher groaned as he came to, naked except for the threadbare blanket wrapped around him on the glazed-ice floor of the cell he'd called home for...how long now? Six months? Seven? A hundred?

Fuck.

But not to be a total whiner, he did get breaks from the cell. Sometimes he got to visit the Isle of Torture, which was exactly what it sounded like. Lord Bael, the fallen angel who ruled the region, had constructed an island in the middle of a lava river and dedicated it to the art of pain. The question, every time Cipher was put in chains and led from Bael's glacial palace's dungeon to the scorched island, was whether he'd be a participant or a spectator.

Cipher generally preferred being a spectator. But every once in a while Bael would drop him into the arena and force him to fight for his life, and that...that gave him a fucking rush. Who wouldn't love a chance to brush up on fighting skills and let off some steam? Not to mention the fact that his change in status from an Unfallen angel into a True Fallen angel had given him an appetite for dishing out pain to his enemies.

Not that, as both a Heavenly and an Unfallen angel, he hadn't enjoyed serving up some well-deserved death. But now he enjoyed serving his opponents their own innards before they died.

So yeah, the arena gave him a brief taste of pleasure in this realm of perpetual misery. But even during those precious moments of ecstasy, when his opponent grunted in pain or bled from a wound, two voices whispered in his mind.

The first belonged to his buddy Hawkyn, laden with disappointment as he uttered the words Cipher imagined Hawk would say if he knew how much evil was seeping into Cipher's body with every new day spent in Sheoul.

This isn't you. You're decent. Honorable. An idiot, yes, but an honorable one. Fight it, Ciph. Don't give in to evil. You know what it did to Satan. And Lucifer. And my father.

No shit. Cipher hadn't met the first two infamous fallen angels, but he'd worked for Azagoth, the literal Grim Reaper, long enough to have seen what eons of exposure to malevolence did to a person.

And now he could add Bael and his bastard brother, Moloc, to the list of sadistic, evil-ravaged fallen angels he had firsthand experience with.

Which brought him to the second voice that spoke in his head when he was getting off on beating down demons in the arena.

Don't die, Cipher. Don't. Die. If you die in Bael's realm, your soul won't be whisked away by griminions *and taken to Azagoth. It'll be trapped here, where Bael can torture you for eternity in ways you can't even imagine.*

Lyre had told him that, but she was wrong. He *could* imagine it. He'd seen what Azagoth could do to a soul. Still, Cipher would prefer that his soul reside with Azagoth, who was an ally and the father of his best friend, rather than spend the rest of his eternal life with a sadistic motherfucker who hated him.

The sound of approaching footsteps outside his cell brought him to his feet. Maybe it was time for food. Or, more likely, it was time for another round of torture. If he was lucky, the torture would come in the form of his newest handler, a pretty raven-haired fallen named Lyre.

His pulse picked up in anticipation, which was a sad measure of how shitty Cipher's life was; he was actually looking forward to seeing one of his captors. Sure, she was gorgeous, but what intrigued Cipher most was that, unlike everyone else in Bael's realm, she hadn't gone completely rotten to the core with evil. Not yet. Which was awesome, because unlike his two handlers before her, she hadn't strung him up with razor wire and beat the shit out of him. Yes, she'd shoved him into a pit full of demonic piranha once, but only because he'd done the same to her on the first day of her assignment.

It had been his twentieth attempt at escape, and it had gone as badly as the nineteen before, ending at the wrong end of a Darquethoth torturemaster's skinning knife. The weird thing was, Lyre hadn't attended his torture. She never did.

But she'd been at the arena last night for his latest death match. Had she hoped he'd win? Or had she wanted to see him die? She'd looked like she was having fun, in any case.

Gotta love good old family entertainment in Hell. He wondered what the concessions stands served. Probably not popcorn and Red Vines.

The heavy metal lock outside his cell clanked, and the door swung open. He shoved to his feet as the hulking eight-foot tall Ramreel guard moved aside to allow his visitor to enter.

Curiosity veered sharply to rage at the sight of the flaxen-haired fallen angel who stepped inside, her thigh-high leather boots clacking on the floor as she strutted to the middle of the cell.

Flail.

She might have changed her hair color, but the she still reeked of deception. Hatred unlike anything he'd experienced before consumed him, rerouting all rational thought and leaving him with only one goal.

"*You.*" Dropping his blanket, he charged her. "You *bitch.*"

He was going to kill her with his bare hands.

He'd wrench her head from her body and impale it on that shard of ice over there, and then he'd—*holy fuck*!

A red-hot bolt of agony detonated inside his chest, blasting him backward like a rag doll. His spine crunched into the ice-glazed wall, and he crumpled to the floor. The impact shook the massive icicles that hung from the ceiling like monster fangs, and he cursed his impulsive mistake as dozens broke loose and rained down on him.

"Hello, baby," Flail purred. "It's been a while."

"It hasn't been long enough," he growled as he sat up, clutching his throbbing chest and wondering where she'd stashed the sledgehammer. "But remind me, how many months has it been since you got me dragged down to Hell?"

Demons had done the actual dragging, but she'd been the one to call them in when he left the safety of Azagoth's realm, Sheoul-gra, to help Hawkyn's sister kill a seriously dangerous demon. As a wingless, powerless Unfallen angel, he'd been exposed and vulnerable, and Bael's minions had done a grab-and-go. He'd been forced to watch helplessly as his friends ran toward him in a futile attempt to save his dumb ass. Twenty-four hours later, he'd morphed into a True Fallen angel, with fangs, wings, and no hope of Heavenly redemption.

Making it worse, the lone benefit of becoming a True Fallen was the restoration of powers, but because his wings had been bound with enchanted twine, he couldn't access either. He didn't even know what talents he'd gained. Some might be the evil counterpart to their Heavenly versions. Some might be unique to Sheoul. He had no fucking idea.

The most maddening part was how he could sense the power inside him, the strength that ran through him like lit kerosene, but he couldn't touch it. Couldn't bring it streaming to the surface in the form of a weapon or a healing wave or a telepathic conversation. It sat there, frustratingly out of reach, like a donut in the window of a closed pastry shop.

Man, he missed donuts.

"Well?" he prompted. "How many months have I been without donuts?"

"Seven, I believe." She shrugged, and one of her breasts nearly popped out of her tight crimson corset. Why did all fallen angels wear those things?

Not all. Not Lyre.

No, Lyre was all about being ready for battle, from her boots to the dagger holstered at her hip to her sexy BDU pants or cargo shorts that emphasized a seriously perfect ass. And always a tank top. She could have stepped out of an action RPG, like his Mass Effect character come to breathing, beddable life.

If his existence ever stopped sucking long enough for him to get an erection even once, she was going to provide him with some serious fantasy material.

The way Flail used to, before she turned out to be a traitorous evil slutbag.

"Seven?" He gulped a pained breath. "You don't know?"

"Like I keep track." She rolled her eyes. Her traitorous evil slutbag eyes. "You were one of dozens of Unfallen I'm contractually bound to deliver to Bael and Moloc."

The mere names of the twin fallen angels was enough to terrify any sane person, and they weren't a threat to be sneezed at.

But if they were a sneeze, Cipher's former employer was the fucking swine flu.

He allowed himself a dark smile at the knowledge that she was going to die even if it wouldn't be at his hands.

"You know you didn't betray only me," he said. "You betrayed Azagoth."

She tossed her head like a high-strung hell mare. "He's powerless outside of his realm, and I don't plan on returning."

That was where she was wrong. Dead wrong. Azagoth's reach extended far beyond the boundaries of Sheoul-gra. He couldn't leave his realm, but there was no corner of Heaven or Sheoul he couldn't touch. With eons of knowledge and secrets gleaned from the souls he interrogated, he had resources beyond her comprehension.

Not that Cipher would tell Flail that. She'd see for herself when she was pissing in those black leggings at Azagoth's feet and begging for mercy.

"Even if he doesn't kill you, you'll die eventually." He breathed deeply as the pain in his chest eased. "Your soul will belong to him."

"Not if he's no longer in charge of Sheoul-gra."

He barked out a laugh. "No longer in charge? You know something I don't?"

Azagoth had ruled Sheoul-gra for thousands of years, since the day he'd willingly given up his wings to create a holding tank for evil souls that were wreaking havoc on humans. He'd *built* Sheoul-gra and created its specialized demons, *griminions*, from the materials given to him by both Heaven and Sheoul. He wasn't going anywhere.

"I'm sure I know a lot of things you don't." She twirled a lock of hair around her finger. "For example, I know that you're going to give me the list Bael wants."

The fuck he was. The list containing the names and last known locations for all of Azagoth's children, those who didn't yet have angelic powers or knowledge that they were anything but human, was safe on his laptop. Bael might have his computer, but neither he nor his minions had been able to even open the case, let alone access the list inside.

And there was no way he was giving it up to Bael. At least, not while he retained even a sliver of his current self. His fear, his crippling fucking fear, was that he'd succumb to evil and willingly spill all of his knowledge of Azagoth and his realm. Or worse, that he himself would be stupid and arrogant enough to use his knowledge against Azagoth.

"Maybe you could tell me why he wants it," he hedged.

"Does it matter?"

"Well," he said, not bothering to hide his sarcasm, "since I doubt Bael wants the names and addresses of Azagoth's children so he can send them birthday cards, then yeah, it matters."

She thought on that for a moment, toe tapping dramatically. Once upon a time, he'd appreciated her love of theatrics in bed, but right now it was getting on his nerves.

Finally, she pasted on a smile. "Bael is planning to spoil them with ice cream and maybe a movie."

"Real sincere, Flail." He rubbed his sternum absently, the curious tingle there adding to his irritation. "Try again."

"*I'm* not the one named for being a liar."

"Lyre? Kinda random to bring her up, but now that you do, I don't trust her, either. But *she* only shoved me into a pit of flesh-eating demon fish. *You* got me dragged to Hell and destroyed my chances of getting back into Heaven."

"Pfft." She nudged his foot with her toe like one might poke a dead thing they found in the woods. "Why would you want to go back there?"

"Because," he said as he kicked her away, "—and I can't stress this enough—no one tortured me there." And what the *fuck* was up with his sternum? It wouldn't stop aching.

"Give up the list and no one will torture you here either."

Something pinched. Hard. Jerking his hand from his chest, he looked down and drew a startled breath at the weird little ivory disk stuck there, a penny-sized piece of fuckery he was sure couldn't be a good thing.

"What. The. Hell."

"Isn't it pretty? It's an *ascerdisc*. Ever heard of one?"

He had. His friends Hawkyn and Journey had shown him around Azagoth's treasure room, and they'd told him it was a mysterious fallen angel weapon so rare that they believed it to be the only one in existence.

He couldn't keep the stunned note out of his voice. "You stole it from Azagoth?"

"Oh, you simple fool. That's not how they work. The *ascerdisc* in your chest was made from my bones, and I alone can control it. If Azagoth has one, it belonged to another fallen angel." She smiled. "I'll bet everything you think you know about them is wrong. Let's see, shall we?"

Oh, shit. This was not going to be a good time. But hey, if he ever saw Hawk and Journey again, at least he could rub in how wrong they'd been.

Yup, as Hawkyn liked to say, Cipher could see the bright side of anything.

Chapter Three

Most of Journey's thousands of adult brothers and sisters thought that spying on their charges was the worst part of being a guardian angel. Specifically, a wingless Memitim guardian angel, bred to live in the human realm as they worked to earn their wings and a place in Heaven. They'd rather be fighting demons or doing research than hanging out in an invisible bubble while their Primori went about their day-to-day lives. Some didn't like feeling like voyeurs, but most were just bored out of their minds.

For Journey, spying was the *best* part of the job. Depending on who he was spying on, of course. Of his current four Primori, only one kept him entertained. The others, two human scientists who sat around in labs all day, and a werewolf construction worker with no social life, were serious yawners.

But he did have to admit to a twinge of shame for watching Declan as much as he did. The guy was his freaking brother-in-law. Which was actually how he justified staying so close. His sister, Suzanne, would be pissed if he let anything happen to the guy.

But the truth was that Declan fought demons for a living with the Demon Activity Response Team, and there was always shit going on. It was even better than *Live PD*. Much, much higher stakes.

And then there was the fact that his father had ordered him to stay close and listen closer. Azagoth had seen an opportunity to gain intel, and he'd been right. Even informal gatherings of DART members such as the one they were having now yielded tasty nuggets of information.

He braced his hip against a wall and nearly stepped on the ferret that ran under his foot. It chattered at him, and he held his breath as the critter's owner and a founding member of DART looked over from where she was seated at the dining room table with the others. Journey knew she couldn't see him, but some animals could, and that noisy little weasel was clearly one of them.

"Hey, buddy. You need to eat your dinner." Tayla scooped up the animal and set him down in the kitchen of the luxury apartment she shared with her mate, Eidolon. She nudged its dish with her foot and turned to the guys at the table. "Anyone want a beer while I'm up?"

There were three "no's" and a silent "yes" from Journey.

Arik Wagner, husband of Limos, the Horseman of the Apocalypse known as Famine, emphasized his "no" with a shake of his head as he tapped on his phone. "Did I tell you guys that Reaver came by the house last week?"

Declan gave a low whistle. He'd only been introduced to the supernatural world recently, and the newness of it still left him awestruck at times. "Must be weird to have a Radiant as a father-in-law."

"You know what's weird?" Tayla asked. "I knew Reaver back when he was a powerless Unfallen angel working at Underworld General Hospital. Now he and his brother are the most powerful angels in the universe."

Even weirder, Reaver's brother, Revenant, ruled Hell even though he wasn't technically a *fallen* angel.

Arik gave Declan a sideways glance. "My father-in-law might be an angel, but yours is the Grim Reaper. Not sure you want to be calling my situation weird."

Declan laughed. "Yeah, but my father-in-law is relegated to his realm and can't drop in anytime he wants."

"Good point," Arik conceded as he looked back down at his phone. "But Reaver's a great source of intel. When he was at the house he said he'd heard that some fallen angel named Bael is gathering Unfallens."

The very name made Journey bristle. Hawkyn suspected that Bael was behind Cipher's abduction, but they hadn't gathered any proof so far. And the bitch who'd deceived them all in order to gain their trust and get inside Sheoul-gra had disappeared without a trace and with

Cipher's laptop.

"Bael?" Kynan Morgan's battle-ravaged voice dipped even lower and rougher. "That's not good."

Arik frowned. "I didn't get a chance to ask Reaver about the guy. Who is he?"

"Bael was one of Satan's most trusted generals." Tayla sank into her seat and wiped her finger over her iPad a few times before spinning it around to Arik. "This is a sketch of him. He and his brother Moloc fell from Heaven and remained loyal to Satan until Revenant and Reaver locked him away. Together, Moloc and Bael control about a quarter of Sheoul."

They also controlled a lot of souls, and Azagoth didn't take kindly to those who denied what rightfully belonged to him. The cold war between Azagoth and the brothers had gone on for over a century, with both sides stepping up their aggressions recently.

"Are they working for Revenant now?" Declan asked. His gaze skipped over to Journey, and Journey swore the guy looked right at him before turning his attention back to Tayla.

"Unknown," Kynan said. "My intel indicates that they've agreed to recognize him as the rightful ruler of Sheoul, so if Bael is gathering Unfallens, he's doing it against Revenant's edict."

Journey had only seen Revenant once, but it had been enough to know that he would be very careful about going against anything the guy said. As a Shadow Angel who had been tutored by Satan literally since birth, he was at the top of the food chain. His power eclipsed even Azagoth's. Only a dipshit who wanted a scythe up the ass would cross him.

"Oh," Arik said as he glanced over at Declan. "Reaver also said something about Bael nabbing an Unfallen who worked inside Sheoul-gra. Thought you might want to tell Suzanne. Sounds like info Azagoth would want to know."

Journey's pulse did an excited little kick. Arik had to be talking about Cipher. Had to be.

Finally, a break.

Declan leaned back in his chair and stretched his long legs out in front of him. "I just hope it's news Azagoth wants to hear. He only yesterday reopened his realm to Memitim and a few Unfallen and fallen angels he trusts, and Suzanne said he's still in a temper over the death of one of his young children inside his realm."

"I can't believe anyone was stupid enough to infiltrate Sheoul-gra and kill a kid right under his nose," Tayla said. "When he finds out who did it..." She let out a low whistle.

Yeah, the general consensus was that Azagoth was going to go supernova on the bastard. All Memitim would. It was just last week that someone had snuck inside Sheoul-gra and slit the throat of a boy who hadn't even grown into his powers yet. He'd been taken from the human realm to a place that should have been nothing but safety, and instead, he'd lost his life within days of arrival.

Journey had no doubt that they'd learn the identity of the perpetrator, but for now he was just going to be happy that he had some information about Cipher.

Feeling hope for the first time in months, he flashed himself to Sheoul-gra's landing pad, and then he found Hawkyn and their brother Maddox exactly where he thought they'd be.

In the kitchen scarfing the Red Devil's Food Cake their sister Suzanne had promised to deliver this afternoon. Maddox had crumbs all over the front of his navy Rick and Morty T-shirt, and Hawkyn had smeared frosting on the sleeve of his leather bomber. Those two didn't need a table, they needed a trough.

"Yo," he called out. "I got a lead on Cipher." He skidded to a halt in front of them as they shoved their faces full of cake.

"Holy shit," Maddox mumbled through frosting. "You serious?"

Journey reached for a plated slice. "I was checking in on Declan while he was meeting with some DART colleagues, and they were talking about the increase in Unfallens being dragged to Sheoul."

Hawkyn drained a can of cola in half a dozen swallows and popped a perfect two-pointer in the nearby garbage pail. "DART is a demonic activity response organization. They fight demons. Why would they even care about angelic issues?"

Maddox gave Hawk a "duh" look. "Maybe because Declan's married to a Memitim?"

"Yeah, I get why *he* would be concerned, but what about the others?"

"Arik was there," Journey explained. "Reaver told him that Bael captured an Unfallen who worked in Sheoul-gra."

Hawkyn let out a nasty curse. "I knew it. That *bastard*."

"Bael?" Maddox let out a low whistle. "No one was tighter with Satan."

"Top tier evil," Hawkyn acknowledged. He turned back to Journey, his emerald eyes bright with hope. "Did Arik say anything else? Did he have a name?"

"No, but it has to be Ciph. No other Unfallen who worked for Father has gone missing."

"That's awesome." Maddox reached for the black leather duster and weapons belt slung over the counter. "Let's get him."

"Easy there, Quick Draw." Hawk shot Mad a "you're kidding, right?" look. "Do you know how big Bael's territory is? Even if we could access that part of Sheoul, we don't know where Cipher's being held." He dug his phone from his jacket pocket. "Although I do have a crude map of Bael's prison region somewhere..."

"You sure Cipher's being held?" Journey hated to even suggest it, but he'd seen what being exposed to evil did to people. "He could be with Bael voluntarily."

The temperature in the room dropped so low that Journey could see Hawkyn's breath as he lifted his gaze from his phone's screen.

"Cipher would never betray us," he said, his voice going as low as the temperature. "If he could be here, he would."

Hawk's faith in his best friend was admirable, but Journey wasn't so sure it was deserved. When an Unfallen entered Sheoul, the act completed his fall from Grace, allowing evil to fully penetrate. No matter how decent Cipher might have been as an Unfallen, evil was now a part of him. His new wings would be formed with it. His powers and abilities would all be tainted by it.

But to what degree? That was always the question when it came to fallen angels. Most had malevolence seeping from their pores and they were giant, radioactive dickbags. But a few, usually those who were only recently fallen, weren't half bad. Maybe if they got to Cipher in time, they could save him from the worst of it. Or at least hold it off for a few centuries.

"Okay, man." Journey held up his hands in a defensive gesture. "Take it easy. I just wanna address the big, awkward demon elephant in the room, you know?"

Hawkyn glared, but a moment later was back on his phone. "I've got the map, and I think I have a file that can help us." He tapped on his phone as he spoke. "Last year Cipher probed the personal networks of about a dozen of Azagoth's enemies to look for back doors into their security systems and tech."

Journey nodded excitedly, knowing where this was going. "I helped him with that. Bael was one of the targets."

"Tell me you guys breached his shit," Hawkyn said.

"We did." Journey grinned at his brothers. "Boys, I think we can help Ciph."

Journey dove into his cake with an enthusiasm that had been missing since Cipher disappeared. They were finally going to help save their friend.

But after seven months in a Hell realm, how much of Cipher would be left to save?

Chapter Four

"Say it, Cipher. Don't make me have to hurt you again."

Cipher's fiery curses didn't melt any of the ice in his cell, but they made him feel better. Flail had spent what felt like hours making him say stupid shit, because if he didn't, she punished him through the bone *ascerdisc* embedded in his skin. Which was seriously gross.

In any case, up until now he'd done what she wanted and said the stupid shit, avoiding major pain. But at some point she was going to stop toying with him and get serious about the torture.

Still, this particular sentence was especially stupid, and he'd initially refused. His chest throbbed like a sonofabitch from that little act of defiance.

"Cipher..."

"Fine." He rolled his eyes so hard it hurt. "My dick is the size of a cocktail wiener."

When she giggled and clapped, he threw his head against the wall and looked up at the remaining hundreds of icicles hanging from the cavernous ceiling, some as big as he was.

They hurt a lot when they fell.

Too bad one didn't fall on Flail.

Carefully, he shifted his weight, keeping his wing anchors from supporting too much weight. The binding rope around the base of his new fallen angel wings, deep inside his back, hurt like hell. Any pressure was agonizing. The worst part about it was that he hadn't even seen his wings yet. Bael had ordered them to be secured before they had a chance to emerge.

"How long did it take you to break, Flail?"

She blinked. "Break? No one broke me. After Heaven rejected me, I entered Sheoul willingly and proudly."

"*Rejected* you." That was too absurd to waste a laugh on. "Next you're going to say you're innocent of whatever got you kicked out."

"I wasn't innocent in the least," she said, her words clipped with irritation. "But it was still bullshit. I mean, so I killed a few humans without permission. So what? Most of them were scum. What happened to me was completely unfair."

"Unfair?" Was she insane? "Killing humans without cause or authorization is the worst offense on a long list of offenses—by far. You broke the number one rule, and you're surprised that you lost your wings?"

She made a sound of disgust. "I understand that I broke the law, but the law is ridiculous. Humans are like an infestation of insects. How can it be wrong to kill them?" He must not have schooled the shock in his expression, because she jammed her fists on her hips and scowled at him. "I'm not alone in feeling that way."

"No shit," he said. "It's kind of why Satan and his cabal of evil assholes were kicked out of Heaven."

"Thanks for the history lesson," she said dryly. "But you're clearly not grasping the size of the anti-human movement amongst Heavenly angels."

"How would you even know?" he shot back. "You've been fallen for what, eight hundred years?"

She eyed one of the icicles above, the pointiest one, and he made a mental note to avoid being under it. "That span of time is but a blink of an eye for angels. You know that. But you're wrong. I lost my wings fewer than three centuries ago."

"Yeah, well, I was in Heaven far more recently than that, and no one was talking rebellion."

Her lips, which had at one time brought him a lot of pleasure, pursed in annoyance. "They wouldn't speak openly of it. Some of the people you think you know the best probably agree with me."

He wanted to tell her how wrong she was, but now that he thought about it, he'd heard stirrings of discontent. Angels of the old guard, those who had been around since before the Earth supported life of any kind, had waited a long time for humans to prove themselves worthy. Many of those who hadn't supported Satan's rebellion and who had preached patience were beginning to rethink their positions. And younger angels who had come along later in human evolution saw only a species that was destroying itself and the planet they'd been given.

It's like humans are devolving, Tuvol, one of Cipher's oldest friends, had said once. *We had such high hopes for them, but they're a failed experiment. It's time Father ends it. The other living things on Earth will be better without their cruelty and selfishness.*

As shocked as Cipher had been, he'd written off Tuvol's opinion as non-mainstream, shared by an insignificant number of fringe malcontents whose influence was equally as insignificant.

But what if that wasn't true? What if the extremists were growing in number and influence?

"Let's say there are more of you than I think," he said. "What is it they want?"

She stared at him like he was an idiot. "How can you not know? They want the Apocalypse."

Now *that* was worthy of a bark of laughter. "I hate to tell you this, psycho, but Heaven has always been working to prevent the Apocalypse."

Flail kicked his foot again, this time harder. "The Apocalypse is inevitable, Cipher. Just as there are religious demon and human radicals who work to bring about the end days, there are angels as well."

"But the point of delaying it is to allow humans time to perfect their souls." That was the entire argument against Tuvol's "failed experiment" bullshit. Yes, humans were awful and seemed to be regressing, but they learned from the bad times—not the good ones. "To become worthy of the eternal life they'll be gifted with after they've lived several earthly lives and experienced all there is to experience."

She made a gagging gesture. "Ugh. You sound like a fucking textbook. Don't you realize that they will never succeed? Why prolong the agony? If Armageddon kicks off before humankind perfects itself, all human souls will be extinguished."

"Bullshit. When the end of days comes, all good souls will cross over, no matter whether they're perfected or not."

She shrugged. "That's what we're all told, isn't it? Now, if we're done with the theological debate, let's get back to why I'm here." She gestured to him. "Stand and strip."

Talk about a change of subject. "Thanks, but I'll pass."

"When did you get modest?"

He wasn't modest at all. He had a great body and he saw no reason to hide it. But he also saw no reason to comply with this particular demand.

He'd always been bullheaded.

And it was exactly that trait that had gotten him kicked out of Heaven.

"I'm not playing anymore, Cipher." A wave of agony spread from the *ascerdisc*. He clutched at his chest and moaned as blood trickled between his fingers and down his sternum. "Stand up and drop the fucking blanket."

"Fuck. You."

The agony retreated, but what it left behind was worse—a sudden, overwhelming need to obey.

"What—" he breathed as his fingers went to the knot at his hips. "What the hell?"

"That's how the *ascerdisc* works. Obey or suffer."

Growling, he snapped his hand back...and instant agony returned. The trickle of blood from the device became a stream, and a new trickle started from his nose.

"Just drop the blanket, you fool."

Yeah, okay, he was stubborn, but he liked to think he wasn't a total moron. This was a minor battle he was willing to lose in order to save strength for the next one, which would probably have higher stakes. He pushed to his feet and dropped the sucker. The pain faded.

Flail ogled, even though she'd seen him naked before.

"That is definitely no cocktail wiener," she said before letting out a resigned sigh. "Bael sent me to seduce you. But I know how much you hate me. You'll never fall for any of my tricks."

"Duh."

"So I'm going to make you want me."

He laughed. "That will never—" He broke off with a hiss as his body flooded with sexual need that bordered on pain.

"There you go," she murmured, her gaze becoming drowsy, full of erotic promise.

And he knew well that she kept her promises.

Damn her.

Hatred boiled up and merged with the lust burning hotly in his veins. His body wanted to fuck her. His brain wanted to kill her.

"Why—" he gritted. "Why are you doing this?" She could have beaten him with chains, flayed the flesh off his bones, smashed his organs with a sledgehammer, but instead, she was taking the one thing he had left: his free will.

This was so much worse than any torture he'd suffered so far.

"It's all about self-loathing, my boy." She walked toward him, slowly, deliberately, each hip kicking out in invitation. "You're going to fuck me, and you're going to hate yourself later."

"I'll know it wasn't my choice."

"But that won't be true, will it?" She poked one long, black-lacquered nail into the hollow of his throat. "Deep down, you want me with more than just your cock. And that will eat away at you. Which will let evil in." She smoothed her finger down his chest, through the wet blood. "Every day you give in a little more, but with an emotional wound like that? You'll succumb within days and give Bael what he wants."

"Never," he ground out. But each of her words chipped away at his conviction and tapped into his own secret fear.

"You fell for a reason, Cipher. You fell because you have no self-control, especially with females." She used his blood to paint his skin, and revulsion started to swallow the runaway lust. "You know that if you give in to me now, you're still the same piece of shit you always were, no matter how hard you tried to get back into Heaven."

"Bitch," he hissed. His fangs throbbed with the desire to rip out her throat, but his cock was throbbing for an entirely different reason.

Dropping her hand, she palmed his shaft, and he nearly jumped out of his skin. He stumbled backward out of her grip, and pain crushed his body in a vise of invisible pressure.

"When you resist my order, you suffer. Come to me and there will be only pleasure."

"No." He doubled over and shouted as another round of agony shredded him.

He'd been tortured on a weekly, and sometimes daily, basis since he'd been dragged here. He'd never been close to breaking. But Flail was somehow doing what the others couldn't. She was ripping beyond his flesh and into his soul.

"How?" he rasped. "How are you doing this?"

"We all have superpowers." Her hand came down on his neck, and no matter how hard he tried, he couldn't move. "Why do you think I'm called Flail? It's because my special power, the one that makes me indispensable to anyone who pays me enough, is that little thing buried in your chest. With it, I can use my thoughts like a whip, flaying emotions open."

Her superpower was horrific. Cipher had no idea what his unique fallen angel power was yet, but he hoped it was just as nightmarish.

And then, he swore, he'd use it to kill Flail.

Chapter Five

Cipher's shouts of agony echoed in the dark halls as Lyre hurried toward his cell. The tower guard said Flail was with him, but if that were true, why would Cipher be in pain? She'd been sent to seduce him, not torture him.

Unless...

Shit.

She started past the cobra-faced guard at the cell door, but the big asshole blocked her. "Sssorry. Flail gave ordersss to not allow anyone in."

"I'm not anyone," she gritted out. "I'm his handler, and I outrank Flail in this."

The guy's slitted eyes narrowed even more in confusion, but he still shook his three-horned, hooded head. On the other side of the door, Cipher moaned. Time for a different tack.

Summoning every ounce of power she could muster, she used her one major play and dematerialized into a wisp of gray vapor. In her smoky form she could squeeze through any opening, and the keyhole was just perfect.

She heard the guard's shout of "Hey!" as she slipped inside the cell and rematerialized.

When she'd fully formed, her jaw dropped at the sight of Flail, standing near the center of the small room like a dominatrix, her spike-heeled boots digging into the ice, her arms crossed under her bare breasts. On the floor, puddled like blood, was her corset.

Cipher's glassy gaze jerked over at Lyre as he stood slumped against the icy wall, one hand clutching the *ascerdisc* in his chest. Fury knotted in her own chest as blood ran in thick streams from the device and from Cipher's nose and mouth.

"Bitch!" Without thinking, she slammed an invisible fist of power into the other female's gut, knocking her off her feet and into the remains of a giant fallen icicle behind her. "How dare you torture him."

Flail laughed, flipping to her feet as if Lyre's power punch had been a mere slap. To add insult to injury, Flail shot her a mocking smirk that all but screamed, *Your powers are feeble and you're a pathetic excuse for a fallen angel, and everyone knows it.*

So embarrassing.

"I'm not torturing him." Flail curled her finger at Cipher in a come-here gesture. "He's torturing himself." With a pained hiss, he staggered a couple steps closer to Flail, his hands clenched, rage burning in his eyes. Even his erection, engorged and pulsing with thick veins, seemed angry. Impressive, but angry. "The more he resists, the more it hurts."

"He's not torturing himself and you know it. You're forcing him into it." Lyre cursed. "This is sinister, even for you."

Flail made a sound of disgust. "Such a human thing to say. Next you're going to tell me that this is mind rape." She waved her hand dismissively. "Or rape rape. Whatever."

Well, yeah, technically...

As a fallen angel who had allowed the malevolence of Sheoul inside her, Lyre should embrace all acts and all things evil. But every once in a while, like now, her past and her memories rose up, all inconvenient and shit.

Her ex had been a vigilante of sorts, a demon who'd put his ability to cause nightmares to good use. Anyone who harmed others could find themselves victims of his gift, but rapists had been his favorite targets. He'd have *paid* to haunt Flail's dreams until she went insane.

Lyre couldn't haunt Flail's dreams or drive her insane, but she could put a boot up the skank's perfect ass.

"Get out, Flail." She sent a mental flare at the door, and it creaked open. "He'd rather die than screw you, so this is pointless."

Ignoring her, Flail again gestured to Cipher, inviting him closer. He snarled, his hatred hanging in the frosty air with his breath. But he shuffled toward her, his efforts to resist making his steps jerky and uncoordinated.

Son of a bitch. "I'll call the damned guards," Lyre ground out.

"And you'll answer to Bael," Flail shot back. "He ordered me here."

As a baby fallen angel with weaker powers than most, Lyre was always outranked by every fallen angel she encountered, including Flail. But not here. Not as long as Cipher was in her charge.

Lyre came at Flail, ready to take the skank down with her bare hands. She might be pathetically weak when it came to angelic powers, but she'd spent a lifetime training in physical combat to help make up for her lack of supernatural ability.

"Bael ordered you to seduce him," she said, halting at the very edge of the other female's personal space, "but he ordered me to train him and care for him, and I say he's had enough."

Flail's jaw tightened, her lips mashing into an angry slash, and Lyre summoned power to have at the ready if the other female struck out. Lyre was hopelessly outgunned and outclassed by Flail, but within the confines of the power-dampening cell where only low-level abilities could be used, Lyre could hold her own enough to avoid a serious ass beating.

Plus, she had a really sharp dagger at her hip.

"I'll leave," Flail said in a shockingly peaceful capitulation, "but only because you ruined the mood." She leveled a warning look at Cipher. "I'll be back tomorrow, and we will finish what we started. But your handler's little stall tactic is going to cost you. We're gonna do all of this again...but we'll do it in the arena in front of an audience."

Flail flicked her wrist, and the *ascerdisc* tore out of Cipher's chest with a wet, ripping sound. He grunted and clutched at the bleeding wound as she stalked out of there, not even bothering to take her corset. No surprise. Flail had always been an exhibitionist.

Which was why she was probably already drooling over tomorrow's arena sex show starring Cipher.

For some reason, the idea repulsed Lyre in every way.

She'd attended a lot of Bael's erotic displays—he used the arena to host both pain and pleasure, and if they happened at the same time, even better. And she'd seen Cipher in the arena, fighting battles that could have killed him. But this would be a fight he couldn't win, and death might actually be kinder.

After closing the door, she turned back to Cipher, who watched her with wild eyes, a wounded predator, in pain and more dangerous than ever.

"Let me heal you." Like all her abilities, her healing power was limited in scope and strength, but she could at least take the edge off and jumpstart the process.

He bared massive fangs dripping with his own blood. "*Don't touch me.*"

Of all the times she'd seen him following a death match, or torture, or forced hard labor, he'd never looked like this. Exhausted, yes. Bleeding and barely conscious, sure. Trembling and puking, yeah, once or twice. But no matter how battered he'd been, defiance had burned in his eyes. That same unyielding hatred still smoldered there, but now it shared space with doubt. And maybe a little anxiety.

Flail had gotten to him. She was famous for it. But what deep, emotional scar had she ripped open to do it? Cipher wasn't going to survive the arena mentally intact, was he? He'd come out of it as evil as any fallen angel. And then he'd give Bael what he wanted, and Flail would take the credit.

No way. Lyre was tired of waiting to get back at her enemies. She needed this win, and she needed it badly.

"Listen to me," she said as she kicked Flail's corset into a corner. "Flail is going to destroy you in the arena—"

"Never," he spat.

His fire was magnificent, but fires could be put out.

"You know it's true, Cipher." She met his tortured gaze, hoping he'd recognize her genuine concern. He just had to mistake concern for her own situation for concern for his. "You *know* it is. She's going to crack the shield you've got around yourself, and evil is going to pour in and turn you into someone your friends and family won't recognize. And then you'll willingly give up the list Bael wants. But if you give *me* the list, you won't have to go through the hell Flail will put you through. You can hold on to your sanity and yourself for a while. Let the effects of being in Sheoul seep into you gradually instead of pouring in like a dam breaking."

"You think I'm stupid?" he rasped. "You don't give a shit about me. You just want to deny Flail a victory while scoring one for yourself." He inhaled a gurgling breath, his fingers tightening around his gaping chest wound where the *ascerdisc* had been. "And fuck you for making sense." He spat blood onto the floor, where it froze instantly, little drops of color on a canvas of white. "Is that how it went down for you?"

"I wasn't forced to give up anything, if that's what you're asking."

Nope, she'd entered Sheoul with a heart full of screw-you-Heaven enthusiasm. She'd expected evil to take her immediately given that she'd come here of her own free will. Instead, she could barely feel the slow creep of it and sometimes she wished it would happen faster. She'd love to be devoid of empathy. Too much of that crap got you in trouble. Having her own emotions sucked enough as it was. Having to feel for others bordered on overwhelming.

It was why she tried to avoid being anywhere nearby when Cipher was being worked over by torturemasters. It was also why she interfered with said torture as often as she could without looking suspiciously sympathetic. She wasn't squeamish; some people deserved what they got. But during the months she'd spent with Cipher she'd grown to realize that he didn't deserve any of this. The most offensive thing she could find about him was that he liked black walnut ice cream when everyone knew rocky road was the best.

"What about Bael?" He made a gesture that encompassed the glazed ice walls of his cell. "Did he lock you up in the Hellton hotel?"

Lyre almost laughed. If Cipher thought this was bad, he should see the prison where Bael kept the people he *didn't* want to work for him. His true enemies. People who he thought might have slighted or cheated him. People who looked at him the wrong way. The suffering that radiated from the mountain complex fueled entire villages of demons who thrived on the pain of others.

This, the Hellton, as Cipher called it, was downright luxurious in comparison.

"I was never imprisoned," she said, surprised she hadn't told him this before.

They'd talked a lot over the last couple of months, keeping the conversation light as she tried to pry information out of him about Azagoth's realm. Cipher had always deftly shifted the topic away from Sheoul-gra, but in truth, she hadn't minded. She'd been stuck in Bael's territory for years, prevented from leaving by a magical barrier that wouldn't allow her to flash, walk, or take a Harrowgate out. Cipher's stories had given her a tiny sense of freedom in a place where all she knew were shackles.

"I knew of Bael because I'd studied him as an angel," she continued. "I came to him for employment. Now, let me heal you."

He backed up so fast he hit the wall. "I said no."

"You've let me do it before."

His gaze dropped to his erection, just for a second, and her heart skipped a beat. He'd been naked in front her before, but he'd never been...aroused. Was that Flail's angle? Had he been traumatized sexually and she was trying to exploit his pain?

As an angel Lyre would have proceeded from here carefully, with tact and sensitivity. As a fallen angel she didn't have to do any of that. Hell, she could use that little suspected tidbit of information like an instrument of torture the way Flail seemed to be.

She chose to just be blunt. "Is it sex? Is sex your trauma? I wouldn't have guessed that."

"What? Are you kidding?" He looked horrified by the very thought. "Sex is awesome. I just don't want to have sex with *her*. Talk about trauma." He glanced down at his erection again. "But this won't go away, and my blood...burns."

"Oh." Well, this was awkward. "Um...I'm not entirely sure how Flail's ability works, but I think it takes a couple of hours for the pain to subside." Her gaze fell to his hips, where the thick column of engorged flesh curved upward, the glossy tip nearly touching his hard abs. Sweet baby Lucifer, that was impressive. "Or, you could, ah..."

Her cheeks flushed with heat, which was ridiculous, given that she was a couple of centuries old and a fallen angel. She'd watched orgies before, and she couldn't tell Cipher to jerk off?

I so want to see that.

The heat in her face spread to her breasts and pelvis, and she shifted uncomfortably.

"I could what?" He leveled his sharp gaze at her, so intense it took her breath. All his focus was on her. He didn't even seem to be in pain anymore. "I could..." He grasped his shaft, his long fingers wrapping around the thick length. "Take care of it myself?" His fist made a slow pass from the head to the base and back up, and her throat clogged with lust. "Or I could fuck you instead?"

"*Of course not, you worm*!" she said. Silently. In her head. Where Cipher didn't hear it.

Suddenly, he was on her, knocking her back against the door.

She hadn't even seen him move. Her first instinct as he bit into her throat and pressed that enormous erection into her belly was to hit him so hard that even the wings he'd lost would feel it. But when the erotic purr in his chest reached her ears, her body betrayed her.

Months of watching this magnificent creature perform in the arena and stand up to every form of torture thrown at him had put the tiniest chip in the wall she'd erected when she'd lost everything and everyone she'd loved. On the day she'd lost her wings, she'd sworn off love and friendship, tenderness and compassion, and then she'd let evil in, hoping it would fill the empty space inside. Her anger had been, and still was, a shield, protecting her from the cruel reality in which she now lived.

But now, for the first time since she'd fallen, there was a pleasant distraction from the perpetual misery of Sheoul. A distraction who, as coincidence would have it, could help her get revenge.

You need to step up your game, Lyre. I expected more from you.

Bael's words from yesterday in the arena rang in her ears. Shuddering, she clung to Cipher, her nails digging into his rock-hard biceps as if holding him close would block the memory of Bael showing her how much more he expected by chaining—literally chaining—her to his side until this morning. She'd witnessed how he did everything from getting a blow job to taking a shit to skinning an Oni demon alive, so yeah, she saw what happened to those who disappointed him. He didn't handle failure well.

And she had a head full of disturbing memories to process.

Buck up, girl. You can dissect your trauma later. You're working with a ticking clock right now.

She had to get Cipher to give Bael what he wanted, and she had to do it before Flail did it. Because even if Cipher didn't break in the arena, he *would* break eventually. Everyone did. The question was who got credit for it.

Lyre *needed* the credit. Maybe Bael would finally give her the freedom to leave the realm now and then.

Resolved to this course of action, which really wasn't a hardship, she let her head roll to the side so he could deepen his bite, and the rush...oh, yes, the rush was incredible. She'd never been fed on before, had never had anyone ask. No one wanted to feed on a weakling like her. And as a weakling, she didn't even need to feed much. When she did, she fed from humans after being escorted to the earthly realm by other fallen angels who never seemed happy to have to babysit.

During the time she'd been Cipher's handler she could have taken his vein at any time. It hadn't even occurred to her.

Now it was on her to-do list.

Adrenaline rushed through her veins like erotic fuel as Cipher's lips and tongue ravaged her neck. *More of this.* She needed much, much more of this.

Heart pounding so hard Cipher surely must have felt it against his teeth, she slid her hand between their bodies. His warm skin twitched as the backs of her fingers slid across his steel-hard abs, and his breath hitched as her thumb brushed the underside of his shaft.

Her own breath lodged in her throat. She'd never done this before. She and Dailon had been interrupted before they could consummate their love on the physical plane.

Anger at the stupid sentimental glitch roared back, and she roughly took Cipher's cock in her palm. There was nothing to wait for. No prince in angelic armor was going to sweep her into the pillowy embrace of his wings and gently take her maidenhood.

She lived in Hell now. Gang rape or having her virginity sold to the highest bidder for use in some sort of power spell were the more likely scenarios if it ever got out that she was a virgin. She might as well make it happen on her own terms and now was as good a time as any.

Besides, it was only a matter of time before Bael forced her into his bed. Honestly, she couldn't believe he hadn't already.

She squeezed Cipher's shaft, and his gasp of pleasure created an unexpected throb of need deep in her belly.

Stop it.

This was a task. A means to an end. Not a meaningful exploration of her sexuality or some crap.

Oh, but it felt so good.

She squeezed again, adding a slow pump of her fist. Cipher shuddered and rocked into her hand.

A low moan dredged up from his chest as he lifted his head from her throat. "Hurts," he whispered.

She froze, then hastily released him. "I'm sorry—"

"No." His big hand closed around hers and guided it back to his shaft. "Not that." He shuddered again. "That is the only thing that feels good. The only thing in...months."

Sadness mingled with the pain in his voice, and her heart clenched.

No. No clenching of hearts. She was doing this for a purpose.

If she gave Cipher what he wanted, maybe he'd give her what she wanted.

Information.

And, of course, an orgasm.

* * * *

Pain. There was so. Much. Pain.

Even with Flail gone, Cipher's pain was still crippling. It was as if every cell was being alternately crushed then sliced, cycling over and over, with breaks only when he'd willingly moved closer to either Flail or Lyre. Resisting meant that someone dialed up the pain intensity.

But worse than the pain was the desire. The ball-throbbing, dick-tingling, soul-crushing desire to bury himself first in Flail, and now Lyre.

At least Lyre hadn't betrayed him. He didn't completely hate her. And she was hot.

He'd fucked worse.

Probably shouldn't say that out loud. Or think on it too much. Didn't say anything good about him, that was for sure.

Whatever. He was just glad Lyre was here instead of Flail.

How had Lyre gotten in here, anyway? He hadn't seen the door open.

And why the fuck was he thinking about random shit when he should be concentrating on how Lyre's hot blood circulated through his body and her warm hand pumped along his shaft, the only real heat he'd felt since he'd been dragged to Sheoul. It spread across his skin and into his muscles all over his body, and for the first time in forever, misery wasn't the only thing he was feeling.

"Just like that," he rasped as he thrust into her grip.

He wanted to haul her legs up around his waist and take her, right against the door. She'd let him; he could tell by the way she rocked into him, the way her breathing came fast and hard, the way the scent of her arousal wrapped around him like satin. But then she did some kind of twisty thing as she squeezed him from the base of his cock to the head...and he was done.

He threw his head back and shouted as the climax hit him, a giant, rolling wave of pleasure that, for the briefest moment, made him forget everything shitty in his life. More waves followed, weaker, just lapping at his pleasure centers as he came down.

Then someone in a nearby cell screamed, jolting him out of his bubble of bliss and reminding him where he was. Reminding him that pleasure was nothing but an illusion in Bael's prison, a sick joke, a fleeting sliver of time meant to make you hate normal life even more.

God, he hated it here. This was why few Unfallen angels willingly entered Sheoul to complete their fall from grace. Most of them lived a nomadic life, constantly fleeing those who would capture and drag them into Sheoul, just as Cipher had done. He'd spent a couple of decades on the run, hiding in the human realm in the guise of a homeless man, until he'd run into Hawkyn.

Unlike the last time he'd seen Hawkyn, the Memitim hadn't tried to kill him for what Cipher had done to his Primori. Instead, Hawk had offered him sanctuary. Well, he'd offered it after an epic battle in which they'd beaten the shit out of each other in a good old-fashioned fistfight.

Life had been good in Sheoul-gra. He'd rarely had to leave, and when he did, he was usually with powerful friends.

Unfortunately, he'd let down his guard. He'd taken one too many risks, had gotten too far from his friends during a battle, and now he was paying for his mistakes.

He might be reckless, but he wasn't an idiot. He knew this could only go one of two ways. He'd either give in and join Bael's team, or he'd die an agonizing death, only to be fully conscious moments later as his soul found itself at Bael's mercy. Would Bael use it as a plaything? Perhaps trap it inside Cipher's preserved body, put on display while he slowly went mad? Or maybe Bael would keep it as an offering to Satan on the day the King of Demons was released from his prison.

Cipher knew which option was the most likely. Even now he could feel evil seeping into his very cells, darkening his outlook, his sense of humor. Oh, sure, there was always a chance that he could escape and get back to Sheoul-gra, but the reality was that he had only one choice to make.

Pledge fealty to Bael now...or pledge fealty to him later.

Either way, Cipher would give up the list and betray everyone he cared about.

They don't care about you. Flail's voice rang in his head, tapping into his fears. *You've been gone too long. They think you've gone to the dark side already. They've given up.*

No way. They hadn't. They wouldn't. If he could get out of here, they'd welcome him back in Sheoul-gra.

He just needed a plan. A way to contact them.

But to contact them, he'd need his computer. To escape he needed his fallen angel powers. To get his fallen angel powers he needed his wings to be unbound.

There was only one way that was going to happen. He had to give Bael what he wanted.

The scream rang out again, the prod he needed to get his shit together.

Awkwardly, he stepped away from Lyre, grabbed his blanket, and used it to clean up. "Uh, sorry..." He stopped himself before he said anything else. Why should he apologize? Lyre was his fucking captor. Well, she was employed by his captor, anyway.

"Did it help?" She sounded breathy. Turned on. And despite the fact that he'd just come and he was in a prison in Hell's asshole, he started to get hard again.

"Did what help what?"

She huffed as if he was a complete idiot. "Is the pain gone?"

"Oh. Yeah." But he wasn't sure if he felt better thanks to the nourishment her blood gave him or because of the sex. Maybe both.

He looked down at his chest. Blood still streaked his skin, but the *ascerdisc* wound had sealed and was only a little tender. His wings still hurt, strangled by ensorcelled rope, but that was nothing new.

She started toward him. "Cipher—"

"Ooh, hey, watch your step."

She did a jaunty little hop to avoid slipping on the result of her hand action, and he hid a smile at the way her cheeks turned pink. "Thanks."

"Don't thank me. I warned you before I had a chance to consider how hilarious it would be if you fell in my jizz." Why *had* he warned her, anyway? Should have let her break her ass on the ice.

But it was such a nice ass.

"You know tomorrow's going to be worse, right?" she asked, sounding a little flustered. "Flail is probably drafting invitations right now."

She's going to crack the shield you've got around you, and evil is going to pour in and turn you into someone your friends and family won't recognize. And then you'll willingly give up the list Bael wants. But if you give me the list, you won't have to go through the hell Flail will put you through. You can hold on to your sanity and yourself for a while. Let the effects of being in Sheoul seep into you gradually instead of pouring in like a dam breaking.

As much as Cipher hated to admit it, Lyre's words made sense. And if he'd been here for seven months, like Flail said...yes, this might work.

He tossed the blanket aside. "If I give Bael the list, he'll unbind my wings, right?"

"That's the deal."

"Then bring me my laptop." He paused. "And some clothes. Real clothes. And a shower would be great."

Lyre jerked like she was a marionette and someone had yanked her strings. "Are you serious?"

"I'm covered in blood and I'm naked. What do you think?"

"No, I mean the list." Her silver eyes were wide, glinting with surprise. "You're willing to give Bael the names he wants?"

Hearing her say it out loud made his gut churn. If he was right about this, he could buy time to escape without anyone getting hurt. If he was wrong, Azagoth's wrath would make Bael's cruelty seem downright merciful.

And so, with a deep breath and a silent prayer to anyone who would listen, he nodded.

"Yeah," he growled. "I am."

Chapter Six

"Ever seen the inside of a soul?"

Azagoth frowned at the speaker over the rim of his highball glass filled with Scotch. "You're kidding, right?" He lowered the glass to his desktop. "You're asking me, the Grim Reaper, a fallen angel who hasn't found a new thing to do with a soul in at least two centuries, if I've ever seen what's inside one?"

Jim Bob, an angel whose real name and identity Azagoth didn't know, shrugged, making the hem of his hooded black robe whisper against his boots. "Supposedly, most souls are filled with light. But what about the souls you keep in the Inner Sanctum?"

This was a weird conversation, but Azagoth couldn't work up the energy to be annoyed by something so minor. Not when *big* shit was going on all around him. Big enough that he'd been scattered and sleepless and distracted for days.

Last week, one of his sons, a boy barely in his teens whom Azagoth had only just met, had been murdered inside Sheoul-gra.

Inside Sheoul fucking Gra.

The bastard responsible for Niclas's death hadn't yet been identified, but he—or she—would be. Azagoth wouldn't rest until he knew who had dared to kill one of his children inside his own realm and right under his nose.

One thing of which he was certain: whoever it was, they weren't working alone.

Three of his grown children, trained, powerful Memitim, had also been slaughtered recently, and just this morning he'd learned that, without a doubt, the deaths were connected.

The remains of the demon who'd delivered the message were still splattered on the wall, and his soul was in Hades's capable, cruel hands.

That demon's soul was definitely not brimming with light.

"Most of the souls I deal with are full of blackness," Azagoth replied. Since not all demons were evil, some didn't possess a dark inner void, and a rare handful even radiated light.

Jim Bob walked slowly around the office, his gaze settling on the splatter. "When a good soul full of light is destroyed, the light returns to the Creator unless the soul is trapped, devoured, or used as fuel for a spell. What happens when an evil soul full of darkness is destroyed?"

Azagoth propped his hip against his desk and relaxed although, as always, he kept his powers locked and loaded. Jim Bob was a prime source of Heavenly intel, but he was also an angel. Which meant he could never be fully trusted.

"Same, basically," Azagoth said. "The dark void inside a soul is fuel for a soul-eating demon. But if I destroy a soul, the darkness returns to Satan and makes him more powerful. That's why so few have the power to destroy souls and why I don't do it on a whim." He'd also signed a contract stating he'd pay a hefty price for every soul he destroyed, and that price generally wasn't worth it. Very little was worth giving up a measure of his power or a slice of his realm. "Why the sudden interest in the internal plumbing of a soul?"

Jim Bob swung slowly around, his expression, while always serious was downright grim. "There are rumblings of a plot to free Satan from his prison. I wonder if enough souls were destroyed if he'd gain the necessary powers required to escape."

Azagoth studied Jim Bob's carefully schooled features but, as usual, there was nothing there to read. Still, his question wasn't an idle one; he was probing Azagoth's feelings on the matter. Maybe even his involvement.

"Possibly," Azagoth mused. "But it would take hundreds of years even for *me* to destroy that many souls. By then Satan most likely would be free. According to prophecy, of course."

"Of course." Jim Bob casually waved his hand in front of the fire as he spoke, but if he was looking for heat, he'd have to go elsewhere. Azagoth's fireplace was as cold as his heart and it had been since the day Lilliana walked out on him. "Have you heard any of this talk?"

That *talk* was what got the demon in the corner all kinds of dead. Azagoth had known there were multiple plots afoot to rescue Satan, and now he knew that he, himself, was central to many of them.

His children's deaths were a message: help us, or else.

Azagoth had a scythe full of "or else" for every motherfucker responsible, but he wasn't going to let Heaven in on this. The less they knew about the pressure being placed on him to back the *#FreeSatan* cause, the better.

They actually had a fucking hashtag.

What the Free Satan movement didn't have was a single leader to bring cohesiveness. The most powerful demons and fallen angels in Sheoul were all campaigning for followers who could get behind their unique visions for making Hell great again.

And they all seemed to think Azagoth's help could be bought.

Or compelled.

He waved his hand in a dismissive gesture. "As long as Satan is imprisoned there will be talk of breaking him out. When he was free someone was always plotting his demise. It's the circle of life. I wouldn't worry."

Jim Bob snorted. "You have more important things to worry about than the End of Days?"

The lives of his children and his mate were more important, so...yes.

Especially now that Lilliana was coming home. Ares's child just needed to hurry the fuck up and be born. He had no idea why Lilliana had insisted she be there for the birth, but by Satan's balls, it felt like the Horseman's mate had been pregnant for years.

Lilliana had been gone for nine months now, and every single day, every single minute, had been torture. Not that he had anyone to blame but himself. It had taken him a long time to realize that, but now that he had, he'd been working on becoming the male Lilliana deserved.

"...and then I was abducted by alien angels from an alternate universe," Jim Bob said. "They gave me pizza before the anal probe."

"What?" Azagoth snapped, re-focusing his thoughts. They went to Lilliana at the most inappropriate times. She really needed to come home. Fucking Ares. "Did you say something about pizza?"

Jim Bob rolled his eyes. "Pizza? *That's* what snapped you out of your funk? Not the alternate universe or anal probe?"

Azagoth shoved away from his desk. "I'm hungry, not horny." Actually, that wasn't entirely true. Sure, he could go for a couple of large pepperonis. He hadn't eaten in days. Hadn't eaten much at all since Lilliana left.

But he really was horny as hell. It had been eons since he'd gone this long without sex, but more than that, he'd never gone this long without Lilliana.

In the past, he'd had an endless parade of sexual partners. Demons had thrown themselves at him and Heaven had kept him supplied with angels to make baby Memitim with, so no, there'd been no shortage of sex. Which was fortunate because, as his fallen angel Chief of Operations, Zhubaal, liked to say, "There's nothing more frightening than the Grim Reaper when he's horny."

Yup, he was horny as fuck. But for all the evil that ran through his veins, he'd never even so much as glanced at the females who tried to seduce him while Lilliana was away. And there had been thousands, most of them demons who wanted to trade sex for mercy. But mercy wasn't his thing, and he'd laughed as his *griminions* whisked them away, ushering their souls to their new, nightmarish digs.

He'd never been tempted, not once. Even his evil side wouldn't betray Lilliana for a blow job from a succubus.

But his evil side did enjoy the game. It enjoyed toying with the angels and fallen angels who came into his office thinking that with Lilliana gone they could get their claws into him.

Jim Bob's fingers snapped in front of his face. "Yo. What the fuck, man? Put your horns and fangs away. And stop snarling. Makes my wings itch."

Azagoth blinked as he once again climbed out of the mire of his own thoughts. His body vibrated with a dark lust as the memories of toying with prey collided with a sexual awareness that burned deep in his muscles. Warmth crept into his cold flesh, and his cock, already excruciatingly hard, began to throb to the beat of his pulse.

His pulse.

Holy hell, his heart had started beating again.

"Lilliana," he breathed, joy taking his breath as her presence filled his soul. "She's here. She's home."

Another spike of awareness pierced him, a powerful energy signature he'd never felt before.

What the fuck?

A possessive, smoky growl rattled his chest, and his hackles rose with his wings. Someone else was here. Someone crazy strong.

Lilliana wasn't alone.

Chapter Seven

Lilliana inhaled a shaky breath as she stood on the portal pad inside Sheoul-gra, the symbols engraved into the stone glowing hotly. A breeze swirled around her, rattling the leaves on the perpetually blooming citrus trees and bringing their tangy and sweet scents to her nose. Grassy lawns stretched for acres, broken by babbling streams and worn paths—and the occasional ancient Greek column or demonic statue that rose into the featureless gray sky.

Several yards away, a fountain that once ran with blood splashed crystal water onto pavers leading to outbuildings that housed dozens of Unfallen angels and Memitim. And beyond the fountain, Azagoth's palace towered over all, its pale walls gleaming.

Relief sifted through her, temporarily replacing her nervousness. The realm was attuned to Azagoth's moods, and she wasn't sure what she'd have done if she'd come back to find the kind of decay and evil that had once held court here.

The Grim Reaper's realm could be beautiful but disconcerting; look, but not too closely, touch, but don't feel.

Her gut turned over, and inside her rounded belly, the baby stirred as if sensing the return of her anxiety.

Except that *anxiety* was too mellow a word for what she was experiencing. Really, she was flat-out terrified, mere moments away from seeing her husband for the first time in months. For the first time since she'd left him.

And he didn't have a clue that she was pregnant.

She almost regretted telling Reaver that she didn't need him to accompany her down here when he'd flashed her from Ares's Greek island to the outer portal. She should have at least allowed Maleficent, a hellhound that had shadowed her everywhere on the island, to come with her. The hound had refused to leave her side until Cara distracted the beast long enough for Lilliana to get away. She was going to miss the moose-sized canine, but Cara assured her that Mal would find her if the hellhound had bonded with her.

Lilliana was going to have a hard enough time trying to explain bringing home a baby, let alone a pet that ate people.

Resting her palm on her baby bump, she stepped off the landing pad and started toward the palace, her heart pounding wildly. Azagoth would have sensed her presence by now.

Before that thought even faded, the skin on the back of her neck tingled, and she stopped in her tracks.

He was here.

He was behind her.

She should turn around and face him. But damn, she wasn't ready for this.

Closing her eyes, she let out a long, ragged breath, and when she spoke, she could only manage a whisper. "Azagoth."

"Look at me, Lilliana."

The sound of Azagoth's voice, commanding but soft, sent a tremor of emotion through her. They'd spoken almost daily via Skype, so she knew he wanted her to come home. But how would he feel about their child after he'd once told her he didn't want any more children? How would he feel about the fact that she'd kept this from him for nine months?

Bracing herself for anything, she swung around.

Dark power emanated from Azagoth as he stood a few feet away, his glossy obsidian wings folded rigidly behind him, his short hair as black as his shoes, slacks, and shirt. He'd rolled up the sleeves, revealing tattoos he'd stolen from Thanatos, and his hands were clenched at his sides.

She couldn't read him at all, and she wasn't sure how to process that.

His emerald eyes met hers for a mere heartbeat and then dropped to her belly.

"I guess I have something to tell you..."

The sound of laughter came from somewhere behind her, and Azagoth's head snapped back up as two of his sons, Journey and Maddox, came into view just up the path. The two Memitim were goofing off with their cell phones, oblivious to the fact that in a moment they were going to be in the middle of something they didn't want to be anywhere near.

Azagoth hissed, his wings unfurling as he swept her into his arms and lifted her into the air. The breath whooshed from her lungs as the ground fell away, but Azagoth tucked her close, his grip secure but gentle even as he dive-bombed his startled sons. He banked hard, forcing them to the ground before shooting across the courtyard to land on the balcony outside their bedroom.

Lilliana swayed a little as she found her footing, but Azagoth's arm remained in place, a solid band of support. "Azagoth—"

"Shh." He covered her mouth with his in a desperate kiss. "I've missed you," he whispered against her lips.

God, she'd missed him too, and with a cry of relief, she melted against him.

* * * *

Azagoth moaned at the taste of Lilliana on his lips. It was as if he'd been starving for months and had finally been given a morsel of gourmet cuisine.

It wasn't enough, was merely an appetizer, and he cursed as he broke the kiss and stepped back to avoid crushing her belly.

Her *pregnant* belly.

Holy shit.

She looked up at him with big amber eyes. "So you aren't angry?"

Fuck, yeah, he was. But no. How could he be? Yes. No. Fuck. There were so many emotions tangled up inside him that he wasn't sure how to answer. Obviously, she'd been pregnant for months and hadn't told him. Had she known she was pregnant when she left him? Who else knew while he'd been kept in the dark like a fool?

Yeah, he was a little steamed. But he was also a jackass who'd pushed her away in the first place.

Screw it. It was too complicated and frankly, he didn't give a shit right now. He had other needs to address, like the fact that Lilliana was home and even his evil side was thrilled.

And it wanted to claim its mate.

"I'll sort it out later," he said roughly as he fisted her skirt and yanked it up. "Right now I need you."

"*Yes.*" She threw herself against him, wrapping her arms around him as she hooked his thigh with her leg. "Hurry."

Her nails dug into his shoulders and her swollen belly pressed into his abs and there was no way this was going to work.

As carefully as his desperation would allow, he spun her around and braced her against the railing.

She looked around at him from over her shoulder, her long chestnut hair draped across her back, her mouth quirked in a naughty smile that hit him right in the cock. "Right here?"

Snarling with impatience, he spared a second to look out at his domain. A group of Unfallen and Memitim were wandering around and glancing up at the balcony while trying not to look obvious. Journey and Maddox must have a fucking loudspeaker.

With a thought and a whisper, a thick black fog rolled in from the outer edges of his realm, shrouding the land in darkness and his balcony in privacy.

"Nice," she murmured.

No, there was nothing nice about it. That fog could have contained acid, poison, or millions of flesh-eating creatures if he'd wished it. As it was, it would leave an ashen residue on everything it touched. He'd have to summon rain later.

Then they could make love in that, too.

She left you. She lied to you.

Yes, she had. But he hadn't been a pillar of virtue either, so he quashed his inner voice, because right now he needed to connect with her, to re-establish their bond...if not their trust.

She seemed to agree, her hand stretching back to grip his thigh and pull him even closer. The heat of her palm though his slacks was nearly his undoing. It had been so long. Too long.

As he reached beneath her skirt and tore away her panties, he swore they'd never be apart like that again. Never.

His fingers found her wet and swollen, so ready for him it made his knees weak.

Lilliana squirmed with anticipation, her slender shoulders rising and falling with every panting breath. Her nails dug into his leg so hard that it was painful. Deliciously, sinfully painful.

"Hurry," she whispered again.

Some part of him wanted to deny her request—the part of him that was angry about being lied to. It wanted to drag this out, to punish her with pleasure.

The logical part of him realized that wasn't much of a punishment.

The horny part of him just couldn't freaking wait.

With a growl, he ripped open his fly.

She moaned as he pressed the head of his erection against her center, but even though he wanted to drive into her with a frenzied thrust, he was careful. His child was inside her, and he wasn't going to risk hurting either one of them.

Very slowly, he eased inside her welcoming heat, her slick walls gripping his shaft in an erotic caress.

He wasn't going to last long, but that was okay. The love of his life had come back to him, and they had eons to make up for lost time.

She sighed his name as he filled her, and the sigh became a husky "Yes" when he began to move, initiating a slow rhythm that was still almost too fast.

"I missed this," he rasped, his grip tightening on her hips.

He pumped into her, his thrusts coming harder and faster as the pleasure spread and intensified. The soft sounds Lilliana made as she pushed against him, meeting every stroke with enthusiasm, drove him even higher. They'd been a perfect sexual match from the beginning, and after almost a year of separation, nothing had changed.

The first stirrings of climax tingled in his balls and the base of his spine, and before he got too carried away, he thrust his hand between her legs and found her swollen bud. She cried out, bucking at the instant orgasm.

Her pleasure triggered his, and he roared in ecstasy that went beyond the physical. It was mental, emotional, so powerful his wings erupted and shrouded them in a cocoon of passion as he emptied himself inside her. His release peaked, ebbed, and peaked again, repeating the cycle over and over until he lost count and his legs would barely support him.

Finally, as his lust eased, another hunger roared into focus. The intensity of it shocked him, and without thinking, he twisted her head and bit into her throat. She moaned as he took a powerful draw, starved for both the connection and the sweet nectar of nourishment only she could give.

Somewhere in the back of his mind he knew he should be more gentle, but before he could tame his inner beast, another voice pierced his awareness.

Father.

The baby. Holy hell, he could *feel* the baby.

He was a father thousands of times over, but he hadn't even met most of his children. Those he did know hadn't come into his life until they were decades, if not centuries, old. This was the first time he'd hold his own infant offspring. The first time he'd fathered a child with a female he loved.

This was *everything* to him.

The fog dispelled and the sky above turned brilliant blue as his world became right again. He tightened his massive wings around their bodies, shielding them from view.

"Azagoth," she gasped. "The sky. It's never been so bright."

Sated and riding a killer dopamine high, he swiped his tongue over the bite wound to seal it and gathered her against him. After nine agonizing months of separation from his mate, hours of bone-crushing loneliness was at an end.

"Lilli," he murmured, as he gently pulled her upright so her back was to his chest and they were still connected. "I love you so much."

She brought one of his hands down to her belly, and his heart fluttered at the movement beneath his palm. "I love you too."

They were going to have to talk after this. Talk a lot.

But right this minute he was going to revel in the gift he'd just been given.

His mate.

His *baby.*

Chapter Eight

His computer.

His *baby.*

As Cipher grabbed his laptop from the pedestal of ice it had been sitting on, he didn't think he'd ever been happier to see anything in his entire life.

"You assholes better have taken care of it." He ran his hand over the smooth protective case. "There's a scratch. See, right there. Fuckers," he muttered.

"Leave us," Lyre said to the demon assholes who'd unlocked the room containing Bael's confiscated loot. "I can handle it from here."

The demons, who looked and smelled like bloated human corpses wrapped in burlap bags, shuffled across the ice floor and fur rugs toward the door. Before this, Cipher had seen very little of Bael's castle, but now it seemed that everything had been constructed of either ice, bones, or fur, and nothing melted...not even the working fireplaces made of ice.

Even the door they'd come through had been constructed of opaque, charcoal-colored ice. According to Lyre, Bael missed the extravagant crystal palaces in Heaven, so he'd created a replica of his former home out of enchanted ice that could withstand the intense heat from the nearby volcano and the moat filled with lava.

Cipher doubted the stronghold was a genuine, exact replica, though, given the scenes of torture carved into the walls by an incredibly talented artist. Everything was so...graphic. Had Bael been a sick, twisted bastard as a fully-haloed angel too?

Cipher waited until the door closed behind the ugly bastards to fire up his baby. When he did, the whirr of the CPU fan damn near made him orgasm.

But it wouldn't have been like the one Lyre gave you.

He nearly groaned out loud at that thought.

Lyre stood nearby, her lush midnight hair tied up in a severe high knot, her mouth little more than a grim slash. She didn't seem nearly as excited to be here as he'd figured she'd be. Bael was going to reward her for this, give her a promotion or some shit. She should be grinning like Flail did when she caused him pain. Instead, ever since Lyre picked him up after he'd showered and dressed, she'd been distracted. Maybe a little sad.

Not that he cared.

When the password screen popped up, he covertly turned the laptop away from Lyre's prying eyes and entered the code. A code that also needed to be entered with *his* fingers, and none other. It was the reason none of Bael's minions had been able to break into it.

They hadn't known about the tech he'd both developed and installed on his computer.

Dumbasses.

"I can't believe you're going to do this." Lyre handed him a flash drive she'd dug out of her side pants pocket.

"I'm tired of living in a deep freeze," he said, and that wasn't a lie.

But mainly...mainly he needed to buy a little freedom. And some goodwill. He wasn't a fool—Lyre and Flail were in a competition to see who could get the list from him first. He wouldn't save Flail if she were being roasted over a Neethul fire pit, but if he helped out Lyre he might get something in return. A favor, or maybe even a measure of trust, which he could exploit when the time came.

If he played his cards right, he could actually escape this hell.

The screen flashed, giving him an option to select one of three private blocks on his hard drive. His gaming partition wasn't protected, but he didn't need that one. He'd password-protected the second partition, but he'd set it up so that if, on the insanely minuscule chance someone got into his computer, they'd eventually be able to get into his basic work files. There was some sensitive shit in there about Azagoth's realm and tech, but nothing so critical that Sheoul-gra would be compromised if it were to get out. There were also some nasty booby traps and a computer virus that would execute once the file was downloaded to another computer.

The third partition required blood to open. Blood and a password spoken only in his voice as he typed it.

"I need you to turn around," he said.

"Why?"

"I want to look at your ass."

She blinked. "Really?"

Yes, but that wasn't the main reason. Also, she was seriously gullible. How had she survived this long in Sheoul?

"Do you want the list or not?"

Rolling her eyes, she spun on her heel and faced the wall. "Oh, and in case you had any ideas about contacting Azagoth or your friends, think again. The ice in this room blocks all electronic signals, including WIFI."

Fuck. There went a major piece of his plan. The *heroes ride in and save the day* part. Guess he was on his own.

Unfortunately, lack of access also meant he couldn't disable Bael's security systems, which would render escape far more difficult, especially since Bael had embraced tech in ways other wretched warlords in Sheoul hadn't. Most still lived in the Dark Ages.

Cursing silently, he nicked his thumb with a fang and smeared a drop of blood on the touchpad. His fingers settled over keys so worn that most of the letters had faded as he whispered, "Han Solo."

Take that, Hawkyn. Star Wars beats Star Trek. Every. Single. Time.

Hawk would probably break his jaw for that, but it would be worth it.

A twinge of regret pricked him. He missed Sheoul-gra. He missed his buddy. Missed all of his friends.

But they were looking for him. He knew they were.

Doubt came roaring in on the heels of that thought. Hawkyn, Maddox, Journey, Emerico...they had been his anchors after his fall from Heaven, but as Hawkyn liked to say—taken from Trek, of course, "The needs of the many outweigh the needs of the few...or the one."

Which meant that if the risk of rescuing him was too great, he'd become a sacrifice for the greater good. It made sense. But that didn't make it suck any less.

"Can I turn around?" Lyre's smoky voice startled him into the present.

"No."

He tapped on the keyboard, the sound of clicking keys as satisfying as a cold beer on a hot day. He even typed out a few unnecessary strokes just so he could hear the sweet music as he brought up the files containing all the research he'd done to find Azagoth's children in the human realm.

The thousands of files on hundreds of kids had been organized into age groups, with the largest collection being the oldest of his Memitim children. The plan had been to bring in the oldest first, allowing them to get the lay of the land and get settled in before bringing in the younger ones who would need more care. Before Cipher was kidnapped and dragged to Sheoul, they'd been in phase one of the operation.

It had been several months since then. The oldest children should have been collected and safely ensconced inside Azagoth's realm by now. He'd give Bael that list, and while the bastard's minions were hunting the children, not knowing they'd already been gathered and taken to Azagoth, he could be plotting an escape.

He punched a few keys, and the list popped up. Forty names, kids in their teens spread out all over the world. Hopefully, all were safe.

Please let them be safe.

He couldn't be responsible for the death of a single one of them.

"What's the matter?"

He started, glancing over at Lyre, who had turned around at some point. "Nothing. Why?"

"You look like you're having second thoughts."

"Second thoughts?" He snorted. "About giving a monster access to the Grim Reaper's innocent children so he can do God knows what with them? No, it's really no problem."

"Innocent? Memitim?" She waved her hand in dismissal. "They're warriors, same as every other angel."

He frowned at her. "You're kidding, right?"

"No." Her long fingers drifted to the blade she always kept at her hip, and he suddenly wondered how good she was with the thing. Was it for show, or could she really dance with danger? "I mean, they aren't full angels with wings, but they do have powerful fighting abilities."

She didn't know. She truly didn't have a clue. "This isn't a list of adult Memitim. It's a list of the little ones still living in the human realm with human parents. They don't even know they're angels, and they don't get their powers until they're adults."

"What?" Her fingers faltered. "I didn't know it was those ones. I thought he wanted Memitim."

"Would it make a difference?"

She gave a haughty sniff as she looked down at her boot. "Of course not."

"Of course not," he muttered. "Do you know what he plans to do with them?"

"No idea." She glanced back up at him. "So what is this list anyway? I mean, obviously it's a list of his children, but why is there a list of them at all? Doesn't Azagoth have thousands of them?"

Many thousands. The dude had been prolific over the eons. "You know how he sired over seventy children a year for thousands of years to create Memitim, right?"

"Of course. That's basic angel knowledge." She gazed up at the ceiling as she recited Azagothic knowledge straight from the history tomes. "His children, born to full angel mothers, are given to human families to raise. They don't learn the truth until adulthood, when they're told the truth about their roots. As their new angelic powers emerge, they're trained to be earthbound guardian angels, working to keep special humans called Primori safe until they eventually earn their wings and ascend to Heaven." A fierce blush spread across her cheeks when she saw him staring at her. "He was one of my favorite historical characters, so he was my focus in my history courses and research."

"Research?"

"It was sort of my job when I was an angel."

Sounded boring as fuck.

"Yeah, well, now that he's mated, he's no longer siring Memitim and wants to bring all children who remain in the human realm to Sheoul-gra." Cipher casually deleted all remaining files related to Azagoth's kids and then ran the virtual shredder program he'd developed. "It took forever for Heaven to agree, but they finally gave him the names and last known locations of those children."

"Hmm." Lyre's pert nose wiggled as she ran the information through her processor. It was cuter than it should be. "Maybe he's going to blackmail Azagoth for something. He's had a bug up his ass about Azagoth ever since I arrived."

Interesting. "And when was that?"

"Not long after the near-apocalypse."

Which was just a few years ago. "That explains it," he murmured as he looked back down at his screen.

"Explains what?"

"Why you don't radiate evil." He deleted more files related to Azagoth and his realm. "You're not completely saturated with it yet."

"I am too," she said, a little defensively. She might as well have stomped her foot, and he gave her a skeptical glance.

"How much time did you spend as an Unfallen?" he asked.

"None."

"None?" Ooh, he should probably delete that porn file. "You were captured and dragged down here right away?"

"No." Her sterling eyes flashed as her defenses came up. This seemed to be a touchy subject for her. He'd have to file that information away. "I came of my own free will."

So she was another Flail. She'd *wanted* to expose herself to the evils of Sheoul. He had absolutely no respect for shitbags like that.

Although he had to admit that she didn't strike him as being anything like Flail. Aside from wanting the list of Azagoth's minor children, anyway. Not that it mattered. He was going to get out of this hellhole and would hopefully never see either of them again.

He jammed the flash drive into the USB port and downloaded the file containing the names that would hopefully buy him some time.

"Done." His gut churned as he unplugged the drive and held it out to Lyre. "Tell Bael to shove it up his ass."

The merest hint of a smile teased her lips. He shouldn't find it sexy, but he did. A lot.

"As much as I'd love to say that, I'll let you tell him yourself." She bounced the little drive in her palm, and her expression grew serious. "Cipher, I hope whatever you put on this drive isn't a trick, because if it is, we'll both pay with blood. And when I recover, I'll show you just how saturated with evil I am."

He doubted the threat would have sounded as cute coming from Flail. But in any case, she didn't have anything to worry about. There were no tricks on the flash drive.

At least, none Bael would find out about until Cipher was long gone.

Chapter Nine

The flash drive felt like victory in Lyre's palm as she walked Cipher toward Bael's throne room. *Take that, Flail. I won. Big time.*

She glanced over at Cipher, whose expression was stony. Unreadable.

But it hadn't been that way when he'd downloaded the list or talked about the names on it.

Names of children.

An unexpected wave of guilt engulfed her. She'd known Bael and Moloc were after Memitim, trained adults who could handle themselves. But the revelation that these were young children left her spinning and struggling to conceal it.

Dammit, it shouldn't bother her. She was a fallen angel. A willing fallen angel. She should be sweating evil from her very pores by now. Evil that would allow her to not care. To maybe even enjoy the suffering of innocents.

Instead, she was slow-walking the damned list and wondering what Bael was going to do with it.

But she couldn't stall forever, and they finally arrived at Bael's residence. Two sleek, black-haired Canis demons, drool dripping from their canine jaws, let them inside.

Bael and his brother Moloc were huddled over a map with Rancor, a female fallen angel who had gained control of the Horun region after a coup backed by the brothers.

All three fallen angels had sworn allegiance to Revenant, but before Lyre had fallen, she'd uncovered evidence that they were secretly working against him. At the time and as a historian, she'd been fascinated by the political dynamics in Sheoul, even as she was disturbed by the Satan loyalists. The Powers That Be in Heaven didn't openly admit they were backing Revenant as the King of Hell, but he was definitely preferable over the imprisoned alternative.

But as a fallen angel betrayed by her Heavenly family, Lyre had intentionally chosen to sell her services to an enemy of Revenant. Hell, she'd come to Bael within an hour of falling.

She'd regretted it by the next day.

But there was no point in dwelling on the consequences of her rash decision, and as long as she got what she wanted out of the deal, she'd consider her choice well made.

Probably.

The three fallen angels turned as a unit to face her and Cipher.

As she held out the flash drive, Bael grinned, his fangs glistening in air made smoky by the torch sconces. He had access to the best technology demons could devise or steal from humans, but his taste in decor ran medieval drab.

"Finally." He pinned Cipher with an intense stare. "You're ready to serve me."

"Serve *you*?" Cipher laughed, and Lyre cringed. Bael didn't appreciate being mocked. "You don't deserve my loyalty. I'll serve Sheoul's cause, but not yours."

Bael's lip curled, revealing wicked, lion-sized fangs. "Sheoul's cause *is* my cause."

"Then tell me how my list is going to be used." Cipher's deep voice was calm, steady, but his gaze smoldered with hate. "I can't imagine that hurting Azagoth's children is in Sheoul's ultimate best interest."

"That," Bael said, "is none of your concern." He fingered the drive. "If this is a trick, I'll kill you."

"Fuck you," Cipher growled, and this time Lyre nodded in approval. Bael might not like being mocked, but he respected good, old-fashioned aggression. "Those are the names of all Azagoth's children who remain in the human realm."

Bael tossed the drive to his brother Moloc, who plugged it into a tablet on a nearby table. After a moment, Moloc looked over. "There are only forty names here. How can there be so few?"

"Most of the children have already been gathered and taken to Sheoul-gra."

"If you're lying—"

"Yeah, yeah." Cipher tucked his hands in his jeans pockets, all casual, as if he wasn't standing in a nest of vipers. "You'll kill me."

Moloc's dark eyes went as black as a poisonous Sheoulin rose. Of the two brothers, he was the calmest, the one least prone to irrational actions. But he was also the smartest, which made him far more terrifying than Bael.

"Killing you will only be the beginning," he said as he shoved the tablet aside.

Rancor eyed Cipher the way Lyre eyed a juicy burger, and the creepy eyeballs dangling from her bracelet and necklace matched her hungry stare.

"What do you plan to do with him now?" Rancor licked her lips, and Lyre bristled. "Come work for *me*, and I'll treat you well."

"He's mine," Bael snapped. "I risked a lot to steal him from Azagoth."

"I belong to no one." Cipher looked each of the three fallen angels in the eye, and Lyre had to give him points for bravery. Or stupidity. Time would tell, she supposed. "I've given you what you want. Now give me what you promised. My freedom."

Bael reached for his favorite cup made from the skull of an angel. Looked like it was full of blood. "Until you've proven your loyalty, your freedom will be limited."

The anger smoldering in Cipher's eyes sparked blue fire. His growing ire shouldn't be sexy, but it was. It was that same intense but quiet fury that she'd found attractive in Dailon before he went vigilante on someone.

"That wasn't the deal, Bael."

"You didn't come to us willingly," Moloc said, sounding all reasonable and calm. "You have to earn your freedom."

Bael lowered the cup from his mouth and licked blood from his lips. "Worry not, worm, I'll find a use for you. One befitting your cyberskills."

"Yes," Rancor purred. "With your fallen angel powers, you could wreak havoc through the demonweb and human internet, and the viruses you could create, ones that can infect living creatures...yes, you'll be invaluable."

For a moment, Lyre thought Cipher would balk, but then he shrugged. "Sounds fun."

Bael watched Cipher over the rim of his cup as he drank, and when he lowered the vessel from his mouth, blood dripped from his lips. "I'll give you more freedom, only with Lyre by your side. Betray my goodwill, and I'll eat your intestines for breakfast." He flicked his wrist. "Begone, worm. Lyre, stay."

Lyre bowed her head in acknowledgement and said to Cipher under her breath, "Wait outside for me. Go. Before he changes his mind." Bael was likely to do breakfast now if Cipher didn't get the hell out of there.

With one last glare at everyone, including her, Cipher left. And she might have watched his retreating backside a little longer than appropriate before turning back to the three regional bosses.

"I did what you asked," she said. "What Flail failed to do. I want to talk about how I'm going to get my revenge."

"This again?" Bael curled his lip in contempt. "I have more important things to do."

"Like what?" Disappointment made her words curt, but dammit, she was tired of waiting. "What are you using those names for?"

Rancor looked up from poking one of the blinking eyeballs on her bracelet. "It's all part of the plan to release Satan from his prison."

Release Satan from prison? She'd heard talk of it, but as far as she knew, no one truly believed such a thing was possible.

"How can that be?" she demanded. "According to prophecy, he's got nearly a thousand years to go before he's released."

"Prophecy." Moloc scoffed, waving his claw-tipped hand. "There are endless interpretations of every prophecy. Even if we must wait until then, we will need all of the souls in Sheoul-gra on our side for the Final Battle between Heaven and Hell."

"Bullshit!" Bael threw his cup across the room, splashing blood all over the ice wall and freezing it instantly. "We will not wait! Azagoth will release the souls, and he'll—"

Moloc's hand came down on Bael's shoulder, easing his frenzy within seconds. Bael was prone to sudden angry fits and, somehow, his brother could always bring him down with something as minor as a touch.

"You should go," Moloc told her.

Only a fool would stay after being told to leave.

Apparently, Lyre was a fool. "Not until Bael tells me how he plans to help me get revenge on those who wronged me."

"Patience, female," Moloc said. "The war between Heaven and Hell will draw out the angels you seek to destroy."

Wait...*that* was the plan? Do nothing? She could have done that herself. "That's nothing but a byproduct of a war destined to happen! I don't want to wait a thousand years!"

"Neither do I," Moloc murmured. "Neither do I."

"Go, my love." Bael broke away from his brother. "Unbind Cipher's wings and let him discover his fallen angel talents. We will have use for them soon enough."

Bastards. All of this for nothing. Well, not nothing. She'd outmaneuvered Flail and gained some points with Moloc and Bael.

But still, none of this felt like a win.

Chapter Ten

Lyre had emerged from Bael's residence with one hell of a scowl on her gorgeous face. She'd said only that she was going to unbind his wings, and then she'd been silent as they hurried out of the massive ice castle. Once outside on the drawbridge that spanned a lava moat, she flashed them both to a bizarre land of gray desert sand, craggy hills, and weird, scrawny vegetation.

"Where are we?" He sidestepped to avoid a spiky black vine slithering toward his crude leather boots.

A prison guard had thrown the blister-spawning footwear at him, along with a pair of seriously beat-up jeans and a T-shirt that must have belonged to some other prisoner, on the way to the shower. Which was really just a drain in the slaughterhouse and a bucket of tepid water. Damn, he hated Sheoul.

"We're in the middle of nowhere."

"I can see that." Another vine, this one red and pulsing like a vein, followed them for a few steps. "I thought you were going to unbind my wings."

"I am. Somewhere safe." She led him toward a flat expanse of sand and gravel, her expression still creased with whatever disappointment Bael and his cohorts had dished out. "Your powers and wings didn't develop the way they should have, over the course of months or years. So when your wings pop out, who knows what's going to happen? Besides, we don't even know *why* your wings developed practically overnight."

Yeah, he'd love an answer as to why he'd woken up with the wing anchors on his back sewn shut, his wings bound inside, the day after being abducted. The official story, that they'd emerged while he was unconscious and that a sorcerer had been immediately called to bind them, seemed fishy to him. No one grew wings that fast, and binding them before knowing what powers they brought with them struck him as short-sighted.

Then again, Bael didn't always operate on logic or with forethought. Impulsive, narcissistic, and emotional, Bael was a dictator whose personal whims took him on wild boondoggles. If not for Moloc's restraining presence, Cipher doubted the guy could preside over his own bowel movements, let alone an entire territory.

"So you brought me to this wasteland so I wouldn't destroy anything."

"Exactly." She stopped in the center of the clearing, and all around them, the vegetation quivered as if excited by their presence. "Take off your shirt and turn around."

He'd say something blatantly inappropriate if he weren't vibrating out of his skin in anticipation of feeling his wings explode from his back. Of feeling power flood him once more. Yes, it was going to be dark energy, but after going without that unique ecstasy for so long, he was eager to experience any kind of power again.

Would it be different than the sensation of letting in Heavenly power? Would it be as addictive?

Lyre slid the blade from the sheath at her hip. "Are you ready?"

He opened his mouth to say yes, but his anticipation suddenly mixed with doubt. This would be the first step toward acceptance of his new life as a fallen angel. There would be no going back once he opened the floodgates to the evil that surrounded him.

But what choice did he have? Without the wings, he was powerless here, and he needed every advantage he could get to escape Bael's clutches.

"Cipher?" Lyre's hand came down lightly on the small of his back, and he jerked out of his thoughts.

"Yeah," he said roughly. He needed to do this, but he swore he'd do whatever it took to keep evil from consuming him completely. "But what's to keep me from flashing out of Bael's territory and escaping?"

"The same thing that happens to all Unfallen brought here against their will." Pity turned the silver in her eyes liquid, like a spoon full of water, and he knew he wasn't going to like whatever she had to say. "Bael had an Orphmage curse your wings with a tethering spell. You can't leave his realm until he trusts you and the curse is lifted."

Well, shit. That trashed his immediate plans for escape. But he wasn't going to give up. If he could get a message to Hawkyn, he could warn him about the list Cipher had given to Bael, and his friends could find a way to get him out of here.

He peeled off his T-shirt and bared his back to Lyre. "Do it."

He felt a whisper of air as Lyre brought the knife up to the twin scars near his shoulder blades, the wing anchors from which his new flappers would emerge. The blade's cold tip sliced into his skin, and he gritted his teeth against the pain. Lyre made two cuts and worked quickly, severing the binding twine that had kept his wings imprisoned.

"Done."

She hadn't needed to tell him that.

Every cell in his body sang with power, as if he'd just been plugged in to Sheoul's main battery. Pleasure-pain tore through his back and shoulders as pale gray, bat-like wings erupted in a violent spray of blood-red gelatinous membrane.

Nasty.

That was *not* how his lemon-tipped white Heavenly wings had popped out the first time.

He didn't have a chance to ponder more. An ice cold stream of energy shot down his arm and blasted from his fingertips, launching him backward in a tumble of dust and flapping, leathery wings.

"What the fuck?"

"Oh, wow!" Sheathing her dagger, Lyre jogged toward him. "That was dissolving ice. Look."

A column of ice had encased one of the tentacle shrubs, freezing it solid. But as they watched, it melted rapidly, turning the plant to liquid as it went. Within moments, there was nothing but a puddle where the shrub had been.

The other shrubs were frozen too, but not in ice. In fear.

That was pretty badass.

"I told you this could be chaotic—"

He threw out a hand to warn Lyre off. His control sucked, which he proved as a fireball shot at her from the palm of his hand.

Fire engulfed her, demon-faced flames that laughed and bit at her. No! Oh, shit. He felt her screams all the way to his gut as she fell to the ground and writhed in violent agony.

"*Soretay*! Stop!" He yelled commands in Sheoulic as he rushed toward her, but his words were useless.

He dove on top of her, covering her with his body. He tried to wrap his ugly-ass wings around her, but the fuckers didn't behave, instead fanning the flames, beating the both of them as they flapped uselessly.

Then, for no reason he could figure out, the shrieking apparitions flickered out. Lyre went limp beneath him, her exhausted, panting breaths puffing hot air against his neck.

"Wow," she rasped. "That was unexpected."

He pushed himself up on one arm and looked down at her. Scorch marks streaked her face and her clothes were singed. The hemline of her shirt was completely gone, leaving her flat belly exposed, a smudge of soot forming a crescent under her navel.

He wanted to clean it off with his tongue. Too bad she was playing for the wrong team.

You're playing for the same team now.

No, he wasn't. He might be a fallen angel, but not by choice. And, until evil took him over completely, he wasn't in league with them yet. And he'd never play for Bael the Seriously Unstable. Right now he had no choice, but once he figured out these new powers, he was going to get the fuck out of here.

"You can let me up anytime now," Lyre said softly. "Preferably before one of your new powers incinerates or melts me."

"Right." He jumped up and offered her a hand.

"Thanks, but no." Eyeing his hand like it was a viper, she pushed to her feet and backed away from him. "I'm just going to watch from...over there." She pointed to a bluff in the distance. The far distance.

It was probably for the best. With little to lose, he was going to test his limits and push his boundaries.

And boundaries? Well, those were something he'd never believed in, and for once, that little personality flaw was going to work for him instead of against him.

Chapter Eleven

Lyre watched Cipher try to get his powers and wings under control for just over twenty-four human hours.

It hadn't gone well. His wings, grotesquely veined with serrated claws at the tips, seemed to have minds of their own. His fallen angel gifts were powerful but unpredictable, like natural disasters spawned by a child's imagination.

Finally, after he exploded a tree with a superheated stream of blue light and nearly fried himself with the blowback, she called down to him.

"You hungry?" she yelled. "Because I could eat."

He let out a frustrated shout accompanied by a stomp of his foot, and a crack appeared in the ground under the sole of his boot. A deafening boom and a slow rumble started up, and within seconds the crack lengthened and began to widen as the walls collapsed and chunks of earth tumbled into the fissure.

That couldn't be good.

"Run!" she shouted.

He sprinted toward her, away from the growing gap. And then, suddenly, he spun around and ran toward it.

"Cipher! No!" What the fuck was he doing?

She extended her wings, ready to go after him as he leaped across the fissure. He wasn't going to make it to the other side of the sheer cliff face. Not if his wings wouldn't work—

His great wings flapped, lifting him easily skyward. He banked and soared in a glorious, elegant arc. A shout of pure joy rang out as he flew toward her, reminding her of the excitement she'd felt the first time she'd tried out her fallen angel wings. Hers had taken a year to grow, but it had taken only minutes to get them working. Cipher had to be thrilled to finally have his under control.

Folding her own black leather wings against her shoulders, she watched him come in for a landing, but as he did, one wing went rogue, freezing in a closed position. He clipped a tree and went into an unrecoverable spin before hitting the ground and tumbling to a stop next to her.

She coughed at the resulting cloud of dust. "That was graceful."

He eyed her from where he lay sprawled in the dirt. "Tell me you got that on video."

She didn't want to be charmed, but she laughed anyway. Humor was something she missed since entering Sheoul. No one had a sense of humor here. And those who did seemed to have found it puddled on the floor of a torture chamber.

"No such luck," she said.

"S'okay. But I'll bet it would have gone viral." Wincing, he shoved to his feet and tried to push his left wing into the retraction position. "I don't get it. I can't control these things. It's like they're fighting me. They don't feel right."

They didn't look right, either. Marred by what seemed to be scars and ragged edges, they weren't like any newbie wings she'd ever seen.

"Hmm. Maybe they were damaged by the restraints." She moved around behind him, silently admiring his broad, muscular back. It would look even better with scratch marks from her fingernails after a long, sweaty round of sex.

She blinked, surprised by her runaway thought. Yes, she'd been prepared to get down and dirty with him in his cell, but that had been nothing but a way to get the list of names from him. A means to an end.

Mostly. It wouldn't have been a hardship, anyway.

But things were different now. She didn't need anything from him, and while he was still a ward of Bael's realm he wasn't exactly a prisoner anymore. And now that his wings were unbound, the strength and power emanating from him wrapped around her like an aphrodisiac.

Didn't hurt that he was gorgeous, either.

Carefully, she nudged his right wing down so she could inspect it, running her palm over the long, flexible bones and thick, rugged expanses.

"How does that feel?"

"I can't feel anything." He looked over his shoulder at her, one lock of blond hair falling across his forehead and giving him a sexy, playful expression. "Are you touching me?"

Not in the way I'd like to be.

Nodding, she flexed one of the joints. "You can't feel this?"

"Not at all."

"Okay, try extending your wing."

Nothing happened. He let out a frustrated curse, and then, finally, the wing shot out before folding in again.

"It shouldn't have taken that much effort, should it? Is this normal?"

"I don't think so."

"You don't *think* so? You're a fallen angel, right?"

She jammed her fists on her hips. "No one is going to want to have sex with you if you're snarky with them, you know."

"*What?*"

Ignoring him, she stretched out one of his wings. "I told you, I've only been a fallen angel for a few years. It's not like I know everything about every fallen angel's experience." She poked at a blemish in a large expanse of the tough, leathery membrane. "But from what I've heard, once the wings erupt for the first time, it only takes a couple of hours to figure out the basics. You should have been flying hours ago." She dragged her finger down the long bone toward the base, her finger tingling from the electric sizzle emanating from it. "Were they sensitive at first?"

"Not at all. Should they have been?"

That was one thing everyone, including herself, remembered about their new wings. Sensitivity to the point of agony at the lightest touch. After the sensitivity eased, wings became erogenous zones. Cipher should be practically groaning in pleasure right now. Hell, she was nearly there and they weren't even her wings.

"Mine were crazy sensitive," she murmured as she zeroed in on a scar that circled the base of the wing, right where it emerged from the skin. She palpated it, feeling for deformities. "Does that hurt?"

"No. Why?"

"It's a scar. Like a ligature mark, maybe. Must be where the twine was wrapped." She checked the other wing and found a twin scar. Yikes. Her own wings throbbed in sympathy. He must have been in so much pain when his wings were bound. "Same thing on the other one."

"Makes sense." He rolled his broad shoulders, and she nearly drooled. "My wings aren't sensitive now, but they hurt like hell until you took the rope off."

Once, while researching the great demonic war of 263 BC, she'd interviewed a fallen angel whose wings had been bound after capture by an enemy. He'd said the pain was so great he'd taken a sword to his own back in an effort to cut the twine. Would Cipher have done the same if he'd had access to a weapon?

She shuddered. "I'm sorry they did this to you."

"Are you?" he asked as he turned to face her.

"Why would I lie?"

He looked at her like she was an idiot. "Because you're a fallen angel."

"I hate to point out the obvious," she said, "but so are you. And who did you trust before? You were Unfallen, living with the Grim Reaper and his unholy *griminions* and fallen servants. Did you trust them?"

"Some of them," he said, going on the defensive. "A lot of them are Memitim. Memitim who are working toward becoming full-fledged Heavenly angels."

She shook her head, knowing exactly how *un*-trustworthy angels were, fully-haloed or not, *family* or not. "If you trust any angel, you're a fool."

"I trust my friends." His big wings flapped in irritation, and a lightning bolt shot from one of them. The bolt vaporized a nearby cactus, and he gave her a sheepish smile. "Oops."

His wings folded and obediently disappeared.

"So where are they now, these friends? Do you think they're searching for you?" She raked him critically with her gaze, from his muscular legs and hard-cut upper torso to his square, masculine jaw and intelligent eyes. She appreciated all of that, but his friends would see him very differently. "What do you think they'd do if you showed up looking like this? Fallen angel wings and a dark soul? They'll turn on you. They'll kill you, Cipher."

"No, they won't."

She'd had faith in her own friends and family once too. And, like Cipher, she hadn't listened to warnings. "Like I said, you're a fool."

"Sounds like someone is a little bitter." One blond eyebrow went up in a quizzical arch. "Betrayed by friends, I'm guessing?"

"Family." She looked out over the scorched and cratered field of destruction Cipher had wrought upon the earth and vegetation. "But friends abandoned me too. It was fun. Lots of fun."

At least none of her family had *enjoyed* watching as she was held down and her wings severed. They'd been devastated. Her sisters, even the one who had betrayed her, had cried. Her mother, wracked by sobs, had collapsed in grief. And her father, ever stoic and suffering from a perpetual stiff upper lip, had managed to scrounge up a tear to shed.

Although she couldn't be sure if the tear was for her or for his reputation.

How could you, he'd whispered just loudly enough for her to hear as guards escorted her to the chopping block. She'd brought so much shame and dishonor down on her family, and all for a male.

But that male had been worth the risk. If not for her own poor judgment in confiding in her sister, no one would have found out that she'd fallen for a demon.

She'd played that day over and over in her head, wishing she'd never told Lihandra about him, and she definitely regretted arranging for them to meet. If only Lihandra could have seen the good in him, a champion for those who couldn't get justice any other way. For those who couldn't stand up for themselves.

And now he was dead, Lyre was disgraced, and her sister got to justify what she'd done by saying she'd done it for Lyre's own good and that she hadn't meant for Lyre to lose her wings.

Right.

As an angel named Lyresiel, Lyre had a contentious relationship with her older sister. She and Lihandra had never agreed on anything, had gone almost a century without speaking once, and had driven her parents and younger sister, Bellagias, mad with their fighting. But Lyre had never believed Lihandra hated her so much that she'd turn Lyre in for "copulating with a demon."

Lyre hadn't "copulated" with anyone, but that hardly mattered to the angelic council that presided over such matters. That she *would* have copulated with said demon was what mattered. Oh, yes, she'd admitted all the things she'd wanted to do with him.

I'd have let him take my virginity, and then I'd have ridden him until we both passed out. And then we'd have done it in our dreams, because he had the power to connect us that way, too.

Every member of the council had gone apoplectic. But her erotic agenda wasn't what had gotten her kicked out of Heaven. Nope. They'd been willing to cut her some slack and write her dalliance off as a youthful transgression. Oh, there would have been some severe punishment, of course, but compared to losing one's wings, it would have been a slap on the wrist.

No, she'd have gotten off easy.

If they just hadn't gone and killed her demon.

* * * *

So Lyre had been betrayed by her family.

That had to suck.

Cipher, for all his faults, had been lucky enough to have a supportive family. Sure, when he'd fucked up and lost his wings they'd been disappointed, but neither his parents nor any of his twenty-two siblings had trashed him. A couple had even reached out to him during his time in Sheoul-gra, keeping in contact and relaying messages from his parents.

But that was before. When he'd been an Unfallen trying to earn his way back into Heaven. How would they react to his becoming a True Fallen? Was Lyre right? Would his friends and family turn on him? Try to kill him?

Lyre seemed lost in thought, her gaze going somewhere he couldn't go. The weird thing was that he wanted to. Because as much as he figured he should hate her, he didn't.

Maybe he just didn't know her well enough to hate her.

Dammit, he wished he had access to the internet or demonweb. He'd love to do a little cyberstalking to find out more about her.

Guess he had to stick with the old-fashioned way. Ugh. Digging up dirt online was so much easier and less talky.

"So," he said, taking the plunge. "How did you lose your wings?"

She jammed her fists on her hips, just above where her low-slung waistband sat. She'd flashed away at some point while he'd been practicing his new powers, and she'd come back with clean clothes free of scorch marks. He definitely approved of the outfit. In the months he'd known her, she'd always worn earth or muted tones, but today's black cargo pants had been paired with a purple tank top that emphasized her perfect, rounded breasts and slender waist. And her combat boots had matching purple laces.

He wondered what color her bra and panties were.

"You know that asking someone how they fell from grace is considered a rude question," she huffed.

Yeah, he had totally sick social skills. "Do I look like I'm concerned about being rude?" He looked down at his palm and summoned a ball of crimson light in an attempt to use his new powers without his wings extended. Maybe he'd have more control this way. One thing that didn't change was the oily, malevolent vibe that skated over the surface of his skin when he was using one of his fallen angel powers. "You don't have to answer if you don't want to."

"No, it's okay," she sighed. "I fell in love with a demon."

"A demon?" His hand jerked in surprise and his ball of light fell to the ground, exploding into a thousand shards of light on impact. "Was he hot? Like, not all scaly and snouty?"

"Of course he was hot," she said as she leaped backward to avoid a spark of super-heated light. "He was a...what are they called? *Tertaceo*? He looked like any other human male model."

"He was a model?"

"He was a psychotherapist."

Sounded boring as shit. Lots of talky. And he'd bet the guy wasn't even that attractive. "What species?"

"Somniatus."

He revised his thought. *Not* so boring. "A nightmare devil."

Demon slayers claimed they were one of the most dangerous demons there were, attacking their victims in their dreams where they were vulnerable.

She smiled wistfully, and Cipher cursed the trickle of jealousy making its way through his body. He had no reason to be envious of a freaking demon.

Had it fed on her like Cipher had? Had it tasted the sweet nectar that had flowed over his fangs and tongue? The very idea that the guy might have taken her like that made him a little prickly. Again, for no freaking reason.

"He was a nightmare," she said softly, "but only to those who deserved it."

"So he was a benevolent demon? Really?" Color him skeptical. "Somniati feed off of terror."

Her smile turned wicked, matching the gleam in her eyes. "And who better to terrorize than those who hurt others?"

Okay, yeah, he'd give her that. There was no sport in hurting innocents. Bringing a tough-guy asshole to his knees, though...*that* was satisfying.

"So you lost your wings for fucking a demon?" Cipher regretted asking the moment it was out of his mouth, because now he couldn't stop picturing her naked. With another male. "I thought Heaven stopped doing that a few centuries ago."

"They seem to pick and choose," she muttered. "But no, that's not why I got a one-way ticket out of Heaven." She looked off into the distance again, beyond the lake bubbling with shit-brown liquid and the mountain range shaped like skulls, but this time, her expression was etched in anger. "I was to be confined to the Heavenly realm as punishment, so before the sentence was carried out, I went to say goodbye to him. But while I was at his place, we were attacked."

"The Aegis?"

"I *wish* those demon-slaying idiots were the ones who attacked us. They were angels. I fought back. I had to protect him, you know?" She didn't wait for his acknowledgment. "I accidentally killed a novice battle angel who was there to assist in Dailon's capture."

Oh, fuck. "Yeah, that would do it." He made another light ball, but smaller this time. "So they booted you after that?"

"Oh, no," she said, her voice dripping with bitterness. "That would have been too easy. First they forced me to watch as he was tortured and killed."

He winced, having witnessed a few executions by angels making a point. "That had to have sucked."

A few strands of silky hair had escaped her messy bun, and a hot breeze spun up, whipping them around her cheeks, softening her expression. She didn't belong in this hellscape, and for the first time, he wanted to know about her background not for tactical reasons, but for personal ones.

"I knew going into our relationship that we didn't have a shot at a meaningful future, but I wanted time to figure that out, you know?"

She cocked her head, watching him with curiosity. "You seem pretty chill about this. You're the most laid-back fallen angel I've ever met."

"Well, I *have* only been fallen for a few years. True Fallen for a few months. You know, since the day I was dragged down here and imprisoned in Bael's ice jail."

A shamed blush bloomed in her cheeks, surprising the shit out of him. "I remember when Bael sent Flail on a mission to infiltrate Azagoth's realm. I was jealous for a while." She gave a bitter laugh. "As a historian, I was dying to meet him."

He frowned as the implications of what she was saying took a dark turn. "So Flail wasn't sent to nab me?"

"Not at first. Bael wanted intel on Azagoth. You just happened to be the best way to get it."

Well, fuck. If he hadn't invited Flail into his bed and, therefore, his life, she'd never have known how important his cyber skills had been to Azagoth. This was all his fault.

Which didn't change the fact that Flail needed to die.

Lyre studied him for a moment, her expression thoughtful. "I'm curious. What were you like as an angel?"

Ah, those were the days. He'd spent them surfing on the Beaches of Paradise, skiing in the Infinite Mountains, and feasting on dishes crafted from decadent ingredients available only in Heaven.

"I was a laid-back son-of-a-bitch," he said. "Pissed off all the Type-As, you know?"

"Is that why you fell?" She tucked a strand of hair behind her ear, and he suddenly wondered if they were sensitive to being nibbled. "Pissed off the wrong asshole?"

"Nah. I slept with a Primori."

"Oh...shit." She stared. "Human?"

"Human virgin whose virginity was the reason she was Primori." His actions had also screwed over Hawkyn, who had been her guardian. He hadn't known Hawkyn at the time, so he hadn't really cared. To this day he couldn't believe Hawk had forgiven him.

"Did you know she was Primori when you slept with her?"

"Yeah."

She stared harder. "Did you know what a Primori was? Like, that they're guarded by Memitim because something about them is important to the fate of the world?"

"Well, I didn't know her virginity was the thing that made her a

Primori. And I didn't know she was a virgin until afterward." Still, it was forbidden for any angel to sleep with a human, let alone a human under the protection of Memitim. "But yeah."

"Damn. You're an asshole."

He snorted, because hello, that was obvious. "Yeah."

But if he could take it back, he would. He'd met the human, Felicia, in Fiji, where she was on her honeymoon. Alone. Her fiancé had left her at the altar, and since the honeymoon was paid for, she'd gone alone. She'd been angry and hurt and ready for a vengeful wild fling to give someone else what she'd saved for the man who'd left her.

He'd been at the resort keeping tabs on a demon plotting a cyber attack on several countries, and Felicia had set her sights on him. Being young, arrogant, and really, really easy, he'd been all about hooking up with the hot, tight-bodied woman looking for a way to forget her jackass of a fiancé.

Then Hawkyn had showed up, all, "*Hey, she's Primori, and you need to back the fuck off, Halo.*"

No one told Cipher to back the fuck off.

So he'd ignored the Memitim, and when Hawkyn showed up again, knocking on Felicia's hotel room door just as they were starting to get down and dirty, Cipher had enough. As a full angel, he'd been far more powerful than Hawkyn, and he'd put the Memitim into a temporary coma and flashed him to a deserted island.

Then he'd given Felicia a night to remember.

He had a lot of regrets about that day, but taking care of Felicia wasn't one of them. He shouldn't have had sex with her; that much was clear. But he didn't regret everything else he'd done to help her get through the pain of being betrayed by her fiancé. It wasn't much, but when she'd cried afterward, he'd held her. He'd brought her food and nursed her through a hangover. And when she'd talked about hurting herself, he'd talked her off the ledge.

The day she'd flown back home, he'd been summoned to Heaven for a quick judgment and a wingectomy.

No, sleeping with Felicia hadn't been worth it. He didn't know what her destiny would have been if he hadn't, but just a year ago he'd checked up on her and found that she was a happily married Connecticut dietician with two grown children, grandchildren, and a beach house in Florida. Hopefully, at least for her, her life was better than it would have been if Cipher hadn't interfered.

"Well, come on, asshole," Lyre said, mercifully pulling him out of his past. "We have things to do."

"Food?" he asked hopefully. His stomach was starting to rebel.

"Right after I show you your new home."

He shouldn't be excited about getting a residence in Sheoul, but anything had to be better than where he'd spent the last seven months. "You mean I don't have to sleep on a slab of ice in a prison cell anymore?"

"Nope. If you were a demon, you'd get a filthy hut in some shanty town somewhere. But lucky you, you're a fallen angel, so you get an upgrade." She waggled her dark brows. "In Sheoul, fallen angels are the elite. Like the super-rich in the human world. Different rules apply. Like how you were in the luxury prison."

That had been luxury? He didn't even want to know how much worse it could have been.

"Where do you live?" he asked.

Her wings, midnight black with elegant arches, erupted from her back. "Give me your hand and I'll show you."

He took her hand, liking the way they fit together. "We're going to fly?"

"The curse on your wings prevents you from flashing, even within Bael's realm, so you might as well get used to flying."

He gestured to the dents in the ground where he'd hit it hard. "You saw how well that went."

"That's why I'm holding your hand," she explained. "I'm going to help you."

He didn't have the chance to process his surprise that she was going to take the time to help him get his flying shit together before she'd lifted off, yanking him into the air with her. But he did give a silent thanks, because the quicker he became proficient at this fallen angel stuff, the faster he was going to get out of here.

Maybe she'll come with you.

Startled by that sudden thought, he faltered in flight and nearly took a dive. But Lyre's capable, strong arms caught him, and her wings buoyed them into the endless sky with effortless grace.

Yeah. Maybe she'd come with him.

Or maybe he'd have to kill her.

But it was definitely a predicament for later.

Chapter Twelve

The flight to Lyre's place took twice as long as it should have, but it certainly had been interesting. And sometimes terrifying. Like a test flight of an airplane built by someone who had never seen one.

Cipher definitely failed at Fallen Angel Flying 101, but Lyre gave him an A for effort and an A+ for cursing.

"Mother...*fuck*!" He shouted as one wing crumpled and he rolled hard. Lyre barely caught him before he spun out of control and nailed one of the housing structures they were trying to avoid as they flew toward her apartment. "This is bullshit!"

"We're almost there." Clinging to his arm, she guided him between two fifty-story statues of Satan in his ugly beast form. She shuddered, as always, as the statues' eyes followed them. "Bank right."

"Are these apartment buildings?" He flapped his wings hard, but he could barely stay aloft. "They look like giant termite hills turned into beehives."

She'd always thought so too. "Right there." She guided him through an opening near the top of one of the structures and landed on the baked clay floor.

Cipher set down surprisingly gracefully and put away his wings as he looked around. "Nice place."

"I guess." She kicked off her boots. She'd always preferred to go barefoot at home, even if she was only there for a minute. "It's no Heaven."

No, the dwelling was an insult, and not entirely because, as a weakling and a newbie fallen angel, she'd been assigned the tiniest quarters available. It was also just a flat-out affront to the senses. Her house in Heaven had been sprawling and colorful, nestled in a private cloud that floated over a vast, turquoise sea. This...this was small and boring, but she didn't have the motivation to decorate beyond the plush Persian rug in the middle of the room.

Decorating would signify some kind of permanence, and for some reason she didn't want to give in to that kind of thinking, even though she'd basically sold her soul to Bael.

"It's kind of like the dorms in Sheoul-gra." He glanced over at the dining table with seats for two that had never been used. "Except you have a kitchen area."

"Where did you get your meals?"

His sensuous lips curved into wistful smile. "Cafeterias. But the food was good." He noticed that she'd taken off her boots, and he did the same. The polite gesture both amused her and left her off balance. No one in Sheoul was polite. Ever. "It wasn't always that way, though. When I first got to Sheoul-gra, it was a wreck. It was like living in a Tim Burton movie. The Nightmare Before Lilliana."

"The what?"

He chuckled and took in the demon version of cave paintings on the walls that she'd cover up if she wasn't worried about awakening some ancient curse or something. "Life before Azagoth met his mate was way different than the way it is now. Lilliana's awesome."

The sad note in his voice knocked a few bricks out of the wall she was trying really hard to build around her heart. Evil wasn't doing it nearly as quickly as she'd like.

"You really miss Sheoul, don't you?"

"Yeah."

Another brick took a tumble, and that was enough of that. Time to shift gears and subjects.

"Well, I can't do anything about that," she said, "but I can get you your own place. Since I'm still in charge of you, you'll take the apartment next door. Bael had it warded so you can enter but you can't leave through the main entrance." She gestured to the narrow door at the back of her place. "You have to use the doorway connected to mine."

"Are all of these hive-holes connected?"

"Yep." She padded past the bed and headed toward the icebox in the kitchen. She could get a real fridge, but unlike most of the other apartments, hers didn't have electricity.

"How do you keep other people out?" Cipher's footsteps followed behind her. "Wards, I'm guessing?"

"You guessed right. Are you hungry?" Bending over, she opened the little icebox and pulled out a couple of *bludbeouf* wraps she'd picked up yesterday at one of the local markets. "These are kind of like human gyros, except they're made with demon cows. And maybe a little hellrat—"

She broke off when she straightened and caught Cipher staring at her ass. And he didn't even have the decency to pretend that wasn't what he was doing. Instead, he gave her a cocky grin that made heat spread through her pelvis and suspicion spread through her brain.

"What?" he asked, all innocence and charm. "You asked if I was hungry."

She handed him the sandwich and tossed hers to the table. "I'm not buying it."

"What? That you have a fine ass?"

"I'm not buying...this." She gestured to all of him, down to his bare feet. "You're being too nice. Bael had you tortured for months. He forced you to betray your friends and ex-boss, and now you're standing in my apartment with a hard-on and a bad boy smirk? Do you really expect me to believe you're just falling in line like a good little minion of Satan?"

"Revenant," he said as he unwrapped his food.

"What?"

"Revenant is king now." He poked at a dripping shaving of meat hanging from one end of his wrap. "You should have said minion of Revenant."

Not if Bael and Moloc have their way.

"Whatever. What's your game, Cipher?"

Suddenly, her spine was kissing the wall and Cipher was kissing her neck, and where the hell was his sandwich?

"My game," he growled against her throat, "is called Stay Alive. And that means feeling alive. It means taking pleasure where you can so you can survive the shit when it hits. And after seven months of shit, I have one hell of a pleasure deficit."

He was lying. Oh, as his hands tugged her close and his lips sucked at the tender skin at the crook of her shoulder, she knew he was being honest about what he'd said. But he wasn't telling the *entire* truth.

He was distracting her from the truth. He was biding his time until he could either earn his freedom, make his escape, or get revenge before the evil of Sheoul took the choice from him.

And the thing was, she didn't care, because he was right. She needed to feel alive. Needed to fuel up on pleasure, because the bad down here was *really* bad.

Lifting her leg, she hooked it around his thigh. The hard bulge behind his fly rocked against her center as he undulated slowly, a masculine body wave that drove a tingle of excitement from her scalp to her toes. Damn, he was good at this. They hadn't even started and every feminine instinct she had was on board and demanding more.

Cipher lifted his head, a flush staining his cheeks, a primitive hunger in his eyes. She knew how that felt, because she was starving too.

"You okay with this?" His mouth quirked in a teasing smile. "Or do you wanna eat first?"

Was he kidding? "You want to eat?"

"Food? No." He dropped to his knees and in three smooth, fast moves, he unbuttoned her pants and yanked them to her ankles. In two more moves, he had them flung across the room.

He gazed up at her, the stark, male need in his expression making her glad for the wall behind her. It had been so long since anyone had looked at her like this.

No, not like this. Dailon had viewed her with lust, but it had seemed...tamer somehow. Maybe because her virginity had sat between them like a chaperone. He'd been willing to fool around, but he was less willing to "foul an angel."

The memory of Dailon pricked her heart. Maybe now wasn't the time to do this. "Cipher—"

His warm mouth covered her mound through the silk of her panties, and she had to bite her tongue to keep from shouting. Okay, she was wrong. This *was* the time to do it, and she moaned as his tongue probed her valley, the dampness from his licks blending with her wet arousal. He stroked her with his tongue, and at the rasp of sensation across her clit she rocked her hips and let out a strangled sound as the first tremors of bliss snuck up on her.

But he denied her, the bastard, his impish gaze catching hers as he sliced a fang through the elastic leg of her panties. An erotic growl rolled in his throat as he spread her legs roughly, splitting the fabric with a delicate rip. Now she was open to him, her hot flesh exposed to the cool air and his gaze. Her face went hot and her instinct was to close her legs, but he held her prisoner, and she didn't have the willpower to fight it. Especially when he glanced up at her, his blue eyes ablaze.

"You're so beautiful," he said, so reverently she nearly broke down in tears. Holding her with his gaze, he captured her sex in his open mouth and kissed her deep.

"Cipher," she whispered as she threw her head back against the wall and allowed herself to simply feel something other than the cold misery of life in Sheoul. "This is...so...good."

He made a humming sound that vibrated through her flesh, taking her breath and her thoughts. Gripping his hair, she arched into him, riding his lips as they nibbled at her swollen bud. He brushed them from side to side and suckled gently before licking at her with the flat of his tongue as his thumb dipped inside her. Waves of ecstasy pummeled her as he rimmed her opening, spreading her juices and teasing her out.

"Yes," she moaned. "Oh, *yes*."

She cried out as his tongue carried her over the line, hurling her into orgasmic bliss. Sharp bursts of pleasure spread from her pelvis to her breasts, taking her breath and, nearly, her consciousness.

Her legs went jelly as the climax ebbed, but he caught her, lifting her as he spun her toward the bed. The backs of her legs hit the mattress, and they both tumbled onto it in a messy tangle of limbs. His masculine weight pinned her deliciously, and she wrapped her arms around him as she spread her thighs to accommodate his big body.

Smiling up at him, her gaze locked with his, she wedged her hand between their bodies to tear open his jeans. He shifted, bracing himself on one elbow to allow her access. Her fingers found the outline of his hard length under the fabric, and he gasped as she squeezed him, toying with him before she flicked open the top button.

The click of the button popping accompanied the soft whisper of a cool breeze.

Oh, shit.

She froze, sensing a presence. Cipher's head cranked toward the entrance and he snarled, a bloodcurdling rumble that echoed off her walls.

Son of a bitch.

Lyre didn't need to look to know that Flail was standing in the doorway.

* * * *

Cipher leaped to his feet and put himself between Lyre and Flail, his wings sprouting before he could stop them. But fuck it, they were shielding Lyre from Flail's view as she dressed, and they made a pointed display of *neener-neener, my wings are bigger than yours*. And if he accidentally zapped Flail with one of his uncontrollable weapons, even better.

Petty? Yes. Did he care? No. Because once he had his powers under control, he was going to zap her intentionally and fatally.

"Did I interrupt something?" Flail asked, all fake innocence and wide eyes as Lyre scrambled to throw on her pants. She gestured at the entrance to the apartment. "Lyre, you know you can set wards to protect your place from prying eyes and unwanted visitors, right?" Fake innocence turned into mocking pity. "Oh, I forgot. You can't."

Cipher had no idea what she meant by that, but Lyre's red-faced fury made clear that she knew.

"What do you want, Flail?" He moved toward her, preparing to toss her off the balcony. He wasn't confined in a cell anymore, his wings weren't bound, and he held a hell of a grudge.

An aura of energy bloomed around her. She was prepared for him to attack, which proved she wasn't stupid. "I come bearing good news."

"Let me guess." Cipher stopped, curious enough to hold off tossing her into the abyss below. It would be pointless anyway, given that she could fly. But it would be fun, and like he'd told Lyre, he was operating with a pleasure deficit. Especially since the bitch had interrupted what would have been a *lot* of pleasure. "You're suffering from an incurable disease that will slowly and painfully kill you. Is that it? Because that would be *great* news."

She didn't look amused. She'd always been lacking in the humor department. "Sorry to disappoint you, but this might be even better. You've earned Bael's trust. To some degree," she amended. "He has an assignment for you."

"Okay, I'll bite," he said, his voice laced with skepticism. "Why the sudden change of heart?"

"Your list panned out." Cipher's gut hit the floor as Flail plopped down on the leather sofa and kicked her feet up on the makeshift coffee table made from an old crate. "We took out one of Azagoth's children. Nearly got a second, but the damned Memitim arrived and ruined everything."

Oh...damn. Oh, fuck. Oh...*fuck*!

Cipher's knees went liquid, and he had to force himself to stay upright. To pretend he wasn't affected by the news. But in reality, he wanted to puke.

He was responsible for an innocent child's death. And not just any child. Azagoth's child. An angel.

"Anyway, congratulations. You've proven your worth." She tossed him the flash drive he'd downloaded the damned list onto. He wanted to step on it. Break it. Smash it to bits. "That contains the names of a few of Bael's enemies. He wants you to devise a computer virus that will kill them. He also wants a virus that will spread through the human population. Something gruesome. Can you make zombies?"

Still sick to his stomach, he stared blindly at the drive. "That's not how computer viruses work." His voice was flat, numb, and he hoped Flail didn't notice.

"You'll make them work. We have confidence in your abilities. And your wings will help you."

His wings? "What will help me is my laptop and access to the internet and demonweb."

"That," Flail said with a knowing smile, "is not an option. You can use your laptop, but it stays where it is. If you need access to the webs, Bael's is available to you."

Screw Bael's devices. No doubt the fallen angel was watching every keystroke on every computer in the region. But Cipher made sure his computer was unhackable and essentially invisible on a network.

"Now," she said as she came to her feet. "I have Memitim to hunt. Azagoth *will* join our cause, or he'll lose everything he loves."

"You *bitch*."

Uncontrollable rage slammed into him. He knew he should control it. Knew he couldn't let these evil fucks know that he still gave a shit about his old life. His old friends. But knowing they'd killed an innocent child and were still planning to kill Azagoth's offspring boiled off all his logic and laid-back nature.

Opening himself up to the evil surrounding him, he roared in ecstasy and fury as the oily burn of malevolence seeped into his cells. Then he struck out at Flail with whatever fallen angel ability surfaced first.

A stream of fire shot from his palm, but Flail blocked it with an invisible shield. He changed tacks, pummeling her defense with a series of ice shards. She fell back under the intense assault, but suddenly his powers went crazy, and the shards turned into fucking snowballs that burst into acid powder on contact. Powder that burned holes in Lyre's floor, walls, and ceiling, but didn't do a damned thing to Flail or her shield.

"Is that all you can do, Cipher?"

"You'd better hope so," he ground out.

Grinning victoriously, Flail raised her hand to deliver what would probably have been a devastating strike, but Lyre charged, throwing herself into the other female. Flail, caught off guard by the attack, stumbled, and a heartbeat later, she disappeared over the balcony with a scream.

"Ward the opening," he shouted, remembering too late that apparently Lyre couldn't do that. He cursed, unsure how to do it himself.

Turned out that there was no need. Flail rose up in flight, gave them a jaunty wave, and disappeared into the dark sky.

Trembling with rage, adrenaline, and frustration, he shot her the finger. She was going to kill Memitim, and he was helpless to so much as warn Azagoth.

"Damn, I hate her," Lyre snapped, her gaze locked in the direction Flail had gone.

"She needs to die."

Lyre turned to him, her fangs bared. "Then maybe you should get to work on those viruses," she suggested, the silver in her eyes darkening into gunmetal death. It was sexy as hell, and his evil side, growing larger every time he opened himself up to it, stirred.

Simmer down, buddy. We have fallen angels to kill.

That seemed to satisfy his inner sex fiend, and he reached for his uneaten sandwich. A guy had to keep up his energy, after all.

"I'm ready when you are," he said. "Let's go make a plague."

Chapter Thirteen

"Please, my lord, I've told you everything!"

The demon screamed, blood bubbling from his parched, swollen lips, as Azagoth wrenched the horn out of his skull with a wet crack of bone and flesh.

"That was the last one." Azagoth tossed the bloody length of ivory to the floor, where it clattered to rest against another horn. "The next protruding body part I rip off will be located a little farther south. So tell me what I want to know."

The demon moaned, slumping from exhaustion and the strain of hanging by his bony wrists from Azagoth's favorite torture rack. A gift from Malachi, a powerful demon from the Islith region of Sheoul, the mahogany rack was a thing of beauty, perfectly sized to grace the far wall in his office, and conveniently located next to the soul tunnel. This Croucher demon had not, however, come through the tunnel, his soul escorted by a *griminion.*

Nope, his sons Journey and Maddox had dragged the bastard in themselves.

Azagoth's cell phone beeped from his desk. Inconvenient timing, but he swore to Lilliana that he would always get back to her immediately, especially now that she was close to giving birth.

"Hey, Hawk," he called over his shoulder. "Is that a text from Lilli?"

Hawkyn had arrived a few minutes ago with news about Cipher. Somehow, he and Journey had been able to crack into Bael's demonweb, and they'd left a message for the fallen angel. So far, there'd been no response.

Azagoth wasn't sure what to think about Cipher's situation. Bael had taken Cipher for a reason, and Azagoth suspected the kidnapping had something to do with him. Lilliana had pointed out that Unfallen angels everywhere were, in general, being hunted and forced into Sheoul, and that was true. Demons and fallen angels everywhere were preparing for the End of Days now that there was a time table.

But Cipher's abduction had felt personal, because no one in their right mind would abduct anyone under Azagoth's protection.

Which meant that whoever had done it wanted Azagoth's attention.

Azagoth was going to show them why drawing his attention was a very bad thing.

Hawkyn flipped Azagoth's phone over and glanced at the screen. "Yup, it's Lilliana. She wants to know what time to plan for dinner. She's got a recipe of Suzanne's she wants to try on you. Says it's...oh, I see. She wants to try it *on* you." Hawk's face went crimson as he put the phone down and backed away as if it were a poisonous Croix viper. "She's very graphic about it."

Azagoth laughed. Damn, it felt right to do that again. At least, it felt right to be laughing at anything good and pure and pleasant. The only thing that had been funny while Lilliana was gone was the suffering of people who deserved it.

"Suzanne recently did an episode about aphrodisiacs and food," Azagoth said. "Lilliana thought it was interesting."

Hawk cringed the way he always did when his sister and sex came up in the same conversation. Azagoth got that. Suzanne was his daughter, so he didn't like to go there either.

"I don't want to know." Hawkyn gestured to the demon. "Shouldn't you be torturing that guy anyway?"

"I didn't think this was your kind of thing." Not all of Azagoth's offspring had inherited his special interests. Maddox and Emerico showed promise, though.

Hawkyn's expression turned dark. "The bastard tried to kill one of my sisters. The sooner we know who he works for, the sooner we can destroy them."

Azagoth nodded in approval. Maddox had said something similar when he'd asked to stay for the Croucher's interrogation. He'd been disappointed when Mad was called away to watch over one of his Primori.

He turned back to the demon. "So," he said, as he watched his hands form the claws that were going to do the ripping he'd promised, "are you still insisting that you and your demon buddies just happened to stumble upon my daughter while you were innocently roaming the streets after a night of terrorizing humans? That you didn't know I was Gretchen's father?"

Azagoth had never met Gretchen, one of his young children who had been raised in the human realm, but she was safe in Sheoul-gra now, and once she was settled in and had gotten over the shock she'd been through, he'd introduce himself.

Fear flickered in the demon's eyes as Azagoth dragged one sharp claw down his skeletal chest.

Lower, and the demon began to tremble. Lower, and he swallowed hard, the veins in his scrawny throat bulging.

Lower.

"Okay, okay," the demon blurted, his eyes wild now.

Azagoth dug his claw into the soft abdominal skin. "Okay...what?"

"W-we were sent to kill her," he said in a rush, and now they were finally getting somewhere. "But we didn't know she was your daughter! I swear!"

That was most likely true. It would be stupid to tell underlings too much, especially if the information might make them balk at following an order.

"I believe you," Azagoth said in a pleasant, calm voice. He even paused his finger, letting the demon relax for a moment. Letting him feel hope.

Hope was for fucking morons. This creature was going to die a terrible, painful death, no matter what.

Obviously.

"How unlucky for you that Memitim are rounding up all of my children in the human realm, and Gretchen was next in line." They'd gotten to her just in time. Five minutes later, and her body would probably have been found partially eaten and dumped in a German forest or field. "But you can change your luck." He leaned in, baring his fangs as he lowered his voice to a husky whisper. "Tell me who sent you to kill my daughter."

Silence hung in the air, and for a long moment, Azagoth thought the demon would refuse. But just as he began to drop his hand to start squeezing things until they popped, the Croucher let out a resigned groan.

"Bael," he rasped. "The fallen angels Bael and his brother, Moloc."

Azagoth went taut. The names weren't surprising; Moloc and Bael had been testing Azagoth's patience for centuries in their quest to find ways to keep souls that rightfully belonged to him. But that wasn't what made anger singe the edges of Azagoth's patience as he turned to Hawkyn.

"Bael," he snarled. "The bastard who took Cipher."

"Then this is all connected," Hawkyn said, but he was missing the real link.

Azagoth laid it out, crystal fucking clear. "Cipher has access to the locations of all my human-realm children."

Hawkyn's emerald eyes—Azagoth's eyes—shot wide as the implication sank in. "No way." He shook his head. "*No* damned way. Cipher wouldn't have given Bael anything."

"Are you certain?"

"Yes. I know it," Hawk insisted. "He would never betray us. He'd never betray *you*."

Hawkyn was so convinced of his friend's innocence. Azagoth wished he could be as sure. Or even a little sure. Cipher had been an asset, and he'd been loyal. But in Azagoth's thousands of years of life, he'd seen loyal people turn. Everyone had a price...or a breaking point.

Someone banged on the door. "Hawkyn! Father!"

The urgency in Journey's voice raised the hair on the back of Azagoth's neck. With a mental flick of his mind, the heavy office door swung open.

"What is it?" he asked as Journey rushed inside.

"It's Amelia," Journey breathed.

"Who?"

"Amelia," Hawkyn repeated miserably. "Dammit."

"She is—was—one of your...ah...fuck." Journey dropped his gaze to the floor and Azagoth's gut went with it. He knew where this was going. "She was a sister in the human realm. I was with Jasmine. We went to get her. She...she was the last one on the list. She's dead."

Sudden rage turned Azagoth's blood to acid. Everything inside him burned as he rounded on Hawkyn.

"Still think this is a coincidence?" His voice was warped, spoken through clenched teeth. "Find Cipher. Find him *now*."

"But Father—"

Azagoth's inner demon clawed at his control, and he wasn't in the frame of mind to restrain it. The monster was about to be loosed.

"I offer this one mercy, my son," he growled. "Find Cipher. Find him and kill him. Because if you don't, I will." His sons just stood there. "*Go*!"

They scrambled out of the office, and Azagoth let his beast loose. He was going to break some rules and people were going to pay for killing his children. Eyes for eyes.

He started with the Croucher's.

Chapter Fourteen

In the hour it took for Lyre and Cipher to get from her place to his computer, Cipher's fury had dulled enough that he could temporarily relegate his part in Azagoth's child's death to the background.

Revenge, though, was very much in the foreground.

He fired up his laptop with the single-minded focus of a vampire on the trail of a bleeding human.

"Do you think you can do it?" Lyre asked as she locked the door behind them.

"What, write a virus? Sure."

"The kind of viruses Bael wants?"

Cipher let out a bitter laugh. "No. People have been trying since the internet began."

"But there are stories about people being possessed or cursed after opening emails or files."

He nodded, familiar with those. He'd written code for dozens of types of viruses like that, but as a powerless Unfallen he'd lacked the ability to execute them. Now, maybe he could. They'd be perfect to kill individuals like the enemies Bael wanted dead.

"Those are useful for individuals, but they're limited in scope and expire quickly. Not to mention that the spells can be broken by deleting the emails or closing out the app or whatever. But Bael also wants me to create an enchanted computer virus that can spread from the computer to the human world, and then keep on spreading. It can't be done."

At least, he hoped not.

"Then what are you doing? You said you were going to make a

plague."

He'd said that, but really, he was going to *cause* a plague. Because once Azagoth knew Bael was behind his children's deaths, Azagoth was going to become an epidemic. All Cipher needed to do was hide a message inside one of the viruses meant for Bael's enemies. When the virus activated, a subprogram would deliver a warning to Azagoth via the demonweb. Bael would never know.

"Cipher?"

Oh, right. He was supposed to answer her. Probably shouldn't tell her his real plans. He opened his mouth to spew some bullshit he hoped she'd buy. But before he could say anything, his wings sprouted from his back, wrenching and twisting with so much force that he grunted in pain.

"What is it?" Lyre rushed toward him. "What's going on?"

"I don't know," he gritted out. "They popped out on their own and—"

He broke off as an electric tingle sizzled across the surface of his skin and pinprick points of light filled his vision.

"What the hell..?" Transparent cyan glyphs appeared before his eyes. Random numbers, letters, and symbols took shape in the air, some skimming the floor and hugging the ceiling. Holy shit.

"It's code," he whispered.

"Code? Ciph? Are you okay?"

Ciph. She'd called him by his nickname. Felt intimate. Felt...right.

And that was so not what he should be concentrating on right now. No, the programming language floating around was way more significant.

Because weird.

He blinked. Maybe he was hallucinating. What had Lyre said was in the sandwiches? Demon beef and hellrats? Maybe they'd gone bad.

"Hey, Lyre...how old were those sandwiches?"

"I bought them yesterday." She frowned. "Why?"

Closing his eyes, he shook his head. Maybe he could reset his operating system. But nope, when he opened his eyes again, the atmospheric graffiti was still there.

"Can you see this?" he asked.

Lyre glanced around. "See what?"

"The symbols." He pointed at a group of them. "The greenish-blue symbols."

She looked right through them and then turned to him like he'd lost his mind. "I don't see anything. What's going on? You're weirding me out."

"I don't know. It's language of some sort."

"Language? Like a demon language?"

"Like programming language." As he watched, character sets and entities rearranged themselves. A Greek omega symbol spun into a tilde operator squiggly mark and caused a cascade of code into lined formation. "Holy shit," he breathed, as what he was witnessing started to make sense. "It's a spell. Fuck me, I'm *seeing* a spell!"

"How can you see a spell?" She grabbed his arm to get his attention, but he couldn't look away. "What kind of spell?"

"I don't know." It was fascinating how the symbols unique to demonic computer language vibrated while the others were static. "I'm not even sure how I know it's a spell. Or maybe a curse." He remembered a theory he'd hashed out with Hawkyn, and he finally looked down at her. "You know, some people believe that everything in the universe is really made up of mathematical code, and if you could just see and access it, you could control it. Reprogram it. Delete it."

"That's insane." She frowned, appearing to rethink that. "Do you think it's true?"

"I didn't," he admitted. "But I also didn't believe that active spells had source code, either." This was so crazy. Was it his unique fallen angel ability? If so, it was majorly awesome.

"Well, what's the spell you're seeing?" Lyre moved toward a book shelf. "Maybe one of the books is enchanted."

He glanced over at the books, and sure enough, tiny rows of code surrounded a leather-bound tome lying on its side. But that wasn't related to the millions of lines of programming language floating in the room.

"Dammit, I need access to the internet. If I can just plug some of this into the translator I stored in my cloud—" He sucked in a harsh breath, his mind reeling at the sudden clarity. "It's the spell that blocks internet access."

Lyre wheeled around, and he cursed his stupidity at blurting it out. He kept forgetting she was the enemy.

She doesn't feel like the enemy.

No, she didn't. But Flail hadn't felt like an enemy either...until it was too late.

"You're kidding," she said, and just as he was about to say that yes, he was full of shit, she added, "Can you break it?"

Well, that was unexpected. "Are you asking me to?"

"Yes, of course. You can put it back, right? Cipher, this is your gift." Her excitement made him wonder what hers was. "You need to practice with it."

"So Bael can force me to use it? Yeah, great."

She hissed and grabbed his arm. "Bael can never know about this. Never tell anyone about your gifts. Especially not someone like Bael."

"You're not going to tell him?" He looked at her sideways. "I can't believe he didn't tell you to report every one of my abilities to him."

"He did," she admitted. "But what he doesn't know won't hurt him."

Oh, yes it would. Cipher swore it.

"You don't like your boss much, do you?" As he waited for her answer, he concentrated on a few individual characters in the code, using his thoughts in an attempt to rearrange them.

Nothing. Maybe the spell was voice activated.

Lyre plopped down on a fur-lined ice bench. "I hate him."

They could start a club. "Then why are you working for him?" He studied the code and considered another tack. "And what's the Sheoulic word for delete?"

"*Altun.* And I'm working for him because I want revenge on the people who got me expelled from Heaven."

"Yeah, I get that," he said. "But why a deranged lunatic like Bael? Why not a regular lunatic like Revenant?"

"Because the people I want revenge on are in Heaven, and Heaven backs Revenant."

He looked over at her as she kicked her slender legs up on the bench. Legs he'd been between just an hour ago.

Fucking Flail.

"They don't *back* him," he said. "They just prefer him over Satan."

She gave a dismissive snort. "Same thing."

No, it wasn't. Heaven needed allies like Revenant, but from what he'd heard, the Powers That Be didn't interfere with his rule. If Revenant wanted to help someone get revenge on an angel, Heaven might be miffed, but ultimately, they needed him.

Okay, maybe they backed him.

Not wanting to admit she was right, he focused again on the code, choosing a random ampersand as his victim. "*Altun*!"

The code just laughed at him. Well, not literally, but it felt that way.

Sighing, he turned back to Lyre. "So what happens after you get your revenge?"

"What do you mean?"

"I mean, what do you want to do with your life? Spend it helping Bael torment Azagoth? Spend it preparing for Armageddon?"

She drew her knees up to her chest, her expression troubled. "I hadn't really thought that far ahead."

"So you shackled yourself for all eternity to Bael and his empire of evil for the sole purpose of getting revenge and without any thought about what comes after? Seems a little shortsighted."

She glared, the silver in her eyes glinting like daggers. "Well, hello, did you think about the consequences of ruining a Primori before you did it? Or were you bent on your own self-gratification or self-destructiveness?"

"Touché," he muttered. "But in my defense, I never said I wasn't a hypocrite." That coaxed a smile from her, but it was distant. He'd touched a nerve. Maddox insisted that was the best time to keep pressing for information. Cipher had always found the opposite to be true, but hey, he'd give it another shot. "So, this is off topic, but what did Flail mean when she said you couldn't set wards?"

"Nothing," she said with a jerky shrug. "It's just not my skill set."

Seemed odd. Wards were the most basic kind of conjuration there were. Sure, he didn't know how to set one, but that was because he'd only had access to his fallen angel powers for a day. He should have a firm grasp on them within another day or two. Lyre should have obtained the knowledge years ago.

"So how's your progress?" She jumped to her feet. Clearly, she was ready to talk about something else. "Were you able to delete any of the code?" When he shook his head, she cocked hers and asked, "Can you touch it?"

"I tried earlier. My hand passed through it." He suddenly remembered how he used to manipulate 3-D programs in Heaven, and an idea came to him. "But maybe I don't need to *touch* them."

His wings quivered as he summoned energy to his fingertips and reached out as if trying to swat at a group of characters. They vibrated, and he held his breath as he tried again, harder this time.

Yes!

Three numbers and a demonic glyph spun away from the main group and hung in the air. Refocusing his objective from manipulating symbols to obliterating them, he pointed at each line of code and watched as they broke apart and dissolved into sparkly glitter.

"I did it!"

Lyre sat up straight. "We have the internet in here now?"

He blasted the last remaining lines of code. "We should." He turned to his computer and searched for a connection. When the signal lit up, he let out a whoop. "We have active demonweb, baby."

Excited, hopeful for the first time in months, he went straight for his private inbox. Junk. Junk. More junk.

And an email from Hawk, dated seven months ago.

We're looking for you.

That was all. Four words. But those four words meant everything.

Another one from Hawk, dated six months ago.

We're looking for you.

There were more, one each month, ensuring he'd know they hadn't given up. But it was the most recent one that had his heart pumping a mile a minute.

We found you. Flip the bedora gateway switch.

He grinned like a lunatic. Hawkyn and Journey had hacked into Bael's private network and given Cipher a way to shut down his security system. Cipher just had to access it.

"Um...Cipher? What's going on?"

He looked up, alarmed by the urgency in Lyre's voice. The walls, once opaque, were growing transparent, and suddenly a klaxon rang out.

The code...oh, damn, oh, *shit*!

"I missed the failsafe." How could he have been so stupid?

"What?"

His fingers flew over the keyboard. He had to get a message out. Fast. "There was code in the spell that triggers an alarm if the spell is broken."

The door burst open, and armored guards, their weapons drawn, spilled inside.

He. Was. Fucked.

Chapter Fifteen

Lilliana smiled into her laptop's camera as her friend Cara held up baby Aleka. "I know I've only been back in Sheoul-gra for a couple of days, but I swear she's grown."

Cara cradled the infant, swaddled in a blanket made from the golden wool of Heavenly sheep, in the crook of her arm as she tenderly stroked her rosy cheek. "I think so too."

Longing stirred in Lilliana's chest as she smoothed her palm over her belly. She couldn't wait to hold her own child in her arms. Only a month to go. She and Cara had conceived within days of each other, but as an angel Lilliana had an extra four to five weeks of gestation.

"Well, you both look amazing," she said. "I'm so glad you got a chance to call."

"I just wish you were here." Cara sighed. "I miss having you around. Maleficent misses you too. She's been searching the island for you, and she won't stop whining."

Guilt and sorrow made Lilliana's heart clench. Poor Mal must feel so abandoned. "Maybe you should send her here. I'm sure Azagoth will be okay with it. It's not like hellhounds don't haunt the Inner Sanctum anyway."

"You sure?" At Lilliana's nod, Cara continued. "How *are* things going with Azagoth? I've been dying to know what he did when he saw you."

"I thought he'd be angry," Lilliana said. "But he understood why I left and why I didn't tell him I was pregnant."

That wasn't entirely the truth, since they hadn't talked about it yet. Azagoth hadn't brought it up, but he'd also been really busy. *The talk* was coming, and she knew it.

"So what was his reaction when he first saw you?"

Lilliana's cheeks burned. "He was, um, shocked..."

"And then..?"

"And then he flew me up to the balcony and tore my clothes off."

"He did not!" Cara laughed. "Wow. That sounds deliciously scandalous and totally like something Ares would do after not seeing me for nine months. How does he feel about the baby?"

Lilliana heard the thud of footsteps behind her and knew it was Azagoth. Her bodyguard stationed outside the door would never have allowed anyone else inside. A heartbeat later, Azagoth's deep voice echoed through the room.

"I can't wait for our son or daughter to arrive," he said, as his hands came down on Lilliana's shoulders.

She reached up and laid her hand over his. He'd been so affectionate and attentive since she'd been back. Even better, he'd been open in a way he hadn't been even before his emotions had gone out of control.

"Well," Cara said, "I'll let you two spend some time together." She wrinkled her nose. "I think someone needs a diaper change anyway." She glanced at Azagoth and laughed. "I just pictured the big bad Grim Reaper changing a nappy. That'll keep me in a good mood for the rest of the week." She waved. "Talk to you later!"

After the screen went dark, Lilliana spun in her chair to face Azagoth. He looked so handsome in casual clothes, his black jeans, charcoal Henley, and combat boots giving him a relaxed air that no one would mistake for anything less than lethal danger.

"This was a nice surprise," she said. "To what do I owe this visit?"

"It was time for a break and I wanted to see you." His deep emerald eyes grew serious. "I think it's time to talk."

Oh. She hadn't been looking forward to this. At all. "You want to know why I didn't tell you I was pregnant."

He sank down on the chaise lounge she used for reading, his legs spread, his forearms resting on his knees. "I know why you left, but I don't know why you kept this from me."

She fidgeted in her seat as she thought about what to say. It was weird; every day while she was in Greece she'd prepared for what she'd say to him. Went over and over it in her head. And now she was drawing a blank.

"I guess..." She inhaled, bracing herself. "I guess at first it was just too soon. I wanted you to sort out your issues without having anything else to think about. So I decided to tell you when I started showing, but every time I talked to you, I just...couldn't. You were so worried about all your children. So many were in danger, and then you said we were never going to have one together...I got nervous."

He sat in silence for a long moment. "I remember that," he said quietly. "Maddox and Emerico were being assholes, and then Meera was killed." His voice went low, taking on a smoky tone. "It was a bad day." He reached over and took her hand. "But I was wrong. There is nothing I want more than you and our child in my life, and I swear to you, I will do everything within my power to make sure you're both safe."

"I know," she said. "And I know someone murdered one of your young sons inside Sheoul-gra, and you're freaked out. But is the bodyguard really necessary? You said yourself that the murderer had to be a fallen angel, and you kicked all of them out."

The only fallen angels who remained were his trusted assistants and their mates. A handful of Unfallen remained as well, but again, they were the ones who had been with him for years as they tried to work their way back into Heaven, and that wouldn't happen if they were killing his children.

"I won't take any chances with you." His words were clipped, forceful, and she knew arguing was pointless. She wasn't going to win this battle, and ultimately, having a shadow wasn't *too* annoying.

"Okay." Resolved to her fate, she squeezed his hand. "For what it's worth, I'm sorry I didn't tell you about the baby. But," she added, "I don't regret leaving. I needed to go. And you needed it too."

A low growl rattled his chest. "I fucking hate that you're right."

She laughed as she brought his hand to her lips. This had gone better than she could have even hoped for. "Why don't you take the rest of the day off? I can fire up the *chronoglass* and take us someplace warm and sunny and private."

"Maybe later," he said, shooting her a playful wink that spoke volumes about his mood. Usually his brand of playful was the cat-toying-with-a-mouse variety. "I have some VIP souls coming in."

"VIP souls?"

A shadow flickered in his eyes and he smiled, a morbid, malicious smile that sent a chill down her spine. "Sons of Moloc and Bael. Princes of their territories."

She gasped in disbelief. "What? How? Did you send *griminions* for them?"

"*Griminions* only reap souls. They don't kill." His smile grew even darker. "I sent souls from the Inner Sanctum."

This time her breath clogged in her throat, trapped there momentarily by the intensity of her shock. "Isn't it forbidden to release souls if they aren't reincarnated?"

"It's not forbidden if Heaven doesn't find out." She could argue that it was still forbidden, but his phone beeped, and he dug it from his pocket. "You disapprove?"

"No, of course not," she said fiercely. "Moloc and Bael are monsters who had your children murdered. Their sons are fair game." She paused. "They *are* evil, right?"

"What is it Journey says? Mucho evil? They're that." He grinned at the phone. "They're here."

"What are you going to do with them?" As if she couldn't guess. He was going to play cat and mouse.

"Do you really want to know?"

Not really, but Azagoth's secretive nature was one of the reasons she'd left, and during the months when they'd spoken via Skype, she'd made clear that while she didn't need to know gory details, she didn't want to be "protected" from what he truly was.

"I assume you're going to torture them into telling you why their fathers are killing your children." At his nod, she asked, "Do you have any theories?"

"I suspect they're plotting a coup and want me to play a role in freeing Satan and destroying Revenant."

Well, that wasn't cool. "What are you going to do if you're right?"

"The same thing I'll do if I'm wrong." He shoved to his feet and pulled her with him. "No matter what, Bael and Moloc are going to die."

* * * *

It sucked that destroying souls came with a cost, but fortifying Satan with a drop of strength was a price Azagoth was more than willing to pay today. Bael and Moloc's sons had been monsters, but more than that, their darkness would return to Satan, and that bastard would know Azagoth was responsible. It was a message of sorts, a *fuck you* that could only be better if Azagoth had destroyed Satan's offspring instead.

An hour later, Azagoth was still burning a serious soul-destroyer high as he entered his library, where Hawkyn was pacing a hole in the floor while waiting for him.

"I heard from Cipher," Hawk said before Azagoth had even shut the door.

"Heard from him? You were supposed to kill him." Hawkyn was lucky Azagoth was in a good mood, because he really, really wanted Cipher dead.

Hawkyn held out his phone. "He sent this. I think he was in a hurry, but I got the gist."

The list is out. Save the kids. Bael is after Memitim.

Azagoth rolled his eyes. "He's evil, son. You can't trust him."

"You're evil too," Hawkyn pointed out.

"Exactly. I will fuck over anyone who gets in my way or who tries to harm what's mine. I will lie, cheat, and kill. There is no line I will not cross. Do you not think Cipher would do the same?"

"He hasn't been a True Fallen for long. He's not lost to us." He took his phone back and scrolled. "He also says he thinks he can bring down the wards that prevent *griminions* from entering when he takes out the security system with the bug Journey planted."

He hadn't known about a security system bug, but it didn't really matter. The wards thing was curious, though. Bael and Moloc's ability to keep the *griminions* at bay had meant that no souls had been reaped from their territories in decades. Not even the souls Azagoth had released from Sheoul-gra to grab the fallen angels' sons had been able to enter. They'd had to take the males while they were fucking around in other regions of Sheoul.

"When can Cipher do this?" Azagoth asked.

"I don't know. I've tried contacting him, but he's not replying."

There was a tap at the door, and Z's voice boomed from behind the thick wood. "I just got word that Reaver and Revenant are on their way."

Before Z even stopped talking, Azagoth's bones vibrated like a tuning fork, and a blast of nuclear energy slammed into him. They were here. Fuck. He wasn't in the mood. He was never in the mood when it came to dealing with those douchebags.

"I'll go." Hawkyn beelined for the door, anxious to either miss Reaver and Revenant, or to get away from Azagoth before he told him to kill Cipher again. Maybe both. "I'll let you know if I hear from Ciph."

He whipped open the door, and lo and behold, the Prince of Heaven and the King of Hell were standing right there in the doorway.

They exchanged brief nods, and then Reaver and Revenant strode inside.

"Well, well," Azagoth said. "If it isn't the Wonder Twins."

"The what?" Revenant asked.

"A brother sister superhero team from Saturday morning cartoons," Reaver explained. "Back when I was Unfallen, Wraith made me watch a lot of those things."

"That's cool," Revenant said. "We didn't have fun shit like cartoons in the part of Hell where I grew up."

Reaver shot his brother a look of exasperation. "You just can't let that go, can you?"

Revenant shrugged in his black leather duster. "It's still a sore spot." He plopped down in the overstuffed chair by the fire.

"That's my seat," Azagoth said. "Move."

"Whatever, Sheldon." Holding up his hands, Revenant scooted to the couch. At Reaver's quizzical expression, Rev shrugged again. "I like sitcoms. Sue me."

"Are you two done?" Azagoth asked. Talk about exasperation. "Maybe you could tell me why you're here?"

Reaver turned to him, his body taut, his expression serious. "I'm here to warn you not to push the boundaries of your limits, which were agreed upon in the Sheoul-gra Accord."

"What he said." Revenant kicked his booted feet up on the coffee table, as relaxed as Reaver was strung tight.

"This must be serious if Heaven is sending its most powerful angel and Sheoul's overlord."

Revenant barked out a laugh. "Heaven doesn't *send* me anywhere, Soul Man. I'm here because this concerns my realm too."

The fire in the hearth snapped and hissed as Reaver waved his palm over the flames. Did he notice that the fire burned hot? It had been cold for months, its flames pale blue, reflecting Azagoth's heart while Lilliana had been gone.

He hated that his environment was so connected to his moods, that he could be so easily read by those with an observant eye or half a brain.

Reaver turned away from the fire. "You released souls into Sheoul," he said, getting right to it. "The Angelic Council is apoplectic. So we're here to tell you to knock it the hell off."

"Fuck the council," Azagoth growled. "Bael has been killing my children. I have the right to defend my family."

"Only within the confines of Sheoul-gra."

Azagoth gave a bitter laugh. He'd been stupid to agree to such restrictive rules. "What would you do, Reaver? What would you do if Bael killed Limos? Or Logan? Or any of your children or grandchildren? Would you sit around in Heaven and do nothing, simply because you signed a piece of parchment? You, who haven't followed a rule...ever?"

"There's not a rule I wouldn't break for my family," Reaver said.

"But you can't be all blatant about it," Revenant broke in. "If you're going to do the revenge thing, use your *griminions*. No one would know. But man, you release souls, and it sets off seismic alarms."

"I don't really give a shit about the souls." Reaver shoved Revenant's feet aside and sat on the opposite end of the couch. "The Angelic Council needs to chill out. But Bael...he can't die."

"Oh, he can die," Azagoth promised. He *would* die. Soon.

"I mean that he needs to *stay* alive."

As if that was going to happen. Still, he should probably know the reasoning behind Reaver's ridiculous announcement. "I give. Why should Bael keep breathing?"

Reaver looked troubled. "I don't know."

"You don't know?" Azagoth stared at the angel. "Then why the fuck—"

"The Moirai summoned him," Revenant announced in a bored tone, as if the Moirai, legendary angelic seers who weren't allowed to speak to anyone except in the most dire of circumstances, had casually asked Reaver to tea.

Hell, until now, Azagoth had actually suspected they were a myth. Sequestered angels who lived on another plane and in all timelines at the same time? Yeah, bullshit.

Except, apparently, it wasn't.

"They see instability in the current timeline," Reaver said. "They stressed that Bael's demise would cause even more destabilization."

"And why do I give a shit about the destabilization of a timeline I know nothing about and that clearly favors Heaven in the Final Battle and beyond?"

"I'm wondering the same thing, bro," Rev said. "If something's good for Heaven, that means it's bad for me."

"Not when we have a common goal, and that's to keep Satan from winning the Final Battle."

"Yeah, well, I don't give a fuck what your Fates have to say." When Reaver cursed, Azagoth held up his hand to stay the lecture. "Take it easy, Halo. Bael doesn't have to die for me to get my revenge. I can keep him alive and in agony for all eternity."

Revenant stood, a big grin on his face. "I knew I liked you."

Azagoth looked between the two. "So are we cool?"

"Yeah," Reaver said. "But watch it. I don't give a shit what you do, but I have to be the bad guy when the Angelic Council gets a bug up their collective asses."

"Come on, bro." Revenant opened the door. "I'm jonesing for a burger."

Reaver was all about a fast food lunch, and they got out of there without so much as a goodbye.

The moment they were gone, he called out, "Lilli? I know you're there."

The hidden panel at the back of the library slid open, and a sheepish, gorgeous, pregnant angel stepped out. "I'm sorry. I didn't mean to eavesdrop. I slipped away to see you and heard you guys talking."

"You just felt the sudden need to use the secret passage to come to the library?" He gave her a *don't bullshit me* look. "You were ditching your bodyguard, weren't you?"

She had the good grace to blush. "Maybe."

She walked over to him, her hands on her belly. Beneath her palm, the baby moved, and when he reached out to feel the movement, his heart stuttered at the instant connection that formed between him and the child.

"Is Grim Junior talking to you again?"

He cocked an eyebrow. "Grim Junior?"

"Do you hate it?"

"Yes."

Her laugh filled his office and his heart. It was so good to have her back. "Guess we should talk about names then, no?"

"Soon," he promised. "I've got a lot to do right now."

"Revenge does take up a lot of time, I suppose." She glanced at the door Reaver and Revenant had just gone through. "They seemed to want to put a damper on your plans to get it. What are you going to do?"

"What do you think, my darling?" He palmed her cheek and stroked her smooth skin with his thumb. He'd never take touching her for granted again. "I'm going to ignore everything they said and kill Bael, of course."

And he dared Heaven to try to stop him.

Chapter Sixteen

The antechamber outside Bael's great hall was freezing. Not that Lyre experienced cold the way humans did, what with all the teeth-chattering, hypothermia, and death. But it was still pretty uncomfortable, and when combined with the terror of what might lie ahead, she couldn't help but shiver.

Bael had made her wait out here for almost twelve hours. Cipher's fate was still unknown. The one bright spot in the day had come when one of his minions had brought news of his son's death at Azagoth's hands. Bael's roars of fury and his murder of the messenger had given her the most pleasure she'd experienced in a long time.

Finally, the great hall's massive doors opened, and Bael's Ramreel guard gestured for her to enter.

She did her best to control her breathing, her pulse, and her sweat glands as she walked across the floor, her boots cracking down on the bones and teeth set into the umber tiles.

"My lord," she said, bowing deeply when she reached the dais where the fallen angel sat on a throne made of more bones and teeth. A set of desiccated angel wings formed the back of the throne, the yellowed feathers dotted with ancient dried blood.

He didn't waste any time. "I just found out that Azagoth murdered my son and my nephew, so I'm in a bad fucking mood. Don't piss me off, Lyre," he warned. "Tell me how Cipher disabled the demonweb block."

"I don't know," she lied calmly, relying on one of the few skills she had that was worth anything down here. "He was using his laptop to work on the viruses you requested, and the next thing I knew, your goons were storming into the room."

"You weren't watching him?"

"Of course I was watching him," she snapped. "But I don't know how all that tech stuff works."

Her answer seemed to mollify him, maybe because it was true. She could operate email and search engines, but everything else was as much of a mystery to her as Stonehenge's purpose was to humans.

Bael sat back in the chair, his narrowed gaze locked on her like a weapon. "Did he create any viruses?"

She shook her head. "He says they're complicated and that it'll take time."

"Time?" He made a sound of derision. "With his computer skills and the plague talent that came with his wings, he should be able to snap his fingers and come up with what I want. He's stalling. He's stalling and I'll kill him! I'll slice him and skin him and..."

He went off on an insane, chaotic tangent, and she knew him well enough to stay silent while he let off some crazy steam.

When he was finally done, having promised to maim and/or kill Cipher in a few dozen ways, she asked tentatively, "How do you know what talents came with his wings? Cipher isn't even aware of all of his abilities yet."

Bael reached into a bowl sitting on the arm of his throne and plucked out something oblong and dripping with clotted blood. Repulsed, she swallowed sickly and hoped to hell that when evil began to flourish inside her she wouldn't develop a taste for disgusting things.

"I know what those wings can do because they aren't Cipher's." He spoke calmly, as if he hadn't just screamed about boiling Cipher until his eyeballs burst. "They belonged to Asher."

"Asher? He was killed last year—" She sucked in a shocked breath, remembering the scars at the base of Cipher's wings. "You cut off his wings, didn't you? You cut them off and transplanted them onto Cipher." So bizarre. "But why?"

Bael popped the bloody bit into his mouth and chewed. "We needed Asher's specific skill set, and Cipher was the perfect recipient."

She shouldn't be surprised, but damn, this was some devious shit. She'd never heard of a wing transplant before. But it explained why Cipher's powers and flying ability were so out of control.

"So how, exactly, will you be using your computer virus?"

Bael crunched on something and swallowed. "Depends on what his viruses do."

"Well, maybe you could write up a wish list," she said sarcastically.

"That's a good idea, my love!" He leaped to his feet, startling her into taking a step back. "Imagine if he could make a virus that would be executable in Heaven." He threw his arms above his head in a show of maniacal exuberance. "Wonderful!" He grinned at her. "That's how you could get your revenge."

Yikes. That would be one hell of a revenge. She wanted her sister and the bastards who condemned her to pay, but setting loose a plague in Heaven could invite destruction on a...well, a biblical scale. For the first time, she wished Moloc was here to temper his brother's insanity.

"Yes," he purred as he took his seat again. "Tell Cipher I want a virus that will affect angels. And another that will affect millions of humans. And yet another that can be sent to individual demons and fallen angels." He closed his eyes as if picturing the mass destruction he was talking about. "I will be the most powerful fallen angel in history."

Aside from Satan, of course. And actually, if Cipher could do all of that, *he* would be the most powerful fallen angel—second to Satan—in history. He could rule the world with that kind of power.

"My lord...if I may." She cleared her throat. "Where is Cipher?"

He blinked as if he'd forgotten the lynchpin in his plan for universal domination. "Ah. Cipher. The Isle of Torture, maybe?" He used one long fingernail to stir the contents of the bowl. "Flail wanted to play with him. If you hurry, you can catch her."

Shit!

She started toward the door, but he called her back.

"Cipher can have access to the demonweb, but only on my network," he said. "My people will watch every move."

"Of course." She turned to leave again.

"And Lyre?"

Her insides turned to jelly at his tone. It was his sadistic one. The one that sounded like a dull knife scraping bone. "Yes, my lord," she whispered.

"You know you belong to me."

She swallowed her loathing and the "Fuck you, you piece of shit," that sat on her lips and instead uttered a mandatory, "Yes, my lord."

For the ten millionth time, she regretted agreeing to serve him in any capacity he wished for all eternity if he helped her get the revenge she craved. She'd been out of her mind with anger and grief, and the implications of *any capacity* and *for all eternity* were, for the first time, truly hitting home.

"*Everything* of yours belongs to me," he said, and her mind instantly flashed to Flail, who must have told him about finding them in bed. "Including your virginity."

He knows? Shock stole her breath, and then a blow to her spine sent her sprawling to the floor and gasping for air. His heavy footsteps fell like thunder, coming closer, threatening destruction.

She tried to push to her feet, but something held her frozen to the floor and she could only watch as Bael's gore-crusted boots stopped next to her head. He bent over, his hot, rancid breath blowing in her ear.

"Betray me in any way, and I will take your virginity with a sword. Do you understand?"

"Y-yes," she gasped.

Her skin crawled as he stroked her hair. "But help me use Cipher to free Satan, and you can be our queen as we serve at his side."

Oh, God. She couldn't have heard him right. "*Our* queen?"

"Moloc and I. We are one." He yanked her to her feet with a painful jerk of her hair and tossed her at the door, where she landed in heap. "Go. Make my viruses."

She had her feet under her and was out the door in a heartbeat.

The Ramreel guard watched her with beady eyes until she got around the corner, where she stumbled to a halt, grabbed her knees, and struggled to catch her breath.

What had she gotten herself into?

Her conversation with Cipher earlier came back to her. Haunting her.

You shackled yourself for all eternity to Bael and his empire of evil for the sole purpose of getting revenge and without any thought about what comes after?

At the time, what he'd said hadn't really sunken in. Her daily life since falling had been about one thing: revenge. But what would happen later? Was becoming some sort of brother-wife demon queen truly what she had to look forward to? Why her? Why wouldn't they choose Flail, who seemed to enjoy the brothers' penchant for vile acts?

And was revenge really even all that important anymore? Merely surviving filled most of her life, and helping Bael try to jumpstart Armageddon filled the rest.

The same impulsivity that had gotten her wings sliced off had gotten her an eternity of hell, and her only hope was that evil would take her so completely that she didn't care anymore. Because right now, she did care.

She was a fallen angel. She should be thrilled to hear of Bael's plans for Satan, Heaven, and her enemies. But this was too much.

This was *way* too much.

This was the kind of shit Flail should be excited about, and if she wanted to—

Flail.

Bael said she'd been heading to see Cipher. Screw that. Cipher was *hers.*

Heart thundering in her chest, Lyre sprinted toward the castle's main exit.

Hold on, Cipher. I'm coming.

* * * *

Of all the beatings Cipher had endured during his time in Sheoul, the ones he'd gotten over the last few hours had been the worst.

Oh, he'd dealt with far more painful, off-the-scale torture, but in his mind, that was different than a beating. A beating involved fists and feet, maybe a blunt object, and a whole lot of taunting.

It was fucking annoying. At least when he was in agony, the pain shut down his brain. But today he'd been hung like a punching bag to endure the chatter of demons who'd used him as practice before they were ushered into the arena for their fights to the death. He was the warm-up.

And he wondered if, at some point, he was going to be tossed in the arena too.

Even as the thought filtered through his battered brain, Flail showed up.

No. Fucking. Way.

Today was not his lucky day.

"Looks like you got yourself into hot water," she said, sounding far too happy about it.

"You know me," he drawled. "Always out of the fire and into the pot."

"Mmm." She flicked the door to the training room closed with her mind. "Is that why you got kicked out of Heaven?"

He wasn't going to tell her jack shit about why he lost his wings.

Weird that he'd spilled all to Lyre, though. Just spit it out like it was no big deal. But then, Lyre hadn't betrayed him or tortured him, so there was that. Plus, he couldn't help but like Lyre. Other than the time she'd fed him to demon fish, she'd been pretty cool. They'd spent months talking about mundane things, like the topography of Bael's territory, the locations of the Harrowgates scattered through his realm, and the best flavor of ice cream.

The ice cream talk wouldn't help get him out of here, but the other shit might. Not that Lyre had given him intel when he'd asked, or even all at once. He'd pieced it together over time, keeping mental notes on anything that might prove useful. But in the course of the information-gathering, he'd learned enough about Lyre to not hate her. And now he actually felt something for her. A protective instinct that made him grateful she hadn't been here while the demons had pounded on him. And that she wasn't here now, when Flail was going to do whatever it was she liked to do. Which he guaranteed wouldn't be something *he* liked to do.

He tested the rope binding his hands as he hung from the ceiling by his wrists. Nothing had changed. The rope held, preventing both escape and his ability to use any of his powers. He couldn't even break the damned rope to get to one of the hundreds of weapons locked on racks around the room.

Too bad, too, because he'd love to shove one of those spears right through Flail's evil heart.

"I guess I'm getting the silent treatment," Flail said as she plucked a dagger from a rack. "I wonder if you can scream in silence."

He already knew the answer to that.

It was no.

The door banged open with such force that a piece splintered and lodged in the wall. Then, in a whirlwind of energy, Lyre burst in like he'd summoned her. Forget wanting her to stay away. She was a badass bundle of fury with lasers for eyes, and it was hot. As. Fuck.

"*Get away from him, you bitch.*"

Yes! Bonus badass points for quoting *Aliens*, intentionally or not.

Flail laughed, but Lyre threw a swing and decked the bitch, cutting her off mid-guffaw. The surprisingly powerful blow sent a couple of Flail's teeth clattering to the ground.

Lyre didn't back off or even slow down. Like a battle-seasoned warrior, she pressed her advantage, swiping a sword from a rack and attacking while Flail was off balance. Flail fell back under the assault, and just as she summoned an elemental sword of her own, a massive blade of fire, Lyre disappeared in a puff of vapor.

What the hell?

Then he saw it. The vapor *was* Lyre. Flail shouted in frustration as she whacked uselessly at the wispy rope of smoke that circled her, taunting her, *laughing* at her. He could actually hear soft giggles as Lyre made a joke out of the other female.

Abruptly, Lyre shot upward and dove down, wrapping her misty form around his wrists.

"No!" Flail ran toward him, but the rope broke and he dropped to the ground, his hands free, power singing through his veins.

Now Flail was going to pay for everything she'd done to him.

And then it was Bael's turn.

Chapter Seventeen

Lyre had had enough of that skank.

So she loved it when Cipher hit the ground, popped his wings, and slammed Flail with a summoned wave of scalding water.

That was a new power. And it was all kinds of awesome.

Flail screamed as her skin blistered and peeled, steam rising from her body. Somehow she managed to strike back with her fire sword, catching Cipher in the ribs. The stench of burnt and boiled flesh mingled in the air like a demon chef was preparing some sort of savory fallen angel soup.

Clutching the cauterized wound, Cipher hit the ground and rolled into Flail, bowling her over and knocking the wind from her lungs. As she gasped for air, Lyre, still in her vapor form, had an idea. Like, why the hell not?

Mind set on a course of action, Lyre darted into Flail's open mouth.

Flail tried to scream, but she was choking and gagging, and Lyre wondered what would happen if she slid right into the bitch's lungs.

Blind to whatever was happening outside Flail's mouth, she squirmed around, plugging the other female's windpipe and making her squeal in rage and panic. There were grunts, flailing, and then everything went still and quiet.

"Lyre?"

Lyre slid between Flail's motionless lips and materialized next to her as she lay on the ground.

There was a spear through her chest.

Awesome.

Cupping the back of Lyre's head, Cipher drew her in for a kiss that was as hot as it was quick. "That was one of the coolest things I've ever seen." His fierce, admiring gaze held hers. "Awesome gift."

She shrugged awkwardly, a little dazed and flustered by his unexpected kiss. Not that she was complaining. He could do that anytime he wanted to.

"It's kind of useless. I can't manipulate things very well. But every once in a while it comes in handy." Which was a good thing since it was pretty much her only fallen angel ability. She gestured to Flail. "She's not going to be unconscious for long."

"I know," he said grimly. "We have to finish her off."

As much as she'd love that, killing Flail right now was impossible.

"We can't. Bael will know as soon as her soul goes to him." She glanced around the room, thinking they could tie her up to buy some time, but when she spotted the coffin-like chest in the corner, she got an idea. "Let's shove her inside the torture casket."

His brow knit together in confusion. "What's a torture casket? I thought that chest was for storing weapons."

"Nope." She grabbed Flail's wrists and started dragging her toward the stone box. "Once you put someone in it, it seals for twelve hours. The poor bastard inside gets twelve hours of terror. Nightmares of the things they're most afraid of."

"Huh. Demons are really creative, aren't they?" He gestured for Lyre to stand back, and then he hauled Flail's unconscious body up over his shoulder. "I'd rather kill her, but I'll just make that a future goal."

"Everyone needs aspirations, I guess." Although it had occurred to her that, beyond revenge, she had none. It made her feel...empty.

He dropped her unceremoniously into the box and slammed the lid closed. The gold lock on the front spun and glowed, and a moment later, Flail's muffled screams assured them it was working.

"Come on." She took Cipher's hand. "We need to get out of here." She stopped, an idea sparking in her brain. "Wait. You were able to see the spell that kept you from accessing the internet. Can you see the one on your wings that keeps you from being able to flash inside Bael's territory?"

He frowned. "I don't know."

As if his wings knew they were talking about them, they flapped crazily, nearly knocking him off his feet. She should probably tell him the truth about them, but right now might not be the best time. He cursed as he tried to get the dead fallen angel's wings under control. Finally they remained still, although they quivered with the effort it must have taken him to keep them that way.

"I can see the spell," he said, "but not all of it." With Flail's cries for help as background noise, he concentrated for a little while, and then shook his head. "I think I need to be able to see the entire code in order to alter it. Dammit. And why the fuck won't my wings behave?"

She started to answer, but at the sound of voices outside the door, she thought better of it. "I'll tell you, but not here. Come on."

Quickly and without incident, she led him out of the building Bael had dedicated entirely to imprisoning and torturing his enemies...and anyone else he felt like slaughtering for fun. As soon as they were outside, they took flight, which went about as well as the last time, with Cipher struggling to maintain altitude and course.

He cursed the entire way to the nearby Valley of Asshole Trees, as she called it, a rift between two volcanoes that had developed into an orchard of spiky trees that produced round blackish-purple fruit. She'd discovered the valley about a year ago, one of the few places in Bael's realm that wasn't completely nightmarish. Even the lizard-monkeys that lived in the trees were kind of cute.

Well, they weren't terrifying carnivores, anyway. That had to count for something.

"What is this place?" Cipher turned in a slow circle on the stubby but lush yellow grass, taking it all in. "It's beautiful. In a weird, grotesque way. Those apples probably eat people, don't they?"

If they did, demons would have found a way to weaponize them by now.

"No, but they're gross. They're like raw hamburger inside. Hell stallions and hell mares love them." Sobering, she looked up at the plume of ash that had puffed out of the top of the one of the distant volcanoes. "Do you want out of here? Out of Bael's realm, I mean. Out of Sheoul."

He pivoted around to her. "Is that a trick question?"

It wasn't, but trying to explain herself wasn't going to be easy, and it took her a moment to put the words together. When she finally did, her voice sounded tired, as if she hadn't slept in years. It felt that way, too.

"I fucked up, Cipher," she sighed. "I don't want any part of Bael and Moloc's plans."

"What plans?"

"All of them." Her fists clenched in anger at the memory of what Bael said he wanted to do to the populations of Earth and Heaven. "I was so pissed off, so hateful after I lost my wings that I wasn't thinking straight. I signed on with Bael and Moloc because I wanted revenge, but you made me rethink that." At the skeptical arch of Cipher's brow, she jammed her fists on her hips. "What, you don't believe me?"

"I want to, but this could be a trick."

Given Flail's betrayal almost a year ago, she understood why he'd think that. "You've seen how I live. What life is like here. How Bael treats people. I have no reason to lie."

"Saving your own skin is a reason," he pointed out. "Revenge is a reason."

A hot, stale wind ruffled his hair and made her long ponytail flutter against her neck. She watched as the breeze knocked a fruit to the ground, where a lizard-monkey snatched it before scampering up the tree.

"I chose the wrong team, Cipher. I should have remained an Unfallen."

"I can see the appeal of entering Sheoul," he admitted. He looked up, his expression thoughtful, his strong, masculine profile nothing short of majestic as he took in the sky made orange by volcanic activity. "As an Unfallen, most angels don't have powers, and those who do got them through sorcery."

"I still don't."

He turned his gaze back to her, and she shivered at the intensity of it. Sometimes he was super laid back, and others, like now, he carried an aura of authority that made her feminine side take notice in the most inopportune ways.

"You still don't what?"

"Have powers." She hated admitting this, but it was time to lay it all on the line. If she wanted out of here, he was her best hope, and he wasn't going to help her if he didn't trust her. "I mean, I have a couple, but they're weak."

"I saw your little vapor trick. That didn't strike me as weak."

"Today it came in handy, but it's mostly useless. I can fit through small cracks and keyholes, but any fallen angel can get past locked doors and stuff like that anyway. Remember I told you never to reveal your unique power? Well, that's mine, and everyone here already knows about it."

She'd been so stupid, so happy to have any ability at all that when it manifested as her very first power, she'd shown it off. In her extreme naïveté, she hadn't realized it would be pretty much her only gift, and that other fallen angels delighted in sharing fellow angels' secrets. Acting on her desire for allies after losing her Heavenly friends and family had been so incredibly foolish.

"You've healed me several times," Cipher pointed out. It was nice of him to try to make her feel better, but it didn't do much good.

"The healing power I used on you? It only worked because your healing abilities were already powerful. I can't set wards. I can barely swat a fly with mental strikes. The one unique ability I have is all but useless."

"Must have been awful to go from being a Heavenly angel to a fallen angel with limited powers."

She laughed bitterly. "You'd think. But I was a weak angel, too. It's why I got assigned as a historian and researcher. You don't need angelic powers for that."

He seemed to think on what she'd said. "So you want to escape Bael's clutches, and you want me to help. Is that what you're saying?"

"I don't deserve your help. But I'm asking for it."

"And then what? You'll want help to get your revenge?"

"I'm over that," she said. "I don't care anymore." For some reason, her eyes stung, and tears welled up.

"Your tears say you do," he said, as he caught a drop with his finger, his touch so gentle it didn't even seem real. Not in a place like this. Not in a Hell realm.

"I think...I think I'm...I don't know." Drawing in a ragged breath, she searched her brain for the right words. "I feel...relieved. Like I don't need to hold on to that anger anymore."

"Yeah, well, I'm still pissed." His wings flared and flapped for no apparent reason. "And these stupid things aren't helping. Seriously, what the fuck?"

"Oh, ah, about that..."

He shot her a *what now* look. "Do not tell me that they're cursed or some shit."

How could she put this gently? "Do you know of a fallen angel named Asher?"

"Why would I—" He broke off, and then nodded. "As an angel, he was from the Order of Thrones. He was lead on the Ten Plagues of Egypt debacle."

"That's the one. Terrible mess. Humans got the stories all wrong." She blew out a breath. "Anyway, after he got the boot, he joined up with Moloc and Bael. Revenant killed him last year."

"What does that have to do with me?" Realization dawned, and his eyes shot wide. "Oh, shit. My wings—"

"They belonged to Asher."

Chapter Eighteen

Numb with shock, Cipher wheeled away from Lyre. His wings—*Asher's* wings—folded and spread of their own accord, and he had the sudden desire to rip them off. No, not even a desire. A desperate *need.*

With a roar of anguish and fury, he reached over his shoulder and seized one by its bony ridge. Pain streaked through the wing and up into his neck as he tried to wrench it from his body. He was going to rip it in half. Shred it. Break it. Whatever he had to do in order to free himself of a dead angel's wings, he'd do it.

"Cipher, no!" Lyre tried to restrain him, but he threw her off like she was one of those freaky little reptile-primate things.

"How long have you known?" he yelled, the sense of betrayal hitting him harder than he figured it should.

He knew she'd been employed by Bael all this time, knew she'd do anything to get the revenge she yearned for. But this...this was sick.

"I just found out." She came toward him again.

"Bullshit!" Rage throbbed through him and he tugged harder, gritting his teeth against the agony. The other wing struck at him as if defending its partner, its claw ripping at his head.

Lyre grabbed the thing in an effort to make it stop, but it fought her as hard as it fought him. Son of a bitch! This was creepy and twisted, and what kind of sicko transplanted *wings*?

It was a stupid question given where he was. Sheoul was filled with sickos, and he was bound to become one of them if he didn't get the fuck out of here.

His struggle with the wings knocked both him and Lyre off balance, and they went down on the grass, his wings wrapping him in a tight cocoon. Increasing pressure compounded his muscles and made his bones ache as the wings tried their best to squeeze the life out of him.

"Roll onto your back." She grunted as a wing kicked out and struck her in the gut, but she managed to wrestle the thing and hold it against his shoulder.

He rolled, pinning the bastards under him. Finally, he could take a breath. Lyre stretched out next to him, panting with exertion.

"I swear to you, Cipher," she said between breaths. "Bael just told me and I went straight to you." Her hand came down on his forearm, and he found himself hoping she'd leave it there. After being so alone for so long, he craved more than a fleeting touch. More than the usual pain others doled out every time they laid hands on him. "I tried to tell you back on the island, but things were kind of crazy."

Were crazy? The crazy was still well underway. And despite his freak-out, he was grateful Lyre was here to help. She didn't have to tell him the truth, and she didn't have to rescue him from Flail's evil clutches. Hell, she'd been his sole link to sanity for months. What would his life have been like without her? His other handlers had been as depraved as Flail, bringing him food that was either too long dead or too alive, torturing him for fun, fucking with his head every chance they got.

There's no way they would have saved him from Flail or told him his wings weren't actually his.

And what the hell was up with that, anyway? Now he understood why Flail had said his wings would help him create viruses. That had been Asher's specialty. Combined with Cipher's tech skills, Bael had been counting on some serious computer-borne plagues.

As he lay there on his back, staring blankly up at the sky, he watched the programming code circling in the air far above him. He'd noticed it the moment he and Lyre had stepped outside the training facility and again here in this weird valley, but he hadn't been able to decipher it yet.

Some of it looked familiar, as if he knew the subject, if not the purpose. *Griminions*. Souls. There would be no reason to cast spells for those things unless...unless they were the spells that kept the souls of the dead inside Bael's territory and that kept *griminions* out.

"Cipher? Are you okay?"

"What? Oh, yeah." He gave a reluctant nod. "I'm just pissed. This is insane." He growled as his wings bucked beneath him. "That whack job gave me someone else's wings, and as if that wasn't bad enough, he made sure they were ensorcelled so I can't leave his realm."

"They're actually ensorcelled so you can't flash around *inside* the realm. No newbie fallen angel can leave."

He cranked his head to look at her. "So you're trapped here too?"

"Yup. I'm still on probation."

She rolled onto her side and propped herself up on one elbow, her thick ponytail draping over her shoulder and falling across her breasts. Was it wrong of him to notice that and the way her full breasts filled out her tank top?

Nah.

"Do you think part of the reason Bael gave the wings to you was to accelerate the process that turns fallen angels evil?" A breeze whipped her ponytail around until it settled in her cleavage, and he went utterly parched when she absently brushed her fingers over the thick lock of hair. "I mean, those wings are already steeped in malevolence. It should be bleeding into you."

"Maybe," he mused, refocusing on the subject and not on how much he wanted to drag his tongue along the neckline of her top. "But you'd think I'd feel more of it." He'd been shocked at how *not* evil he felt. He'd expected to be slammed with it, to have to fight it more than he had.

"I should feel more of it too." She toyed with a piece of the yellow grass, her liquid mercury gaze downcast. "I don't know what's wrong with me. For so long I felt like I should want to do evil things. I wanted evil to fill me with so much hate that I wouldn't be miserable down here."

He got that. He'd let despair get to him once or twice, making him wonder, for a split-second, how much easier life would be if he just gave in to the dark side.

Heh. Dark side. Between his Star Wars reference and Lyre's Aliens line, he figured that if they survived the next twenty-four hours they'd have to do a science-fiction marathon. With popcorn and pizza and beer. Damn, he could practically taste garlicky pepperoni and feel ice cold liquid pouring down his throat. He could invite Hawk and Journey, and—

A sinking sensation tugged at his insides. What if they hated him? What if they couldn't forgive him for giving up the list of their brothers and sisters? He didn't have to survive just the next twenty-four hours, he had to survive all his friends and the Grim Reaper.

"I think it wouldn't have been long before I got to that point." He swallowed dryly. "Knowing I'm responsible for the death of one of Azagoth's children would have fucked me up."

Still might.

"I'm so sorry." Her palm traveled up and down his arm in long, soothing strokes, and his skin tingled at the gentle touch. "I didn't know what Bael intended."

He tempered his voice, driven by curiosity, not malice. "Would it have mattered?"

"Honestly? At the time, no."

"And now?"

She closed her eyes, and he wondered if she was conscious of the way her nails dug into his skin. "Now I just want to get out of here. I don't want to be responsible for any of the catastrophic things Bael and Moloc plan to do." Her sable lashes flew up, and her eyes mirrored her sudden anger. "Now the only evil I want any part in is aimed at those assholes," she growled.

Okay, he could work with that. "Wanna do evil things together?"

"Like what?"

"Like...open Bael's realm to Azagoth." God, he hoped this wasn't a trick. He was going to lay it all out, and if she reported back to Bael, he'd be dead. But ultimately, he needed her. He couldn't do this without her. And, most significantly, he *wanted* to trust her.

"Are you serious?" she asked.

He nodded and went down the rabbit hole. "My buddies slid a code into the backdoor of Bael's security system. If I can get to my computer I can shut it down." He looked up at the sky, its eerie orange depths streaked with gray tendrils of ash. "And I think I can destroy the spell that prevents *griminions* from getting inside and that keeps souls in. If I can send a message to Hawkyn, we could coordinate everything. We can escape."

"But your wings are still enchanted. They won't let you leave his territory."

Which was why he had to lose them. "You're going to have to cut them off."

Abruptly, she sat up and stared. "Are you serious? Cipher, that'll be excruciating. And you won't be able to recharge your powers until you grow new wings. All you'll have is what's stored in your anchor bones."

All that was going to suck. Hard. But he'd gotten lots of practice being in pain, and he'd spent decades without powers while he was an Unfallen. He could do it again. As long as he had enough juice in his power battery to execute his opening salvo, his recharge could wait.

"That's why we'll need Azagoth's help. And an *aural*," he added. "I'll stab Bael myself if I get the chance. Do you know where he stores the one my opponents used in the arena?"

"He keeps it locked in the armory nearby. But it's impossible to get into. It's locked with a spell."

"Sounds right up my alley."

"Oh, yeah." She grinned. "You have a really cool gift."

He could see it coming in handy quite a bit, actually. "I just hope I don't lose it with the wings."

She nibbled her bottom lip thoughtfully. "The wings were attached to your existing bone structure. Most of the non-plague related abilities should be yours, not Asher's. But just in case, maybe you should delete the spells that keep souls in and *griminions* out now."

Made sense. Looking up at the bazillions of lines of code, he concentrated. It took longer than he would have liked to reprogram the spell and insert a timer, but after about an hour, he was finally satisfied.

He gripped Lyre's hand and squeezed. "You ready?"

"To slice off your wings?"

He suspected that they weren't going to *slice* off, all polite and easy, like a tender shaving of roast beef. But sure. "Yes."

"No."

He wished he could laugh, but the best he could do was reach across his body and snag the dagger from the sheath at her hip. "Just hurry. They're going to fight you."

Taking a quick, deep breath, he rolled onto his stomach and held onto the ground, trusting Lyre with his body, his future, and his very life.

Chapter Nineteen

Lyre had never been squeamish, and years in Sheoul had made her even less so. But sawing wings off Cipher had left her shaking with adrenaline and horror. The wet crunch of the blade sawing through bone, the resistant vibration of the knife hitting gristle, the metallic stench of his blood.

And through it all, Cipher had been silent.

She'd screamed when her own wings had been severed, and hers had been taken off neatly, with a blade meant for the task. Her wings also hadn't fought like pterodactyls caught in a net.

He knelt a few yards away, where he'd stumbled and collapsed after the second one flopped to the ground, his back bleeding, his chest heaving. She dropped the knife and ran to him.

He reached blindly for her as she went down on her knees in front of him. "Is there anything I can do?"

"No." The pain etched in his expression broke her heart. He squeezed her shoulder, using her as a brace as he straightened. "It's already getting better."

She doubted that. Taking his hand, she channeled healing waves into him. Every little bit had to help, and within moments, his color had come back a little and the flow of blood to the ground slowed to a drip.

Suddenly, he hissed and went stiff, his back arching so violently she thought his spine might snap. "Fuck...hurts..."

"I want to help, Cipher—"

He dropped forward again, catching himself on her arm. His forehead fell to her shoulder, and he spent a dozen heartbeats like that, his labored breathing rocking his entire body.

"Thank you," he rasped.

For what? Maiming him? Hurting him? She knew she'd done what was necessary, but it didn't change the fact that she'd brutally severed a fallen angel's defining feature and the source of his power. Didn't matter that they weren't his. He felt it as if they were.

"Shh," she murmured. "Rest. Heal."

Without his wings, the healing process would take longer, but already the edges of his wounds were less ragged and starting to seal up, and his skin had lost the ashen tone.

He relaxed against her, the tension in his big frame draining with every passing minute.

Gently, she held him, stroking his damp hair until he looked up at her, his tormented gaze locking onto hers. "I'm sorry."

Her mouth fell open with shock. "Are you kidding? For what?"

"For making you do this." He reached up, his hand trembling as he cupped her cheek. "It couldn't have been easy."

No, it hadn't been. But she'd definitely been on the less horrible end of the blade, and it amazed her, humbled her, that his concern wasn't for himself, but for her. What a magnificent male he was.

The last of her walls crumbled, and she leaned into his touch, selfishly taking comfort from him when she was the one who should be comforting him. His mouth was just inches from hers, his breath fanning her lips, and she found herself wanting even more from him.

"Lyre?" His deep voice was soft, and yet, it hung in the air as a resonant echo.

"Yes?" she whispered.

"If we don't make it out of here alive, I don't want the last thing we did to be...this."

She melted. All her emotions melted, just puddled in the lower chambers of her heart at his tender words.

"What are you saying?" she whispered back, even though she knew.

She hoped. This might not be the ideal place, but it was the perfect time. Nothing in her life had been under her control for years. She'd basically signed everything over to Bael, including her virginity, apparently.

Well, screw that. She'd just thrown in with Cipher, and if they failed in their attempt at escape, she'd either die or end up in Bael's bed. She didn't want to do either of those things without having experienced the kind of passion Cipher promised.

His mouth closed on hers, and as if he'd lit a fuse, her body sparked to life. Sizzling, fiery life, brought back from the cold, dead ashes of her past.

She opened to him, and his tongue slid between her lips and stroked hers, deepening the kiss as he pushed her onto her back. He wasn't rough, but he wasn't gentle, either. There was a desperate urgency to the way he tore open first her pants and then his, and as he kissed his way down her jaw and along her throat, tiny, hot nibbles left her moaning for more.

He gave her exactly that, making love to her with his mouth all the way to the top of her breasts, where he swept his tongue along the edge of her neckline.

"That's so sexy," she whispered, arching to help him shove her bra-lined tank up.

"No," he said, as he gazed at her bare breasts. "This is."

Lowering his head, he opened his mouth over her breast and sucked gently, sending a series of erotic tingles spiraling through her. His tongue was magic, stroking and licking each breast as his hands shoved her pants down her legs.

Eagerly she helped him, clawing at the stupid cargoes and then kicking at them when they tangled around her ankles. Finally, she flung them aside and welcomed Cipher between her thighs.

His hands were everywhere, tickling her ribs, stroking the sensitive skin at her hipbones, and delving lower to her swollen sex. She rolled her hips to meet his touch as she wrapped her arms around him. Her hands slid through slick smears of blood, and when she cried out in sorrow that she might be hurting him, he shifted and grasped her wrist, holding it at his back.

"No," he breathed against her collarbone. "Your touch only makes it better."

Oh, damn. He was so sweet, so strong, so out of place in this awful world. She fell for him right then and there, her pledge to remain emotionally detached gone up in the flames he was stoking in her as he slipped a finger between her folds.

She nearly sobbed with emotion and pleasure as he caressed her, his fingertip circling her clit with alternating measures of pressure, and adding feather light flicks at the tip and a few heartbeats of intense, steady pressure at the base.

She couldn't bear it, the way he manipulated her body with the same nimble precision he used with a keyboard. Her climax hit her so hard she couldn't breathe, could barely even gasp for air as ripples of ecstasy spread all the way to her toes and scalp.

"That's it," he murmured. "Keep coming."

Keep coming? Her body was all over that command, and another explosion rocked her.

"Again," he whispered, and damn if she didn't ride his hand to another orgasm.

"What are you doing to me?" she cried out as she peaked, because whatever it was, he could keep doing it.

His hot breath fanned her neck as he shifted, positioning himself at her entrance. "Programming you." His deep voice rumbled with masculine need. "This is how you'll always respond to me."

Oh...yes.

Hooking her ankles around his thighs, she arched into him, moaning at the sensation of his broad head pushing past the tight ring of her core. The stretching sensation was bearable; the wait was not.

Panting with exertion and anticipation, she managed a breathless, "Are you saying you hacked my network?"

He looked down at her, his blue eyes glowing with intensity, a hint of a smile on his lips. "You had a strong password, but I haven't met one yet that I can't crack."

His hips rolled as he eased inside her. Pain and pleasure mingled, and this was so much more than she could have hoped for. She'd always regretted that she and Dailon had never consummated their relationship, but now she knew why they hadn't. As an angel she'd always believed that everything happened for a reason, and that there was always a plan.

But she'd lost that faith to bitterness in recent years. Maybe this was a sign that she'd been right all along, because she knew, without a doubt, that this was the moment an intimate connection was needed.

An intimate connection that reminded her to live, to love, to fight for life.

Hers, *and* his.

* * * *

This was the best sex Cipher had ever had, and he hadn't even come yet.

Holy hell, Lyre was tight, her slick channel barely accommodating him, squeezing so hard he didn't even have to move. She was doing more than enough to make him clench his teeth and hope for control.

That lasted about two seconds.

With a groan of shame, he rocked against her, sliding in and out in a slow, easy rhythm that had her making soft, sexy sounds as she clenched around him. She was close again, so responsive to his touch and his body, and shit, he needed to play with that. A lot. When they got out of here, he was going to find every erogenous zone and he was going to make her come until they both passed out.

"Cipher, I-I'm..." Her sexed-up voice put him over the top as she shouted in release.

He let himself go, lunging into her and sliding her backward in the grass with the force of his thrusts. Surging, his hips driving home as if he needed to claim her so deeply she'd always feel him, he came hard, the ecstasy reaching every part of his body.

It didn't stop, and at the height of it, his wing anchors, raw and exposed to the elements, rolled into the position they would have taken for an angel's embrace, the cocoon of wings around an angel and his partner.

Ah, damn, he'd gone all in with Lyre, hadn't he?

He could hear Hawkyn now, all, "Cipher, the consummate playboy, the jackass who got my Memitim sentence extended with his uncontrollable need to nail everything that moved, finally got his angel ass plucked."

Or Hawkyn would kill him and never have to the chance to call him "plucked." Such stupid terms the young punk Memitim were using these days.

The last ripples of pleasure wrung him out, leaving him heaving above Lyre, his arms trembling with the strain of holding himself up as she undulated through her waning climax. Her sixth, maybe? He wasn't sure, but he loved watching her expression and the way her glistening lips parted with each delicate cry.

Finally, she went limp, her fingers caressing his tender back as she pulled him down on top of her.

"Wow." Turning her head, she kissed his cheek as he lay at the curve of her shoulder. "That wasn't what I expected."

"Better or worse?" If she said worse, he was never telling Hawkyn this story.

She chuckled. "Better. Way, way better."

Okay, somehow that answer wasn't any more desirable. "Ah...what were you expecting?"

"More pain, I guess."

He pushed himself up on one elbow, ignoring the stabbing discomfort where his wings used to be.

"Did you *want* pain?" He really wasn't into that, but he figured he could get some tips from Journey. That guy liked his whips and chains and nipple clamps. "And why were you expecting it? Do I scream Dom, or what?"

Her half-lidded, satiated smile stroked his masculine pride. Stroked his cock too, and it stirred. How, he had no idea. His muscles were basically soup right now.

"No, I don't think I'm into pain, and no, you don't scream Dom." She wriggled onto her side, and he slid from her warm body, to his acute disappointment. "It was my first time. I just thought it would be less enjoyable. But it was *really* enjoyable."

First time? He stared, unsure how to respond. Or how to feel. She'd given him something she'd held on to for over a century. Something she'd managed to safeguard while living in Sheoul, where innocence and purity were ultra-rare commodities to be selectively ruined in the most useful or evil way imaginable.

Finally, he managed a lame, "Why me? Why now?"

"It had to be you." She reached over and twined her fingers with his. "I know, because I was ready to have sex with you in your cell and later in my flat."

She averted her gaze, and he hated it, reached out and tilted her chin up so their eyes met. "Why now?" he repeated. "Tell me, angel."

Strength and resolve swam in her liquid mercury eyes. "It's because I needed it. If I'm going to fight, I need a reason to win."

He inhaled deeply, thankful that she'd been assigned as his handler. Thankful for *her*. What she lacked in angelic ability she more than made up for with her brains, her fiercely protective nature, and her determination.

"We'll win." Reluctantly, he grabbed her pants and slid them over her feet, enjoying the intimacy of helping her dress. That small act was somehow even more personal than sex. "If Azagoth helps us escape, we can't lose."

"You think he'll help after—" She broke off, biting her lip.

"After I betrayed him and got one of his kids killed?" He buttoned his own jeans as she buttoned hers. "He won't be *helping* me. He'll be *using* me to kill Bael." And then he'd probably kill Cipher.

Small details.

He suppressed a groan at the ache in his back as he stood and held out a hand to her. "You ready?"

Taking his hand, Lyre nodded. "Whatever happens...thank you."

"For what?" Needing an excuse to touch her, he tucked her tank top into her pants, letting his fingers linger on her firm rear. "I'm probably going to get you killed."

"For reminding me that there's more to live for than revenge." She smiled wanly. "The downside is that now dying would suck."

Pretty much. Holding his breath, he looked up at the sky, afraid of what he'd see.

Or *wouldn't* see.

Relief nearly knocked him to his knees. There, in the gray-streaked orange sky, were the transparent characters that made up the spell codes. He didn't want to waste the power remaining in the stems of his wings since he had no way to recharge now, but just a teeny bit couldn't hurt. He opened himself to a trickle of power and zapped a character out of existence before replacing it a heartbeat later.

Fucking awesome. It was *his* power, not Asher's.

Now he just had to survive long enough to use it.

Chapter Twenty

A dull pain throbbed in Cipher's wing anchors as he and Lyre slipped inside the room where his poor laptop sat, all cold and alone. But his body felt revitalized, his mind refreshed.

Amazing what sex can do for a guy, huh?

It wasn't just the sex that had him hopped up on positive energy. Ridding himself of the heavy taint of malevolence that had come with Asher's wings had been like a weight off his shoulders. Literally.

He remembered how bereft he'd felt after losing his heavenly wings, how depressed and physically ill he'd been. But if losing his heavenly wings had dragged him down, losing the transplanted evil ones had filled him with power that had nothing to do with angelic energy.

He was, once again, his own master.

They'd also successfully gotten in and out of Bael's armory with clean pants and a tee he'd pilfered from a guard he'd knocked out, as well as with a weapon protected by a nasty spell that would have turned them both inside out if he hadn't been able to break it.

But beneath the bliss was a thread of fear. Not for his life, but fear for Lyre. And the world. If they didn't stop Bael, the crazy motherfucker was going to trash human life, Heavenly life, and Azagoth's entire world. And once Satan was free, the trash pile was going to get even bigger.

That guy had a score to settle.

"Can you really bring down his security systems?" Lyre asked.

"Even with your powers diminished?"

"Yup." He fired up his baby. "It's all about the computer. No magic involved."

She paced around the room, her nerves showing with every quick step, every nibble on her nails. "How long will it be before the soul barrier spells are down?"

He checked the clock on the computer. "If I didn't screw anything up, we have about ten minutes."

"Is that enough time to bring down his security systems?"

He tapped his way into Bael's security backdoor and looked for the trigger Journey had installed. "It should be."

"Should be?" Her fingers went absently to the *aural* tucked inside her waistband, covered by her shirt. It was still visible, but it was more likely to be mistaken as a dagger than recognized as a rare, ancient angel-killing stake. "Bael is going to know the moment the protective spells are gone, and he's going to know who did it."

"I know." There was Journey's backdoor. All Cipher had to do was flip a virtual switch, and every bit of Bael's tech would fail. If Journey himself had written the program, it would take Bael's best technicians hours, if not days, to get it up and running again. The Memitim was that good.

"Can Bael repair the spells?"

"I fucked them up pretty bad. If he tries to use the same spells again, they'll fail. Eventually his sorcerers will try new formulas, but I bought us some time to escape." He looked over at her. "Your inability to flash out of Bael's realm is tied to the spell barriers, right?" At her nod, he continued. "Then all you have to do is flash us out of here once they're down."

She snorted. "First we have to make it out of the building and across the drawbridge. No one can flash in or out of his castle or the surrounding grounds, and you know he's going to lock everything down."

Which was why they'd have to run really, really fast. While being completely inconspicuous.

"We just have to trust that Azagoth will come through," he said, and she gave a skeptical snort.

"I still don't understand how you can trust any of those people."

"Not everyone is out to hurt you, Lyre," he said softly.

He popped open his message app and shot Hawkyn a note.

Glanced at the computer clock. The spells should break outside in 3...2...1.

"It's time."

He flipped the switch.

* * * *

"Father!"

Hawkyn ignored Zhubaal's warnings that Azagoth was not only busy but also not in the best of moods, and he burst into Azagoth's office.

"I got a message from Cipher," Hawkyn said breathlessly. "He's brought down Bael's security system and the soul barrier."

Azagoth turned away from the *griminion* he'd been speaking to. "So I've been informed." He'd probably felt the soul barrier's collapse himself.

"So what are we going to do? Cipher needs help, and none of us can enter that part of Sheoul." It was damned inconvenient, too. There were a lot of places inside Sheoul where angels couldn't—or wouldn't—go. Most parts of Sheoul, in fact. "Whatever it is, we need to hurry. Bael will have everything up and running again soon."

And then Cipher, if he couldn't escape in time, would die.

"I'll take care of it." Azagoth gestured to the little robed *griminion*, and the critter skittered away.

"Take care of what?" It could be dangerous to question the Grim Reaper, but Hawkyn had found that if he didn't nail down specifics, Azagoth found loopholes. Azagoth could find a loophole in a straight steel rod.

"Bael." Azagoth's voice dipped low, daring Hawkyn to ask another question.

Hawkyn dared. This was too important not to. "What about Cipher?"

"I'll take care of him too."

Azagoth's tone was chilling, and Hawkyn growled. "I want him back alive. Not barely alive. Not mostly alive. Alive and *well.* With a physical body."

Crimson streaks flared in Azagoth's black eyes as his anger and malevolence escalated. "*He killed my daughter.*"

"No, he didn't." Hawkyn dug his phone out of his pocket. "Just before Hawkyn's message, I got word from the Memitim Council. Amelia was Primori."

"What?" Azagoth's shock morphed instantly into doubt and anger. "How can any of my children be Primori?" he snapped. "They're Memitim. They can't be both."

Hawkyn had been as stunned by the news as Azagoth was. As far as he knew, no Memitim had also held the protected status of Primori.

"I don't know, but the Council confirmed it. Amelia had a Memitim guardian from the moment of her birth. He was taken off the job just hours before she was killed." When Azagoth just stood there, his fury congealing in his eyes, Hawkyn beat him over the head with the obvious. "Father, she was *meant* to die."

And what *that* meant was anyone's guess.

With a hiss, Azagoth turned toward the entrance to the Inner Sanctum, but Hawkyn grabbed his arm.

"*Please*, Father. He's my best friend." He tempered his tone, not caring if he sounded like he was begging. Because that's what he was doing. "Cipher's been through a lot with me. He's an honorable male."

Azagoth shook off his touch but didn't turn around. When he spoke, he spoke to the wall. "And if becoming a True Fallen has changed that?"

Hawkyn swallowed, knowing the correct answer but not wanting to say it. Hell, he didn't even want to think it. But if he wanted his father to give Cipher even half a chance, he had to.

"If Cipher has turned evil," he said, "I'll put him down myself."

Chapter Twenty-One

Alarms blared as Cipher and Lyre crept through the ice hallways and narrow, winding stairwells of Bael's castle. Armored Ramreel guards charged toward duty stations, exits, and Bael's residence, their crude axes and spiked maces clutched tight in their meaty fists. They weren't specifically searching for Cipher yet, but it wouldn't be long before Bael filtered through the chaos and realized that only Cipher could have been responsible for the failure of not only the security system, but the downing of the soul barrier as well.

"This way." Lyre tugged him down a corridor lit by flickering torch sconces that cast snarling, demonic faces in shadow. "There's a side door. We can take the staircase into the outer dungeons."

"Dungeons?" He glanced over his shoulder at a Ramreel that had followed them into the passage. Maybe it was coincidence. "Isn't that what we're trying to avoid?"

"There's a tunnel from there that leads into the Bowel Mountains. Once we're out, if the barrier is still down, I can flash us out of Bael's territory. If the barrier is up again, we'll still be ahead of his troops, and I know where we can access a Harrowgate that'll get us into the human realm."

A horde of several species of demons rounded the corner ahead, the leader's dozens of eyes lighting up when he saw them.

No coincidence there.

"Shit!" She pulled him down another hallway. "Plan B."

"What's Plan B?"

"Run fast."

He hated that plan. They took off at a dead run, the demons closing the distance behind them way too quickly.

"Hurry!" he shouted, putting on a burst of speed as the sound of snapping teeth rang out so close to his head he felt hot breath on the back of his neck.

"Out the front," she yelled. "We can lose them in the chaos."

Ahead, the giant double doors were open. Beyond the doorway in the courtyard, confused demons milled about beneath decorative corpses swinging overheard.

Cipher risked a glance behind him and instantly regretted his mistake. The number of pursuing guards had doubled.

He summoned the precious remains of his power, holding it at his fingertips and ready to strike. He was weaker without the wings, but even now he could feel the increase in control. A tradeoff, but really, in a fight it might be better to have uncontrolled strength than controlled crumbs of power.

This was not going to be a piece of cake.

But if they made it out of this alive, he was going to ask Suzanne to make one to celebrate.

They burst outside, jumping into the midst of hundreds of beings who clearly had no idea what was happening but wanted to be in the middle of the action.

Demons were stupid.

"There!" Lyre pointed toward the bridge that spanned the lava moat. "Once we're across, I can flash us out of here."

Okay. This might work. Hope trickled through him.

And then he looked up and jerked to a stop. "Oh, shit," he breathed. *Oh, fuck.*

"What is it?"

"The spells. They're not down. Azagoth can't get help in here and we can't get out—"

A massive explosion rocked the ground ahead. The bridge collapsed as giant boulders of rock and ice spewed into the air and cratered all around them, crushing demons, carts, and the stands where they sold their wares.

With shrieks of terror and pain all around, Cipher knocked Lyre to the ground, covering her with his body as debris rained down. Basketball-sized chunks pummeled his back and legs, but he'd survive.

Unlike that poor bastard with his hooves sticking out under a Volkswagen-sized block of ice, his blood spreading in a pool beneath him.

"*I will slaughter you where you stand*!"

Bael's voice, sounding way too close, froze the blood in Cipher's veins. He leaped to his feet, heart pounding and pushing that frozen blood like slush that left him feeling like shit was in slow motion.

A crack of thunder shattered his eardrums a split-second before a lightning strike sizzled through him, paralyzing him where he stood. Agony became everything, his feelings, his thoughts, his vision. Because apparently, you could *see* pain. It was red and shiny and twisted as fuck.

Distantly, he heard Lyre's shouts for mercy. Not mercy for her. Mercy for him.

"Stop," she yelled. "I'll do anything!"

"Yes," Bael hissed. "You will."

No! Cipher inhaled, coughing on blood as he staggered forward blindly, his only goal to reach Bael and choke the life out of him with his bare hands.

He heard a grunt, a thud, and suddenly the electrocution stopped. His ears rang and white spots floated in his vision, but the pain died to a dull roar, and as his eyes focused, he saw why.

Lyre had tackled Bael.

But she'd paid for it, was now trying to pick herself up off the ground, blood pouring from her nose and ears. Bael laughed as he punched down, hitting her in the back of the neck and dropping her as if she'd been hit with a bolt.

His fist tangled in her hair, and he brutally wrenched her head up, putting his mouth to her ear. Cipher couldn't hear what he was saying, but he heard Lyre's cry of terror.

"Bastard!" Cipher roared in fury and released the first weapon that came to mind, a barrage of voracious summoned demon locusts that swarmed Bael in a whirlwind of teeth.

Bael howled in pain as he was cut to ribbons, giving Lyre a chance to push to her feet.

"Come on!" Cipher held out his hand to her. "Hurry!"

She started toward him, but suddenly, the locusts fell dead. Son of a bitch! The locust swarm had drained his power by half, and Bael had circumvented it as if the locusts had been no more than a nuisance.

Bael, his ire taking on a life of its own, transformed, his body tripling in size, his skin hardening into black armor, his face taking on nightmarish, oversized features and teeth the size of Cipher's fingers.

They couldn't score a freaking break.

With the very last of his power, he blasted Bael with his ice melt weapon, encasing the bastard from head to toe. "Lyre, run!"

"No!" She sprinted toward him, and he wanted to scream at the futility of it. She couldn't help him. She'd just die with him.

"Go!"

A detonation of ice sent piercing shards into the demons who had gathered to watch, and by some miracle both he and Lyre had escaped unscathed. Some of the demons dropped dead while others hit the ground and thrashed in pain. Still others ran.

Bael, completely ice-free, roared in fury and blasted Cipher and Lyre with some sort of weapon that sliced a million tiny cuts into the skin and peeled it away.

Agony became the very air Cipher breathed, and through his own shouts of misery, Lyre's screams punched through, flaying his insides as well.

"You're going to die," Bael shouted above the thunder that rolled in from the blood-red storm clouds above. "You're going to die, and then I'm going to feed your souls to my Orphmage while I dine on your flesh." The fallen angel sauntered toward him. "But not before you get to watch what Moloc and I do to your precious Lyre."

No. Please no...

Darkness started to fall. Maybe not in the realm, but in Cipher's head. He couldn't lift his arms, his legs, his head. Hell, he could barely open his eyes.

He saw Lyre writhing on the ground, and his heart, already riddled with wounds, bled. Tortured by the sight, he put all of his strength into reaching for her. If he could just touch her...

A demon shrieked and ran between them, nearly stepping on his arm. Then another. All around, terrified wails rose up. Suddenly, Bael spun around, his attention and restraining powers no longer focused on Cipher and Lyre.

What the hell?

Groaning, Cipher glanced at the sky. The spells...the spells had broken!

Something, or some *things*, were attacking the demons, and for the first time, Bael looked afraid.

"Lyre," he croaked as he pushed himself to his hands and knees on shaky limbs.

She looked over at him. Looked at Bael.

And then she looked back at him again, determination mirrored in her glittering eyes. What was she going to do?

"Lyre?"

She vaporized into a puff of smoke, and before he could even blink, she shot into Bael's nostrils. His eyes popped wide and he grabbed his throat, choking and gagging.

And Lyre, that wily little angel, had left the *aural* on the ground.

Cipher staggered to his feet. His legs were rubber and his steps leaden, but he managed to palm the *aural* and somehow make it to where Bael was struggling to exorcise Lyre.

Clutching his throat, Bael wheeled around to face Cipher, the hatred in his expression making his face bulge grotesquely. He lifted a clawed hand, shocks of electricity sparking between his fingers, and Cipher knew that this next blow would kill him.

There was no time left.

He lunged, slamming the *aural* into Bael's chest.

And nothing happened. The weapon slid uselessly off his armor.

Fuck!

Still coughing, Bael grinned, raised his hand once more.

Then, from out of nowhere, a transparent gray, shapeless form wrapped around Bael, its eyes empty, its mouth screaming silently.

Bael's scream was *not* silent.

One of Azagoth's souls. Way to go, Hawkyn!

Lyre's vapor form ejected from between Bael's lips as the fallen angel returned to his original, angel-sized body. He writhed in misery as the soul spun around him, doing whatever it was souls did.

But no, that soul wasn't going to claim this kill.

This kill belonged to Cipher.

With a battle cry soaked in vengeance, Cipher buried the *aural* in Bael's heart. This time the weapon slammed home.

Bael gasped as his body shuddered and convulsed, smoke rising from the cracks forming in his skin. The sizzle of burning flesh accompanied his death cries, and the evil inside Cipher was transfixed by it all.

Finally, as Lyre wrapped herself around Cipher and held him tight, the fucker collapsed.

Bael was dead. The monster who had terrorized this region of Sheoul for eons was gone.

Somehow, they'd survived this, but Cipher still had one more monster to face, and his name was Azagoth.

Chapter Twenty-Two

Azagoth hated waiting.

People were always amazed by his patience, but they only saw what he wanted them to see. His exterior was very much different than his interior.

Inside was a high-strung, restless beast that didn't like to wait for things like vengeance. Or pleasure.

At least now that Lilliana was home, it didn't have to wait for the latter. Her presence had soothed the monster until now, as he waited for news coming out of Sheoul. He'd sent hundreds of souls to destroy Bael, and with any luck, Moloc would be with his brother as well.

But so far his *griminions* hadn't brought him their souls. They'd delivered dozens of other souls they'd reaped from Bael's realm, but not the ones Azagoth wanted.

This was taking too long.

A massive power surge forced the hair on Azagoth's neck to stand up, and before he could even blink, another, equally powerful wave of energy slammed into him.

Fuck.

Reaver and Revenant had just popped in for a visit, and Azagoth had no doubt that this wasn't going to be a friendly one.

Which meant that he was going to meet them in the place of his choosing, the place that gave him a strategic advantage.

He threw open his office door just as Zhubaal skidded to a stop in front of it. "My lord—"

"I know. Send them to the Inner Sanctum."

Z jerked. "M-my lord?"

"Do it. And send someone to keep Lilliana occupied. I don't want her near Reaver or Revenant." He doubted either male would harm Lilliana, but he wouldn't put it past them to use her in some way if they had to.

"Yes, sir."

Quickly, he went through the passage to the Inner Sanctum, and within moments of stepping across the threshold, Hades materialized.

"Hey, boss man," Hades said, his blue Mohawk cut close to his head today. "Who are you here to torture?"

"I'm not torturing anyone. We're expecting guests, and we only have about sixty seconds to prepare."

"Guests?"

"Reaver and Revenant."

Hades's eyes shot wide open. "But won't their presence weaken the veil between Sheoul and Sheoul-gra?"

"I'm counting on it," Azagoth said. "They know they can't destroy me here without blowing out the barriers and releasing millions of demon souls."

There was no way either angel would risk that. The resulting chaos would spread quickly, affecting not just the demon realm, but the human one as well. They wouldn't stay long, either, knowing that their mere presence would burn holes through the veil like acid.

Hades nodded. "Understood. I'll put my repair crew on standby."

"No." Azagoth glanced over at the portal the angels would be coming through at any moment. "I don't want you to fix any damage their presence causes."

"The fuck you say?" If Hades had ever been more stunned by anything, Azagoth wasn't aware of it. He cleared his throat and added a hasty, "My lord?"

Not in the mood to either explain his command or be questioned about it, he snapped, "Go. They'll be here in a moment."

Hades popped his wings and lifted off just as Reaver and Revenant stepped out of the portal.

Reaver stalked toward him like a bull, his expression shadowed with fury, his pristine white and gold wings flared high above gleaming crimson and gold armor. Revenant flanked him, his black and silver wings folded tamely against the backplate of his light-absorbing ebony armor, but there was nothing tame about his bared fangs. Both angels were prepped for battle, and Azagoth flooded his body with power in response.

"I warned you not to release souls." Reaver's voice, singing with strength, vibrated the very air. "I warned you not to kill Bael."

Guilty as charged on point A. But point B was a bust. Not for lack of trying though. His disappointment in not being brought Bael's soul was almost crushing.

"Chill the fuck out, boys," Azagoth said. "If Bael was dead, his soul would have come to me, and I'd be dissecting it right now."

Sure, it was possible that another incredibly powerful demon or fallen angel had destroyed or devoured his soul, but the odds of that were so low as to be preposterous.

Reaver looked out over the stark terrain of what was basically the antechamber to the rest of the Inner Sanctum, and Azagoth wondered if he noticed the demons in the distance, slowly moving toward them, drawn by the power emanating from the two angels.

"You're wrong." Reaver turned back to Azagoth. "*Griminions* couldn't have harvested his soul. He and his brother Moloc were...aberrations."

Azagoth scoffed. "What do you mean, aberrations?"

"They're twins," Reaver said. "But they are one."

Revenant's head cranked around to stare at his brother. "Say what?"

"They share a soul," Reaver explained. "To kill one of them means reuniting their two halves and making the remaining 'brother' whole. And much, much stronger."

Well, wasn't that interesting. Azagoth *had* succeeded in killing Bael's physical body. Unfortunately, the fucker was still alive inside another body, and even stronger than before.

Fan-fucking-tastic.

"You couldn't have shared that information sooner?" he gritted out.

Revenant jabbed Reaver in the shoulder. "No shit."

Reaver glared at them both. "I didn't know either, assholes. I just found out a few hours ago when I looked them up in the Akashic Library."

Man, Azagoth missed the Heavenly library that contained details about every human, every event, every *thing* in the history of the universe.

"So?" Revenant crossed his arms over his chest, his spiked gauntlets clanking against his armor. "What's their story?"

Azagoth was curious as well. Not because he gave a shit, but because information was a weapon.

"Apparently," Reaver began, "their split-soul is why they were banished from Heaven as the youngest angels in history. According to the texts, they were devoid of empathy, and they delighted in hurting others. Humans, animals, other angels. They were going to be executed, but Moloc escaped. Bael couldn't be executed for fear of reuniting the souls, so the archangels cut off his wings and kicked him out. Moloc performed a ceremony and his own wingectomy, and he fell too. Both joined up with Satan, and here we are."

Minor setback. Azagoth just had to kill Moloc now. MolocBael? BaelMoloc? Whatever. Minor. Fucking. Setback.

So why didn't it feel so minor? Alarm bells were ringing hard on this.

"Listen to me, Azagoth," Reaver said. "I know you killed Bael. You fucked up. Don't do it again. Don't kill Moloc."

"Or what?"

"Or you'll cease to exist."

Klaxons joined the alarm bells, and an entire symphony of warnings vibrated his body now. "You're threatening me?"

"No, Azagoth, I'm telling you." Reaver's voice went low, ominous, his wings quivering with the force of it. "If you kill him, all that you know, all that you are...will be destroyed."

Sudden fury seared Azagoth's veins, hot and potent. "Do you not understand what Bael and Moloc want? They want Satan freed and Revenant deposed, and they're killing my family to make it happen!" He rounded on Revenant. "Why can't you do anything about this? You're the fucking King of Hell. Surely you're not going sit back and lose your throne to an insurrection."

"Oh, I have plans for Moloc," Revenant drawled. "I'm more concerned about you."

"Isn't that sweet."

Revenant smirked. "Not that kind of concerned."

Of course not. Why would he give a shit about Azagoth's family? "You'd better *get* concerned," Azagoth growled. "Or the entire underworld is going to read your inaction as cowardice."

Revenant bared his fangs, his eyes went nightmare, and before Azagoth could even blink, the guy was in his face. "Call me a coward again."

"Step off, asshole," Azagoth warned. "This is my fucking realm, and you have no power here."

A flash of light nearly blinded him as Revenant lit up like a supernova, proving just how wrong Azagoth was.

"I can *melt* you if I want to, soul boy."

An invisible force knocked Azagoth into a mausoleum, triggering his temper and his inner demon. He unfurled into his beast, his horns and great wings reaching skyward.

"*How dare you.*" His voice, warped by his fury and his form, made the very ground shift under their feet. "How dare you attack me inside my realm."

Revenant hissed and shook off Reaver's restraining hand. "You attacked my realm by sending souls to do your bidding in violation of the treaty. What's your next move? Freeing Satan?"

"Never," he snarled, his shock at the very idea bringing his fury down a notch.

Revenant's wings spread wide, the bony claws at the tips clenching as if they wanted to shred Azagoth like pulled pork. "Are you sure?"

Was he sure? Satan had blackmailed Azagoth for eons, threatening his realm and his children if Azagoth refused to reincarnate the souls Satan wanted. He'd slaughtered *griminions.* He'd demanded loyalty Azagoth refused to give, and always it was one of Azagoth's children who paid.

So fuck Revenant and the hell stallion he rode in on. "Do not question my hatred for Satan," Azagoth roared.

Blood boiling, he attacked. He could have used any of a thousand weapons at his disposal, but what he wanted was to feel flesh rending between his teeth and blood streaming between his claws.

Revenant hit him head on. The shockwave of the impact blew structures apart for as far as Azagoth could see in the brief glimpse he got before Revenant's fist pounded his face and broke every bone in his head.

The pain as his skull knitted itself back together only pissed him off more, and he clamped down on Rev's throat in a bite that crushed the angel's windpipe and spine. Blood poured down Azagoth's throat, hot and powerful, and then Reaver wrenched them apart, blasting them both a hundred yards in opposite directions.

"*Enough*!"

Suddenly, Azagoth found himself hanging in the air at the end of Reaver's fingers. Revenant was at Reaver's other hand, clutching his mangled throat. Good. Fucker. Inside the Inner Sanctum, he wasn't healing as quickly as he should have.

Reaver dropped his brother to the ground. "Are we done?"

"He started it," Revenant rasped.

Shaking his head in exasperation, Reaver turned to Azagoth and dropped him next. "How can we know you won't conspire with someone to release Satan?"

Baring his teeth, he put everything he had into what he was about to say. He felt this to the depths of his soul and in the blood that ran in his veins.

"I. Will. Die. First."

Silence stretched as the stench of char swirled around them. Then, finally, Reaver nodded. "Okay. Give Lilliana my best. And congratulations on becoming a father again."

"Ditto," Revenant rasped. "Asshole."

Azagoth inclined his head and watched the brothers leave before surveying the damage to the Inner Sanctum. As he'd noted earlier, everything all around had been flattened and scorched. A few souls might have been disintegrated, but he didn't care. What he cared about was the fact that a small section of the barrier between the Inner Sanctum and Sheoul had weakened. Just a single, tiny, hairline crack in the veil that no one else but Hades would be able to see.

Smiling, he brushed himself off and whistled a jaunty tune as he headed toward the portal back to Sheoul-gra. But when he stepped into his office, he checked up hard.

Lilliana was sitting there in his chair, her expression drawn, one hand clutching a sweating glass of ice tea.

"What is it?" He rushed to her. "What's wrong?"

"I don't know," she said softly. "You tell me."

"Nothing is going on."

She looked at him like he was a dumbass. "I'm not a fool. You're covered in blood, your horns are out, and something rocked Sheoul-gra hard enough to topple statues and break dishes just minutes after Reaver and Revenant arrived. So don't bullshit me." She came to her feet, and when he reached to help her, she swatted his hand away.

"You released souls to kill Bael, and they found out, didn't they?"

Azagoth had always kept his work and his home life separate. He'd never wanted Lilliana to be exposed to the ugly part of his job...or the ugly part of himself. He didn't want her to see how the soul sausage was made, when it came down to it.

"I don't want you to worry, Lilli. You've got enough to deal with as it is."

"Don't," she warned. "Don't shut me out. Never again. You swore."

He wanted to deny that he was shutting her out. And if he was, he wanted to assure her that he was doing it for her own good. But shutting her out was part of what had led to her leaving him in the first place. He'd held her hostage emotionally, not giving her that bit of him that she craved. And then when he had expressed emotion, it was anger. Always anger.

He'd promised he'd do better. It was time to fulfill that promise.

"You're right." He inhaled softly. "Bael's dead, and the Wonder Twins know about it. But they're the least of my concerns. Moloc's still alive, and he's more powerful than ever. He's going to come after me with everything he's got."

"That's why you've put a rush on bringing in the last of your human-realm children, isn't it? To get them out of the way."

He nodded. "And it's why you always have a guard. Moloc will stop at nothing to get what he wants from me."

Earlier, Lilliana had mentioned that the hellhound she'd befriended on Ares's island might be joining them, and the mutt was welcome. He wasn't fond of the beasts, but they were fiercely loyal, and no one would fuck with Lilliana with one at her side.

"Why does Moloc need you so badly?" Lilliana asked.

He reached for his favorite bottle of rum. "Because I have the key to Satan's prison."

"The key?" She lost color in her face and sank back into the chair. "Satan is in Sheoul-gra?"

"Yes and no." He abandoned the bottle and moved to her. He needed her more than the alcohol anyway. "When Revenant and Reaver trapped Satan, they created an inter-dimensional prison using the same basic frequency as the Inner Sanctum. Satan's cell is both inside Sheoul-gra and not inside it. I, alone, can access it." Leaning against the desk, he rethought that. "Well, Reaver and Revenant can too, but only if they can find it."

Lilliana looked down at her belly. "I don't like this, Azagoth."

Which was why he hadn't wanted to tell her about any of it. He'd wanted all the stress, all the ugliness, on his shoulders. Not hers. But no matter what, he'd protect her, and he'd keep her safe, no matter what it took.

"I don't either, Lilli," he said, dipping his head to give her a kiss that was more than affection. It was a promise. "But I won't let anything happen to you or our child."

Stepping back, he pulled a gold-tipped white feather from the sleeve of his right arm, and a silver-tipped black feather from the left and laid them on the desktop. Neither Reaver nor Revenant had noticed when he'd lifted them from their wings.

Lilliana reached for them, her slender fingers skimming over the delicate glitter. "What are these? I mean, obviously they're feathers, but what for?"

"Insurance," he said grimly. "They're insurance."

Chapter Twenty-Three

Cipher held Lyre's hand as they stood near the portal that would get them into Sheoul-gra. Well, it would if they had permission. Apparently Azagoth had recently sealed it after the death of one of his children.

"Can you see it?" Lyre asked, referring to the spell that kept the entrance closed.

"Yup."

"Having second thoughts?"

"What, about breaking a spell that the Grim Reaper put in place to protect his realm?" He snorted. "Nah."

She squeezed his hand reassuringly, well aware that he was having second thoughts. Third thoughts. Fourth thoughts.

There were a whole lot of thoughts going through his head right now.

"We don't have to do this," she said. "We could disappear somewhere. Live away from everyone else." She shrugged one battered shoulder, still bruised and bloodied from the battle. Her major wounds had healed already, the fractured bones and lacerations, but without wings his damage was taking far longer. "I heard Pestilence lived in a cave for centuries. So, you know, there's that."

He knew she was kidding about the cave—probably—but no matter what, life as a fugitive from Azagoth's wrath and his friends' scorn wouldn't work for him. He'd always been an *act first, ask forgiveness later* type of guy, but he did always ask forgiveness.

"I can't run, Lyre." Both literally and figuratively. He was pretty sure his right femur was shattered.

"I know," she sighed. "It's just...I saw enough of you being tortured. I don't want you to go through that again, and I'm guessing that if anyone is an expert at causing pain, Azagoth would be it."

"And you would be right." He brushed a lock of hair back behind her ear, needing an excuse to touch her where Bael had put his filthy mouth. "Lyre?"

"Hmm?"

"What did Bael say to you? You know, right before you did your vapor thing?"

Lyre gave a casual shrug, but he'd seen the look of terror on her face when Bael was bent over her, his teeth grazing her ear.

"Apparently, virgin fallen angels are hard to find," she said. "He and Moloc decided to use me for some kind of mating ceremony to make themselves whole." She shook her head. "I have no idea what that means. Anyway, when Bael sensed that I was no longer 'pure,' he got a little cranky."

"I wish the bastard wasn't dead," he growled. "I want to kill him again."

"Well, there's always Moloc and Flail," she said as she channeled a wave of healing power into him. She'd been sending pulses through him every couple of minutes as her power recharged. He wished he could do the same for her, but there wasn't any guarantee that he'd develop that skill. He couldn't wait for his new wings to find out.

"I'm sure Azagoth will handle Moloc." Flail, however, was his.

The mention of Azagoth's name put a shadow of worry in Lyre's eyes, and he wished he could reassure her, but he wasn't a hundred percent on the likelihood of surviving the rest of the day.

"So who are we going to talk to first?" she asked. "Azagoth? Your friend Hawkyn?"

"I don't know. Whoever we see first, I guess. I have to apologize to everyone. I'm responsible for the death of a child who was the sibling of every Memitim in Sheoul-gra. I owe them all an explanation."

"Okay." She went up on her toes and kissed him, her warm lips giving him the courage to get this done.

Except "getting it done" took longer than expected. The battle with Bael had drained him of power, leaving him with a single drop that was barely enough to interrupt the spell protecting Sheoul-gra's entrance. He was so weakened, in fact, that he couldn't completely bring it down. He could only pause it.

"We have five seconds," he said. "Let's go."

They materialized on the landing pad, and almost immediately, Zhubaal arrived, his expression a storm cloud. Cipher stepped in front of Lyre, putting himself in the path of Azagoth's chief enforcer. No one got to manhandle Lyre but Cipher.

He was about to make that clear when he heard Hawkyn call out his name.

"Cipher!" Hawk charged past Zhubaal and tackled him in a massive bear hug. "You're alive! Fuck me, I didn't think I'd ever see you again." He stepped back and looked him up and down. "Are you evil? Tell me you're not evil. I don't want to have to put you down."

Cipher laughed. "I'm surprisingly myself."

Z watched from the periphery, his hand at his sword hilt, his gaze watchful but non-threatening. He was ready to take Cipher out, but he was trusting Hawkyn to handle the situation.

Cool. Cipher had always liked Zhubaal. The fallen angel had a good head on his shoulders and he was a total dick. What wasn't to like?

Journey, Maddox, Emerico, and Jasmine, a few of Hawkyn's siblings, sprinted toward them, all smiles. Word was spreading fast. It wouldn't be long before Azagoth either sent for him or showed up.

Cipher wasn't sure which would be worse.

Hawkyn shifted his gaze to Lyre. "Ciph's last message said he had inside help to escape Bael's territory. You must be Lyre. I'm Hawkyn."

"It's good to finally meet you," she said. "Cipher has a lot of faith in your friendship."

"Yeah?" Hawkyn looked like he was about to say something that would be completely humiliating to Cipher—because what else were friends for—but the group of loudmouthed Memitim led by Journey stormed the landing pad.

They tackled him the way Hawkyn had, all smiles and "welcome back" and "tell us everything."

And for the first time in months, Cipher truly relaxed.

He was home.

He glanced around, frowning as he realized that shit was a mess. Statues were toppled, pillars smashed, and even a couple of trees were down. Memitim were working to clean up, although several had stopped what they were doing to watch the Cipher Show.

"What happened?"

Maddox jerked his thumb toward Azagoth's mansion. "Pops got into it with Reaver and Revenant."

"Why?"

Jasmine shook her dark head. "Dunno."

"Where is he?" He was almost afraid to ask, and Lyre gave his hand a comforting squeeze.

"Last time I saw him he was with Lilliana," Rico said.

Well, that was interesting. And potentially good news for Azagoth's mood. "I thought Lilliana left him."

"Dude, she's back," Journey said. "Like, last week. And get this, she's pregnant!"

Cipher stared in disbelief. "No. Seriously?"

Hawkyn nodded. "She just showed up one day, nine months pregnant."

Holy shit. "How did your father take it?"

"I've never seen him happier." Hawkyn gestured toward all the destroyed shit. "I mean, you know, as happy as he gets."

"I have a theory." Maddox took an enormous gulp of the soda in his hand. "What if the baby's not his?"

All heads swiveled toward Mad.

"*What*?" That came from everyone.

"Think about it, yo. She was gone nine months. She's nine months pregnant. She could have boned some dude after she left, like she was getting back at him or something, and bam! Preggo. She had to come back so he'd think it was his. You watch. This baby will be 'late.'" He added a wink to the last bit.

Journey scowled at his brother. "You're such a jackass."

"And how." Hawkyn opened his mouth to say something else, but abruptly, the ground shifted and the air went still and cold.

Oh, fuck.

"Uh-oh," Maddox said in a quiet, singsong voice. "Daddy's here."

Cipher shot Hawkyn a look, and Hawk dipped his head in understanding. Knowing his friend would keep Lyre safe, Cipher moved toward Azagoth, a cold knot of anticipation tightening in his chest.

At least he's in his fallen angel suit.

It was a small comfort that Azagoth was striding down the path in black slacks and a matching shirt instead of wearing scales and horns, but Cipher would take what he could get. Especially because, even from twenty paces away, he could see flames dancing in Azagoth's unyielding emerald eyes.

The Grim Reaper was extra grim today.

Adrenaline shot through Cipher as he prepared for whatever Azagoth was going to do to him. In Sheoul-gra, most angelic and demonic abilities were muted or useless, and even if they had been allowed and Cipher was at full strength, he couldn't stand up against the Grim Reaper's awesome power.

Azagoth's boots cracked the pavers as he stopped a mere three feet away, well inside Cipher's comfort zone. Of course, Cipher's comfort zone with Azagoth was three *miles*, not three feet.

Swallowing dryly, Cipher bowed. "My lord—"

"Not. A. Word." Azagoth's voice sounded like it had been filtered through the walls of a coffin. "You're still breathing for one reason. And that reason is Hawkyn."

Of that, Cipher had no doubt. He inclined his head in a respectful nod and looked back, meeting Hawkyn's gaze.

Thank you.

Again Hawkyn gave a solemn nod of acknowledgement before a flash of humor crossed his face and he mouthed, *You owe me.*

A thousand times over, buddy.

"Tell me why you gave the names of my children to my enemy," Azagoth continued, his expression as cold as his eyes were hot. "*Now* you may speak. And be careful. Hawkyn only holds so much sway with me."

Cipher took a deep, bracing breath, and when he spoke, it was with determination, sincerity, and a need to show Azagoth that he wasn't the devil-may-care playboy he used to be, but he was as loyal as he ever was.

"My lord, I'm sorry about your daughter. I'm so sorry." He raised his voice, needing everyone to hear this. "I gave the names of Azagoth's children to Bael in exchange for a chance to escape. I thought I was tricking him. I thought all of those children had already been brought to Sheoul-gra. I didn't know any were still out in the human realm." He met the gaze of every single Memitim before turning back to Azagoth, who stared in silent judgment. "I'm sorry," he repeated, even though it wasn't enough. There weren't enough apologies in the universe for this. "I'd take it back if I could."

"It's true!" Lyre shoved past the ring of Memitim before Hawkyn could grab her. "He didn't know. He was devastated when he found out. He wanted revenge as much as anyone."

"*Not* as much as anyone," Azagoth snapped.

Lyre cursed as Hawk snared her arm and gently reeled her in. "Cipher killed Bael with an *aural* from Bael's own armory."

Azagoth's sharp eyes bored into Cipher. "*You* killed Bael? It wasn't my souls?"

Cipher would have been content to let Azagoth believe that his souls had taken down Bael, but Lyre would have none of it, and she shrugged out of Hawkyn's grip.

"He could have waited for one of your souls to do it," she said boldly. "But he didn't. He wanted Bael to pay for what he'd done."

Cipher swore storm clouds were brewing over Azagoth's head. "Who *are* you?"

"My lord," Cipher said, moving to intercept, "this is Lyre. She helped me escape, and if not for her, Bael wouldn't be dead." He turned to her, awed by her bravery. She might claim to have weak powers, but she was a warrior from the tips of her wings to the depths of her heart. "And if she'll have me, I would have her as my mate."

Lyre's eyes flared, her mouth fell open, and he nearly groaned. Was it too soon? What if she rejected him in front of all his friends? What if she rejected him *anywhere*? He was alive because of her. He wasn't drenched in evil because of her. He was home because of her.

He owed her everything, and he'd already given her the one thing he never thought he'd surrender.

His heart.

"Yes," she whispered. "I would love to be your mate."

Relief and elation left him momentarily frozen, but once his feet could move again he gathered her in his arms. He wanted to celebrate properly, but it could wait.

Azagoth wouldn't.

Cipher kissed her, a peck with a promise of more later, and turned back to Azagoth. "Lyre didn't have to help me, but she did. When she learned all that Bael and Moloc planned to do, including murdering your children, she turned against them."

Azagoth's gemstone eyes once again flashed with intensity, but when he spoke, the razor edge in his voice had dulled. "The daughter on the list, my daughter who died...she was part of a plan. I can accept that. I don't like it, but it's beyond my ability to change. Prove to me Amelia didn't die in vain."

"I will," Cipher vowed. "I swear."

Silence stretched, a make-'em-sweat tactic Azagoth had trademarked. "Hawkyn insists you'll be an asset to Sheoul-gra," he finally said. "Time will tell. But if you do anything, and I mean *anything*, to make me regret this..." Azagoth paused, his lips peeled back from deadly fangs. "I don't need to go on, do I?"

"No, sir, I'd rather you didn't."

With a hint of a smile and a nod so shallow Cipher questioned whether it happened at all, Azagoth flashed away, leaving him with all he'd ever wanted.

His home, his friends, and now, Lyre.

Chapter Twenty-Four

Life inside Sheoul-gra turned out to not be horrible.

Cipher was right: his friends were decent people, and while many of the Memitim were a little chilly toward her, she couldn't blame them. She and Cipher were fallen angels with a history of working for one of the worst overlords Sheoul had to offer, and given the recent murder within Sheoul-gra's borders, trust didn't come easily.

But she was willing to do what it took to gain that trust. Azagoth was going to be a hard sell, and frankly, she chose to just avoid him when possible. Bael had been terrifying, but the Grim Reaper made him look like a kitten in comparison.

Cipher had gone straight to work for Azagoth, hacking into enemy computers. Once his wings grew in and his powers were restored, Azagoth said he'd make use of his spell-coding skills, as well. At least his ability to flash had come back, so things were moving along.

Lyre...she wasn't sure where she'd fit in yet. Her powers were so weak she feared she'd never get a job, but just this morning, one week after escaping Bael's clutches, Azagoth came to her with a proposal. She'd listened in silent terror as he explained that her lack of strong abilities had the potential to make her all but invisible to power-sensing demons in the Inner Sanctum, and in addition to using her for intel into Bael and Moloc's methods, he had some spy work for her. Her gift of turning into a wisp of vapor would give her even more ways to ensure she went undetected.

She could do that. It sounded fun, actually.

And as she was sitting in their apartment inside Sheoul-gra, reading up on everything she could find about the Inner Sanctum, Cipher offered her a break.

"I have a surprise for you," he said, taking her hand and pulling her up from the sofa.

She beamed. "Really?"

"I'm not sure it's a good surprise," he hedged, "but it might be what you need."

Uh-oh. That didn't sound great. Sounded terrible, in fact. "So where do we have to go for this unnecessary surprise?"

"I'll show you."

He escorted her to the portal, where they dematerialized and re-formed at the earthly forest clearing they'd used when they'd first entered Sheoul. Once topside, he flashed them to a dusty hilltop in Israel, and she cursed. Megiddo. He'd brought her to a place of angelic importance. Where executions and battles and expulsions from Heaven had taken place.

"What the hell is this, Cipher? Why are we here?"

A hot wind spun up, and a split-second later, Lihandra materialized alongside Lyre's other sister, Bellagias.

Anger, as hot as the wind, blasted her, but the funny thing was that she didn't experience the murderous rage she'd felt for years while she was in Sheoul. This was just good old-fashioned pissed.

"I asked Hawkyn to contact your family," Cipher said. "I hope that's okay."

It wasn't, but she nodded anyway. "It's good to see you, Bella." All she could muster for Lihandra was a glare.

Bella, always a softie, threw herself at Lyre, wrapping her arms around her in an enormous hug. "I'm so glad you're okay. I've been so worried about you."

Lyre pulled back. "Really?"

She nodded. "Mother and Father, too. And, believe it or not, Liha."

Lyre laughed, but when she looked over at her other sister, Lihandra's expression was serious. "I'm having a hard time believing that."

"I wouldn't be here if it wasn't true," Lihandra said. "I...regret what I did."

Lyre could have been knocked over by one of Lihandra's lacy ivory feathers. "Seriously?"

"I could have handled it better," she admitted. "I don't regret the demon's death, but you shouldn't have lost your wings."

Ah, well, that was more like it. Anger steamed through her again, but when she glanced over at Cipher, his calm, strong presence brought her down. Nothing from her past mattered anymore. Holding this grudge wouldn't hurt her sister; it would hurt only her, and possibly her relationship with the male she loved.

She had to let it go.

"I forgive you, Lihandra," she said, and it was her sister's turn to be shocked. "But I don't want to see you again. Not for a while. Maybe not ever."

"What kind of forgiveness is that?" Lihandra said in a clipped, stung voice.

"Considering that just a week ago I wanted you dead, I figure it's a pretty huge development. I'm sorry, did you *want* a relationship with me?" Lihandra's mouth opened. Closed. Yeah, that's what Lyre thought. As usual, she was playing the wronged party, but this time she got called out on her fake outrage. "I didn't think so. Let's just walk away from this with a fresh start. Agreed?"

Lihandra bowed her head. "Since I'm no longer welcome in your presence, I'll go. Take care, sister."

With that, Lihandra launched into the sky and flashed away.

"She's such a bitch," Bella said. "But I should go too. Call me and we'll do lunch sometime."

She and her sister used to *do lunch* all the time, and Lyre truly hoped her sister was sincere. Especially because now that Lyre was no longer bound to Bael's realm, she could flash anywhere she wanted to inside the demon and human realms.

They'd just have to keep their lunches secret. While it wasn't strictly forbidden for a Heavenly angel to have lunch with a fallen angel, it was a reputation-killer.

She waved as Bella lifted off, and then she turned to Cipher, who watched with what looked like envy. It could take months to regrow wings, and until then, he'd be earthbound. Maybe she could keep him distracted. With sex. Yep, that sounded like a plan.

"That was the nicest thing anyone has done for me in a long time," she said.

He shrugged as if it was no big deal, but it was. It *so* was. "After all those years of wanting revenge, I thought you might need some closure."

She flew into his strong arms, her heart singing. "You're amazing. I love you so much."

Emotion poured out of her as she held onto Cipher, and her wings erupted of their own accord, surrounding them in the most intimate of angelic embraces.

Swallowing a lump of his own emotion, he traced the edge of a wing with his finger. "I love you too." Tenderly, he pressed a kiss into her hair. "And now I have a favor to ask of you."

"Of course," she said. "Anything."

Shadows of hesitation danced in his eyes before he blurted, "Someday we'll have kids, right?"

She hadn't really thought that far ahead, but yes, she absolutely wanted to have Cipher's babies. Lots of them. "I can't see why not."

His lips curved into a happy smile, but his eyes remained shadowed. "If we have a girl, and it's all right with Azagoth, I'd like to name her Amelia. Would that be okay?"

"Oh, yes," she whispered. "What a wonderful tribute to Azagoth's daughter." And what an incredible male he was to want to honor her that way. How had Lyre gotten so lucky? She held him tighter, putting their hearts together. "Thank you, Cipher. Thank you for hacking my password and rebooting my system."

He laughed at the computer reference and pulled back just enough to look down at her, his gorgeous eyes mirroring the joy she felt. "I can say the same about you. I can even thank Flail. If she hadn't gotten me abducted, I never would have found you or discovered my unique power."

She wondered where Flail had gone after the torture box had opened. Who was she working for now? And was she going to seek revenge? The female would be crazy to attempt it, but she'd never struck Lyre as all that stable. They were going to have to be on guard.

Lyre playfully drummed her fingers on Cipher's chest. "So Flail's forgiven?"

The dark, deadly smile tipping up one corner of his mouth gave her delicious shivers. "Oh, I'm still going to kill her. But I'll thank her before I do."

"That's my evil boy," she teased.

But really, the good/evil battle they both were facing as True Fallens was something everyone, from demons to humans to angels, had to endure on a daily basis. It was part of life, and there was a reason for it. There was a reason for everything, and for the first time in years, she believed that again.

She believed in a lot of things again.

Epilogue

Moloc stared out the window at the glorious scorched earth and burning corpses that surrounded his stronghold. One would think there had been a battle, but it had been better than that.

The explosion of his soul merging with Bael's had caused a catastrophic blast he still felt inside him. And oh, it was good.

He was whole for the first time in his life.

He and Bael had always had a strange relationship, knowing that they were both brothers and a single person, and he'd wondered how it would feel when they were finally melded together inside one body.

Now he knew. It felt like power.

He reached for the vial next to him, a vial he'd been saving for thousands of years. A gift from Satan himself, the little glass tube contained the Dark Lord's blood, meant to strengthen him and, he hoped, give him a psychic connection with his king.

As he brought it to his lips, there was a tap at the door. The chaotic half of his soul that had been Bael wanted to strike out at the interruption, but the calm half, the one Moloc had possessed, overruled.

"Come in," he said, but added for Bael, "but if you displease me, you die."

The door swung open and Flail strutted in, a smile on her usually pouty lips. "I have news from our agent inside Sheoul-gra."

"I'm listening."

"Cipher and Lyre are there," she growled. "Azagoth has accepted them."

"Disappointing, but not entirely unexpected," he said. "What about his young human-realm children?"

"They've all been taken to Sheoul-gra. We won't be able to kill more of them."

He smiled. "No matter. I have a new a plan. One that is guaranteed to force the Keeper of Souls to release Satan from prison."

"You won't be able to kidnap Lilliana," she warned. "Not even with your insider. She's guarded all the time."

"That's the beauty of it, my love," he said, Bael's influence already affecting his choice of words. "I won't need to abduct her."

"Why not?" Confusion pulled her brow down. "I don't understand."

That was because she was beautiful but not all that bright. Females never were.

"Because," he said, his heart racing with anticipation, "when the time is right, Lilliana will come to me, and Azagoth will be mine."

* * * *

Also from 1001 Dark Nights and Larissa Ione, discover Bond of Destiny, Reaper, Cipher, Dining With Angels, Her Guardian Angel, Hawkyn, Razr, Hades, Z, and Azagoth.

* * * *

Bond of Destiny: A Demonica Novella

By Larissa Ione

Coming August 24, 2021

New York Times and USA Today bestselling author Larissa Ione returns with a new story in her Demonica series…

Sold into slavery mere hours after his birth to werewolf parents, Tracker spent decades in service to cruel underworlders. Then the fallen angel Harvester transferred his ownership to a human woman who gave him as much freedom as the unbreakable bond would allow. Still, thanks to his traumatic past, he's afraid to trust, let alone feel love. But when an acquaintance shows up at his door, injured and in need of help, he finds himself longing for a connection. For someone to touch. For someone to care.

Stacey Orr has had it bad for Tracker since the day her best friend, Jillian, was forced to hold his unbreakable slave bond. At first, the fact that he's a werewolf seemed weird to Stacey, but hey, her best friend was married to one of the Four Horsemen of the Apocalypse, so weird is definitely a matter of perspective. Stacey knows the depths of Tracker's trauma, and she longs to help him even as he helps her, but breaking through his walls isn't easy.

And it only gets harder when the only blood family he has, the pack that gave him away, lays claim to him…and everything he loves.

About Larissa Ione

Air Force veteran Larissa Ione traded in a career as a meteorologist to pursue her passion of writing. She has since published dozens of books, hit several bestseller lists, including the New York Times and USA Today, and has been nominated for a RITA award. She now spends her days in pajamas with her computer, strong coffee, and fictional worlds. She believes in celebrating everything, and would never be caught without a bottle of Champagne chilling in the fridge…just in case. After a dozen moves all over the country with her now-retired U.S. Coast Guard spouse, she is now settled in Wisconsin with her husband, her teenage son, a rescue cat named Vegas, and her very own hellhounds, a King Shepherd named Hexe, and a Belgian Malinois named Duvel.

For more information about Larissa, visit www.larissaione.com.

Also from Larissa Ione

~ DEMONICA/LORDS OF DELIVERANCE SERIES ~
Pleasure Unbound (Book 1)
Desire Unchained (Book 2)
Passion Unleashed (Book 3)
Ecstasy Unveiled (Book 4)
Eternity Embraced ebook (Book 4.5) (NOVELLA)
Sin Undone August (Book 5)
Eternal Rider (Book 6)
Supernatural Anthology (Book 6.5) (NOVELLA)
Immortal Rider (Book 7)
Lethal Rider (Book 8)
Rogue Rider (Book 9)
Reaver (Book 10)
Azagoth (Book 11)
Revenant (Book 12)
Hades (Book 13)
Base Instincts (Book 13.5)
Z (Book 14)
Razr (Book 15)
Hawkyn (Book 16)
Her Guardian Angel
Dining With Angels
Reaper

~ MOONBOUND CLAN VAMPIRES SERIES ~
Bound By Night (book 1)
Chained By Night (book 2)
Blood Red Kiss Anthology (book 2.5)

Discover More Larissa Ione

Reaper: A Demonica Novel
By Larissa Ione

He is the Keeper of Souls. Judge, jury, and executioner. He is death personified.

He is the Grim Reaper.

A fallen angel who commands the respect of both Heaven and Hell, Azagoth has presided over his own underworld realm for thousands of years. As the overlord of evil souls, he maintains balance crucial to the existence of life on Earth and beyond. But as all the realms gear up for the prophesied End of Days, the ties that bind him to Sheoul-gra have begun to chafe.

Now, with his beloved mate and unborn child the target of an ancient enemy, Azagoth will stop at nothing to save them, even if it means breaking blood oaths and shattering age-old alliances.

Even if it means destroying himself and setting the world on fire…

* * * *

Dining with Angels: Bits & Bites from the Demonica Universe
By Larissa Ione
Recipes by Suzanne M. Johnson

In a world where humans and supernatural beings coexist — not always peacefully — three things can bring everyone to the table: Love, a mutual enemy, and, of course, food.

With seven brand new stories from the Demonica universe, New York Times bestselling author Larissa Ione has the love and enemies covered, while celebrity Southern food expert Suzanne Johnson brings delicious food to the party.

And who doesn't love a party? (Harvester rolls her eyes and raises her hand, but we know she's lying.)

Join Ares and Cara as they celebrate a new addition to their family.

See what Reaver and Harvester are doing to "spice" things up. Find out what trouble Reseph might have gotten himself into with Jillian. You'll love reading about the further adventures of Wraith and Serena, Declan and Suzanne, and Shade and Runa, and you're not going to want to miss the sit down with Eidolon and Tayla.

So pour a glass of the Grim Reaper's finest wine and settle in for slices of life from your favorite characters and the recipes that bring them together. Whether you're dining with angels, drinking with demons, or hanging with humans, you'll find the perfect heavenly bits and sinful bites to suit the occasion.

Happy reading and happy eating!

* * * *

Her Guardian Angel: A Demonica Underworld/Masters and Mercenaries Novella

By Larissa Ione

After a difficult childhood and a turbulent stint in the military, Declan Burke finally got his act together. Now he's a battle-hardened professional bodyguard who takes his job at McKay-Taggart seriously and his playtime – and his play*mates* – just as seriously. One thing he never does, however, is mix business with pleasure. But when the mysterious, gorgeous Suzanne D'Angelo needs his protection from a stalker, his desire for her burns out of control, tempting him to break all the rules…even as he's drawn into a dark, dangerous world he didn't know existed.

Suzanne is an earthbound angel on her critical first mission: protecting Declan from an emerging supernatural threat at all costs. To keep him close, she hires him as her bodyguard. It doesn't take long for her to realize that she's in over her head, defenseless against this devastatingly sexy human who makes her crave his forbidden touch.

Together they'll have to draw on every ounce of their collective training to resist each other as the enemy closes in, but soon it becomes apparent that nothing could have prepared them for the menace to their lives…or their hearts.

* * * *

Hawkyn: A Demonica Novella
By Larissa Ione

As a special class of earthbound guardian angel called Memitim, Hawkyn is charged with protecting those whose lives are woven into the fabric of the future. His success is legendary, so when he's given a serial killer to watch over, he sees no reason for that to change. But Hawkyn's own future is jeopardized after he breaks the rules and rescues a beautiful woman from the killer's clutches, setting off an explosive, demonic game of cat and mouse that pits brother against brother and that won't end until someone dies.

Aurora Mercer is the half-wytch lone survivor of a psychopath who gets off on the sadistic torture of his victims. A psychopath whose obsessive psyche won't let him move on until he kills her. Now she's marked for death, her fate tied to that of a murderer…and to a sexy angel who makes her blood burn with desire…

* * * *

Razr: A Demonica Underworld Novella
By Larissa Ione

A fallen angel with a secret.

An otherworldly elf with an insatiable hunger she doesn't understand.

An enchanted gem.

Meet mortal enemies Razr and Jedda...and the priceless diamond that threatens to destroy them both even as it bonds them together with sizzling passion.

Welcome back to the Demonica Underworld, where enemies find love...if they're strong enough to survive.

* * * *

Z: A Demonica Underworld Novella
By Larissa Ione

Zhubaal, fallen angel assistant to the Grim Reaper, has spent decades searching for the angel he loved and lost nearly a century ago. Not even her death can keep him from trying to find her, not when he knows she's been given a second chance at life in a new body. But as time passes, he's losing hope, and he wonders how much longer he can hold to the oath he swore to her so long ago…

As an *emim*, the wingless offspring of two fallen angels, Vex has always felt like a second-class citizen. But if she manages to secure a deal with the Grim Reaper — by any means necessary — she will have earned her place in the world. The only obstacle in the way of her plan is a sexy hardass called Z, who seems determined to thwart her at every turn. Soon it becomes clear that they have a powerful connection rooted in the past…but can any vow stand the test of time?

* * * *

Hades: A Demonica Underworld Novella
By Larissa Ione

A fallen angel with a mean streak and a mohawk, Hades has spent thousands of years serving as Jailor of the Underworld. The souls he guards are as evil as they come, but few dare to cross him. All of that changes when a sexy fallen angel infiltrates his prison and unintentionally starts a riot. It's easy enough to quell an uprising, but for the first time, Hades is torn between delivering justice — or bestowing mercy — on the beautiful female who could be his salvation…or his undoing.

Thanks to her unwitting participation in another angel's plot to start Armageddon, Cataclysm was kicked out of Heaven and is now a fallen angel in service of Hades's boss, Azagoth. All she wants is to redeem herself and get back where she belongs. But when she gets trapped in Hades's prison domain with only the cocky but irresistible Hades to help her, Cat finds that where she belongs might be in the place she least expected…

* * * *

Azagoth: A Demonica Underword Novella
By Larissa Ione

Even in the fathomless depths of the underworld and the bleak chambers of a damaged heart, the bonds of love can heal…or destroy.

He holds the ability to annihilate souls in the palm of his hand. He commands the respect of the most dangerous of demons and the most powerful of angels. He can seduce and dominate any female he wants with a mere look. But for all Azagoth's power, he's bound by shackles of his own making, and only an angel with a secret holds the key to his release.

She's an angel with the extraordinary ability to travel through time and space. An angel with a tormented past she can't escape. And when Lilliana is sent to Azagoth's underworld realm, she finds that her past isn't all she can't escape. For the irresistibly sexy fallen angel known as Azagoth is also known as the Grim Reaper, and when he claims a soul, it's forever…

Dining with Angels: Bits & Bites from the Demonica Universe

By Larissa Ione, Recipes by Suzanne M. Johnson

In a world where humans and supernatural beings coexist — not always peacefully — three things can bring everyone to the table: Love, a mutual enemy, and, of course, food.

With seven brand new stories from the Demonica universe, New York Times bestselling author Larissa Ione has the love and enemies covered, while celebrity Southern food expert Suzanne Johnson brings delicious food to the party.

And who doesn't love a party? (Harvester rolls her eyes and raises her hand, but we know she's lying.)

Join Ares and Cara as they celebrate a new addition to their family. See what Reaver and Harvester are doing to "spice" things up. Find out what trouble Reseph might have gotten himself into with Jillian. You'll love reading about the further adventures of Wraith and Serena, Declan and Suzanne, and Shade and Runa, and you're not going to want to miss the sit down with Eidolon and Tayla.

So pour a glass of the Grim Reaper's finest wine and settle in for slices of life from your favorite characters and the recipes that bring them together. Whether you're dining with angels, drinking with demons, or hanging with humans, you'll find the perfect heavenly bits and sinful bites to suit the occasion.

Happy reading and happy eating!

* * * *

The rich, sweet aroma of vanilla made Runa's mouth water as she turned on the professional quality electric mixer her mate, Shade, had gotten her for Christmas. She wasn't a big fan of cooking meals, but she did enjoy baking sweet treats, and her family didn't complain a bit.

Boots clomped on the floor down the hall, and she turned off the mixer as Shade sauntered into the kitchen. He'd donned his black paramedic uniform for his afternoon shift at Underworld General Hospital, and she had a powerful urge to rip it off. Right here in the kitchen. She could finish making cookies to go with the smoothie pops she'd just put in the freezer to celebrate Stryke's A+ in science class later.

"Where are the boys?" he asked as he reached for a bottle of water in the fridge.

"They're at Stewie's pool party. Serena just sent a picture of them playing on the big float. It's on my phone if you want to see it."

"We should get a pool," he said as he swiped his finger across her phone's screen.

"We're welcome to use theirs anytime," she pointed out.

A smile ruffled his lips at the sight of the three dark-haired, espresso-eyed boys, the spitting images of their father, splashing in the water.

"Wraith and Serena made their house *the* place to be when they put it in, didn't they?"

It was probably the very reason they put in the pool. "Well, they love parties and kids."

"That's because they only have one," he muttered, but he was joking. Shade adored children, and when they were around, he could always be found nearby.

She fetched a can of cooking spray from a cupboard. "Speaking of kids, this morning a witch at the hospital told me I'm going to have twins in exactly eight years."

"Only twins?" Shade twisted the cap off his water. "Awesome."

She shook a spatula at him. "I remember when you wanted a whole bunch of kids."

"I remember too," Shade said. "And then we had triplets."

"Are you saying you don't want more?"

Pausing with the bottle at his lips, he shrugged. "We've got centuries ahead of us. I'm not in a hurry."

Neither was she. She loved being a mother, but she only had so much time between volunteering at the hospital and taking care of triplets, a mate, and two homes. Granted, one of the homes was a cave in a jungle, but it still had modern appliances and conveniences like hot running water and toilets, and modern things needed to be cleaned.

"I still can't believe your drive to impregnate me hasn't kicked in since the boys were born."

"That's how it works when we're mated." He grabbed a granola bar from the pantry and tucked it into the leg pocket of his BDU pants. "The drive only kicks in when our mates are ready. You're clearly not ready."

"You think? I barely have time to shower, let alone have more kids. But I'm sure everything will be different in eight years," she added, with more than a little sarcasm.

"You never know." He waggled his brows. "Wanna practice making our twins?"

Always up for a little practice, Runa eyed her mate, her body already heating at the thought of watching him strip out of his uniform. Or maybe she'd make him leave it on. It was sexy as hell.

"Don't you have to be at work in fifteen minutes?" she asked.

"Con will cover for me. Sin's working late with DART today."

Smiling, she peeled off her shirt and tossed it at him. "Then by all means...let's get some practice in."

Rescuing Macie
A Delta Force Heroes Novella
By Susan Stoker

1001
DARK
NIGHTS
RESCUING MACIE
A Delta Force Heroes Novella
NEW YORK TIMES BESTSELLING AUTHOR
SUSAN STOKER

Author's Note

The first time I saw a 1001 Dark Nights book, I wasn't sure what it was about. But after reading a few of the stories, I was hooked. It had been a dream of mine to be invited to write in the series and when Liz Berry did ask if I was interested, it took me about two point one seconds to say, "Yes!"

This wasn't a book that was supposed to happen. I had planned on ending the Delta Force Heroes series with Mary and Truck's book. But after being invited to write in the 1001 Dark Nights world, I had to think of whose story I should write.

Deciding to give Truck a sister who suffers from anxiety feels like a right choice. I asked my readers who have anxiety to try to explain some of what they go through when they're having an attack. I used a lot of what they told me. I know I probably made some mistakes, but I tried to keep to the facts and show what people who have anxiety suffer from on a daily basis.

This book is for all my Delta Force Heroes fans who didn't want to see the series end.

It's for anyone who ever has experienced an anxiety attack and felt like less of a person as a result. You deserve love just like everyone else and if you haven't found it yet, please don't give up.

And lastly, this is for Liz. Thank you for inviting me to be a part of your family. For your advice and encouragement and for being so wonderful.

Chapter One

Mercedes Laughlin was in bed reading when she heard the noise.

At first she didn't think much about it. She heard random noises at night all the time. The apartment building she lived in wasn't exactly quiet. There were people coming and going at all hours of the day and night, and she'd definitely heard her share of domestic arguments.

Macie's apartment was on the second floor and toward the back of the building. She loved how she could see a creek meandering through acres of trees from her living room. And since she spent most of her time there, sitting at her desk and working on her computer, it was soothing. It wasn't the most expensive apartment complex in Lampasas, but it wasn't a shit hole either. All in all, she'd lucked out in finding a place where she felt safe and could be near her brother.

But the noise she'd heard was unusual. It wasn't like the sounds she heard from outside...cars driving by, people talking, it sounded as if it was right inside her apartment.

Putting her ereader aside, she held her breath and waited to see if she'd hear the odd sound again.

When she did—and it sounded closer—Macie froze. Then she heard a voice.

"Shut up, you idiot! We don't want her to wake up until we're in her room."

"She's not going to hear me shuffling across the floor, but she *is* going to hear your dumb ass talking. So *you* shut the fuck up!"

Without thought, Macie threw back her covers, grabbed her cell phone, and headed for her closet and the sort-of safe room she had there. But the next words from whoever was in her apartment made her stop in her tracks.

"Remember, if she's not in bed when we get there, check the back of the closet. He said that's where the shit'll be and where she'll probably hide anyway. If we push on the right side, the door'll open up."

"You gonna let me have first crack at her?"

Macie was breathing hard now, and she felt dizzy, but she didn't hesitate as she changed course and headed for the window instead.

As someone who suffered from anxiety, she'd made sure she had a place to feel completely safe inside her apartment. She'd hired a local carpenter to build a false wall in the back of the walk-in closet. There was just enough space behind it that she could sit and be comfortable. She used the space when she needed absolute darkness and quiet, or when she was simply overwhelmed with whatever was going on in her life.

But that hidey-hole wouldn't keep her safe tonight. Whoever the men were in her apartment, they knew about it, and it was obviously the first place they'd look for her.

She definitely didn't like the sound of the one man wanting "first crack" at her.

So she was resorting to Plan B.

Her first choice would always be to hide inside. Away from the world. Cocooned from prying eyes and judgmental stares. But being pragmatic, she also knew if a tornado came through, or if there was a fire, she couldn't hide inside the apartment. She needed an escape route. And that was the other reason why she'd chosen this unit.

Right outside her bedroom was a large tree. It wasn't easy, but she could jump from the window ledge onto the large branch that grew perpendicular to the ground, toward the building. She knew she could do it because she'd practiced. Always in the middle of the night, when no one was around to see what she was doing and judge her.

Every moment of her life, Macie worried about what people thought of her. Were they looking at her and laughing about her clothes? Did her hair look weird? After she met someone, she always wondered if she'd said the right things, if they were talking about her to their friends.

It was a curse, and she hated feeling the way she did, but she couldn't turn it off. She took Lexapro daily to try to control her anxiety and to quiet the voices in her head that were constantly telling her she wasn't good enough, smart enough, or capable of doing her job. And when needed, she took a Vistaril tablet, which made her feel nothing at all, and that was bliss when her anxiety got the better of her.

Knowing her apartment wasn't that big and she had mere seconds before the men came into her room, Macie quickly raised the window, thankful that she'd recently made sure it was in good working order, and eyed the tree branch. Her breaths came out in short puffs and she could feel the tips of her fingers begin to tingle. She really wanted to run back in and grab her meds, but she had no time.

"Remember, he's not sure if she's already found the stuff, but if we get it tonight, we'll earn an extra grand. So don't spend too much time with the bitch."

"Awwww, come on. I love it when they cry and fight. It makes it that much better."

There was a muffled smacking sound and a quiet *umph* before the first man said, "We get the shit first. Then if there's time, you can have your fun."

The men were whispering, but she could still hear them clearly. Macie didn't have to be a rocket scientist to know what they were talking about. At least when it came to the "fun" the one man wanted. She had no clue what they could possibly be looking for, but she'd run out of time to even think about it.

If she'd been asleep, she wouldn't have heard them until it was too late.

Shoving her cell phone in the waistband of the sleep shorts she had on, Macie ducked and climbed onto the windowsill. It was second nature to make sure she always had her phone on her. She needed the security it provided. The small electronic device was a way to get help if her anxiety completely overwhelmed her...which it had more than once.

She wished that she could find a way to close the window after she jumped, so the men in her bedroom wouldn't know where she'd gone, but it was too late to think of that now.

Hyperventilating, Macie eyed the branch—and jumped.

She let out an *umph* when she landed on her stomach on the limb. She held on for dear life, but felt extremely shaky and wasn't sure she could hang on. She vaguely felt her inner thighs burning from scraping along the rough bark, but the pain barely registered. She had probably thirty seconds or so, tops, before one of the men looked out the window. They'd probably see the empty bed and go straight to the closet first. At least she hoped that's what they would do. It would buy her a bit of time.

Scrambling to her feet quickly and carefully, Macie shuffled along the large branch, holding on to the smaller limbs above her as she made her way toward the trunk. She began to climb downward as fast as she could, mentally counting the seconds. When she'd practiced this, she'd always been wearing jeans and sneakers. Bare feet and pajama shorts weren't exactly conducive to a middle-of-the-night escape.

Macie was trying to be quiet while still moving as fast as possible. Climbing down was harder because of her lack of proper clothing and the way her entire body was shaking. Stretching her leg down to the final branch, she sighed in relief, thinking she'd made it.

"Hey!" a low voice shouted from above her.

She startled so bad, she missed the branch and tumbled the three feet or so to the ground, landing on her ass. Without looking up at her window, Macie leaped to her feet and took off running. As she ran, she pulled out her cell phone—which had miraculously not fallen out of her shorts as she'd climbed out of the tree—and frantically pushed one of the saved numbers as she tried to figure out where she could hide.

* * * *

Colonel Colton Robinson ran a hand over his face wearily. It was oh-two-thirty in the morning and both Delta Force teams were finishing up their debrief of the mission they'd just returned from. The fourteen men, from two different teams, had worked together to bring down a high-value target who had been hiding out in Africa. Logistically, the last week and a half had been a bitch, but Colt had never doubted the men under his command for a second.

Ghost's team was older and more experienced, and tended to err on the side of caution. All seven men were married, some had children, so their main concern was getting home to their families safe and sound. Trigger's team, on the other hand, was younger, mostly late twenties and early thirties, and all of them single. They had no problem taking risks and doing everything necessary to get the job done.

Together, the fourteen men were the best he'd ever had the pleasure to command. Colt trusted each and every one of them, and the latest mission had been no exception. The HVT was neutralized and they'd done it without blowing their cover. As far as the African government and the terrorist organization was concerned, the man had died in a local skirmish, not at the hands of the US military.

Colt knew everyone was anxious to get home, but debriefing was required. He listened as Lefty explained how they'd exited the compound where the HVT had been holed up. Colt knew all the details, but protocol demanded they review it one more time.

He heard the unmistakable sound of a phone vibrating and turned to frown at the man sitting to his left. Truck knew they weren't supposed to have their phones on, but at least he'd had the decency to put it on vibrate. Colt wouldn't reprimand him—if *he* had a wife or kids at home, he'd want them to be able to get ahold of him at any time—but he glared at Truck to let him know that he was walking a fine line.

Truck looked down at his phone and frowned. He brought the phone to his ear. "Mace? What are—"

The second Truck said his sister's name, Colt straightened in his chair and all his attention was on the soldier sitting next to him.

So many times in the last two months, he'd wanted to ask Truck for his sister's number, but he didn't want to pressure Macie with his attention if she didn't want it. And he had to assume she didn't, because he'd flat-out asked her if he could see her again the last time they'd been together—and she'd snuck out of his house without a word or leaving him a way to contact her.

The memories of the last time he'd seen Macie were interrupted when Truck stood and moved toward the door, the phone still to his ear.

Without thought, Colt stood and followed Truck. At the last second, he turned to the group of men still sitting around the table. "Dismissed," he said absently. They'd finish the debrief later.

"Sir?" Ghost called as Colt was about to disappear.

He waved at the man and said, "I'll call if we need you." And then he was rushing after Truck down the hallway.

"Mace, slow down. What's wrong?" Truck asked.

Colt's blood ran cold. He hurried to catch up, trying to control himself and not rip the phone out of Truck's hand.

"I'm coming!" he said urgently. "Find a place to hide. I'm on my way."

That was it. Colt was done. "Give me the phone," he ordered.

Truck's gaze went to his, and his brows drew down in surprise and annoyance.

Colt wiggled his fingers. "Give her to me. You drive. I'll talk."

Surprisingly, Truck nodded and handed him his phone. Both men ran down the hall to the door that led out to the parking lot. Colt reached in his pocket and threw his keychain at Truck even as he brought the phone up to his ear. "Macie?"

"Yeah?" was the weak answer.

"It's Colt. From Truck's wedding. What's going on? Where are you?" He could hear her wheezing as she hyperventilated, and it only increased his concern.

"My apartment. Men broke in. I got out but I don't know where to go!"

Colt's heart dropped at her words. He and Truck arrived at his Jeep Wrangler and both jumped in. He pulled out his own cell and dialed 9-1-1, then handed it to Truck. The other man started the Jeep and began talking to the dispatcher at the same time. Within seconds, they were racing out of the parking lot and headed for the front gate of the Army post.

"What do you see around you?" Colt asked Macie. "Look around, Macie. Tell me what you're looking at," he ordered.

"A big open parking area. Trees at the edge."

"Are there lights? Cars parked close together?"

"Lights near the buildings, not as many farther out. There's lots of cars. Oh shit..." she said.

"What? Macie, talk to me," Colt barked.

"I hear the men," Macie whispered. "They're looking for me."

The terror in her voice made panic rise within Colt and he held the phone against his chest for a second to try to regain his composure. He turned to Truck. "Hurry. Drive as fast as you fucking can. They're hunting her."

The second the words left his mouth, Colt felt the Jeep lurch forward. It was a good thing it was the middle of the night and no one was on the streets. Truck was driving like a bat out of hell.

It was thirty miles to Lampasas. There was no way they could get there in time to help if the assholes got their hands on her. Truck had called the cops, but Colt knew what he told Macie in the next couple minutes could be a matter of life and death.

"Head away from the lights. If it's dark, they can't see where you are exactly," he told her urgently. "Do you understand?"

"Y-yeah."

"Have they seen you?"

"I-I don't think so."

She was breathing hard and still wheezing. Colt's chest hurt for her. "Good. Head for a row of cars as far away from the lights as possible. Get under one. Not behind it, but under it. Then if you need to, you can crawl under the one next to it. Then the next. Keep moving if you have to. If it's possible, work your way around the cars until you get to a section of vehicles they've already checked. As a last resort, head into the trees, but *only* if they don't see you. The last thing you want is to go farther away from civilization where the men could do whatever they want to you without someone hearing or seeing. Understand?"

She didn't answer him, but he heard her breaths coming quick and shallow through the phone.

"I'm here," he said, forcing his voice to lower and calm. She needed him to be her rock right now. He couldn't let her hear one ounce of panic in his tone. "I've got you, Macie. You're doing great. Just listen to me. You're amazing. I'm sure they didn't expect you to outsmart them. Just keep doing what you're doing. You've got this." Colt kept up the litany of praise even as he gripped the phone so tightly his fingers were cramping.

He glanced at the speedometer and saw that Truck was doing ninety-five. The Wrangler shook slightly from the speed, but the only thing Colt could think was, *Go faster. God, just go faster.*

"They're coming this way," Macie said—and Colt lowered his chin to his chest, closed his eyes and prayed harder than he'd ever prayed before.

* * * *

Macie had no idea what Colt was doing with her brother at two-thirty in the morning, but she couldn't deny that she was extremely grateful. She didn't even flinch when Colt called her brother Truck. He'd apparently been given the nickname when he'd joined the Army. She was trying to remember to call him that, but because he'd been Ford to her as long as she could remember, it was tough.

And as much as she knew her brother would've helped her, hearing Colt's steady voice kept her grounded. She remembered after

Truck's wedding, when she'd been having an anxiety attack, he'd held her against him and talked to her in his low, rumbly voice. How much it had helped. He'd calmed her and helped pull her out of the dark place her mind had gone.

The same was happening tonight. She'd been panicking and running headlong through the parking lot, with no idea what to do or where to go, when he'd forced her to pay attention to her surroundings. He gave her something to concentrate on, and it felt good to let him take over and tell her what to do.

She had no idea why he hadn't called her after her brother's wedding. He'd asked her out and she'd badly wanted to spend more time with him, but he hadn't called. Hadn't gotten in touch with her. His rejection had hurt, but she really wasn't surprised. She was a pain in the ass and no one as amazing as Colt would want to be with her.

At the moment, however, she had more pressing issues to think about. Looking back toward the building, Macie didn't see any sign of the men who'd broken into her apartment, but she could hear their footsteps. Macie ducked behind a car and dropped to her knees.

She winced but ignored the pain and crawled between a row of cars, making sure to stay out of sight. Then she lay down on her belly and crawled under one of the cars in the lot. She was wearing a tight tank top and her sleep shorts, because she hated to feel constricted by clothing when she slept.

"Macie?" Colt asked.

She opened her mouth to respond when she heard one of the men saying to his friend, "She has to be this way. We've checked all the other cars."

It felt like she was having a heart attack. Her chest was tight and she couldn't get enough air into her lungs. But she couldn't gasp for oxygen because they'd hear her.

Macie mentally berated herself for calling her brother and not the police. If she'd called 9-1-1, they'd probably be here by now.

"Easy, Mace," Colt said in her ear. She ground her teeth together and forced herself to listen to him rather than the two men who were still looking for her. "You can do this. You told me that you used to play Army with Truck when you were younger. This is the same thing. Remember when you hid in that bush one afternoon and he couldn't find you anywhere? See if you can do that again. It's dark where you are, right? If you're quiet, they'll never see you. They'll walk right on by."

Macie nodded, even though Colt couldn't see her. She'd told him about hiding from her big brother when she was at Colt's house, the night of Ford's wedding. She'd crawled under a bush next to a neighbor's house and her brother hadn't been able to find her. Eventually she'd fallen asleep, and Ford had been beside himself with worry, thinking that she'd been snatched off the street. He'd walked by her hiding place dozens of times without knowing she was there.

It was only a matter of time before one of the men found her under the car, though. This wasn't a game, and she wasn't a kid anymore. Macie was sure they were looking under each and every one of the vehicles. It wouldn't work to simply roll under the one next to her; eventually she'd run out of cars and be stuck.

Quickly, still trying to be as quiet as she could, Macie backed up. Her knees were getting torn to pieces, but she barely felt the rough asphalt digging into them. She wiggled her way to the back side of the SUV she was huddled under and turned around. She was at the edge of the parking lot, and there was a row of hedges, then the trees and creek she so loved to look at while she was working.

Remembering what Colt had said, she resisted the urge to get up and run into the trees. Instead, she stayed on her hands and knees and hurriedly crawled to the thick hedge. She pushed her way between the leaves, thankful it wasn't winter and there were actually leaves to hide behind. The branches scratched at her arms, but again, she didn't feel the slight sting. At five-seven, she wasn't exactly small, but she brought her knees up to her chest and wrapped an arm around them. She brought the phone to her ear and ducked her head into her knees, trying to make herself as small as possible.

"I crawled into a bunch of bushes," she said in a toneless whisper. "Colt?"

"Yeah, Mace? I'm here. Are you hidden? Are you safe? Are the men still looking for you?"

"I can't breathe."

"Yes you can. You're doing amazing. In and out. Remember how you breathed with me that night? Close your eyes. Imagine we're back in my bed. I'm behind you, and my hand is on your chest. In…and out. Slow down your breaths, Mace. That's it. They're gonna walk right by you. They can't see you. In…and out. That's good. You're doing great."

Amazingly, his voice in her ear, along with the way she was pinching her thigh to try to force her attention away from her situation, was working. She breathed with him, not making a sound. Macie could feel her lungs loosening up a bit.

"You start on that side, I'll start over here. If she's not under the cars, I'm guessing she ran into the trees. We can catch up with her and make sure she hasn't found the shit and blabbed about it to the pigs."

"Then I can have my fun?" the other man asked.

"Jesus, you have a one-track mind. Yes, once she spills her guts, you can do whatever the fuck you want with her."

Their voices were loud enough that Colt heard them.

"Don't listen to them, Mace. Concentrate only on me. You're good. We're almost there. You just have to hang on for another couple minutes. You can do that. Piece of cake."

Colt's voice was almost as good as the drugs she used to control her anxiety and panic attacks. Almost.

Macie heard the men getting closer and closer to her hiding spot, and she felt her breathing speed up once more. She couldn't help it. They were going to find her and torture her until she gave them information. She had no idea what they were looking for when they'd broken in, but she'd tell them whatever they wanted as long as they didn't hurt her.

"Eaaaaasy, honey. You've got this."

That was the thing. She *didn't* have this. But by some miracle, Colt thought she did. His voice was still even and controlled.

"Shit. She's not here!" one of the men complained after they'd passed by her hiding spot.

"Come on, she's got to be here somewhere. She's barefoot and in her fucking pajamas. No cars have left, so she hasn't driven off. Stupid bitch is just hiding from us. You go that way and I'll—"

His voice abruptly cut off when the sound of sirens wailed in the distance.

"Fuck. She called the fucking cops!" the man who wanted to "have his way with her" said. "We gotta get out of here."

"Dammit. There goes that extra thousand," the other man complained. "We'll come back after the cops leave. She won't get away again."

Macie didn't move a muscle after she heard the men run off. She stayed where she was, refusing to do something stupid, like come out of her hiding place too soon and have the men catch her after everything she'd done to keep away from them.

"Are those sirens?" Colt asked in her ear.

Macie nodded, knowing he couldn't see her, but not able to speak. Her vocal cords had closed up and refused to work. Her lips were dry and she didn't have enough spit in her mouth to even lick them.

"Don't come out, hon. Just stay where you are. We'll be there in"–there was a pause and Macie could imagine him looking over at her brother—"less than ten minutes. Even if you hear the cops, just stay put. Truck'll tell the 9-1-1 operator that you're too scared to come out. You won't get in trouble. Hear me?"

Macie nodded again, but didn't speak.

"I'm proud of you, Mace. You're doing great. You did the right thing. You got out of your apartment, called for help, and stayed hidden. That's exactly what you should've done."

His praise was like a balm to her soul. She wasn't sure she believed him—she felt like the biggest coward ever—but for now, right this second, she chose to take his words to heart.

She could hear the sirens getting louder and louder, but she kept her concentration on Colt. If she didn't, she knew she'd completely fall apart.

* * * *

Colt ignored the looks Truck was shooting him from the driver's seat. He knew the other man was going to have a lot to say to him later…not that he could blame him. He was just getting to know his sister again, and obviously hadn't known about the fact she suffered from anxiety—or that his commander had spent the night with her after Truck's wedding.

They hadn't *done* anything, but Colt didn't think that was going to matter to Truck.

His entire focus right now was on Macie. He could hear her breathing on the other end of the line and could hear the sirens wailing in the background, but most importantly, he no longer heard the men who were searching for her.

He continued his litany of soothing words, not wanting her to move until he could get to her, holding on to the handle over his head as Truck continued to drive like a man possessed. Truck wasn't fucking around. He'd pushed the Wrangler as far as it could be pushed. It was a miracle they hadn't been stopped by a cop. Even with his credentials and the fact that Truck was on the phone with an emergency operator, he didn't think a police officer would be amused at how recklessly Truck was driving.

Truck clicked off the phone and Colt looked over at him. The other man's lips were pressed tightly together, and he looked like he was about two seconds from losing his shit. Colt wanted to tell Truck to pull himself together, that the last thing his sister needed to see was him freaking out, but he couldn't, because he was still talking to Macie.

"Macie? We're almost there. I can see your apartment complex ahead. It's lit up like a Christmas tree with all the blue and red lights from the police who are there. You're safe. We're here. Stay put until I come and get you though, okay?"

She hadn't been answering him, but for that question, he got a slight murmur. Even that made him feel better.

He didn't know exactly where she was, but once Truck pulled into the lot, he looked around and tried to see it from Macie's perspective. "Where's her apartment?" he asked Truck. The other man pointed toward a building to the left.

Nodding, Colt climbed out of the Jeep and headed in that direction. He was stopped by Truck's hand on his arm. "You get my sister and I'll speak to the cops. But we need to talk. *Sir.*"

The rank was tacked on at the end of his sentence in such a way that it more than communicated Truck's irritation with his commanding officer.

Nodding at him, Colt turned to head toward a row of cars on the back side of the parking lot. There weren't lights covering the entire blacktop and he could see dark shapes in the distance that he imagined were the trees Macie had described to him.

He remembered her talking about how beautiful they were and how she liked to look at them when she was working at her desk in her apartment. She'd recovered from her anxiety attack after the wedding reception and had been relaxed and warm in his arms. Right afterward, Colt had told her that he wanted to take her to dinner, and she hadn't agreed or disagreed. He'd taken that as a good sign, but of course he'd been wrong, as she'd left the next morning without a word and without waking him up.

Shaking off his memories, Colt concentrated on finding Macie.

"I'm here," he told her quietly through the phone. "You're going to need to come out so I can get to you. If those other men couldn't find you, there's not a chance in hell that I will." He was lying, but he wanted to reassure her that her hiding place was secure. That she'd done a good job.

"Mace? You can come out now. Your brother is here. You're safe."

He waited a heartbeat…then he heard rustling coming from his left. He turned toward the row of hedges that looked way too skimpy to have concealed a full-grown woman, but sure enough, Macie was crawling out of the bushes.

Clicking off Truck's phone, he shoved it into his back pocket even as he jogged toward Macie. She was on her hands and knees, and she looked up at him with wide eyes.

Without thought, he dropped to his knees and took her into his arms. Instead of recoiling, she latched on to him so tightly, he couldn't tell where she ended and he began. He could feel her heart beating way too damn fast against his chest, and she buried her face into the space between his neck and shoulder. Her arms wrapped around him and she clutched at his back. It felt as if she were literally trying to crawl inside him.

"Shhhh," he murmured. "I've got you. You're safe."

Macie didn't cry. She simply held on to him as if he was the only thing between her and certain death. And in a way, he supposed he maybe had been.

How long they stayed like that, he couldn't say. All he knew was how good she felt in his arms and how fucking relieved he was that she was okay. Finally, Colt forced himself to loosen his hold and draw back from her. She resisted, but he reached up and took her wrists in his hands. Her pulse was still hammering as if she'd run a mile.

"Hi, Mace," he said with a smile.

She did her best to return his smile, but it quickly faded from her face.

"Are you hurt?"

"No. At least I don't think so," she said softly.

Colt looked her over as best he could, but as it was dark in this corner of the parking area, he couldn't see much. She was wearing a dark-colored tank top and shorts that matched. He absently had the thought that he was glad she hadn't been wearing white before he eased to his feet, pulling her with him.

"Oh!" she exclaimed when she was standing and her knees suddenly buckled.

Colt didn't waste time asking what was wrong. He simply put an arm behind her back and one under her knees and picked her up.

She grabbed at him. "Don't drop me!"

"Of course not. You don't weigh any more than the packs I used to carry on missions," Colt reassured her. "I've got you." He saw that she still clutched her cell phone in her hand and didn't bother telling her to put it away. First, he had no idea where she'd put it, but second, it had been her lifeline, and he'd let her hold on to it for as long as she needed if it made her feel more secure.

He started walking toward the spinning lights of the cop cars, where they'd no doubt find Truck.

She rested her head on his shoulder, and Colt felt as if he were ten feet tall. He loved the way Macie fit in his arms, how she felt. He didn't care about her anxiety. Nobody was perfect. And if he could make her feel better about herself and about things going on in her life, he'd be satisfied.

Chapter Two

Macie sat sideways in a chair at her dining room table and watched with wary eyes as the police and detectives wandered through her apartment. Truck was standing off to her left with his arms crossed over his chest and a scowl on his face. After draping a blanket around her shoulders, Colt sat in front of her, holding her hand. In fact, he hadn't let go of it since he'd carried her away from her hiding spot.

"Why don't you tell me everything that happened tonight," the detective sitting across from her said in a no-nonsense tone.

"She needs to take her medicine first," Colt insisted, then turned to Macie. "Are your pills in your bathroom?"

She nodded. "I can go and get them," she told him quietly.

"I got it. What am I looking for?" Truck asked.

Macie looked down at her lap. This wasn't the way she'd wanted Truck to find out how messed-up she was. He was strong and brave and amazing, and the last thing he'd want to deal with was a sister who was crazy. He'd—

"Macie," Colt said firmly, making her raise her head to look at him. "Where are your pills?"

"In the cabinet to the left of the sinks. I need one of the Vistaril tablets," she told him.

"Be right back," Truck said.

"I know this is hard, but you're doing great," Colt said. "Just hang on a little longer and we'll get you to a quiet place where you can relax, okay?"

Macie nodded. She had no idea where that would be, but she knew Colt wanted her to agree, so she did. Her head was pounding and she felt shaky from her anxiety attack. And the worst thing was that her nightmare wasn't over. She was going to have to talk about what happened and what she'd heard. Then her brother, Colt, and the cops would leave, and she'd be alone again, and the men said that they'd be back and—

This time Colt simply threaded his fingers with hers and held on tightly. He always seemed to know when she was lost in her head, when she was over-worrying.

Truck was back within seconds, holding a small pill in his hand. He handed her a cup full of water and she swallowed the pill gratefully. If there ever was a time when she needed to be numb, it was now.

"Take your time," Colt said gently. "When you're ready, walk us through what happened tonight."

Wanting to get it over with, Macie didn't hesitate. "I couldn't sleep so I was reading. I heard a weird noise, and then heard two men talking. They were being quiet, and if I had been asleep I wouldn't have heard them, but because I was up, I did." She knew she wasn't being very articulate, but no one interrupted her, which she was grateful for.

"What were they saying?" the detective asked.

Macie's hand tightened on Colt's involuntarily. She didn't want to repeat what they'd said. What if Colt decided she was somehow to blame for what had happened tonight? What if Ford decided she was too much trouble and wouldn't want to keep talking to her?

"Breathe," Colt said softly. "You're safe. Your brother and I won't let anything happen to you."

She looked up at him and saw the sincerity in his eyes. She had no idea what a man like Colt was doing here with her. She was fucked up. *Seriously* fucked up. But she was also weak enough to not give a damn right now. She needed him.

"At first, they were arguing about whether or not I could hear them. They knew about my safe room. They were going to see if I was in bed, and if not, the first place they were going to look was my room in my closet."

"You have a safe room?" the detective asked, sitting up straighter in his chair.

"Sort of. It's not *really* a safe room. It's just a place I like to go when I need complete darkness. I get migraines, and it helps to be somewhere with no light," Macie explained. She could've gone on and told the police officer about how sometimes it was the only place she felt safe, how she liked to hide there when her anxiety overwhelmed her, but, ever aware of how people perceived her, she kept her mouth shut.

"How big is it?" the detective asked.

"Not big at all. Maybe around six feet long by three feet wide. I just had a false wall put in the back of my closet," she explained.

"Okay. Go on. What happened next?"

Macie took a breath and continued. "The men were there to pick something up. They said if they got it tonight, they'd get a bonus from whoever hired them."

She glanced at her brother and saw him run a hand through his hair in agitation. Just seeing him so stressed out made her own anxiety level climb.

Macie used her free hand to pinch the skin at the top of thigh. Sometimes the slight pain helped keep her in the moment and not completely freak out. "Yeah. They said they were there to pick something up."

"What were they looking for?" the detective broke in.

Macie knew this question was coming. She'd been trying to think of what in the world someone could want of hers, but had come up blank. Knowing it was important the officer believed her, she raised her head and looked him in the eyes. "I don't know. I don't know who the men were who broke in. I don't know what they were looking for. I don't know how they knew about my safe room. I don't know why they'd be interested in someone like me. I'm nobody. I don't meet a lot of people. I work from home. Most days, the only people I talk to are online. I don't understand *any* of this."

She felt Colt squeeze her hand. Then she felt him nudge her other hand off her thigh and rub the spot she'd pinched. It was almost uncanny how much he *saw* her. It made her uncomfortable, but at the same time it felt good.

"How'd you get out?" Colt asked.

She turned her gaze on him. She liked looking at his warm, compassionate eyes more than looking at the hardened face of the detective. She could tell the cop didn't believe her. That he thought she was hiding something. If she knew what the men were after, she'd give it to them, no questions asked. The last thing she wanted was someone hunting her.

"I jumped out my window," she said matter-of-factly.

"Jesus Christ," Truck swore.

Macie flinched at the harsh words from her brother.

"More, Macie. Give us more," Colt said firmly.

She took a deep breath and kept her eyes on Colt. "You know I need to have an escape route. I did it at your house, too."

He nodded. "The first thing you did was look out the windows, test to be sure you could open the one in my bedroom, and scope out how you could get out of the house."

"Right. Because if there was a fire or an earthquake, I needed to know where to go. What to do."

"Makes sense. Go on," Colt urged.

"There's a big tree right outside my window. I picked this apartment because of it. It's close enough to my bedroom, and has branches big enough that if I needed to, I could jump out of my window and get down."

"Is that how you got these?" Colt asked, running his fingers lightly over the scrapes on her legs and arms.

Macie shrugged. "Some. The ones on my knees I got from crawling in the parking lot."

"Mace," Truck said, then he was kneeling in front of her. "God, I'm so sorry. But…you also have to know, I'm so fucking proud of you."

She blinked. Proud of her? He was *proud* of her?

"I was a coward," she told him. "I was so scared. I didn't even call the cops. Those guys would've gotten me if it wasn't for you and Colt."

Truck brought a hand up to her head and brushed her hair back from her face. "You are *not* a coward," he scolded. "You did what had to be done. You got out of the situation. Believe me, that's the most important thing you could've done."

"Okay. So you jumped out your window and climbed down a tree. Then you hid, right? And the men came after you?" the detective asked, obviously wanting to move the interview along.

Truck gave her one last caress, then stood back up and leaned against the wall once more.

Macie cleared her throat. "Yeah. Colt told me to hide, so I got under a car in the far part of the parking lot. But the men figured out that's where I'd most likely be and started looking for me there. I crawled out from under the car I was hiding under and went into a bush. I hunkered down there until the men were scared away by the sirens."

"Did they say anything else?" the detective asked. "Can you give us anything that will help us find these guys?"

She hated the sound of impatience in his voice and wished she could tell him exactly who the men were, and why they'd been in her apartment. "They said they'd be back to get what they were looking for."

"There's no way in hell you're staying here tonight—or in the near future," Truck said firmly. "You can come and stay with me and Mary."

Macie was shaking her head before he'd finished his sentence. "I can't stay with you guys. You just got married!"

"Well, you're not staying here," Truck repeated. "Mace, they said they'd be back. It's not safe here."

She *knew* that. She was the one who'd had to jump out her window. She was the one who'd had to listen to the one guy talk about wanting to hurt her. She was the one who'd had to crawl around the parking lot to try to stay hidden.

For the first time in a long time, she was furious. At the situation, at Ford saying something she knew. But as soon as the feeling swept through her, she pushed it away. Anger was what had pushed her brother away all those years ago.

"She can stay with me," Colt said, successfully diverting Macie's attention.

"What?" she asked.

"That's a good idea," the detective said.

Macie looked from one man to the other, not sure what to say.

"Macie, look at me," Colt said quietly.

She turned to him.

"What do *you* want to do? What are you thinking?"

"I don't want to stay here," she blurted. "One of the guys was determined to get his hands on me, and not in a good way, if you know what I mean. But I don't want to stay with my brother because he and Mary just got back together again, and I don't want to mess that up. But I also don't want to make him mad by staying with *you*." Her voice dropped to barely a whisper. "The last time I got in a fight with him, I didn't see him again for almost twenty years."

And with that, Truck was at her side again. "Mace…what are you talking about?"

Macie bit her lip and couldn't look at him. She stared at his shoulder instead. "We fought before you left for the Army, and you were so mad at me you never came home. You didn't write or talk to me for years. I don't want to do anything to make you that mad at me ever again."

"Mercedes Laughlin," Truck said gently but sternly. "Look at me."

She didn't want to. She *really* didn't want to. She could already feel his condemnation. Her breaths sped up and she pinched her thigh again, trying to stave off another anxiety attack.

"Easy, Truck," Colt said.

"Macie," her brother said in a gentler tone, leaning closer but not touching her. "We fought the night before I left, but I was already over it by the next morning. Brothers and sisters fight. It happens. I was worried about you. You know I didn't like that guy you were seeing. But we were teenagers. And I wrote you. For *years*. But when I didn't hear anything back, I thought you were still mad at *me*."

Macie's head came up and she stared at her brother. "You did?"

"Yeah, Mace. I love you. I always have, and I always will. I even called. Several times. On Christmas. Your birthday. But Mom always told me you didn't want to talk to me," Truck said.

"I didn't know you called," she said in shock. "And I didn't get any letters."

Truck's face got hard then. "Damn our parents," he said under his breath.

"They said you never came home because of *me*. Because I was a terrible sister. Because of the—"

She caught herself and snapped her mouth shut at the last second.

"The what?" Truck asked.

Macie shook her head.

Truck sighed. "I was worried about you then, and I'm worried about you now. But I'm not mad at you. I just found you again; *nothing* is going to keep me from talking to you. From getting to know you better. I love you, sis."

"But you don't want me to stay with Colt. Why not?"

She watched as Ford took a deep breath. He looked over at Colt, then back to her. "You're my sister. No one is good enough for you. I don't like that I didn't know you guys had gotten…close, at my wedding."

Refusing to look at Colt, she somehow got up the nerve to ask, "Is he not a good person?"

She felt Colt squeeze her hand, but he didn't interrupt or otherwise put in his two cents.

"He's an amazing person," Truck said immediately. "I trust him with my life. I have no doubt that he'll take good care of you and make sure you're safe. But you're my *sister*. And I don't like the thought of you being with *any* man. I didn't like it when I was eighteen and you were dating that douchebag, and I don't like it now."

"I've dated," Macie told him. "In fact, I just broke up with a guy before your wedding."

"That's not the point—" Truck began.

"Actually," the detective interrupted. "I think that's a *great* point, and one I was going to get to. Who is he? What's his name? Could he have had anything to do with what happened tonight?"

Macie turned to look at the police officer. Amazingly, she'd forgotten he was sitting there listening. Her mind was still reeling with everything her brother had told her.

"Yeah, Mace. Who is he?" Truck asked, standing once more.

"We broke up a while ago." The last thing she wanted to do was talk about Teddy.

"What'd he do to you?" Truck growled.

Macie shook her head. She really *really* didn't want to discuss Teddy, especially not with Colt and her brother there. "Nothing."

"Hon," Colt said, "It's okay. We aren't going to judge you. We need to know if he had anything to do with this."

She looked down at her leg and almost laughed out loud. Not judge her? She felt as if every single person she met, every single day of her life, was judging her…and finding her wanting. Intellectually, she knew it was probably the anxiety messing with her head, but what if it wasn't? What if she really was an awful person?

She felt somewhat out of it after taking the Vistaril tablet, but not so out of it that she wanted to talk about what a colossal mistake she'd made in dating Teddy.

When no one said anything after a long pause, she sighed. They weren't going to give it up. It was better just to get it over with. "I met Teddy online. He seemed nice. We started dating. He came over and watched movies with me a few times, but I never really felt comfortable with him. We went out for lunch one day, and I had an anxiety attack. He got embarrassed and left."

"He *left* you there? When you needed him? What an asshole," Colt said.

Macie looked up at him in surprise. His hand had tightened on hers and it was obvious that he was upset on her behalf.

"He came over later that night but I wouldn't let him in. I broke up with him. He was upset, but he left without protest. I haven't heard from him since."

"What was his last name?" the detective asked.

"Dorentes." Macie said.

"Theodore Dorentes?"

"Yeah."

The detective whistled long and low.

"What?" Truck asked. "Do you know him?"

"Yeah, you can say that," the detective said dryly. "Possession, possession with intent to distribute, assault, larceny, and disorderly conduct…to start with."

Macie sucked in a breath. "Seriously?"

"Seriously," the detective confirmed.

Macie turned to Colt. "I didn't know. I swear I didn't know." Then she turned to her brother. "I didn't!"

"Shhhh, we know you didn't," Colt soothed.

"Okay, so I think we know who ordered her house broken into," the detective said dryly. "The question is why. What was he looking for?"

All three men looked at Macie.

She gulped and shrugged. "He was only here a few times."

"He obviously stashed something somewhere," Truck said.

Macie felt her chest getting tight and her fingers began to tingle once more. She looked around and didn't see anything that looked out of place. "What? Where? I haven't seen anything."

"He probably hid it so you *wouldn't* find it. Thought he could get it next time he came over, but then you broke up with him," the detective mused.

"There are drugs in my apartment?" she practically screeched. So much for her anti-anxiety meds working.

"Why take so long to come back?" Truck asked.

The detective shrugged. "No clue. Maybe it wasn't important until now. It makes sense that he knew about her safe room. I'm assuming you told him about it?" he asked Macie.

"No! I hadn't been dating him that long," she said vehemently. "But..." Her voice trailed off.

"But what?" Colt asked.

Macie sighed. "One time when he was over I got up to get us something to drink and Teddy said that he needed to use the restroom. He was gone a really long time and I just figured he was having...you know...stomach issues. I didn't want to embarrass him so I didn't say anything about it."

"He was probably snooping around looking for somewhere to stash whatever he wanted to hide. I'm guessing he was under pressure from another dealer and was desperate," the detective said. "Then when Macie broke up with him he didn't have an opportunity to get back into her room to collect his stuff."

Macie shivered thinking about Teddy snooping around her place and finding her safe room. She wasn't sure she'd ever feel safe again.

"I think we're done here," Colt said. "Macie's about at the end of her rope. Truck, can you drive her car to Killeen? I can take her with me."

Truck eyed his commanding officer for a heartbeat, and Macie thought they might start arguing right there, but eventually he gave a quick nod.

"You have nothing to worry about," Colt told him. "Nothing is going to happen to your sister."

"It better not," Truck said under his breath. Then he kneeled next to Macie once more. He put his hand on her thigh, and the weight and heat of it felt good on her chilly skin. "Thank you for calling me tonight, Mace. I'm so glad you're all right."

"Thank you for coming," she said.

"Anytime you need me, I'm here," he responded. "And I know this will be impossible, but I'm asking anyway—forget *everything* our parents told you about me and about what happened back then. Not one fucking word was true. They are awful human beings, and I hate like hell that I didn't try harder to stay connected with you. My only excuse is that I was young and dumb and didn't want anything more to do with them. I'm ashamed that I thought for even one second that you might've had a good reason for not wanting to talk to me. I shouldn't have let my feelings about them interfere with my relationship with you. And for that, I'll forever be ashamed of myself."

Macie's eyes filled with tears. He was right, it was impossible to block out the years of hurtful words her parents had hurled at her. But she hated that he felt responsible for what happened.

"I should've come and seen you when you were injured." Her eyes went to the gnarly scar on her brother's face. "I didn't think you'd want to see me. But you should know I cut off all ties with Mom and Dad when they got home from visiting you. They said some truly horrible stuff, and even though it was one of the hardest things I'd ever done, I told them that they were dead to me. I haven't spoken to them since."

Truck's eyes closed for a second before he nodded. He stood and kissed the top of Macie's head. "I'll bring Mary over to see you tomorrow."

"I'm not sure—" Colt started, but Truck interrupted him.

"Tomorrow," he repeated firmly.

Macie looked from Colt to her brother, then back to Colt. He finally nodded.

"I'll call Ghost and have him pick me up at your house after I drop off Macie's car," Truck said, then he turned and headed for the front door of the apartment.

"After we check out this safe room of yours, my guys will be about done looking around," the detective said, standing as well. "I think it goes without saying that if you find anything that doesn't belong, don't touch it and *call* me."

Macie was nodding when Colt said, "We will. Thank you."

Colt looked down at her. "You ready to go pack? I want to look at those scrapes too. Get them cleaned up before we get out of here."

Macie swallowed hard and took a deep breath. Her head hurt and her fingers were still tingling, but the thought of going home with Colt comforted her. She stood up and swayed on her feet. She clutched the blanket around her shoulders when she'd sat down to talk to the detective and closed her eyes.

"Easy, Mace." Picking her up as if she weighed no more than a child, Colt headed for the hallway which led to her bedroom.

Instead of worrying about whether or not he would drop her or where she should put her hands, Macie lay her head on his shoulder and kept her eyes shut.

It had been a long time, maybe forever, since she'd felt as calm as she did right now. Some of it had to do with the meds she'd taken earlier, but most of it was Colt. There was something about him that made her feel more grounded.

Chapter Three

Colt did his best to control his anger. He was pissed way the hell off. When he got his hands on this Teddy person, he was going to wish that he'd simply walked away from Macie. Seeing her hunched over in the chair and worried that Truck was going to leave and not talk to her again made him want to punch something.

He didn't know her parents, but he hated them all the same.

He knew he had to get a handle on his emotions or he was going to worry Macie even more than she already was. He'd talked to his aunt about his cousin's anxiety issues. There was a lot he didn't understand, but he did know that this wasn't something Macie could control. She'd constantly worry about any and everything.

But he had no problem reassuring her when she needed it. Being anxious wasn't a deal breaker for him. From what little he knew about her, she was an amazing person. He'd looked at some of the websites she'd designed and was highly impressed. She was creative and generous, and he would do what he could to protect her from anything that might cause her distress in the future.

When he'd started thinking long term, Colt didn't know, but he also wasn't stressed out about it either. He'd connected with Macie when she'd been at his house after Truck and Mary's wedding. He'd thought he'd have time to feed her breakfast and get her number so they could continue to get to know each other. At some point, he was going to have to ask why she'd left the way she had...but right now wasn't the time.

He sat Macie gently on the counter in her bathroom. He leaned close and placed his hands on the cool tiles next to her hips and waited for her to open her eyes. It took several moments, but when she finally brought her beautiful brown eyes up to his, he wasn't prepared for the jolt of electricity he felt.

Bringing one hand to her cheek, he was encouraged when she tilted her head and rested it on his palm. "You okay?" he asked softly.

She nodded and said, "No."

He smiled at the contradiction. But he had a feeling she was being completely honest. "Where is your first-aid stuff?"

She lifted her head and gestured to a cabinet behind him.

Colt got to work getting the Band-Aids and hydrogen peroxide ready. When he turned around again, he had to take a deep breath. He'd purposely kept his mind off the fact that she was wearing only a tank top and a pair of short-shorts. But she'd dropped the blanket, and he couldn't stop his eyes from tracking from her feet up her long legs to her curvy thighs. Her belly wasn't flat, but she wasn't overweight either. And her tits were lush and full. Even as he stared at her, he saw her nipples tighten under the cotton.

He finally looked up and saw she was examining him just as openly. Waiting until her gaze had traveled the length of his body, he finally said, "Let's get you cleaned up so we can get out of here."

She blushed when she looked up at him, but nodded.

Turning his thoughts away from how sexy he found her—but loving that she seemed to be just as interested in checking him out as he was her—Colt concentrated on cleaning the scrapes on her body. He put the bottle down on the counter and picked up one of her hands. The palm was scraped and red, and he hated knowing it was because she'd leapt out her fucking window into a tree. He hated every single bruise and mark on her smooth skin. Throughout his ministrations, she didn't cry and didn't make a sound. He knew he had to be hurting her, but she was stoic and calm as he tended to her wounds.

When he was finally satisfied that he'd cleaned the worst of her scratches, he helped her stand and wrapped the blanket back around her shoulders. "You need help packing?"

She considered his offer for a second, then shook her head. "How long will I be staying with you?"

Forever was on the tip of his tongue, but he held back the word, knowing it would stress her out…and that it was crazy. "At least a couple days. We need to give the detective time to find Teddy and find out what this is all about. The police department will increase patrols of the area, but they can't be here every minute. Those assholes who were here tonight *will* probably come back, and I don't want you anywhere near here when they do."

"Okay," she said a bit hollowly.

Colt wasn't too concerned about her tone; he had a feeling the pill she'd taken earlier was finally kicking in. She walked to the doorway of the bathroom, then turned back.

"Um…while I'm changing and packing some clothes, will you do me a favor?"

"Anything," Colt said immediately.

That got a smile out of her. "What if I asked for something crazy?" she retorted, with a tilt of her head.

"I'd do what I could to do whatever you needed," Colt told her.

She shook her head and a small smile curved her lips. He loved that he could make her smile after everything she'd been through.

"What do you need, hon?"

"In my safe room is a box. Will you get it for me? I'd like to take it with me…if that's okay."

"Of course it is. Can I ask what's in it?" He was planning on checking out this safe room of hers anyway. He knew the cops had checked it for anything Teddy might've left, but he wanted to look at it himself as well.

"It's nothing expensive or illegal," she said. "It's just a shoebox of keepsakes. Stuff from when I was younger and from college and stuff." She shrugged. "It's not a big deal, but I'd rather it not get destroyed if those guys come back."

Colt was curious as to what keepsakes she had that meant so much to her, but he didn't want to push. "Anything else?"

"Can I bring my computer? And my work files? Oh, and there's a box of CDs and my headphones in the other room that I'd love to bring with me, if possible."

Colt smiled bigger now. "No problem. What else?" He actually hoped she'd continue to list her most prized possessions, because the more stuff she moved over to his house, the more comfortable she'd be there. And the more comfortable she was, the less she'd feel inclined to come back to *this* place. As far as he was concerned, she could move her entire fucking apartment. He had plenty of room for her things. For her.

"Um…" She looked into the bedroom then back at him. "I'm not sure."

Colt walked up to Macie and put his hands on her shoulders. "Whatever you want to take with you is fine with me. If there's not enough room in my Wrangler, we can come back tomorrow."

"Why are you being so nice to me?" Macie asked, her brows drawn down in confusion.

"Because I like you, Macie Laughlin. You didn't do anything for this to happen to you tonight. I want to make sure you're as comfortable as you can be in my house. I know it will be stressful for you, and I want to mitigate that as much as I can."

"Oh."

He could tell she was still unsure. So he added, "And because you're Truck's sister. And all the men under my command are like brothers to me."

She nodded, as if that response made more sense than him liking her.

"Go pack," he ordered gently, turning her around to face the bedroom. "I'll grab the box from your safe room, which I can't wait to see, by the way. Then I'll go and pack up your computer and CDs. You change, and call me when you're done. I'll come back and grab your suitcase so you don't further hurt those hands. Okay?"

"I can carry my suitcase," she protested.

"Hon, I said I've got it. There'll be plenty of times in the future when I'll let you carry your own shit, but tonight isn't one of them. Got it?"

She studied him, but eventually nodded. "Can I ask something else?"

"Of course."

"Why were you up and with my brother when I called? Did I interrupt something important?"

He had a feeling she'd been worrying about that. "My two teams of soldiers just got back from a mission tonight. We were debriefing."

Her eyes widened in horror. "I interrupted you working?"

Colt couldn't have stopped himself if someone had a gun to his head. He leaned down and covered her lips with his own in a brief caress. He rested his forehead on hers and linked his fingers together at the small of her back. He felt his heart jolt when her hands landed on his chest, but she didn't push him away.

"You didn't interrupt anything," he told her. "We were almost done. But even if we weren't, you're more important than work. I don't care what time it is or what you think I'm doing, if you need something, you call. Got it?"

She didn't answer for a long time, and Colt lifted his head to stare at her. "Got it?" he repeated.

"I can't promise. I mean, you know how I am. I'll worry that I'm interrupting you, or that you'll be annoyed, or that your *boss* will be annoyed. And that you'll think I'm being stupid or weak."

"Macie, I won't—"

She cut him off. "So I can't promise to *always* call, but if it's a true emergency, as it was tonight, I'll call."

Colt wanted to protest. But it was a big deal for her to tell him what she was feeling. What her anxiety made her feel. "Okay, hon. But would you mind if I called *you* when I needed something?"

"You want to call me?"

"Yeah, Mace. There might be times when I need help with something. But, like you, I don't want to interrupt you if you're working or doing something important."

"You can call me," she said softly. "I don't think anything I do is nearly as important as what you do."

"I'm sure the authors and other people you work for would disagree. I've seen some of the websites you designed. That couldn't have been easy, and I know that you also keep them updated as well. I *know* that can get crazy, considering how fast some authors write."

That earned him another small smile.

Forcing himself to step back, he gestured to the bedroom. "Do not carry that suitcase yourself. I'll be back here in a bit. Okay?"

"Okay. Colt?"

He smiled. "Yeah?"

"Thanks. I was really scared tonight."

"I'm glad I was there," Colt said simply, then forced himself to turn and leave her to change and pack. If he stood there any longer, there was no telling what would pop out of his mouth. He was a seasoned soldier. Had seen and done way more shit in his life than anyone should ever have to. He wasn't proud of some of his actions in the past, but he couldn't change what he'd done.

But it was the thought of arriving to find Macie dead that haunted him more than any of the carnage he'd lived through did.

He left her in her bathroom packing up her toiletries and made a quick stop to her closet to grab the shoebox she referenced. Her safe room was just what she said it was, a small quiet space with a sleeping bag rolled up at one end. He found the box she wanted and headed out to the living room.

As he began to gather up the CDs strewn around her laptop on her desk in the main part of the apartment, Colt's mind spun with plans. He wanted to make his house a safe place for Macie. Wanted her to feel relaxed and to do whatever it took to minimize her anxiety when she was there. The safer she felt, the more comfortable she would be. And the more comfortable she was, hopefully the more receptive she'd be to dating him on a long-term basis.

He didn't know what he'd done the night of Truck's wedding to make her back off, especially when things had seemed to go so well, but now that he had a second chance, he wasn't going to blow it.

Chapter Four

Macie nervously rubbed her hands on her jeans as she waited for Mary and the others to arrive. She hadn't seen her brother's wife since their wedding day, and while she liked the other woman, she had a tendency to be extremely blunt. In some ways it was refreshing. Macie never had to wonder what Mary was thinking. But on the other hand, she was terrified of doing something that would irritate her sister-in-law and make her not like her anymore.

Colt had put off the visit for almost a week, which Macie was super grateful for. She'd seen Truck several times; he'd come over to his commander's house to make sure she was doing all right. He'd also gone back over to her apartment to grab more clothes and other odds and ends for her.

She'd barely left Colt's house in a week, but she was more than all right with that. He went to work each morning, but came home for lunch to check on her, and was home by three-thirty every afternoon. He'd explained that since the men under his command had just gotten back from an intense two-week mission, and he'd been monitoring their movements almost twenty-four seven, he had some flexibility on when he had to be in the office.

She didn't like hearing about her brother's mission. Not that Colt actually told her much, but just knowing he'd been overseas doing something dangerous was more than enough for her to worry.

The view from the table she was using at Colt's house was just as nice as the one from her apartment. She sat at the table in his dining room, which overlooked a small park in the neighborhood. Macie had always wanted kids. Always. But before now, she'd stayed away from them because it was too painful. At the moment, however, she found herself staring at the children on the playground for hours. They looked so carefree. So happy. She couldn't remember a time in her life when she was truly that relaxed. Maybe before Ford had left for the Army.

Thinking about her brother leaving—and what had happened afterward—made her anxiety flare. She had no idea how he could still care about her after she'd not returned his letters. She didn't know he'd sent them, but still. It had already been a long time since she'd talked to her parents, but she made a mental vow to never see them again. She'd never forgive them. And not just because they'd purposely kept Ford out of her life.

The doorbell rang, and Macie jumped. Looking at the clock, she saw it was three. Forcing herself to her feet, she went to the front door. She looked through the peephole, saw that it was Mary and the others, and took a deep breath. Colt wasn't here—he said he'd be home as soon as he could—so it was just her. Macie's heart raced and she crossed her arms and pinched her biceps, trying to keep her anxiety under control. This was her sister-in-law. It was fine.

"Mace!" Mary said happily as soon as the door was open. "It's about time!"

Macie opened the door wider to let Mary and the others in. She recognized them, but Mary went ahead and introduced them anyway. "I'm sure you remember, but this is my best friend, Rayne. Behind her is Emily and her daughter, Annie, and Casey. The others wanted to come too, but they were busy. We'll have to plan another get-together with them soon."

Macie smiled at the other women and closed the door behind them once they'd all entered. She gestured to the living room and bit her lip as she followed. She hadn't made anything for them to eat. She probably should've. Especially for Annie. Children were always hungry, weren't they? She should've made cookies. That would've been easy.

And crap. Her stuff was strewn all over the dining room table. She was used to it just being her and Colt, and he'd told her to leave her computer set up at the table, and they'd been eating in the living room on the couch while they watched TV.

Macie was working her way to a full-blown anxiety attack when she felt a small hand slip into her own. Looking down, she saw Annie staring at her with a big smile. Her hair was messy around her head, but the little girl didn't seem to notice or care. She was wearing a pair of jeans that had dirt on the knees and a pink T-shirt with white sequins all over it. Squinting, Macie saw that it said "I like glitter."

Annie saw her looking at it and smiled. "Like my shirt?"

"It's cute," Macie told her.

Annie's nose wrinkled, and she said, "Look what it can do!" And with that, she ran her free hand down her chest and the sequins changed directions and colors. Now they were brown and said, "But dirt is cool too."

Macie smiled. "That's funny."

"I wish the dirt part was what showed all the time," Annie pouted.

"Annie, what did we talk about?" Emily reprimanded gently.

The little girl looked at her mom. "That I should just say thank you when people give me a compliment. But Macie is my friend, I can tell her secrets."

Macie glanced at Annie in surprise. "I've only met you once. At the wedding."

Annie looked at her with big blue eyes and said, "But you're Truck's sister. And he's my favorite uncle. And my brother is named after him. So that means you're my aunt. And thus, we're friends."

Macie's eyes teared up, and she had to look away from the little girl before she lost it completely. For the millionth time in her life, she regretted being so weak. For letting her parents coerce her into the worst decision of her life.

"Thus?" Mary questioned with a laugh.

"She's been reading a lot," Emily said. "It's her new favorite word."

"I'm glad we're friends," Macie told Annie.

"Me too," Annie answered happily.

It had been a long time since Macie felt accepted so readily and without strings. Annie was able to make her feel comfortable in a way she rarely felt around others…children included.

"Where's your brother?" she asked the little girl.

"Daddy and him are having a manly bonding moment and I wasn't invited," Annie pouted.

Macie looked at Emily.

The other woman laughed and explained, "I needed a break. Ethan doesn't sleep much. So Fletch took him to the office for the afternoon."

"I wanted to go to the office too," Annie said dejectedly. "I wanted some manly bonding time too." Then she perked up. "But I also wanted to come see you. So here I am!"

Macie squeezed Annie's hand. "I'm glad."

"I've never been in the commander's house," Casey mused.

"Me either," Rayne said. "And I've known him the longest."

"It's nice," Mary noted. "It feels comfortable."

"Why do you sound surprised?" Emily asked.

Mary shrugged. "I don't know. I mean, I guess because it's the commander. He's always seemed so stern. So cold."

"He's not cold," Macie said, surprised that anyone could think Colt was stern. "He's amazing. Patient and kind. He'd never hurt a fly." She regretted her words when three pairs of eyes stared at her in surprise. "What? He's *not* nice?" she asked quietly.

"Annie, do you want to go play?" Emily asked. "There's a playground right across the street."

"Yes!" the little girl shouted, then got serious. "But don't talk about anything important. I don't want to miss anything."

Macie forced a smile and squeezed Annie's hand once more. "We won't."

"Stay at the playground. I'll be watching from here. If you wander off, I'll take away your obstacle course privileges for a month," Emily warned.

Annie snapped to attention and dropped Macie's hand as she saluted her mom. "I won't, Mommy. Promise. Bye!" And with that, she ran to the front door and disappeared. They all watched as, seconds later, she ran onto the playground and immediately started playing with a group of boys.

"She is way too addicted to that obstacle course," Mary said wryly.

"I know, but it makes an affective punishment to take it away, so I'm not complaining," Emily said with a smile.

"Obstacle course?" Macie asked.

"The guys have a course they use at work for PT sometimes. Fletch took Annie there one day and that was that. She didn't want to do anything else. And she's good at it too. Fast."

Macie had met Fletch and the other men Ford worked with at the wedding. She loved how protective and loving they were with their wives. It was part of the reason she'd had such a major anxiety attack at the reception. She wanted the same. And knew she was too broken to ever have a man like that. A man who could put up with her insecurities and anxiety for the long haul.

"Let's sit," Rayne said, gesturing to the couches.

Macie knew she should be offering everyone something to drink, but she couldn't remember what was in Colt's fridge. What if she offered colas or juice and he didn't have any? Should she offer to see if he had any beer or wine? She was getting overwhelmed, so she kept quiet and followed the others to the living room to sit down.

No one said anything for a moment, and Macie's anxiety spiked. She should say something. Get the conversation rolling…but what should she say? She wasn't a part of these women's lives, even if Ford *was* her brother.

"What do you know about Colt?" Mary asked, as blunt as ever.

Macie blinked. "Um…he's my brother's commander. He's in charge of another group of soldiers too. He manages stuff from here while they go on missions." Said out loud, it sounded ridiculous.

But no one seemed to think her explanation was weird or stupid.

"Right," Mary said. "But do you know why he was chosen as their commander?"

Macie shook her head. "Because he was qualified?"

Mary chuckled. "You could say that. Look, we all like the commander. He's an amazing man, and he's kept our husbands safe more times than we can count. But…he's not exactly… What word did you use…kind?"

Macie stared at her sister-in-law. "Yes he is," she countered.

Mary shook her head. "I'm trying to look out for you. He's got a reputation for being one of the toughest officers on post. He doesn't like excuses, and doesn't like it when his soldiers are late and I heard that when he was at another post, he refused to let a soldier take leave when his baby was being born. I also heard that once he—"

"No," Macie said firmly.

"No, what?" Mary asked.

"I appreciate that you're trying to look out for me, but there's no need," Macie said, trying to sound firm. She knew Mary had a tendency to say whatever she was thinking, but she didn't want to hear gossip about Colt.

Mary's voice gentled. "I'm not trying to be a bitch, I swear. I just think you need to know so you don't have expectations that might never be met. The commander was a Delta Force soldier himself, Macie. He actually left the teams after an incident where one of his teammates was captured. I heard Truck talking about it on the phone one night with Blade. He said the commander went crazy. That he killed forty-two people that day."

"Have you ever been so worried about something you can't breathe?" Macie asked Mary out of the blue.

"What?"

"Have you stood in a room and known deep in your soul that *everyone* was talking about you behind your back?"

"No, but—"

"I know you've been through a lot, Mary. I *know*. There's a saying I try to live by: everyone you meet is fighting an invisible battle you know nothing about, so you should always be kind. I think you and I know more about that than anyone else in this room. If I told you that Truck was an asshole, would you believe me? Would that change how you feel about him?"

"You know it wouldn't," Mary said.

"Right. I can't pretend to know how Colt was feeling when he killed those people. I would imagine he was angry. And scared for his friend. And frustrated, and a hundred other emotions I can't name. How would you feel if *you* were that captured soldier? Wouldn't you want your fellow soldiers to do whatever it took to get to you? What if that was Rayne, and someone was holding her hostage? Wouldn't you kill forty-two people to get to her?

"The night of your wedding reception was a living hell for me. I was pretending to be happy, but I was miserable and freaked out that everyone was staring at me, wondering who I was and why I was there. Colt was the *only* one who noticed. He understood something was wrong and he got me out of there. Spent the entire night making sure I was okay. He didn't pressure me for sex. In fact, not once did I even worry that might be why he was helping me. He held me in his arms all night, making me feel safe, even as I struggled with my brain telling me things that I knew damn well weren't true, about everyone staring at me at your reception.

"I don't give a shit what Colt did in the past. Just as I don't care what *you* did. You aren't perfect either, and what you just told me was rude and bitchy, but I'm going to let it go because I want to be your friend, you're married to my brother and I truly believe you were trying to help me. I don't expect Colt to be some sort of paragon. The bottom line is that he's kind to *me*—and that's what I care about. He's also truly concerned about the men under his command, including my brother, your husband. And when I called last week, freaked out and scared because men broke into my apartment, Colt was the one who got me through that situation. He kept me calm so the men didn't find me. I know *exactly* who Colt Robinson is. I think it's *you* who doesn't."

The silence in the room after her outburst was oppressive, but Macie refused to look away from Mary. It took everything she had to do it, but she held eye contact with her.

"I'm sorry," Mary said quietly. "God, you're right. I was out way of line. But in my defense, I was doing it because I care about you. Because I like you. I'm trying to stop saying whatever I'm thinking, but I'm obviously failing. Forgive me?"

"Of course I do," Macie told her. The last thing she wanted was to fight with her sister-in-law.

"I'm sorry you were uncomfortable at the reception," Casey said. "Was it something someone said?"

Macie took a deep breath. She could either confess about her condition or make up something to blow off the other woman's concern. But she wanted friends. Wanted to be able to open up to them when something good *or* bad happened in her life. If she lied now, it would be almost impossible to explain later.

Making a split-second decision, she said, "I have chronic anxiety. I take meds for it, but sometimes they don't always help." She kept the explanation simple, and held her breath to see how they'd react.

"That sucks," Casey said.

"Wow, I can't imagine how hard that would be," Rayne commented.

But it was Mary who blew her mind. She got up out of the chair she'd been sitting in and came over to Macie. She knelt in front of her and put a hand on her knee. "I'm sorry," Mary said. "I should know better than anyone not to assume things about people. And for the record, you seem as if you always have everything under perfect control. Yeah, you were nervous that day you came to the bank, but I figured it was because you hadn't met me before."

"I went home after that meeting, took a pill I only use in extreme situations, and slept for twelve hours," Macie admitted.

"For what it's worth, I admire you," Mary said. "You've been through hell and you haven't let it beat you. You're tough as nails."

Macie gaped at her. She knew what Mary had been through. Not only her childhood, but with the breast cancer she'd fought…twice. There was no way she thought *Macie* was tough. Most days, she felt like a wreck.

"But I can see it now. You're perfect for the commander."

All sorts of things raced through Macie's head at that comment. That she was perfect for him because she needed taking care of. That she was too weak to get by without a man at her side. But then Mary continued.

"Because your heart is so big, you see the good in anyone. And you worry about things because you care. Too much. I think the commander needs that. He needs someone to care about him the way he cares about all the soldiers under his command."

Macie blinked. Mary was exactly right when it came to Colt. He worked hard. Worried about the soldiers under his command…and their families.

She thought about the last week, how happy he'd been when she'd made dinner for them. When she'd done laundry. When she'd changed the sheets on the bed they'd been sleeping on all week. She'd thought he was being grateful because he was trying to make her feel better about living there temporarily, but she realized now that he'd probably always had to do those things himself.

"Shit," Casey said, wiping tears from under her eyes. "You guys are making me cry. Bitches."

Mary smiled at Macie, then turned to Casey. "That's us. The bitch squad."

Macie couldn't believe she thought someone calling her a bitch was funny. In the past, the insinuation could send her to bed for a few days. But it felt like a compliment to be compared to Mary, who never took shit from anyone. Macie liked her. Ford had talked to her a lot about Mary's background, and had warned her not to take what she said personally. He'd told her that his wife was brash, but it was only to guard herself from being hurt. It made sense then, and it made even more sense now.

She wasn't mad at Mary for saying what she had about Colt. The other woman had been trying to look out for Macie. But the thing was that she didn't give a shit what Colt had done in the past. She didn't know the details of what had happened, but she trusted Colt. Knew he wouldn't hurt anyone if the situation didn't call for it. And curiously enough, what Mary said made Macie feel even safer with Colt. He'd make sure her ex didn't get anywhere near her. Of that she had no doubt.

"Have they found the men who broke into your house, or your ex?" Rayne asked, as if she could read Macie's mind.

"Not yet. Truck went to my apartment the day before yesterday and realized that someone had been in there. They didn't trash the place, but they'd definitely been looking for whatever it was that Teddy had left. The cops didn't find anything in my safe room where Teddy told the guys whatever it was would be," Macie told them, already feeling more comfortable with these women than she had with anyone in a very long time.

"Holy crap!" Mary exclaimed.

"Drugs?" Casey asked.

"That's just it. I don't know. The cops brought a drug-sniffing dog to my place and he didn't find anything. He alerted to a few different places, but the handler thinks it was because Teddy had been there and probably had drugs with him when he was." Macie hated that he'd been in her place and might have had drugs on him, but she was trying to move past that. Colt had been a big help in that arena, reminding her that *she* wasn't the one doing drugs, and that she didn't know what Teddy had been doing.

"Do you need us to go to your apartment and clean up, or get you anything?" Emily asked.

Macie stared at her incredulously.

"What?" Emily asked when Macie didn't answer her question. "Should I not have asked? Does it make you anxious when people are in your space?"

Macie shook her head. "No. I mean, yes, but that's not…you don't know me," she blurted, stumbling over her words.

Emily smiled. "I know you're very important to the commander. I know that he requested our men ask us to come over today because he was worried you were here most days by yourself. I know he told Fletch that he would be off this weekend because he was going to spend it with you. I might not know you that well yet, but I want to. Besides, going to Lampasas will get me out of the house and some peace and quiet for a while. I love my kids, but they exhaust me."

"I'm happy to help too," Casey added.

"Me too," Mary said with a grin.

"I…thank you," Macie said. "But I don't need anything. Truck got me some stuff the other day, and Colt went over there the other night. He said he wanted to make sure my fridge was cleaned out, but I think he was hoping to find one of the men who broke into my apartment lurking around."

"That sounds like something one of our men would do," Casey said with a smile.

Just then, Annie came back into the house. She was out of breath and talking a mile a minute. "Mommy! I made a new friend. Her name is Sam. That's short for Samantha. I taught her how to play soldier and I really like her!"

Emily smiled at her daughter and gave the other women a look as if to say "See? Exhausting."

"That's great, baby. Now, go wash your hands before you get dirt all over the commander's house. I saw a bathroom next to the kitchen."

Without a word, Annie spun and headed for the washroom to clean up.

The rest of the afternoon passed relatively smoothly. Macie was surprised at how comfortable she felt with the three women, but it definitely helped to have Annie there. Her presence kept anyone from bringing up anything that might be upsetting to the little girl. They laughed, gossiped, and talked about what it was like to be an Army wife.

Before she knew it, it was quarter to four and the front door was opening and Colt was home.

Macie looked up and smiled at him. He saw her and came straight to her side. He leaned down and kissed her on the cheek and straightened. "Hey."

"Hey," she replied.

"You look like you're having a good time," he observed.

Macie nodded.

"It doesn't smell like you've started anything for dinner?" He raised a brow, making the statement a question.

Macie frowned. "No, I hadn't thought about it yet. It'll be easy enough to make something though. Grilled chicken? Hamburgers?"

He smiled and ran a hand over her hair. "I have a craving for Chinese. I can go and pick it up. I just didn't want to bring anything home if you'd put in the effort to make us something already."

"Chinese sounds great."

Colt smiled at her. "Perfect. You stay and chat. I have some things I need to finish in my office upstairs. I'll come back in a bit and you can tell me what you want. Okay?"

"Okay."

And it wasn't until then that he turned and nodded at the other women. "Good to see you," he said politely.

Mary was staring at Colt as if she'd never seen him before. Casey and Emily smiled at him and returned his greeting.

"Hi," Annie said boisterously.

"Hey, Annie. How are you? Have you been practicing the obstacle course for the upcoming kids' contest?"

"Yes!" she shouted, and nodded her head so hard, Macie thought it would come right off her shoulders. "I can't wait! I took five seconds off my time the last time I did it."

Colt wandered over and put his hand on her shoulder. "I have no doubt you're going to win that trophy," he said seriously. "I think you can absolutely do whatever you want to."

"I want to be a doctor," she said. "And help soldiers when they get hurt on missions so they can come home to their families."

Macie blinked in surprise. Most eight-year-olds she'd come across still wanted to be ballerinas or actresses. Annie's goal was much more specific…and lofty.

"Anyone who's in your unit will be very lucky," Colt said solemnly. Then he turned, smiled at the others, winked at Macie, and headed upstairs to his office.

"Holy crap," Casey whispered.

"I take everything back that I said," Mary mused with a shake of her head.

"He only had eyes for you," Emily told Macie with a smile. "We might not've existed for all the attention he paid to us."

"He wasn't trying to be rude," Macie defended Colt. "He just wanted to make sure I was okay. I was nervous about today, and he knew it."

Mary shook her head. "He looks at you like Truck looks at me. Like Beatle looks at Casey and Fletch looks at Emily."

Macie wanted to protest. Wanted to deny Mary's words, but she couldn't. She'd seen the way her brother looked at Mary. She'd been at the wedding and seen how *all* the men on Colt's team treated their women. It was true. She'd gotten used to being the center of Colt's attention, and she'd convinced herself he was simply being polite. But deep down, she knew better. They had a connection. A deep one.

She didn't respond, just simply smiled.

"How does Daddy look at you, Mommy?" Annie asked with a confused tilt of her head.

Emily tousled her daughter's hair. "Like I'm his wife, of course."

Annie frowned. "I don't get it."

"You will, baby. When you're older."

Annie rolled her eyes. "You always say that."

"That's because it's true."

"Uh oh, Mommy! Look! It's Ethan time!" Annie said and pointed at Emily's shirt.

There were two wet patches on the front of it.

"Oh crap. You're right," Emily said, then looked up at the group in embarrassment. "He usually eats around this time and even though I pumped"—she gestured at herself—"my body is on the same schedule he is."

The others all laughed, but Macie could only look at Emily in horror. Not because she'd leaked through her shirt, but because if that was her, she would be embarrassed beyond belief. She wouldn't ever be able to face the other women again. She couldn't understand how Emily wasn't completely mortified.

"I should probably get going too," Casey said. "I've got papers to grade for tomorrow."

"And I just want to see my husband," Mary said with a smirk.

Macie walked the women to the door and said goodbye to Casey and Mary. Annie ran ahead to the car so she could start it, apparently one of her favorite things to do.

It was just her and Emily standing in the doorway, and Macie struggled to find something to say and not stare at the wet splotches on her shirt.

"I'm sorry if I embarrassed you," Emily said softly.

At that, Macie's eyes whipped up to hers. "What?"

"I can tell you're uncomfortable. And I'm sorry."

"I just…if that had happened to me, I would die of mortification. Then I'd have to take one of my strong pills and hole up in a dark room with my headphones on for the rest of the night."

Emily chuckled. "Having kids does wonders for my tolerance for embarrassment. Annie has a habit of saying the absolute worst thing at exactly the worst times. And Ethan is always hungry. If I don't feed him on schedule, he screams bloody murder. I've learned it's easier to just find a corner and feed him rather than try to calm him down. And let me tell you, people are *not* that comfortable with breast-feeding in public. And it's not like I just whip out my boob or anything." Emily shook her head. "Annie was so much easier than Ethan for some reason. Anyway, I just wanted to make sure you were okay."

"I'm okay, thank you," Macie told her. And surprisingly, she was. The fact that Emily wasn't upset over what happened with her body went a long way toward soothing Macie's own apprehension about it. It was a natural thing. It happened. "Thank you for coming over today. I had a good time."

"You sound surprised," Emily observed.

Macie shrugged. "I've had a hard time making friends."

"I don't know why. You're funny. You're kind. And you aren't afraid to stick up for your man…which in our circle goes a really long way."

Annie chose that moment to honk the horn a few times.

Emily laughed. "That's my cue. Thanks for having us." Then she leaned over and gave Macie a quick hug, careful not to crush their chests together. "We need to do it again soon. I'll be in touch. Bye!"

Macie didn't have a chance to get a word in before Emily was halfway down the sidewalk and yelling at Annie to hush and to get in the backseat.

Two words stuck out from everything Emily had said. "Your man."

Macie wanted to admit that Colt wasn't her man. That she was only staying with him until he thought it was safe for her to go back to her apartment in Lampasas. That he was simply looking after one of his soldiers' sisters.

She was afraid to think anything else. Especially since she'd left her number for him after the wedding and he hadn't bothered to call.

She waved at Annie as Emily pulled away and went back into the house and shut the door behind her, making sure to lock it. She turned to go back into the other room and screeched in surprise when she almost ran into Colt.

"Everything good?" he asked.

Macie nodded.

"No, Macie," he said as he put a hand on the side of her neck and leaned in. "Are you good?"

She couldn't help the small smile that broke out. "I'm good," she told him. "Really. I liked them. Annie is hysterical, and I loved getting to know Emily and Casey more."

"And Mary? Did she behave?"

Macie must've hesitated a moment too long, because Colt sighed and pulled back. He reached for her hand and pulled her into the living room. He sat on the couch and tugged Macie down onto his lap. He put his arms around her waist and held her firmly.

Macie stared at him in shock. They'd slept curled up next to each other every night, and Colt never hesitated to touch her, to caress her cheek or run a hand over her hair. But he'd never simply hauled her around before—at least, not since the night of the break-in—and she hadn't sat on anyone's lap since she was five years old.

Not sure where to put her hands, she rested them in her lap awkwardly.

"What'd she say?" Colt asked.

"Nothing."

"Mace," he said more gently. "I can tell she said something. I mean, it's Mary, she can't help herself, it's part of her charm." He smiled. "Now tell me, so I can reassure you about whatever it was, and then I'll go get us some dinner. I'm hungry."

It was the last bit that made Macie change her mind about telling him. She had a feeling he would sit there all night if she didn't spill. He was that stubborn. But his stubbornness was one of the many reasons she was crazy about him.

Pushing those feelings to the back of her mind, refusing to think about them right now, she said, "I'm sure she was exaggerating, or that she simply doesn't know the truth."

"About what?"

Taking a deep breath, Macie said, "She was just trying to make sure I knew what this was. What was happening here. And she told me about you killing a bunch of people when your friend was captured."

She felt Colt's thigh muscles tense under her butt, and it seemed as if the air in the room thickened with emotion.

Oh shit. Why had she told him? She should've made something up. She was such an idiot! Now he was going to tell her she couldn't stay at his house anymore, that he couldn't help her. She should've kept her big mouth shut!

Chapter Five

Colt felt Macie begin to tremble in his lap and did his best to relax his own muscles. But it was too late. He could tell by the way she'd hunched in on herself and the way she wouldn't meet his eyes.

He hated doing anything to make her anxiety flare, so he quickly tried to fix it. Her words had surprised him and brought back the memories of that awful day, the day that had changed his life forever.

Tightening his arms around her so she couldn't flee, he began speaking.

"I'm forty-three years old. I've been in the military almost my entire adult life. I have no idea what I'll do when they finally force me to retire. I've never been married. Don't have any children. I've made my share of mistakes in my life, and I won't lie to you, Macie. I've killed people. Lots of them. But if I had to do it again, I would. Every time."

He paused and took a deep breath. He wasn't sure he could relive what had happened at the end of his Delta Force career.

Then he felt Macie relax slightly against him. She put her head on his shoulder and tentatively put her arms around his neck. That was all it took to give him the courage to open up to her. She wasn't rejecting him. She knew the basics, and still she put her arms around him.

"My team was sent into a hostile town to meet with who we thought were loyal supporters. Our intel said they wanted to assist us in taking down the Taliban that had a toehold in that region. Honestly, we were losing the fight there and needed all the help we could get.

The bigwigs thought it would be a good idea to use local strength to fight. So we went in. We were cautious and uneasy, but we were given a direct order, so in we went. I was in charge of my team, and so I was in the lead when an RPG—rocket-propelled grenade—came out of nowhere and decimated the building behind where we were standing. It collapsed right on top of us."

Macie inhaled harshly, but didn't speak. Colt could feel her fingers at the nape of his neck, caressing the short hairs there. He closed his eyes and took a minute to appreciate the feel of her body on his. How good her fingers felt.

"I woke up some time later. I'm not sure how much time had passed. I was completely buried under the stones and concrete of the building, but somehow hadn't been crushed because of the way the walls fell. I don't know if you remember after 9/11 that some people were found alive in one of the stairwells of the collapsed buildings?"

Macie nodded, so Colt continued.

"Yeah, well, that happened to me too. I was relatively unhurt, just sore, confused, and had a raging headache. I pushed the rubble off myself and crawled out. It was almost dark but I could still see all around me. Two of my teammates were lying dead, their heads crushed under rocks from the building. Another had been dragged out of the debris and stripped. Bud was naked, and he had bullet holes throughout his body and a huge puddle of blood around him. Back home, he had two kids and another on the way. I turned my head to puke, and met the eyes of another teammate, Randy. He was alive. Lying in the debris of the building, but his legs and pelvis were crushed and he was pinned under a huge block of concrete.

"I went to his side, and he told me what had happened to our last teammate I hadn't found yet. Randy had witnessed what had happened to everyone, but couldn't do a damn thing to help. He knew he was dying. Could feel it. He said that Sergeant Griswald had fought off the insurgents at first, trying to keep them at bay. He'd used all his bullets and was trying to reload when they overwhelmed him. Bud had shot at them from where he was also trapped under the rubble, but they dragged him out and beat the hell out of him. When he was almost unconscious, they stripped him and began shooting…just for fun. Randy said it seemed like the entire town was there, watching, laughing, participating. Women, kids, men, old and young alike. When Bud was dead, they turned back to Gris. He'd been detained by five insurgents."

Colt huffed out a breath. "Took *five* of those fuckers to contain him. He was strong as an ox, and I can imagine that he was pissed way the hell off. Anyway, they tied a piece of rope around his neck and dragged him away. Randy said Gris had managed to get his hands under the rope, so he wasn't strangled as they dragged him in the dirt, but he didn't know where they'd taken Gris or what had happened to him.

"The last words Randy said to me were to tell his wife that he loved her, and that he was proud as hell to be hers. He died in the middle of that fucking miserable town and there was nothing I could do about it. No amount of first aid would put his legs back together or stop the bleeding. Looking around at the four dead men surrounding me, something snapped. I was *so* enraged that these men—my friends…husbands and fathers, brothers and sons—were dead.

"By now it was fully dark, and I searched through the rubble and found what weapons I could and went on the hunt for Gris. We'd all been trained how to withstand torture, and I hoped like hell the assholes hadn't just killed him outright as they had Bud.

"Every single person I came into contact with on my hunt for Gris, I killed. Some with my bare hands, so I didn't draw attention to myself. I didn't give them a chance to identify themselves, either. Randy said the entire town had participated in the death of my teammates—and they'd laughed while doing it. I showed no mercy for any of them.

"By the time I found Gris, I almost didn't recognize him. They'd stripped him naked like they had Bud, and had tied him to a stake on the back side of the town. He was barely conscious, but I could tell even from my hiding spot that he was still fighting to live. I'd collected various firearms from the people I'd killed on my way through the town and had quite the arsenal set up…including an RPG.

"I didn't hesitate. I aimed that thing at a group standing near Gris and fired. It was stupid. I could've killed Gris."

"But you didn't," Macie said with complete certainty.

Colt jolted under her. He'd been so lost in the memories in his head that he'd forgotten where he was. Forgotten that Macie was even there.

"To confirm what you heard, hon…yeah, I killed a lot of people. Old women, teenagers, adults. I don't regret it, and I'd do it again if I was in the same situation."

"What about Gris?" she asked softly.

"What about him?"

"Did he live?"

"Yeah, he lived. When the air cleared and after I picked off the remaining insurgents who hadn't fled after I'd fired the RPG, I got Gris off that fucking stake and got us the hell out of there."

"You have to be proud of that," she said.

"I might've gotten Gris home, but I left Randy, Bud, and the others there. The one rule we take very seriously is that we never leave anyone behind."

Macie sat up on his lap and turned toward him. She took his face in her hands and looked into his eyes. "You couldn't get Gris and yourself to safety and take their bodies too. They'd have understood, Colt. And I have a feeling, if they were anything like you or my brother, they'd kick your ass for even *thinking* about coming back for their bodies after you'd rescued Gris."

She was right. Randy had been very vocal when it came to safety. About not taking stupid risks. And Bud was completely laid-back. He got his nickname because in boot camp, the drill sergeant accused him of being high because he wasn't fazed by anything. Bud would simply shrug and say that Colt had done what he'd had to do to get Gris home.

Even though he knew she was right, it didn't ease the feelings of guilt he still carried.

"I understand feeling guilty about something," Macie said after she'd put her head back on his shoulder.

Colt immediately snapped out of his own head and focused on the woman in his lap. She was no longer loose in his arms. He could feel her muscles tighten even as she began speaking.

"There are so many things I feel guilty about in my life. I've made so many mistakes it's not even funny. Starting with arguing with my brother before he left."

"You guys were kids. You can't blame yourself for that," Colt said. He moved a hand to rub the small of her back and the other rested on her thigh and kneaded her flesh there lightly.

"I guess I don't blame myself, but I wish I'd listened to him."

Colt stilled.

"The boy I was dating was bad news. Ford knew it, but I thought the guy loved me. I guess I latched on to him as a replacement for the affection I knew I'd lose when Ford left. But he wasn't a good guy. He convinced me that he loved me, and we'd be together forever. I was so young…I thought we were going to get married. I let him convince me to sleep with him. And I…I got pregnant when I was fifteen."

Colt forced himself to breathe, but didn't interrupt.

"I wanted that baby so much," Macie said softly. "We began fighting more and I suspected he was seeing other girls behind my back, but I wanted to make things work so bad. I told him about the baby, and of course he broke up with me. Said he wasn't ready to be a father. Just up and left. I was heartbroken, but determined to raise my baby on my own."

She stopped speaking, and Colt gave her several minutes to continue, but when she didn't, he brought his hand to the back of her neck and massaged her. "What happened?" He was pretty sure she didn't have a child hidden somewhere. He did the math in his head and figured that her child would be somewhere around eighteen.

"My parents made me have an abortion."

Her words were flat, and all the more heartbreaking because of the lack of emotion in them.

"I'm so sorry, hon."

She curled farther into him, bringing her knees up. Colt tightened his embrace, trying to cocoon her with support.

"They said I'd make a horrible mother. Convinced me I had no way of supporting myself, never mind a baby. Said they wouldn't babysit and I'd have to drop out of school. They told me I was a slut and it was no wonder my brother left and hadn't spoken to me since. They said I had no common sense and my baby would probably be deformed or handicapped."

"Assholes!" The word burst from Colt before he could stop it. "Macie, how old you are has nothing to do with whether or not your baby will be born healthy. And I can guarantee that Truck didn't leave because of you."

"I know that…*now*. But I didn't then. I let them convince me it was for the best. They drove me to the clinic and refused to come back to see the doctor with me. When she was aborted…it hurt, Colt. Not physically, the doctor numbed me for that part of the procedure, but it felt as if a part of me was being torn away. The doctor said I was imagining it, that the fetus was small enough that I couldn't feel anything, but it was as if we were spiritually connected. I knew the second she died."

"She?" Colt asked, tears forming in his eyes as he imagined the mental anguish she'd gone through as a vulnerable teenager.

"Yeah. A daughter. She'd be eighteen. Graduating from high school and getting ready for college. I often wonder what kind of person she'd be today. Would she be a pain in the ass and sneaking out every night? Or would she be into math and science? Maybe she'd be an athlete or a singer. I feel guilty for giving in to my parents so easily. I should've stood up to them. Maybe today my daughter would be alive and getting ready to change the world."

"Listen to me," Colt said, turning her chin so she had to face him. "You have nothing to feel guilty about. *Nothing.* Your parents are the ones who should feel guilty. They treated you and Truck like shit for years. The fact that they did what they could to make you feel as if his leaving was your fault was already enough for me to hate them. But the fact that they made you abort your baby when you didn't want to is unforgivable.

"If I've learned anything over the years, it's that we can't go back. We can't change the past. We can only go forward. It sucks, and it's not fair, but it is what it is. You have your brother back now. You have me. You never have to speak to your sperm donors again. You have a whole group of men and women who are more than happy to be your friends.

"I won't say that I'll never look back at what happened to my friends and wish things could be different, but I'm doing my best to move on. To be the kind of man they'd want at their backs. To be the kind of commander who would never send his men into battle without knowing all the facts. Your brother and his team, and the other team I command, will never have to worry about whether they have all the facts before putting their lives on the line. I will *not* deploy them if I'm not sure I know everything there is to know about what I'm sending them into. Randy and Bud didn't die in vain. They live on in your brother, and in every single Delta Force team member I'm responsible for."

"What happened to Gris?" Macie asked.

Colt smiled for the first time in what seemed like hours. "He was medically retired. Lives in this tiny town called Stehekin in Washington state. The only way you can get there is by a four-hour ferry boat ride up Lake Chelan. They don't have any big-box stores, there are only about a hundred year-round residents, and it's buried under snow seven months of the year."

"Sounds like heaven," Macie said with a smile.

"I've been there several times. And it is," Colt agreed. "He and his wife have three kids. His oldest son is named Colt."

Her smile grew even bigger. "I'd love to meet him sometime."

"Done. I'll gladly take you up to Stehekin. In the summer though. I don't like all that snow."

She giggled, and Colt could only stare at her. *He'd* done that. She'd just finished talking about her baby being killed and he'd made her giggle.

Colt had never been a believer in fate. There was no way Randy, Bud, and the others were meant to die how they did. No way that Gris was fated to be tortured like he was.

But sitting on his couch, with Macie relaxed and warm in his arms, he had to reconsider.

He'd done some shitty things in his life. He definitely didn't deserve someone like Macie. And yet, here she was. There were so many decisions the two of them had made over the years, and even one might have meant they never would've crossed paths. But they had.

Colt rearranged them on the couch so his back was against the arm and she was half-sitting, half-lying between his legs, and clicked on the television. They'd disclosed some pretty heavy things to each other today. It was time to rest and simply enjoy being with each other.

He felt Macie relax farther into him and eventually fall asleep. He nuzzled her hair and inhaled its floral scent. He vowed three things, right then and there.

One, if her parents ever tried to contact her, he'd make sure they understood that they were dead to her, and if they ever spoke to her again, they'd regret it. Second, he would not let her ex-boyfriend and his thugs lay one hand on her. She'd been through too much.

And three, he loved her and would do whatever it took to make her happy for the rest of her life. She was meant to be his. She hadn't blinked at his recounting of the way he'd slaughtered so many people to save one man. Hadn't been horrified, hadn't come up with excuses for his behavior.

"Love you, Mace," he said in a barely audible whisper.

"Mmmm," she murmured, and tightened her hold on his arm that was around her chest.

Colt smiled, and finally felt the guilt lift that he'd carried around with him for so long. Raising his eyes to the ceiling, he mouthed, *Thanks, guys.*

Chapter Six

Macie looked up from her computer in surprise when she heard the garage door open. Glancing at her watch, she saw it was only two in the afternoon. She wasn't expecting Colt home for another hour and a half or so. She wasn't panicked though, because it wasn't as if the thugs who'd broken into her apartment would open the garage door if they'd tracked her to Colt's house.

Thankful for the break—she'd been rebuilding an author's website after her old one had been infected with malware, and her eyes felt like they were crossed—Macie saved her work on the computer and stood to greet Colt. It was Friday afternoon, and she was looking forward to him being home for two full days. She felt grounded when he was there. As if he had some sort of magical force field around him that prevented her anxiety from flaring up.

She heard the door to the garage shut and then he was there.

"Hi."

"Hey, hon. How's your day been?"

"Good. Yours? You're home early."

"I am. I thought we could go on a trip this weekend, if you wanted to."

Macie froze. A trip? Together? Would they stay in the same hotel room?

It was a stupid thought. They'd been sleeping in Colt's bed together since she'd moved in. It wasn't sexual, and as the days passed, she got more and more unsatisfied with the status quo. She had no idea how to let Colt know she was ready for more. Didn't want to do anything that might change the comfortable relationship they had. And if she initiated sex, and he didn't want it, she'd be embarrassed and have to move back to her apartment.

As if he could sense her inner turmoil, Colt strode toward her. Macie loved seeing him in his uniform. He looked confident and strong, things that were the complete opposite of how she felt most of the time.

"If you'd rather, we can stay here like we did last weekend," he reassured her as he tucked a piece of hair behind her ear gently. "I just thought you could use a change of pace. You've been cooped up in my house almost since you moved in."

"I like your house," she blurted.

"I know you do, hon. And I like you *in* my house, but I'd like to take us both away for a weekend. The detective in Lampasas hasn't found Teddy yet, though after your place was broken into again, they've really stepped up their searches. I reserved a room at the Four Seasons in Austin. I requested a view of Lady Bird Lake and the Congress Avenue Bridge so we could watch the bats leave at dusk to go feed."

Macie had heard of the famous bats of Austin. It was said that over a million bats lived under the bridge and came out every night at dusk to feed. She'd wanted to go see the phenomenon, but hadn't ever made the time.

Colt went on. "They have an aquarium in Austin that we could do, or we could take a tour of the downtown area. Sixth Street is always an option too. They have a huge multi-block party every weekend, complete with live bands, but I wasn't sure that would be your thing. The stores down there are pretty eclectic, and we could wander around during the day if you wanted. The bottom line is that I just want to spend time with you, Macie. One on one. Continue to get to know you. Have some fun."

Macie took a deep breath and nodded. "I'd like that."

"But?" Colt asked.

Macie smiled a little and shook her head. "How can you read me so well?"

"Because I pay attention. What part of my plans do you not like? Nothing is set in stone. We can change things up however you want."

"There's a store called Uncommon Objects in Austin. One of the authors I work for told me about it. It's an antique store, but it's apparently so much more than that. They have all sorts of stuff, but what I'd really like to get my hands on are the antique photos. Real photos of real people. Memories that are lost to those who experienced them, but I can only imagine the stories that will run through my head when I see them."

Colt was smiling at her and had a look in his eyes that she couldn't interpret. "Of course we can go there."

"And there's a restaurant called Bacon that I want to go to. I saw a rerun of an episode of *Food Paradise* on the Travel Channel that featured it. They make all different kinds of flavored bacon. I think it would be fun to visit."

The indulgent look hadn't left Colt's face. "I've been there. And you're right, the food is amazing. But hon, I have bad news."

"What?" Macie asked.

"They closed."

"Seriously?"

"Yeah. A couple years ago. I guess the street it was on frequently flooded, and they got tired of it. They were supposed to open in a new location, but I haven't heard if they've done that or not."

"Well, darn," Macie said.

"I'll make you bacon if you want it, Mace," Colt told her.

"It won't be the same," she said with a pout.

Colt chuckled. "True. We'll see if we can find another place that sells kick-ass bacon while we're there. How's that? The city's well known for their eclectic, independently run restaurants."

"Okay."

"So you'll go with me?"

Macie looked up at Colt and said seriously, "I think I'd go anywhere with you."

"We won't have time to get there to see the bats tonight, and I figure we'll both be tired by the time we arrive. So I thought we could just order room service."

"Sounds perfect. Colt?"

"Yeah, Mace?"

"I appreciate everything you've done for me. I mean, I know I'm Ford's sister and he's one of the soldiers under your command, but I appreciate it all the same."

He looked confused then. "Macie, you know I'm not helping you just because you're Truck's sister, right?"

Macie heard the incredulity in his voice, and began to get nervous in a way she hadn't felt around him since she'd moved in. "Well, no, because that would be crazy. I mean, you can't move *everyone's* siblings into your house if they need help. But I get that you were there with Ford when I called him that night. And when I refused to stay at his place with him and Mary, you were put in a weird spot. All I'm saying is that I'm thankful."

She couldn't interpret the look on his face now, and that was beginning to freak Macie out. She'd obviously said the wrong thing, *again*, but didn't know how to fix it. So she tried to fill the awkward silence.

"I mean, it's not like we aren't friends, because I think we are. I like you, and I think you like *me*. But when you didn't call after my brother's wedding, I kinda figured out where we stood with each other, and I'm okay with that."

"When I didn't call?" Colt asked, breaking his weird silence. "Mace, I didn't have your number. I could've asked Truck, but I didn't know if that's what *you* wanted. I also didn't want you to feel weird about what happened that night…but I sure didn't. I loved talking to you. Getting to know you. But I wasn't going to force you to go out with me if you didn't want to."

"I left my number," Macie got up the courage to say. "On a note."

The confusion left his eyes, and determination took its place. "Where?"

"Where what?"

"Where did you leave the note?"

Macie's head was swirling with confusion. "Right next to your bed, so you'd see it when you woke up. On the nightstand."

Without a word, Colt grabbed her hand. He turned and pulled her after him as he went up the stairs toward his bedroom. Macie didn't protest or say anything. She was too weirded out by the way he was acting.

When they got into his room, he turned to her and said, "Show me where."

Macie pointed at the small table next to the bed. The same notepad she'd used that night was still sitting there, along with a pen.

Colt looked at the table, then back at her, then back to the table.

Just when Macie was about to completely wig out, he said, "I didn't see a note from you, Mace. And believe me, I looked. When I woke up and you weren't next to me, I was upset. I had been looking forward to having breakfast with you. To talking with you some more. I got dressed then went downstairs to see if you had left a note there. And once again was disappointed when I didn't find anything. I figured you simply didn't feel the same connection between us that I did."

"I did. I *do*," Macie said. "It was hard for me to leave that note because I was scared you were just being nice. That you didn't mean it when you asked if I wanted to have lunch or something. But I liked you. So I left my number. And you didn't call."

He rubbed his free hand over his face. "God, what a clusterfuck," he muttered. Colt dropped her hand and went over to the bed. He got down on his knees and looked under it. Macie had no idea what he was doing.

Then he reached under the bedframe and pulled out a white sheet of paper and held it up.

She held her breath. The paper had some dust bunnies attached to it, indicating that it had been under his bed for a while.

He hadn't lied. It looked like he really *hadn't* seen her note.

He stood and walked back to her, holding the note between them. She looked down and saw her own handwriting on the small piece of paper.

Colt. Thank you for last night. If you were honest about wanting to have lunch sometime, I'd like that. ~Macie

Her number was clearly written under her short note. Swallowing hard, she looked up at Colt.

"Damn it all to hell," he said softly. "I can't believe I didn't get this. I've wasted so much time."

Macie wasn't sure what to say to that.

"I remember shutting my bedroom door that morning and thinking how glad I was that I didn't live in an apartment when it slammed harder than I'd intended," Colt mused. "I bet it blew off then. All this time, I could've been with you, and I fucked it up."

Now Macie felt bad that he was blaming himself. "I shouldn't have torn it off the pad," she said. "I wasn't thinking straight."

"No," he said immediately, shaking his head. "This isn't your fault.

It's mine. I should've manned up and asked Truck for your number anyway. Shit." Colt blew the dust off the note and walked back to the small table. He put the note down, making sure to put the pen on top of it so it didn't get blown off again, then he came back to Macie.

He took both her hands in his and looked down at her. "I would've called that day if I had found the note, Mace. I would've told you then that I had a wonderful night with you, even if it hadn't started under the best circumstances. I would've asked you to lunch. Then after we had lunch, I would've asked you to go with me on a dinner date. I would've asked permission to kiss you at the end of the date, after I'd driven you home. And I would've texted you nonstop after that, and called you when I got home from work, just to hear your voice. I would've bought you silly presents so you wouldn't forget about me. We could've watched movies in your apartment and here at my house. We would've laughed together, and I would've been there for you if you had an anxiety attack. I'm so fucking sorry that I didn't see your note. *So* sorry."

Macie could feel her heart beating fast in her chest, although this time it wasn't a bad feeling. "We can still do all those things," she got up the courage to say. "It's only been a month and a half since we met."

"I *want* to do those things," Colt said immediately. "And more. But I still hate that we've missed out on a whole month of being together."

Not liking the look of regret on his face, Macie brought her hand up to his neck. Her thumb caressed his chiseled jaw and she said, "Ask permission to kiss me, Colt."

And just like that, the regret faded from his face, to be replaced by hunger. "May I kiss you, Mercedes Laughlin?"

"Yes. Please," she responded.

Macie thought he might crush his lips to hers immediately, but he surprised her by leaning down and placing his lips on her forehead. Then her right cheek, followed by her left. Then he took her hand from the side of his neck and kissed her palm. He dropped it and placed his hands on either side of her neck, his thumbs caressing her jawline much as she'd done to him.

"We've somehow managed to screw things up from the get-go, haven't we?" he asked quietly. "But as much as I regret not finding your note and causing you even a second of worry about why I hadn't called you, I love that you're currently living in my house. Sleeping in my bed. In my arms. I haven't pushed for more because the last thing I want to do is rush you—"

"Push me," Macie said, interrupting whatever he was going to say next.

He shook his head. "No. I refuse to rush this. We only have one first kiss. One first time making love. I like this feeling of anticipation. Of knowing that the giddy feeling inside me has returned. It has, hasn't it? You feel it too?"

Macie licked her lips, and loved how his eyes immediately went to her mouth. "Yeah, Colt. I feel it too."

Reverently, he ran a thumb over her lips. Then his beautiful gray eyes met hers and his head lowered.

Macie shut her eyes and waited.

His warm lips brushed hers. Lightly. Achingly soft.

"Heaven," she heard him whisper before his lips were on hers again, this time harder. His tongue brushed against the seam, asking permission to enter. Macie granted him that permission. She opened her mouth and then they were kissing.

Really kissing.

Macie had been kissed before, but nothing compared to how she felt in Colt's arms. His hands kept her head still as he devoured her. She made a noise deep in her throat and gripped Colt's uniform shirt as she took all that he gave her. It was beautiful and carnal at the same time. And the best part was that she didn't feel one inkling of anxiety. Usually when she was with a man, she worried about where she should put her hands, if her breath stunk, if he was enjoying himself…but with Colt, everything else fell to the wayside.

All she could think about was him. And how he made her feel. Nothing else mattered. No one else existed in their little bubble.

Eventually, the kiss gentled. Became less heated. Less desperate. Colt finished their kiss with small pecks and then rested his forehead against hers.

"Wow," Macie said softly.

"Wow, indeed," Colt echoed with a smile.

"You should know something," Macie told him.

He pulled back and took her in, his eyes roaming from her eyes to her mouth, then the slight blush on her cheeks, before returning to her gaze. "Yeah? What's that?"

"There's no way I would've let you kiss me like that a month ago," she said honestly. "And as much as I hate that there was a misunderstanding between us, that kiss made up for it."

He grinned. "It did, didn't it?"

Macie nodded.

"For the record," he added, "I will always remember our first kiss as one of the most exciting, emotional moments of my life."

"Colt," Macie whispered, feeling overwhelmed. He had a knack for saying the perfect thing at the perfect time.

"Pack," he said, running the back of a hand over her cheek before stepping away. "I'll change and meet you downstairs. We'll hit the road at soon as you're ready."

She nodded. Suddenly the weekend seemed even more exciting than before. She'd been to Austin, but seeing it with Colt somehow seemed more special.

Macie headed for the door. Even though she'd been staying in his bed each night, her things were in the guest room, where'd he'd put her suitcases the first day he'd brought her here.

She looked back right before she exited his room to see him running a finger over her note on the nightstand.

He looked up and caught her staring. "Things work out the way I hope they do, I'm going to get this framed so it never gets misplaced again."

Macie's throat closed up with happiness and she couldn't say a word. She simply smiled at him and turned to go pack.

Chapter Seven

Colt held the hotel door open for Macie and followed her inside. He'd reserved a suite on the river side so they could watch the bats. The day had been fun. He couldn't remember the last time he'd laughed so much. As the commander for two Delta Force teams, he wasn't known for being the most jovial man, but spending time with Macie made him loosen up and simply live in the moment.

They'd arrived Friday night and had ordered room service like they'd planned. Then they'd relaxed and watched a movie on pay-per-view. Macie had fallen asleep halfway through and woke up briefly when he'd gathered her in his arms to sleep.

"I missed the movie," she mumbled.

"Yup. Shhhh, go to sleep," Colt ordered, and she'd immediately closed her eyes and relaxed into him once more.

They'd gotten up early and gone for a walk around the lake. Then they'd had brunch, gone to the antiques store she'd wanted to see and spent several hours there. She'd bought an envelope full of old photos and several more knickknacks. They'd found an eclectic place to eat lunch, then enjoyed the rest of the afternoon wandering around Sixth Street. Colt loved watching her eyes light up when she saw something that interested her. She didn't buy a lot of things, simply enjoyed taking in the ambiance of the quirky stores and shop owners.

They'd arrived back at the hotel in time to watch the bats emerge from under the bridge in search of their nightly meals. Colt laughed at the way Macie squealed and proclaimed she was glad they were inside behind a window, because there was no way she would enjoy being anywhere near the animals as they flew off.

Dinner was in the hotel's restaurant, and they were now back in the room. They'd been holding hands and touching each other all day. Colt had even been able to sneak in a few kisses here and there.

The entire day had been building up to this moment, at least in Colt's eyes. It felt like hours of foreplay, which was exciting rather than frustrating. He hadn't been this eager to be with a woman for as long as he could remember. He'd dated, but after the incident overseas, he'd lost the desire for any kind of relationship. He concentrated on being the best commander he could be to protect the men who served under him.

Until now.

Until Macie.

"Today was awesome," Macie said softly. They were sitting on the couch in the spacious suite, each drinking a glass of wine.

"Yes it was," Colt agreed. Her hand was resting on his thigh and he covered it with his own.

She stared at him for a long moment before leaning forward and putting her glass on the coffee table in front of them. Then she took his glass from his hand and placed it next to hers. Colt watched her take a deep breath before she spoke.

"I haven't been this relaxed in a long time, and it's because of you. Usually when I'm in a strange city, I stress about directions, who's around me, and what my plans are for the entire day. But I didn't have to do any of that with you. I trusted you to know where you were going and that you would figure out what we would do all day. It felt good. I like being with you, Colt. I have a question, and I hope you'll be honest with me."

"Of course I will," Colt answered immediately.

"Does the difference in our ages bother you? Or the fact that I'm Ford's sister? I know he gave you a hard time about the night of his wedding. I hadn't told him about it because I thought you saw me as just a friend or something. But now that things are…better between us, I got to thinking about the fact that I'm a decade younger than you are."

"It doesn't bother me in the slightest," Colt told her. "In fact, I hadn't even thought about it until you brought it up. Does it bother *you*?"

"No," she said immediately. "But I don't want you to get in trouble or have anyone at work say anything because I'm only thirty-three and you're forty-three."

"Listen," Colt said earnestly. "We're both adults. I like you, and you like me. I don't give a flying fuck what other people say about us. And, if you *do* care, I'll do my best to shut that shit down if I hear it. What goes on between us is *only* between us. It's no one else's business. And Truck and I talked. He loves you, Mace. Even though you weren't communicating, he still thought about you and worried about you all these years. I'll admit that he wasn't happy with me, but he's not going to be thrilled about *anyone* being with you, simply because you're his little sister."

"Okay," she said.

"Okay?" he asked.

"Yeah."

"Good."

"So, uh…one more thing," Macie said.

"Anything."

"Will you kiss me again?"

Colt smiled. "Absolutely."

He leaned down and took her lips with his, happy that they were alone and he didn't have to worry about anyone looking at them and saying something that would make Macie uncomfortable—or noticing his hard cock.

He pulled Macie onto his lap so she was straddling him, and set about making sure she knew he was in this one hundred percent. That he didn't care about their ages, or what her brother thought, or anything else that might run through her mind as a roadblock to their relationship.

They'd clicked the night of Truck and Mary's wedding, but when she'd called, scared out of her mind, and he'd been able to help her focus and find a place to hide, something deeper had happened between them. Something on a more primal level.

She was his. His to protect. His to comfort. His to make happy. He hoped down the line she would see him the same way…well, at least as someone she could lean on and rely on. But the soldier in him, the man, wanted her in a way he'd never wanted anyone before.

Before he knew it, Macie was grinding her pussy against his dick, and he was holding her hips, helping her gyrate against him as they kissed. Her hands had shoved his shirt up and were caressing his bare stomach and chest. She wasn't hesitant in any way, and Colt loved that.

He pulled his lips off hers long enough to make sure she was on board with what was happening.

"Are you sure?" He could barely form the words.

"Sure about having sex? Yes! Please."

He grinned at her enthusiastic response and groaned when she leaned forward and nuzzled her nose in the space between his shoulder and neck.

"Birth control?" he ground out, wanting to make sure all their bases were covered before things went too far. He hadn't seen her taking any pills, but that didn't mean she didn't have some other sort of contraceptive.

She froze and sat up. Colt could feel the warmth between her legs, and he fantasized about them doing this again, but with both of them naked.

"I…I'm not on anything," she said after a beat.

"I've got condoms," he reassured her immediately. "I'm clean and haven't been with anyone in over a year, but I'll protect you, Macie. Have no doubt about that."

"I'm clean too," she told him, blushing as she did so. "I didn't sleep with Teddy, so you don't have to worry about that."

"I wasn't worried about it," Colt soothed, even though that was a little white lie. He wasn't concerned for himself so much as he was about her. Teddy obviously wasn't a good man, and anything he'd told her about his sex life had probably been untruthful, so for her sake, he was glad she hadn't gone that far with him.

"It's been, like, four years," Macie blurted. "I just…dating is hard when you have anxiety, and sex seems even harder. So I just stopped doing both. I had my vibrator, so…" She cut herself off with a groan and brought a hand up to her face. "Oh crud. Pretend I didn't say that."

Loving the thought of her pleasuring herself, but not wanting to embarrass her, Colt let that go. "Are you worried about us?" he asked. "Because we can wait. We don't have to do anything other than what we've already done. The last thing I want is to be the source of your anxiety. Ever."

Macie immediately shook her head. "No!" she practically shouted, then her cheeks got even redder. "I mean, no, it's not like that with you. This feels right. Good. I don't want to stop."

"I don't want to stop either," Colt reassured her. "But if at any time you need to slow down or take a break, let me know. I won't be upset and I won't be mad."

"I won't. But okay."

He grinned at her and tightened his hands on her hips again. "Now…where were we?"

"You were about to take me into the other room and make love to me," Macie said with a smile.

And with that, Colt helped Macie off his lap and stood. Then he leaned over and picked her up with an arm behind her back and one under her knees, just like he'd carried her through the parking lot at her apartment complex. He entered the bedroom and put her down on the king-size bed—and just stared at her for a long moment.

"What?"

"You're beautiful," he said reverently.

She shook her head.

"You are," Colt insisted. "Your hair is a beautiful shade of brown that reminds me of a thoroughbred. Your eyes are a deep mahogany that hold so many secrets, they make me want to know every single one. You're the perfect height for me…not too short or too tall."

"I'm too fat."

"No," he countered. "You're perfect. Trust me."

Macie bit her lip and nodded.

Colt could tell she didn't really believe him, but he had plenty of time to make sure she knew he was being one hundred percent honest. For now, he would distract her with pleasure.

He reached down and pulled his shirt up and over his head, loving how Macie's eyes didn't leave his body. Wanting to make her feel comfortable, he undid the button and zipper on his jeans and slowly shoved them down his legs. His socks came off next, and then he was standing in front of her with nothing on but his underwear. Briefs that in no way hid his desire for her. He could feel his dick pulsing with desire for the woman in front of him.

"Your turn," he said quietly, not making a move toward her.

Macie looked up at him and, without breaking eye contact, undid the buttons of her light blue blouse one by one. He looked down when she shook off her shirt and stared at the beauty she'd unveiled for him.

Her tits were still encased in her bra, but his mouth practically watered with the need to suck on them. The bra was a lacy thing that showcased her chest rather than hiding it. With every heaving breath she took, her tits looked as if they were going to pop right out and spill over the cups.

Colt watched as her hands quickly unbuttoned her jeans and she lifted her hips to push them down. She kicked them off, and he barely noticed when they landed in a heap on the floor next to the bed. He was mesmerized by the sight of her.

Her legs seemed to be miles long, but he couldn't take his eyes away from the slight scrap of lace between her thighs. He could practically smell her arousal, and it increased his own tenfold.

He took a step toward the bed and thanked his lucky stars that she was his. And not just for tonight, if he had anything to say about it. She was *his*. Forever.

Slowly, he put a knee on the mattress next to her, and she smiled even as she scooted over to give him room on the giant mattress. Colt didn't hesitate; he moved one knee over her body until he was straddling her and lowered himself. He put his weight on his elbows and sighed in ecstasy as they touched from hips to chest. His cock was hard between her legs, but he wouldn't hide his reaction from her.

"Hey," he said when they were face to face.

"Hey," she returned with a small smile.

He felt her hands move up his sides then rest on his naked back.

"You ready for this? For us?"

"I feel as if I've been waiting for this my entire life."

It was the perfect answer. Colt smiled and kissed her. They made out for several minutes, lazy, long sweeps of the tongue, playful and easy. Then the kiss changed. Became more urgent. He felt her hands clutch his back as her hips arched up into him.

He drew back from her mouth and moved down her body. He put his fingertips on the edge of the cups of her bra and looked up. "May I?"

Macie nodded eagerly.

Slowly and carefully, Colt pulled down her bra until her tits popped out. He inhaled deeply at the sight of her erect little nipples. She was plenty bountiful in the chest department, and something about seeing how turned on she was flicked a switch inside him.

He couldn't be gentle anymore.

He'd been trying so hard to be a considerate and easy lover so he didn't scare her in any way, but the second he saw the evidence of her arousal, he lost it.

His mouth descended on one nipple as if it held the elixir of life. Colt didn't lick and tease, either—he sucked her nipple hard, pushing it up to the roof of his mouth with his tongue as he did so. Reaching for her other nipple, he pinched it with his fingers, making it even harder.

She wiggled under him, arched her back to press deeper, and groaned. Loving how responsive she was, Colt continued his assault on her breasts. He couldn't get enough. He pushed them together and switched off, sucking on one nipple then the other.

"Take it off," he mumbled even as he devoured her.

"What?" she asked, dazed.

"Your bra. Take it off," he ordered.

"Oh!"

And with that, she arched her back even more—which Colt took advantage of—and reached under herself to unhook the contraption.

The second she was free, he palmed both breasts and squeezed. "Fuck, woman. Beautiful." Colt knew he wasn't speaking in full sentences, but that was beyond him at the moment.

It took several seconds for him to realize that Macie was attempting to push his underwear down his legs. He wanted to stop her. To tell her that he was on a hair trigger and if he took them off, he'd blow.

But then she looked up at him, her pupils dilated with lust, and said, "I want you inside me."

That did it. He couldn't deny her anything. He was a dead man. If she ever realized the power she held over him, he'd be in big trouble.

Colt rolled onto his back and shoved his underwear down his thighs, wincing as his cock sprang free in the process. He felt movement next to him and looked over at Macie. She'd done the same thing, and now lay naked as the day she was born next to him, smiling.

As quick as a flash, Colt resumed his position over her, this time his cock brushing against the curls between her legs.

"Fuck me," she repeated, lifting her hips in invitation.

Knowing he had no control, and wanting to make sure Macie was slick and ready for him, Colt eased himself down her body, kissing his way from her chest, to her tits, to her belly button and beyond.

Macie tugged at him. "Colt. Please!"

"I'm going to fuck you, Macie. Make no mistake. But first, I'm going to taste you. I'm going to make you come with my mouth and fingers. Then when you're exhausted and sated, I'm going to put my cock inside you and make love to you. You won't know where you end and I begin…and I'm going to make you come again. *Then*, when you're incoherent with pleasure, I'm going to fuck you. That work for you?"

Colt didn't know where the words were coming from. He'd never been a dirty talker. Preferred to just get down to business and get off. But he wanted to cherish every second of this first time with Macie. Wanted her to be as mindless with pleasure as he knew *he* would be.

"Uh…yeah, Colt. That works for me. I'll just lie here and let you…you know…do your thing."

"Thank you," he said with a smile. Fuck, she was adorable. Then he bent his head and did his thing.

* * * *

Macie shook as the orgasm tore through her. Colt had done exactly what he'd said he was going to do. He'd put his mouth on her and made her come. Oh, his fingers had been involved too, but mostly it was the way his tongue curled around her clit and the way he'd sucked the sensitive bundle of nerves that had thrown her over the edge.

She'd never really enjoyed oral sex, because she always worried about what she smelled like, what she tasted like, and if the guy was going to want her to reciprocate. But with Colt, she couldn't think about anything but how good he was making her feel.

And for the first time ever, she wanted to return the favor. She *wanted* to get her mouth on his cock. She'd caught a glimpse of his dick when he'd removed his underwear, and it was quite impressive.

Before she could reach for him, or let him know she wanted to touch him too, he was looming over her once more. She loved the feel of him on top of her. She felt surrounded by him, and it made her feel safe. Loved.

He knelt up and reached over to the table next to the bed and grabbed a condom. She watched him roll it down his length with greedy eyes. She'd been right. He *was* impressive. She must've made a noise in her throat, because his gaze came back to her, and he smiled.

"You want this?" he asked.

"Yes," she said bluntly.

He took hold of his dick with one hand and inched his knees up, spreading her legs wider. Macie looked down and saw the mushroom head of his cock pressing against her folds. She lifted her hips, welcoming him into her heat.

The sound of his groan as he slowly pressed into her hot, wet body was almost as satisfying as the feel of him inside her. Almost.

Closing her eyes at the sensation, Macie arched her spine and threw back her head. She gripped his biceps and sucked in a breath through her nose. He was big, and it had been a long time since she'd had a man.

As if he understood, Colt held completely still inside her, letting her get used to him. She heard him murmuring comforting words as her body relaxed.

"Better?" he asked softly.

Macie nodded.

He pulled out of her body all the way, then slowly pressed inside again, piercing her folds once more. Then he did it again. And again.

She'd never been made love to this way. In the past, the men had just hammered inside of her until they'd come.

But every time Colt pulled away, her hips followed, not wanting to lose him. Then he'd press his cock back inside and she'd feel whole again.

Reaching down, she gripped his ass and dug her nails into his sensitive skin when he left her body once more. "Colt," she griped.

"What?" he asked with a grin.

"Stay inside me," she ordered.

"You're more sensitive this way though, aren't you?" he asked.

Thinking about it, Macie nodded. "Yeah. All the nerve endings down there come to life every time you pull all the way out before pushing back in."

"Exactly," he muttered. "For me too. My cock is all happy and warm, then it's cold and sad, then it's happy and warm again."

Macie chuckled and Colt groaned. "Fuck, I can feel your muscles clenching around my dick when you laugh."

That made her laugh harder, and she wrapped her legs around his thighs, trying to hold him in place. "I thought you said you were going to make me come slow and easy?" she complained.

"You ready for that?" he asked. "I was giving you time to

recover."

"I'm recovered," she reassured him.

Instead of picking up his pace, Colt pressed all the way inside her, then sat up, pulling her ass onto his thighs. Her pelvis was tilted upward and she was resting on her shoulder blades. She was about to ask what he was doing—when his thumb landed on her clit and began stroking, slow and easy.

Squirming, wanting more but somehow less, Macie gasped. "What are you doing?"

"Making love to you. Making you come on my cock."

The movement of his thumb was relentless. No matter how much she squirmed, she couldn't get away from it. His cock was full and hard inside her, and her body bore down on it as she got closer and closer to losing it.

"Damn, hon. You're squeezing me *so* hard. It feels so fucking good. You need to come or I'll lose it."

She barely heard his words. Macie had always thought she needed a fast and hard touch on her clit to come, but Colt was proving her wrong. The orgasm built slowly but steadily until Macie knew she was about to tumble over. She spread her legs as wide as she could as her thighs began to tremble. Her stomach clenched and her toes curled.

"That's it, Mace. Come for me."

And she did.

She thought she might've blacked out for a moment because when she became aware of where she was again, her ass was back on the mattress and Colt was leaning over her once more. He was still inside her, as hard as ever.

"I'm going to fuck you now," he said roughly. "*Hard*. You ready?"

Macie nodded. She was ready for whatever he wanted to do with her. She was his. Completely.

His hips started moving, pressing his length in and out of her. Sweat beaded on his brow as he fought his body's reaction. "I'm not going to last," he informed her. "Watching you come, hearing my name on your lips, feeling your excitement on my thighs…it was too much. Does this feel okay?"

Macie nodded.

"Touch yourself," he ordered. "Make yourself come again."

"I can't," she protested, even as her hips rose to meet his thrusts.

"Try," he croaked. "*Please*. I want to feel you squeeze the come out of me."

Not able to deny him anything, Macie reached down between their bodies and brushed a finger over her swollen clit. She jerked in response. She was so sensitive still. Even though it hurt a little bit, she did as Colt asked. She wanted to please him. Wanted to force him over the edge with her.

It didn't take long. Within a minute Macie felt the telltale signs of her impending orgasm. "I'm close!" she warned.

"I know," he responded. "Do it! Fucking come."

It took another ten seconds or so, but she did. Just moments after she began trembling and shaking from the intense bliss, Colt threw his head back and shuddered. The muscles in his arms next to her shook with the pleasure he was experiencing and his chest heaved with his breaths. It was awe inspiring and hot as hell.

As if a plug had been pulled, Colt relaxed. He dropped down and rolled, taking Macie with him. She lay on top of him now, his dick slowly softening inside her. They didn't say anything for the longest time, not until he slid out of her.

Macie whimpered a protest; she'd liked how he'd felt. How they were connected.

"I know," he whispered. "I liked being in there too."

Macie knew he had to get up and take care of the condom. It had to be uncomfortable, now that they were done, but he didn't make any move to leave the bed.

"Every morning, I wake up in a momentary panic, thinking you'll have left in the middle of the night," Colt admitted softly.

Macie felt awful about that. "I'm sorry."

"Don't be. Just promise that you'll never again leave my bed without telling me. If you have to get up and pee in the middle of the night, fine, but if you can't sleep and are going to go read or work, wake me up and let me know. I can't handle waking up to you being gone, Mace. Not after tonight."

"I promise." It was an easy promise to make.

"I'll do the same. It's much more likely that I'll be the one leaving," he said. "We get called to the base in the middle of the night for missions sometimes, and I always need to go in and monitor my men, but I'll never leave without saying goodbye. That's my vow to you."

"Thank you." Macie couldn't say anything else through the lump in her throat.

Then Colt rolled them over once more and kissed her. It was a long, lazy kiss that felt comfortable and easy. She was exhausted from three orgasms and was on the verge of falling asleep when he pulled away.

He smiled down at her, then kissed her on the forehead. "Sleep, hon. I'll be right back after I take care of this condom."

Macie watched as Colt climbed out of the bed and walked butt-naked to the bathroom. He didn't seem the least concerned that he wasn't wearing any clothes. But why would he? For a forty-three-year-old man, he was in excellent shape. He didn't exactly have a six-pack anymore, but his muscles were clearly defined and his ass was to die for.

Smiling to herself, Macie closed her eyes. She soon felt the mattress depress, and Colt gathered her into his arms. He covered them with a blanket and kissed her temple. That was the last thing Macie remembered before falling into one of the best sleeps she'd had in a very long time.

Chapter Eight

"So you're telling us that you can't find her ex, and you can't track down the men he associates with, who were most likely the ones who broke into her apartment not once, but twice?"

Macie winced at the censure in Colt's tone. They'd driven to Lampasas to grab some more clothes from her apartment and had stopped at the police station to talk to the detective.

"It's not as easy as the shows on television make it look," the man tried to defend himself.

Colt and the detective went into stare-down mode, and Macie shifted uncomfortably. She hated being the cause of this conflict. She didn't really know the detective, but he'd been trying to find Teddy for almost a month.

It was hard to believe an entire month had passed since she'd called her brother needing help. One month since she'd moved in with Colt. The happiest month of her life.

Oh, there were plenty of times when her anxiety overwhelmed her, but somehow, with Colt by her side, things seemed easier. Less stressful. When she went to the grocery store, she worried less if people were staring at her. She went out to eat more because she could sit next to Colt, and if there was something wrong with the food or the service, he dealt with it. And when she'd had a major anxiety attack after one of her clients hated the website she'd spent days designing, Colt had been there to rub her back and reassure her that her entire career wasn't over.

It was nice having someone in her corner.

No, it was more than nice. It was a miracle.

And Macie was scared to death, every day, that she would do or say something to screw things up between them, and then she'd be alone once more. She'd have to move back to her apartment here in Lampasas and worry that the men who'd broken in hadn't been caught yet.

After staring at the detective for a full minute, Colt finally said, "You have my contact information if you find them."

"I'll be in touch with Mercedes, as it's her case," the detective said firmly.

Macie saw Colt's jaw tighten.

She *hated* confrontation. It was one of the things that could easily throw her into a full-blown anxiety attack. "Thank you," she blurted, tugging on Colt's arm. "I would appreciate that. I'm sure you're doing everything you can to find them."

Colt's mouth opened as if he wanted to say something, but after looking at her, he obviously changed his mind. He nodded at the detective, wrapped an arm around her waist and steered her toward the exit.

The second they were out of earshot of the detective, he leaned down and asked, "You okay?"

Macie nodded. She could feel her heart beating way too fast, but she took a few deep breaths to try to control it.

Colt held open the door for her, and his palm at the small of her back felt nice. Comforting. His touch reminded her of how they'd made love the night before. She'd been on her knees in his bed and he'd taken her from behind. His hand had caressed the small of her back, just as he was doing now.

Just the thought of Colt making love to her was enough to help snap Macie out of her downward spiral. He was an amazingly generous lover, always making sure she got just as much pleasure out of their joining as he did.

After Colt had gotten her settled in his Wrangler and climbed into the driver's side, he turned to look at her. "I'm going to see what my team can do to find this guy."

Macie blinked. She'd been lost in her thoughts about Colt and her, naked in bed together, and his mind was obviously in a completely different place than hers.

"You're going to get Ford and his friends involved?" She wasn't sure she wanted that. Macie had no doubt her brother could probably track down Teddy, but she wasn't sure he'd be able to keep his shit together long enough to find out any information from him. Ford was *pissed.* Extremely pissed that Teddy had obviously targeted her as an easy mark. As someone he could use to hide his drugs, or whatever it was he'd stashed in her apartment.

"No, not Truck. He'd lose his shit and do something stupid, which could hurt his career. I'm talking about the other Delta team I command."

Macie nodded in understanding. She hadn't met the men he was referring to, but she knew of them.

"Because Trigger and his crew don't have any connection to you, it will be easier for them to look into this. I'll talk to him tonight. Ask him to have Brain see what he can find."

"Why Brain?" Macie asked.

"Because Brain is a sneaky son of a bitch and is smarter than anyone I've ever met in my life. The man could have been a brain surgeon or a nuclear physicist, but he chose to enlist in the Army instead. He'll be able to use technology the cops don't have to see if Teddy is even still in the area, and then the others can use his intel to track him down."

Macie bit her lip and stared at Colt.

"What?" he asked, reaching out and caressing her lip with his thumb.

"I…I don't want anyone to get in trouble. Least of all you and your men. Maybe, if no one has been back to my apartment since that second break-in and the detective can't find Teddy, he left town."

"Maybe," Colt agreed. "But I'm not taking the chance that he isn't just lying low, waiting for the perfect time to strike against you. We still don't know what it was he was looking for. Maybe those thugs *did* find whatever it was when they searched your apartment that second time, but we don't know for sure. And until I'm one hundred percent certain you're safe, I'm not taking any chances."

Macie's chest felt tight, but this time it wasn't because she was on the verge of panicking. No one in her entire life had ever gone to as much trouble to look after her as Colt. Sure, Ford had done his best to take care of her when they were kids, but this was different. And strangely enough, knowing what Colt had done to get to his friend

Gris, how violently he'd defended him, made her feel confident in his ability to keep her safe.

"Maybe we should go back to my apartment and look through everything again?" Macie suggested.

Colt shook his head. "No. Not today. You've had enough, and if we didn't find anything the first time we looked, then we probably won't find anything the second time."

"Do you think Teddy knows where I've been staying?" Macie asked quietly. She'd been worried about it for a while, which was why she was more than content to stay in the house when Colt went to work every day. He had a security system, and it was easier on her psyche.

Colt looked at her for a long moment before finally nodding. "Yeah, hon. I think it's possible. If he's smart—and I think he is, because he's managed to elude the cops for this long—he probably had someone watching your apartment, and when Truck and the others showed up to get more of your stuff or to check things out, he could've had them follow us back to Killeen."

Macie bit her lip again. Then asked, "Am I putting you in danger?"

With that, Colt leaned over and put his hand on the back of her neck and pulled her closer to him. Macie braced her hand on the console between them but didn't try to pull away from him. "I can handle that punk Teddy. Brain got his rap sheet for me, and believe me, he doesn't scare me."

"But—"

"No buts," Colt said firmly, interrupting her before she could even start to protest. He kissed her briefly, then pulled back to look her in the eyes. "I like having you in my house. In my bed. I like seeing your computer and files on my dining room table. I just plain like *you*, Macie. This isn't a hardship for me. If I had my way, you'd stay even after this is over. So if you think I'm gonna let a punk like Theodore Dorentes hurt you, you're crazy."

She liked everything he'd just said, but one thing stood out. "You want me to stay?"

"Yeah, Mace. I want you to stay," he confirmed.

She *should* tell him he was insane. That she had way too many issues to be a good bet. That he'd helped her feel more normal recently, but her anxiety would always be an issue. That as a colonel, he needed a partner who was outgoing and social, which would never be her. That she always second-guessed people's motives for doing anything.

But she kept quiet. She wanted Colt more than she'd ever wanted anything in her life, and if he didn't understand how fucked-up she was, then she wasn't going to tell him.

"I like you just the way you are," he added after a moment, as if he could see what she was thinking. "There will always be people who misunderstand us, but as long as we're good with who we are together, then fuck them."

She wished she was as confident as Colt, but she gave him a small nod anyway. He leaned forward and kissed her again. "You ready to go home?"

Home. Yeah, she could totally get used to that. "Yes," she said simply.

Even though it had been a weird day, and Macie should be stuck in her head and dealing with her insecurities, she wasn't. She smiled all the way back to Killeen.

* * * *

Colt sat in his office with his hands steepled under his chin as he looked across the desk at the seven men on the second Delta Force team he commanded. He'd asked to speak to Trigger, and told him why, and the next thing he knew, the entire team was there.

"All due respect," Grover had told him, "but if someone is threatening our commander's woman, it's *all* of our concern, not just Trigger's."

Colt couldn't get upset with the men for that. Besides, the more people he had looking out for Macie, the better, in his opinion. So he'd outlined what had happened at her apartment complex and who Teddy was. He explained that Macie was staying at his house, and hopefully would be moving in with him permanently, if he could convince her. He told his men about the Lampasas police not being able to find Teddy or the men who'd broken into Macie's apartment, and he finally touched on the anxiety that Macie fought on a daily basis.

Like the good men he knew they were, not one of the guys in front of him looked discomfited with that last revelation. In fact, Trigger asked, "That's what happened at the reception, isn't it?"

"Yeah," Colt said.

Lefty nodded. "Brain noticed that she didn't look well and was going to deal with it when you beat him to it."

Colt turned his attention to Brain and eyed the younger man.

Brain smiled and held up his hands in a conciliatory gesture. "I knew she was Truck's sister and just wanted to make sure she was okay. That's all."

Colt nodded and tried to calm down. Brain wasn't going to hit on Macie. He was being polite, that's all.

"Yeah," he said, answering Trigger's question. "The wedding and reception were hard for her. Social situations generally are, so I took her home and made sure she was all right."

The men all nodded. "So what's the plan?" Oz asked.

"Brain, I'd like you to see what you can do to find Teddy. Figure out where he likes to hang out, who his dealer is, and who his friends are.

"Doc and Grover, if you can watch her apartment when you can, and see if you notice anyone lurking around, I'd appreciate it. We don't know who the assholes were who broke in and threatened Macie, and I don't like that they're still out there somewhere. Lucky and Oz, I'd appreciate you doing surveillance of my neighborhood. There's no evidence that Teddy or his friends have been to Killeen, but I don't want to take any chances. We don't know what it was that Teddy was looking for, so he might decide to try to get to Macie directly."

"And us, sir?" Trigger asked, referring to himself and Lefty.

"I want you to come over after we leave here and let me introduce you to her."

"Sir?" Lefty asked.

"I told you that she suffers from anxiety. She eventually needs to meet all of you. Needs to get comfortable with you. She's already comfortable with Truck and his team, mostly because of the fact he's her brother. But I want her to get to know all of you, as well. If I have my way, she's going to be around for a hell of a long time, and the last thing I want is for her to feel anxious about seeing any of you. I'm going to need your help in social situations to keep her calm. I won't be able to be by her side at all times, and if she knows you reprobates, then we can both relax."

"Done," Trigger said immediately.

"It's not like I have plans," Lefty added. "I'd love to get to know her."

"What about the rest of us?" Grover smirked. "I want to meet the woman who has our commander wrapped around her finger."

Colt stood and leaned over his desk and glared at his soldier. "Damn straight, she does," he said in a low tone. "And I'll do whatever it takes to protect her. Remember that, soldier."

Grover immediately nodded. "Of course, sir. I didn't mean anything by that."

Colt tried to get his temper under control. He knew Grover didn't mean to be disrespectful, but his comment still rubbed him the wrong way. "She's smart as all get out," he told his men. "Beautiful. Resourceful. And she's been through hell in her life. She's sensitive about the things people say. She assumes they're talking about her, even if they aren't. Watch what comes out of your mouth, and be respectful at all times. Got it?"

A chorus of "Yes, sir" rang out in the room.

"Good," Colt said with a nod. "If you have any concerns, anything at all, you call me first and the cops second. I don't expect you to protect her with your life, that's going a bit far, but I do expect that you'll look after her as you would each others' women."

"Sir," Trigger said, "you don't need to tell us that. We may not have wives like everyone on Ghost's team does, but that doesn't mean we don't respect their women, and even want our own at some point. It's obvious that Macie is important to you, and therefore she's important to us too. She's as much a part of this team as you are. You can count on us to do whatever it takes to make sure she's safe."

Colt relaxed even further. He hadn't realized he wanted and needed their support so much. "Thank you. Dismissed."

The team headed out of his office and Colt took a deep breath.

He had a bad feeling about the entire situation. Too much time had passed since Macie's apartment had been broken into. Men like her ex didn't have a lot of patience…so why hadn't he made a move before now? Every day that went by was another day that his anger could fester and grow. The situation made Colt uneasy, and if he could, he would bring Macie to work with him every day, just to make sure she was safe.

The only thing making him not lose his mind was the knowledge that Macie wasn't the kind of woman to take risks. That was one of the one million and two things he loved about her. He dealt with enough risks and danger at his job. Knowing she had no intentions of leaving his house when he was at work made him feel better about the situation.

He hadn't ordered her not to. Hadn't told her of his suspicions about her ex. She'd actually brought it up one night when they were lying in bed together, replete and relaxed after making love. She'd told him that she felt safer holed up in his house when he was at work because Teddy still hadn't been found. She volunteered to stay safely behind his locked doors during the day and only leave when he was with her.

He hated that she felt that way, but he hadn't argued with her. Hopefully, after they figured out where Teddy was and he was dealt with, he could work with her on feeling more confident about going out on her own.

Taking a deep breath, Colonel Robinson got back to work.

* * * *

Later that night, after he'd reassured himself that Macie was doing well, he told her that Trigger and Lefty would be stopping by. She looked unsure, but nodded.

"These are my men," Colt told her. "Do you think I'd let them into your life if I thought they would do or say anything that would cause you one iota of mental anguish?"

"Well, no, but…that doesn't mean I'm not nervous about meeting them."

"Hon, every single one of my men would do exactly what I did all those years ago if something were to happen to me. If I was captured by the Taliban, I know with a bone-deep conviction that they'd move heaven and Earth to free me…just as I'd do for them. But it's more than that. Just as your brother would do whatever it takes to keep you safe, I'd do the same for him. And for Mary. And for Ghost and Rayne, or Casey and Beatle…or any of them and their wives and children. The bond we have goes deeper than simply soldier and commander. It's because of what we do. How we rely on each other to have our backs in the most intense situations of our lives."

They were standing by the kitchen, and Colt reached out and pulled Macie into his embrace until they were touching from thighs to chest. One hand spanned her lower back and the other buried itself in the hair at her neck. He rested his forehead against hers and continued. "I love you, Macie. It's scary how much. Now that I've experienced life with you, I don't want it any other way. Now that I know how it feels to come home from work to you, I never want to come home to an empty house again. Now that I've been lucky enough to hold you in my arms every night for over a month, I can't go without it. And now that I've been inside you, felt you come on my cock, I can't imagine being intimate with another woman for as long as I live. You're *it* for me. I'm putty in your hands. My men know that—and they'll do whatever it takes to protect you because you're a part of me."

By this time, Macie was crying. She wasn't making a sound, but tears coursed down her cheeks.

"You do *not* have to be nervous about meeting Trigger or Lefty. Or Oz, Doc, Brain, Grover, or Lucky. They will treat you with respect. They will love you. They will be your brothers in every way that matters. They'll have your back and your side and your front. You can trust them to be there for you when you need them, no matter what that means. Eventually, when they find them, their women will be your friends too. I don't know what's in store for them, who they'll find to complete them, but I know those women are out there, waiting. And they'll love you just as much as I do. Want to know how I know that?"

She didn't answer verbally, but looked up at him with her beautiful brown eyes filled with tears and nodded.

"Because you're you," Colt said. "You're considerate, kind, compassionate, down-to-earth, and so damn likable it's hard for me to understand how you don't see it yourself."

"I love you too," she said softly, and Colt closed his eyes, overwhelmed with emotion. He knew how hard it was for her to say the words, and he swore right then and there to never take them for granted.

He opened his eyes again. "I'm the luckiest man in the world," he told her before using his thumbs to wipe away the tears on her cheeks. Then he leaned down and kissed her. It was a slow kiss that started out tender and sweet, but by the time he pulled back, his cock was hard and she was pressing herself into him eagerly.

"As much as I'd like to lift you onto the counter, pull down your jeans and bury my face in your delectable pussy, I don't have time. Trigger and Lefty will be here any minute."

"Rain check?" she asked with a small smile.

Colt grinned. "Fuck yeah. You want to go freshen up before they get here?"

She nodded, but didn't pull away from him. "Colt?"

"Yeah, hon?"

"I can't imagine my life without you in it either."

He couldn't stop himself from kissing her once more. After several moments, he forced himself to stop touching her, and he took a step back. "Upstairs with you, woman."

She giggled at him and nodded, turning and heading for the stairs.

Colt watched her every step of the way. He stood where he was long after she'd disappeared from view, wondering how in the world he'd gotten so lucky.

Chapter Nine

A week later, Macie sat at Colt's dining room table, working on her laptop. Over the last seven days, she'd not only met Trigger and Lefty, but the other men on Colt's second Delta Force team as well.

They reminded her of her brother in a lot of ways. They were funny and polite, but there was an edge to them that was a reminder they were also lethal.

Most of the men were around her age. They varied in height and physical characteristics, but every single one had an intense look that would have made her nervous if Colt hadn't been by her side. But by the time they'd left the house after their visits, she'd felt comfortable with each and every one of them. She could totally understand Colt's devotion to them, and the devotion they had to their commanding officer in return.

It was weird for Macie to think about Colt as a commander. To her, he was just Colt, but it was obvious that he garnered a great deal of respect from his men.

Hearing a noise from her computer that meant she had a new email, Macie opened the program and read over the panicked email from one of her former clients. Somehow, her website had reverted to data that had been on it two years ago and everything was now out of date.

"Shit," Macie muttered, and got to work trying to figure out what the issue was. After thirty minutes, she sat back in defeat. There had been an update to the platform the author was using, but no one had backed up the data on her website since Macie had done the work two years ago. Macie was pretty sure she could fix it, but the coding she'd done in the past was on an older backup drive at her apartment in Lampasas.

She fired off a note to the author, telling her that she was willing to work on the emergency issue and spelling out how much it would cost. Macie might not be good at face-to-face interactions with people, always worrying over what they thought or were saying about her, but one thing she'd learned over the years was that she couldn't beat around the bush when it came to money.

Her clients appreciated knowing upfront how much she charged, and Macie appreciated being paid in a timely manner.

The author immediately emailed back, accepting the price for Macie's help, but insisted that it had to be done as soon as possible. She couldn't wait because she had a new book coming out in a couple days. It was book three in a new series, and as the website stood now, the other two books in the series weren't on there. She had to have her site fixed.

It was a small disaster, and Macie couldn't blame the author for being frantic. She bit her thumbnail and considered her options. She could recode the website from scratch, but that would take forever and would cost the author considerably more. If she could get the work she'd already done from her apartment, there was a chance she could have the website fixed and up and running by tonight.

But the *last* thing she was going to do was drive over to Lampasas on her own. She wasn't an idiot. Not when neither Colt and his teams nor the police had found Teddy yet.

Macie felt her chest get tight as she thought through what she should do. She could tell the author she simply had to wait, but that wouldn't be good for her reputation. The author might turn around and bad-mouth her to others, and she could be blackballed in the profession. Macie knew Colt was busy today. He'd told her that he had meetings with other high-ranking officers on the Army post. They were setting up a new mission for Ford and his team, and the last thing Macie wanted to do was ask Colt to drop that for something that wasn't an emergency.

Well, it was an emergency for the author, but she didn't think that really counted when compared to making sure her brother was safe when he was sent out of the country on a top-secret mission.

Macie thought about Trigger and the others on his team. Trigger had made sure she understood that she could contact him at any time, and had added his contact information to her phone.

Biting her lip, Macie decided to wait for Colt to get home. He'd go with her to her apartment and get the drive she needed. She could just stay up late tonight, updating the website. It wouldn't be the first time she'd lost sleep because of work.

But then another email popped up from the author. She had a newsletter that was supposed to go out that evening, and it had a link to her website for people to preorder the new book, *and* her public relations woman was on vacation and couldn't update the email before it went out to literally tens of thousands of readers.

The pressure built in Macie's chest. She had to have that code today. As soon as possible.

Without thinking too hard about what she was doing, Macie picked up her phone and clicked on Trigger's name.

"Hello?"

"Hi. Uh…Trigger?"

"Macie? What's wrong? Are you all right? Where are you?"

"I'm fine," she reassured him quickly. "I'm at home…er…Colt's house. I…uh…something came up, and I know Colt is busy. Ford too. I wouldn't ask, but it's important." The words were stilted, but Macie was proud that she'd gotten them out at all.

"You're okay? You're not hurt?" Trigger asked.

"No. I'm fine." She heard him sigh in relief.

"Okay. So what's up? What can I do to help?"

"If you can't, I totally understand. I mean, you're probably at work and it's not like you can just leave whenever you want. Isn't that called going AWOL? Absent without leave? I don't want you to get in trouble—"

"Macie. What do you need?" Trigger asked, a hint of exasperation in his tone.

Macie closed her eyes and blurted it out. "I need something from my apartment. I don't want to go by myself, and Colt and Ford are busy. It won't take but two seconds for me to run in and grab it."

"What do you need? Can I pick something up for you on my way to Colt's house?" Trigger asked.

It was a nice thought, but unfortunately unhelpful. She quickly explained the situation, and finished with, "It'll save me hours of work and my client hundreds of dollars if I can get the drive and use what I've already done."

Trigger was quiet for so long, Macie wasn't sure he was still there. "Trigger?"

"I don't suppose you'll let me drive to Lampasas and pick it up for you?" he asked.

Macie sighed. "I would, but I honestly don't know where the drive is. I know I put a bunch of stuff in my front closet, but with the police being there and looking through things to try to find what had been disturbed, plus those men rifling through everything, it could be anywhere by now. I'm not sure you'd be able to find it, especially when I don't remember exactly where it should be in the first place."

"I'm on my way. Do *not* leave the house before I get there," Trigger ordered.

"Of course not."

"I'll be there in ten minutes or less." And with that, he hung up.

Macie sighed and clicked off her phone. She wasn't happy about needing to go to her apartment. The place gave her the creeps now, but she did need her old files.

Macie pushed back from the table and stood—then stilled as something occurred to her.

If she moved in with Colt permanently, she wouldn't have to worry about needing things that might still be at her apartment.

The second the thought crossed her mind, she realized just how much she wanted that.

Things between her and Colt had happened fast, but she couldn't deny there had been something between them at her brother's wedding. There was no way she would've stayed the night with him if she hadn't felt it. And she never would've gotten up the courage to leave him her number either. It didn't matter that he hadn't seen it; the fact that the spark had still been there a month later was enough for Macie to realize he was different from any man she'd met thus far.

Then her shoulders slumped.

She'd never bring it up with him. No way. She wasn't brave enough. She'd never force herself on him. She fought a constant war in her head that things weren't the way she imagined they were. And it would kill her if she brought up moving all her things into his house and Colt vetoed the idea.

Taking a deep breath, Macie did her best to stop her line of thinking before it went any further. She knew she wasn't the best bet when it came to a partner. She'd take more than she'd give. But Colt had said he loved her, and she'd said it back, and the Earth hadn't stopped moving.

She ran upstairs and changed into a pair of jeans and put on a bra before going back downstairs and tidying up her work area. Just when she was about to go crazy from waiting, she heard a knock. Checking the peephole and seeing it was Trigger, she opened the door. "I'm ready," she told him.

Trigger was good-looking. As far as she could tell he was a couple years older than her and even taller than Colt. He had dark hair and an intense look in his eyes that Macie figured someone would take one look at and back off. But, because of Colt's little speech the other night, Macie wasn't afraid of him. She wasn't particularly worried about what he thought of her either, mostly because of Colt, but also due to how friendly and open Trigger had been when she'd first met him.

"The faster we go, the faster we can get back," Trigger said.

Macie eyed him and asked, "Do you think it's too dangerous? I'll wait for Colt if you think it'll be safer. The last thing I want is to put you in danger."

"I can handle your ex," Trigger said with a hint of disgust in his voice. "And I didn't mean anything by that statement. I just know you're more comfortable here than in your own place. And it's hot as hell out here today."

Macie smiled. Texas always seemed to be hot, but today was oppressive even by Texas standards.

She set the alarm by punching the code into the box on the wall then shut and locked the door. She followed Trigger to his vehicle, a sleek black Porsche, and smiled when he opened her side of the car for her. When they were on their way, she asked about the sleek sports car.

Trigger shrugged a little self-consciously. "I'm single and have saved up a lot of money. Why not?"

"I like it," Macie reassured him. "Have you guys found out anything else about Teddy or who he had break in?"

Trigger sighed and ran a hand through his hair. "Not as much as we want. Brain has tracked down a few leads, and we've passed them on to the detective in charge of your case, but either Teddy is the luckiest son of a bitch alive, or he's gotten help from someone we've missed."

"I think it's probably the latter. I mean, I'm not that confident with people, but something about him made me put down my guard faster than I normally would. I have a feeling he's conned a lot of people."

"I know you're right," Trigger said. "And you shouldn't feel bad about dating him. Some people just have more charisma than others, and if he chose to use it to be an asshole, that's on him, not you."

Macie nodded, not completely convinced. The rest of the trip, she worried about why Teddy had singled her out. Did she look that gullible? She tried to remember when she'd first seen him in person, and couldn't. That said a lot about how she really felt about him.

She could remember the first time she saw Colt. It was in Ford's hospital room after he'd been injured at the holdup at Mary's bank. She'd felt the chemistry between them then, but it was at Ford's wedding when she really took notice of him. He was sitting near the front of the church in his dress blue Army uniform. He had a half smile on his face the entire time.

Macie remembered thinking that he looked like a man a woman could count on.

And she hadn't been wrong.

"We're here," Trigger said, snapping her out of the mini trance she'd been in. "I'm going to come around and open your door for you."

Macie nodded and watched as he unfolded himself from the low-slung sports car and strode around the front of the vehicle. He held out a hand to help her out and stayed right by her side as they walked up the stairs to her apartment.

It was the first time she'd been back in a few weeks. The apartment smelled a bit musty. Wrinkling her nose, she turned to smile at Trigger and say something about how it had smelled better when she lived there—but the words caught in her throat when she saw Teddy standing behind him with an evil smirk on his face.

Macie's mouth opened to warn Trigger, but Teddy had already reached out and pressed the prongs of a taser to his side.

The soldier's mouth opened in shock and he fell to the floor with a thump, jerking and moaning.

Chapter Ten

"Trigger!" Macie yelled, then backed up when Teddy calmly stepped over the writhing soldier on the floor.

"You've got something of mine, bitch, and I want it back," Teddy said with deadly intent.

Macie backed up as Teddy kept stalking forward.

"I don't!" she said, feeling the tell-tale signs of a full-blown anxiety attack coursing through her body.

"You do. Where's that stupid box of keepsakes you kept in your closet?" Teddy asked.

Macie blinked in surprise. *That's* where he'd hidden something? She hadn't even looked inside the beaten-up old shoebox because it was the last place she figured anyone would hide anything. It wasn't secure in the slightest, and only held silly, cheap mementoes of her life. Of course, now that she knew that's where Teddy had stashed whatever it was he so desperately wanted, it made sense.

She couldn't come up with an answer fast enough, and he reached forward and wrapped a strong hand around her throat and squeezed.

Macie's hands immediately reached up and tugged at his fingers, to no avail.

She looked into the face, which she had once thought was good-looking, now feeling complete terror. His blue eyes were narrowed in anger and the beard he used to keep trimmed neat was bushy and unkempt. She even saw what looked like food stuck in the hair.

She looked down at the arm she was clawing, still trying to get him to release her, and stared at the tattoo that now adorned it. He hadn't had any tattoos that she'd seen when they'd been dating, but the new ink terrified her. It was a black-and-white design of a naked woman, with her arms tied together in front of her and a knife sticking out of her chest. Blood dripped from the knife, and the words, *Women are like weeds— to be exterminated*, were inked in cursive around the frightening image.

"Where. Is. It?" Teddy bit out, leaning into her and squeezing her neck harder.

Macie's mouth opened and shut, but she couldn't get any words out.

Obviously realizing he was preventing her from speaking, Teddy loosened his grip but didn't let go. "I'll kill you *and* your little friend right here and now if you don't speak up," he threatened.

"Not here," Macie said as soon as she was able. Tricking him didn't even cross her mind.

"You better not be fucking with me," he said.

"I'm not. I took it with me when I left."

"Fucking hell," Teddy swore. "Where is it?"

"Killeen," Macie said. "You can take the keys to the house and go get it. I'll tell you exactly where it is."

"Oh no," Teddy sneered. "You're coming with me. The last thing I want is your fucking boyfriend to walk in on me in his house. You're my ticket to making sure I get what I want and get the hell out of there in one piece."

Macie didn't want to be his ticket to anything. She just wanted him to take his belongings back and get out of her life for good.

Just then, Trigger moaned on the floor next to them, and Teddy swore again.

He raised the taser he still held in his free hand and pressed it to Macie's side. "Nighty-night, bitch," he said, then Macie heard no more as the most intense pain she'd ever felt coursed through her body.

* * * *

Trigger lifted his head and tried to shake off the lethargy he felt. Then he tried to remember where he was and what had happened to him. Everything was confusing at first—until it all came back at once.

He tried to lurch to his feet, but only got as far as his knees before he had to brace himself on the floor and take a deep breath. "Son of a bitch," he swore, then reached into his pocket for his phone. Thankful it was still there, he swore again when he realized that his keys were missing.

He crawled over to the nearest chair and hauled himself into it before clicking on his commander's number in his contacts.

"Commander Robinson."

"He's got Macie," Trigger said, not prevaricating.

"What? Where are you, Trigger?"

"Lampasas. Macie called me because she knew you were busy and she needed a file from her apartment. I didn't see anything to be concerned about when we got here, but her ex ambushed me from behind. Tased me. Just woke up. She's gone. As are my keys."

"You need an ambulance?" the commander asked, and Trigger shook his head in amazement. The man had just learned his woman had been taken, and yet he was still concerned about *him*. "No, sir. I was incapacitated, but I heard her say something about a box with memorabilia in it."

"That's at my house," the commander said. "Call Lefty. He'll come pick you up. I'm taking the others with me. How long?"

Trigger knew exactly what he meant. He looked at his watch. "I'd estimate between twenty and twenty-five minutes."

"Roger."

And then the phone went silent, and Trigger knew his commander was on the move. He sent up a silent prayer that Macie would be able to keep things together and stay smart until her man could get to her.

Because there was no doubt that Colonel Colton Robinson would get to Macie. And the shape he found her in would determine if Teddy was a dead man or not.

* * * *

Colt clicked off the phone with Oz, one of the Deltas under his command, and knocked on the window of a conference room. He made a hand gesture, and the seven men inside immediately pushed their chairs back and hurried for the door.

Colt didn't bother to wait for them. They caught up, and he informed them of what was happening while on the move.

Oz would call the others and have them meet at Colt's house.

There wasn't time for them all to gather and come up with a plan. They'd have to wing it.

Within two minutes, Colt was climbing into his Wrangler, and Truck, Ghost, and Fletch had jumped in as well. He was only half-listening as Ghost discussed strategy and who was going to set up a perimeter around the house to make sure Teddy didn't escape once they made entry.

The only thing he could think about was Macie. If one hair on her head was hurt, there'd be hell to pay.

"So he put whatever it was in a box of keepsakes?" Fletch asked.

"I guess. It's a battered old shoebox. Mace told me she kept mementoes of her and Truck in there."

"I'll fucking kill him," Truck said, and Colt knew he needed to get a handle on his men.

"If anyone is killing him, it's *me*. Hear me?"

He heard two "Yes, sirs," and glanced over at Truck.

"Laughlin?"

"No disrespect, sir, but this is my sister."

"And it's the woman I love," Colt retorted. "I need you to keep your head in the game, because *I* can't. I need you to have my back," he told the much larger man. "If I end up in jail, your sister will be alone, and she'll blame herself."

"She won't be alone," Truck countered. "She'll have me, and the rest of us."

Colt didn't respond with words, merely glared at his soldier.

Finally, Truck relented. "I understand, sir. And I've got your back. We all do."

Colt nodded. It was as good a plan as they were going to have by the time they turned onto his street. There was no more time to talk.

Trigger's Porsche was sitting in his driveway, and every muscle in Colt's body went on red-alert. They couldn't have been at his house very long, but Macie spending even one minute alone with her asshole ex was too long.

Colt stopped his Jeep two houses down and all four men climbed out without a word. He heard a noise behind him, and turned to see three more cars stop and the rest of his men exit the vehicles. Ghost quickly made contact, and most of the men disappeared into the neighborhood. Colt knew they were taking up positions around his house, making sure Teddy—and, God forbid, anyone else with him—

didn't manage to escape.

That left him with Truck and Ghost. Colt looked at his men…and felt an odd calmness settle over his body. Teddy had made the decision to put his hands on Colt's woman and he'd pay the price.

Colt led the way toward his front door. He knew Macie used the security code, and since he hadn't gotten a phone call wanting his passcode, he assumed she'd correctly put in the code when she'd let Teddy inside the house. He very slowly turned the knob on his front door and held his breath as he pushed it open. When the security system didn't immediately start beeping, warning him to put in the code, he thought, *good girl.* Macie hadn't set off the alarm when she'd entered, which would have alerted Colt, but she also hadn't reset it, allowing him and his men to enter undetected.

Colt didn't have a weapon, but he didn't need one. *He* was a weapon. A deadly one.

At first, he didn't hear anyone in the house, and his heart sank with the thought that perhaps he was too late—but then he heard a man's voice coming from upstairs.

Slowly and silently, Colt made his way up the stairs. The farther he went, the clearer he could hear what Teddy was saying.

"You're so stupid! I can't believe you've kept this shit after all these years. What's this? A ticket stub? Fuck…ridiculous. And a napkin? Gross! What's this? A picture? What the fuck *is* this?"

"Don't, Teddy," Macie pleaded, the fear easy to hear in her voice.

"Is this a sonogram? Don't tell me you've got a kid stashed away somewhere?"

"No. *Please*, just give it to me."

"Do you want to know why I picked you?" Teddy asked, but he didn't wait for Macie to reply before he answered his own question. "Because you're *weak*. You're scared of your own shadow. I knew you'd be easy to manipulate, and I was right. But then you had to go and grow a backbone."

"You hid drugs in my apartment," Macie said, her voice shaking.

Colt gestured for Truck and Ghost to pass him and get to the other side of his bedroom door. They needed to make a coordinated entry if they were going to surprise Teddy and get between him and Macie.

"It's not my fault you don't have a shred of human decency in your bones. If you hadn't left me at that restaurant when I had that anxiety attack, I might still be dating you."

"Bitch!" Teddy said.

Then there was the sound of paper tearing, and Macie's anguished voice crying out, "No!"

"Now," Colt whispered—and as a unit, the three soldiers entered the room.

Colt had time to see Macie on her knees on the floor, in front of scattered pieces of paper and other odds and ends.

Theodore Dorentes saw them before Macie did, and he lunged for her with the taser he held in his hand.

Later, Colt mused that perhaps he would've reacted differently if the man had come after *him* with the taser…but he didn't. He targeted Macie, who wasn't even looking at him and couldn't protect herself.

Colt threw himself at Teddy. The prongs of the taser crackled in the oddly quiet room, but Colt didn't even feel them touch his chest. His arm was already moving toward the other man's face and even though the electricity moving through Colt's system jammed up his nerves, he threw his body weight behind his fist and managed to crash into Teddy with his body as he fell.

He felt Teddy's nose break under his fist, and his head snapped back with the power of the punch.

Both men landed in a heap just feet from Macie. In seconds, Ghost was pulling Teddy out from under Colt and kicking the taser away. Colt forced his body to move, thankful that, once his fist had hit Teddy's face, the man had dropped the device.

By the time Colt had regained his senses and turned to Macie, Truck had already wrapped her in his arms and turned his back, protecting his sister from whatever might happen next.

Colt crawled to the siblings and jerked at Truck's arm. Surprisingly, Truck let go of his sister and all but thrust her into Colt's arms. He felt Macie trembling, and assumed the same position Truck had, holding her in his arms and protecting her by turning his back to the room.

Within moments, the room was full of several pissed-off, hyped-up Special Forces soldiers, but all Colt could do was bury his face in Macie's hair and rock back and forth.

Eventually, he realized that instead of being hysterical, she was trying to calm *him*.

"I'm okay, Colt. You got here in time. I'm okay."

Taking a deep breath, Colt picked his head up and realized that he'd been crying, and he hadn't even noticed. Macie shifted in his embrace and wiped the tears from his cheeks. "I'm fine," she whispered.

"He's dead," Ghost said matter-of-factly.

"Dead?" Macie gasped.

It was the tone of her voice that snapped Colt out of the daze he'd been in. He stood and helped Macie to her feet as well. Then he pressed her cheek to his chest and turned to look at Teddy and Ghost.

The man was lying on the floor, his eyes open and staring unseeingly up at the ceiling.

"If I had to guess, I'd say you severed an artery in his brain. The force of his head twisting probably broke the artery, then him hitting the ground didn't help any. He's definitely dead," Ghost confirmed.

"Fuck," Colt said under his breath. He hadn't meant to kill the man, just to keep him from hurting Macie.

"Self-defense," Lucky said definitively.

Colt turned to look at him. "It was, but I'm not sure anyone will believe me."

"They will when they see the video," Lucky said nonchalantly.

"Video?" Macie asked, her voice muffled from being pressed against Colt's chest.

"Never leave home without it," Lucky quipped. "Grabbed your ladder and was going to breach the window after you made your move. I caught it all on video. Commander, you were definitely protecting Macie from being further harmed."

Colt closed his eyes in relief.

He felt a hand on his shoulder and turned to look at Truck. "Owe you, sir. Huge."

Colt eyed the large man and pressed his luck while he could. "I want permission to ask your sister to marry me. Since her dad is an asshole, I've got no one to ask but you."

He heard Macie gasp and felt her tighten her arms around him, but Colt kept his gaze on Truck's.

The two men eyed each other for a long moment before Truck nodded. "One condition."

"Name it," Colt said.

"I want to be there to give her away. Don't care if you do a courthouse quickie, fly to Vegas, or have the full-blown shindig. I want to be there."

"Deal," Colt said without having to think about it. It wasn't even a concession, he'd already planned to ask Truck to be at their wedding, wherever and whenever it happened.

"Ma'am?" Grover said in his deep, rumbly voice.

Colt turned to see his soldier holding pieces of paper that had been torn.

Macie gasped and reached for it with a cry. She held the sonogram of her long-lost baby in her hands and sobbed.

Colt felt helpless. He didn't know what to do to make this better.

"Can I see it?" Brain asked.

Macie let the other man take the pieces from her.

"I think I can fix this," Brain said, once he'd examined the sonogram.

Colt glared at him, not wanting him to get Macie's hopes up.

"You can?" she asked.

"Well, I can't make it perfect, but I can scan the pieces, and put them back together on the computer and reprint it. It won't be like new, but it'll be pretty darn close," Brain said with confidence.

Colt could see Truck looking on with the saddest expression on his face as he realized what Brain was holding, and why his sister was so upset. It was obvious brother and sister needed to talk.

"I'd appreciate that," Macie said, her voice breaking.

"I've called the police," Ghost said, interrupting the moment. "I would advise that everyone but Truck, Macie, myself, the commander, and Lucky disappear. Lucky, we need you to stay since you have the video. Leave everything where it is. Evidence."

Colt knew he should be taking control instead of Ghost, but the only person he was concerned about at the moment was Macie. He picked her up and carried her out of the room and headed downstairs to await the cops.

* * * *

Two hours later, Macie felt as if her head was going to explode. She was sitting on Colt's lap on the couch, with his arms around her. Truck had gotten her a Vistaril tablet, but it hadn't helped the anxiety migraine that had begun the moment she'd woken up in Trigger's Porsche with Teddy driving.

She'd explained to the police at least three times everything she remembered. Teddy had bragged he'd killed the two thugs who'd broken into her apartment because they'd failed in their attempts at recovering her keepsake box. That was why the cops hadn't been able to find them.

Then she'd learned he'd stashed a small amount of drugs in her box, but that wasn't why he was so desperate to get his hands on it again. He'd also put a list of his suppliers in there. He knew if she found it and gave it to the cops, he was a dead man. His suppliers would kill him for being so careless. For someone as desperate as he was, he was also scarily patient. He'd waited weeks for Macie to show back up at her apartment so he could confront her himself and find out what she'd done with the shoebox. It was fairly obvious that he'd planned on killing her, just like he had his "friends," after he got the list back.

Macie was glad to find out Trigger was all right. Apparently, Teddy had beaten him after tasing him a second time, to try to ensure he was knocked out for a long while, giving Teddy time to get to Killeen and collect his list.

She made sure the officers interviewing her knew she believed Teddy when he'd said he was going to kill her. Colt had reassured her before the cops got there that he wouldn't be arrested. The "stand your ground" law that the state of Texas had meant that he didn't need to attempt to retreat on his own property before using deadly force to defend himself or Macie. Colt really had saved her life. Macie had no doubt about that and she also had no doubt Teddy would've tortured her before he'd killed her if he had the chance.

Thanks to Lucky, who apparently always seemed to be in the right place at the right time, and his video, the cops didn't arrest Colt. After checking his background and finding out what he did on the Army post, they'd warned him not to leave town and to be available for any questions they might have, but they didn't handcuff him and bring him to the station to be questioned.

Macie kept her eyes averted when the coroner came and wheeled Teddy's body out of the house. The entire situation seemed surreal to her.

Truck, Ghost, and Lucky had stayed the entire time the police questioned her and Colt. At one point, Truck disappeared upstairs and came back down with her shoebox. He carefully placed it next to her laptop on the dining room table and gave her a look, which Macie knew meant he would want to talk about its contents later.

Looking at her laptop, Macie winced.

"What is it? Are you in pain?" Colt asked.

"No. I mean, yes, but it's not that," Macie said. "I went to my apartment to get a file I needed to help an author with her website, but I never did get it, and she still needs help."

"I'm sure she'll understand," Truck said.

"No. She won't. You don't get it. These authors rely on me to get their work done. Yeah, she might feel bad about what happened, but that doesn't mean she still doesn't need her websites fixed."

"You can do it tomorrow," Colt said softly. "I'll have one of the guys go to your apartment and pack up all your stuff and bring it here. Then you won't have to worry what you have and don't have anymore."

Even though her head hurt, and she wanted nothing more to sit in a dark room and sleep, Macie turned to Colt. "Did you just ask me to move in with you?"

"No," he said. "I *told* you that you're moving in with me."

Macie snorted and closed her eyes. She put her head on his shoulder and sighed. "I'm too tired and my head hurts too much to argue with you right now."

She heard rustling, and she heard Truck and Lefty say their goodbyes to Colt. Then the room was silent, and still Macie didn't open her eyes.

"If you truly don't want to move in, I'm willing to compromise," Colt told her softly.

Finally feeling mellow because of the pill she'd taken, Macie said, "There's nothing I want more than to move in with you, Colt. I just can't help but wonder what everyone else will think. We haven't known each other that long."

"I don't care," Colt said after a moment. "And I don't care what anyone else thinks. I only care about what *you* think. If you honestly think it's too fast, then I'll back off and we can have sleepovers at each other's places. I want you to be comfortable with our relationship. But I'll tell you where I stand—I've already been looking at rings. I've asked your brother for permission to ask you to marry me. I've warned my superior officer that I might need some time off in the near future so I can go on my honeymoon…and I've been asking around to learn who's the best OBGYN in the area. I'm in this for the long haul, hon. I can't replace the daughter you lost, but I can do whatever it takes to give you more children."

"You want kids?" she asked incredulously.

"Honestly? I didn't before I met you. But now I can't stop thinking about what an amazing mother you'll be. I can almost picture your beautiful eyes and features on our children. If you don't mind me being an old fart by the time they get into high school, then I'm willing to give you as many children as you want."

Macie could feel her heart beating fast in her chest, but for once today it wasn't because of her anxiety. Oh, she was still nervous as hell about moving in with Colt, but she couldn't help but be excited about the prospect of spending the rest of her life with him.

"If you get thrown in prison will I get conjugal visits?" she teased.

Colt rolled his eyes. "Thanks to Lucky, I'm not going to prison. Are you… I didn't mean to kill him," Colt said, and Macie could hear the uneasiness in his tone. She hated that he was unsure about her reaction to what he'd done.

Forcing her eyes open, she sat up and straddled the man she loved. She stared him in the eyes and said clearly, "I know you didn't. And you did what you had to do. I feel safer with every day that passes because of you. I know that you'll be the most protective dad any kid could ever have, and that eases my mind."

He sighed in relief.

"But I'm always going to be a nervous wreck," Macie warned him. "And if we have kids, it'll probably get worse. I'm going to need you to balance that out with our children. The last thing I want is for them to learn to be afraid of the world like I am."

"You're not afraid of the world," Colt countered. "And I love you exactly the way you are. You make me feel needed. Sure, I could go out and find a woman who was sure of herself one hundred percent of the time and who could take care of herself and all fourteen of her kids, but that's not what I want. That's not *who* I want. I want you. Every gorgeous, beautiful inch of you. You're not flawed in my eyes, Macie. You're perfect, and I'll remind you every day of our lives if you let me."

"I'd love to move in with you," Macie told him quietly.

"Good. I'll call my men in the morning, and your stuff will be here by noon, and you can fix your author's website, and we can be back in bed trying to make a baby by dinner time."

Macie rolled her eyes and chuckled. He was pushing his luck, but she didn't call him on it. "I'm ready for a nap," she said instead.

Without a word, Colt stood, taking Macie with him. She wrapped her legs around his waist and felt his hands under her ass, holding her to him as he walked toward the stairs. He took her to the guest room and laid her on the queen-size bed.

When she started to ask, he put his finger over her lips. "Just for tonight. Tomorrow is soon enough to face any lingering demons in that room. Okay?"

"Okay," she said. Then, as an afterthought, she asked, "Is there a way out of this room…just in case?"

He smiled down at her and brushed her hair off her forehead and nodded toward the window. "I went out and bought rope ladders after you jumped out of your apartment window. There's one in every room on this floor."

"I love you," Macie said as she shut her eyes.

She felt Colt's lips on her forehead and heard him say, "I love you, too."

Epilogue

"Can I ask you something?" Macie said.

Colt chuckled and tightened his arm around his wife's waist. They were lying naked and replete in each others' arms. They were on their honeymoon in a fancy resort in the Caribbean. It had cost an arm and a leg to rent the room right on the water, but it had been worth every penny when he'd seen how relieved Macie had been.

At six months pregnant, he thought she was the most beautiful woman alive, but she wasn't quite ready to parade around the public beaches with her baby belly.

"I keep telling you that you don't ever have to ask me if it's okay to ask me anything. You can just ask," Colt told her, grinning.

She twirled her finger around one of his nipples, and Colt forced himself to pay attention to what she was saying instead of throwing her on her back and fucking her again.

Macie had gotten pregnant almost as soon as they'd begun trying. She'd been knocked up so quickly, he hadn't even officially asked her to marry him. He'd rectified that immediately, and the same night she'd said yes, he'd called Truck and told him to clear his schedule because as soon as they could get an appointment, they were getting married by a justice of the peace.

Colt knew without asking that Macie would hate a big wedding. She'd hate to have all those people staring at her and she'd worry herself to death over every little detail. So the small ceremony at the courthouse suited him just fine.

That didn't prevent the wives of the men under his command from throwing them a big-ass party. Colt had been relieved that Macie didn't seem to mind, and in fact had the time of her life that night.

"Mary told me about that one mission you went on, and you explained what happened…but I heard her talking with Casey later and she said something else about you."

Colt didn't even tense at the reminder of that day so long ago. Macie didn't love him any less as a result, and he'd finally come to terms with it himself. Gris and his family had shown up at their wedding party as a surprise. Truck had found out about the man and had called to invite him. It was so good to see his friend so happy and settled, it helped with any remaining guilt Colt felt about what had happened all those years ago.

"What'd she say, hon?" Colt asked.

"She was asking Casey if she should tell me about a time when you refused to allow one of the soldiers in your unit to leave when his baby was born."

Colt knew exactly what she was talking about. "Mary's right. I *did* do that."

"Why?"

Colt smiled. He loved that Macie didn't get huffy with him or tell him he was coldhearted. She always gave people the benefit of the doubt. It was one of the million and two things he loved about her.

"The soldier in question was married at the time, and the woman having his baby wasn't his wife. He had been cheating on his wife for months. My hands were tied. Under the Uniform Code of Military Justice, adultery is unacceptable conduct and a soldier can be demoted as a result. This guy wasn't legally separated, and he didn't give a shit who knew about this other woman. Not only that, but the other woman knew he was married, and apparently *she* didn't care either.

"I refused to let the soldier take leave because I knew he was going to lie to his wife about where he was going and why. Not only did I not let him go, I did my best to push for a court-martial as well."

"Wow. Did he get kicked out of the Army?" Macie asked, coming up on an elbow so she could look at his face.

Colt shook his head. "No. He was demoted to private, but he was allowed to stay. Those are the kinds of soldier I hate. They aren't in the armed forces to serve their country. I don't mind the men and women who join for college money, or because they need to support their family, or even because they have no idea what to do with their lives. But I hate the ones who're trying to milk every penny they can out of the government. They're often cowards or bullies, and are part of the reason why I jumped at the chance to command the Delta Force units here in Texas."

Macie put her head back down on his shoulder.

"Any more questions?"

She shook her head. "No. And for the record, I knew you had to have a good reason. It's just not in you to be an ass for the sake of being an ass."

Colt chuckled. "I can definitely be an ass," he told her. "Just ask your brother."

Macie shook her head. "No. That's different. You were doing so to help them become better soldiers."

"He told you stories then, huh?" Colt asked.

He felt Macie smile against him.

"Yeah. I heard some stuff," she agreed.

"You and Truck are good, right?"

Macie nodded. "Yeah. It was tough to talk to him, but I told him all about my baby and what our parents did. He was pissed, like you were, but he didn't judge me like I thought he would. It's good to have him back in my life," she admitted.

"I know he feels the same way," Colt reassured her.

They didn't say anything for a while, just listened to the sound of the waves on the beach outside the screen door of their room.

"I'm worried about Trigger and the others," she eventually said.

"Why?"

"Because they're lonely."

"What? Why do you think that?"

"I can just tell," Macie said.

"I'm sure when the time is right, the right woman will come along for each of them," Colt reassured his wife.

"But what if they're not looking for her? She could be right under their noses and they wouldn't even know it. They'd overlook her, then possibly be lonely for the rest of their lives."

Colt held back the chuckle that threatened. The hormones coursing through Macie's body were making her extra emotional about everything lately. He loved that she was worried about his men, but knew they'd laugh their asses off if they heard her assessment of their love lives. "They'll know her when they see her," he told her.

"Hmmm," she mumbled, obviously not convinced.

Making a mental note to warn Trigger that his wife was on a mission to see him and the rest of the men on his team happily settled down, Colt decided to get her attention off of them and back on him.

He shifted until he was braced over Macie and kissed his way down her body. He spent a lot of time kissing and caressing her beautiful baby belly, and muttering words of love to their daughter nestled within, then continued until he was between her legs.

"Again?" she mock complained.

"Again," Colt confirmed as he lowered his head. He knew Macie loved this, almost more than any other way he made love to her, and he was determined to make sure she *loved* every second of their honeymoon.

He'd do anything for his wife. Move heaven and Earth to make her happy and content. He might've saved her from her ex, but she'd more than paid that back to him tenfold. He was happier than he'd ever been in his life and had never looked forward to the future more than he did now.

Life was good. He held the proof in his hands.

* * * *

Trigger and the rest of his team *will* get their happy-ever-afters starting next year. Stay tuned for a new Delta Force Heroes series featuring the same kind of protective alpha men and strong women you've come to know and love.

In the meantime, if you haven't read about Truck and his team, you can start the series right now for free with Rescuing Rayne!

* * * *

Hopefully after reading Colt and Macie's story you'll want to read more about Truck, the commander, and the rest of the Delta Force team mentioned in the book. Be sure to download Rescuing Rayne. It's the first book in the Delta Force Heroes Series and is FREE on all platforms!

As a flight attendant, Rayne Jackson is used to cancellations, but she never dreamed her latest would lead to a whirlwind tour of

London with a handsome stranger…or a life-altering night in his bed. One evening is all the enigmatic man can give her, and Rayne greedily takes it, despite suspecting it will never be enough.

Heading home after another extreme mission, Keane "Ghost" Bryson hadn't planned to seduce someone during his layover, but Rayne is too sweet to resist. Being a Delta Force member means lying to protect his identity, which is unfortunate, considering Rayne seems made for Ghost, right down to the tattoo on her back. For the first time in his life, regret fills him as he slips away the following morning.

Both are shocked when, months later, they meet again—under the worst possible circumstances. Seems fate has given them a second chance…if they can survive the terrorist situation they're in. If Rayne can forgive Ghost his lies. And if Ghost can trust Rayne to be strong enough to endure the secrets and uncertainty that come with loving a Delta Force soldier.

* * * *

And if you enjoyed Rescuing Macie, you'll like *all* my books because I write much the same way in each of my series. Check out the first book in my new SEAL of Protection: Legacy Series, Securing Caite.

Caite McCallan is a Department of Defense admin working in Bahrain when a glitchy elevator, of all things, leads to an unexpected invitation to dinner by a gorgeous Navy SEAL. When he later stands her up, Caite's understandably upset…until she overhears a plot that confirms Rocco didn't blow her off. Instead, he and two fellow SEALs are in danger—and Caite is forced to put her career and her life on the line to save them.

Blake "Rocco" Wise never expected his routine mission to go sideways, but he was even more surprised to find himself and his teammates rescued by the adorably shy woman he met in a stalled elevator. Caite's selfless act saved his life, but when attempts on her own make it clear someone wants her gone, it's Rocco's turn to protect the brave, sweet, sexy woman. The longer he knows her, the more he wants her…but keeping Caite close could bring her nearer to the enemy than ever before.

* * * *

Also from 1001 Dark Nights and Susan Stoker, discover Securing Jane and Rescuing Sadie.

* * * *

Securing Jane
A SEAL of Protection: Legacy Series Novella
by Susan Stoker
Coming February 9, 2021

From *New York Times* and *USA Today* bestselling author Susan Stoker comes a new story in her SEAL of Protection: Legacy Series…

Over the years, Storm North has witnessed two teams of Navy SEALs under his command find true love. He doesn't expect the same for himself. He's too old. Too jaded. Too set in his ways. Until a woman who's been right in front of him for years manages to impress Storm in a way very few women—or men—ever have.

Jane Hamilton knows it's ridiculous to have a crush on the charismatic and handsome admiral. She's the divorced mother of a twenty-six-year-old daughter. Too old for crushes. Too old for a lot of things. There's no chance she'll ever catch the eye of a man like Storm North.

Until someone delivers a bomb to the base.

As the civilian contractor in charge of the mail room, Jane finds herself in the direct line of fire, enduring a series of events that leads to a budding relationship with the very man she's been longing for. She couldn't be happier, and Storm feels the same.

The only one unhappy, in fact, is the thwarted bomber. Unhappy enough to do something drastic. Now Storm and Jane have to work together to save innocent sailors—and themselves—from an explosive situation threatening their happily ever after.

***Securing Jane* is the 7th and final book in the *SEAL of Protection: Legacy* Series and a part of the 1001 Dark Nights collection. Each book is a stand-alone, with no cliffhanger endings.

About Susan Stoker

New York Times, USA Today, #1 Amazon Bestseller, and Wall Street Journal Bestselling Author, Susan Stoker has a heart as big as the state of Tennessee where she lives, but this all American girl has also spent the last eighteen years living in Missouri, California, Colorado, Indiana, and Texas. She's married to a retired Army man (and current firefighter/EMT) who now gets to follow her around the country.

She debuted her first series in 2014 and quickly followed that up with the SEAL of Protection Series, which solidified her love of writing and creating stories readers can get lost in.

Connect with her at www.StokerAces.com.

Also from Susan Stoker

Badge of Honor: Texas Heroes Series
Justice for Mackenzie
Justice for Mickie
Justice for Corrie
Justice for Laine
Shelter for Elizabeth
Justice for Boone
Shelter for Adeline
Shelter for Sophie
Justice for Erin
Justice for Milena
Shelter for Blythe
Justice for Hope
Shelter for Quinn
Shelter for Koren
Shelter for Penelope

Delta Force Heroes Series:
Rescuing Rayne
Assisting Aimee (loosely related to this series)
Rescuing Emily
Rescuing Harley
Marrying Emily
Rescuing Kassie
Rescuing Bryn
Rescuing Casey
Rescuing Sadie
Rescuing Wendy
Rescuing Mary
Rescuing Macie

Ace Security Series:
Claiming Grace
Claiming Alexis
Claiming Bailey
Claiming Felicity

Claiming Sarah

Mountain Mercenaries Series:
Defending Allye
Defending Chloe
Defending Morgan
Defending Harlow
Defending Everly
Defending Zara
Defending Raven

SEAL of Protection: Legacy Series:
Securing Caite
Securing Sidney
Securing Piper
Securing Zoey
Securing Avery (TBA)
Securing Kalee (TBA)

SEAL of Protection Series:
Protecting Caroline
Protecting Alabama
Protecting Alabama's Kids
Protecting Fiona
Marrying Caroline (novella)
Protecting Summer
Protecting Cheyenne
Protecting Jessyka
Protecting Julie (novella)
Protecting Melody
Protecting the Future
Protecting Alabama's Kids (novella)
Protecting Kiera (novella)
Protecting Dakota

Stand-Alone:
The Guardian Mist
Nature's Rift
A Princess for Cale

A Moment in Time
Lambert's Lady

Beyond Reality Series:
Outback Hearts
Flaming Hearts
Frozen Hearts

Writing as Annie George:
Stepbrother Virgin (erotic novella)

Discover More Susan Stoker

Rescuing Sadie: A Delta Force Heroes/Masters and Mercenaries Novella
by Susan Stoker

Sadie Jennings was used to being protected. As the niece of Sean Taggart, and the receptionist at McKay-Taggart Group, she was constantly surrounded by Alpha men more than capable, and willing, to lay down their life for her. But when she visits her friend in San Antonio, and acts on suspicious activity at Milena's workplace, Sadie puts both of them in the crosshairs of a madman. After several harrowing weeks, her friend is now safe, but for Sadie, the repercussions of her rash act linger on.

Chase Jackson, no stranger to dangerous situations as a captain in the US Army, has volunteered himself as Sadie's bodyguard. He fell head over heels for the beautiful woman the first time he laid eyes on her. With a Delta Force team at his back, he reassures the Taggart's that Sadie will be safe. But when the situation in San Antonio catches up with her, Chase has to use everything he's learned over his career to keep his promise...and to keep Sadie alive long enough to officially make her his.

Eli's Triumph
A Reapers MC Novella
By Joanna Wylde

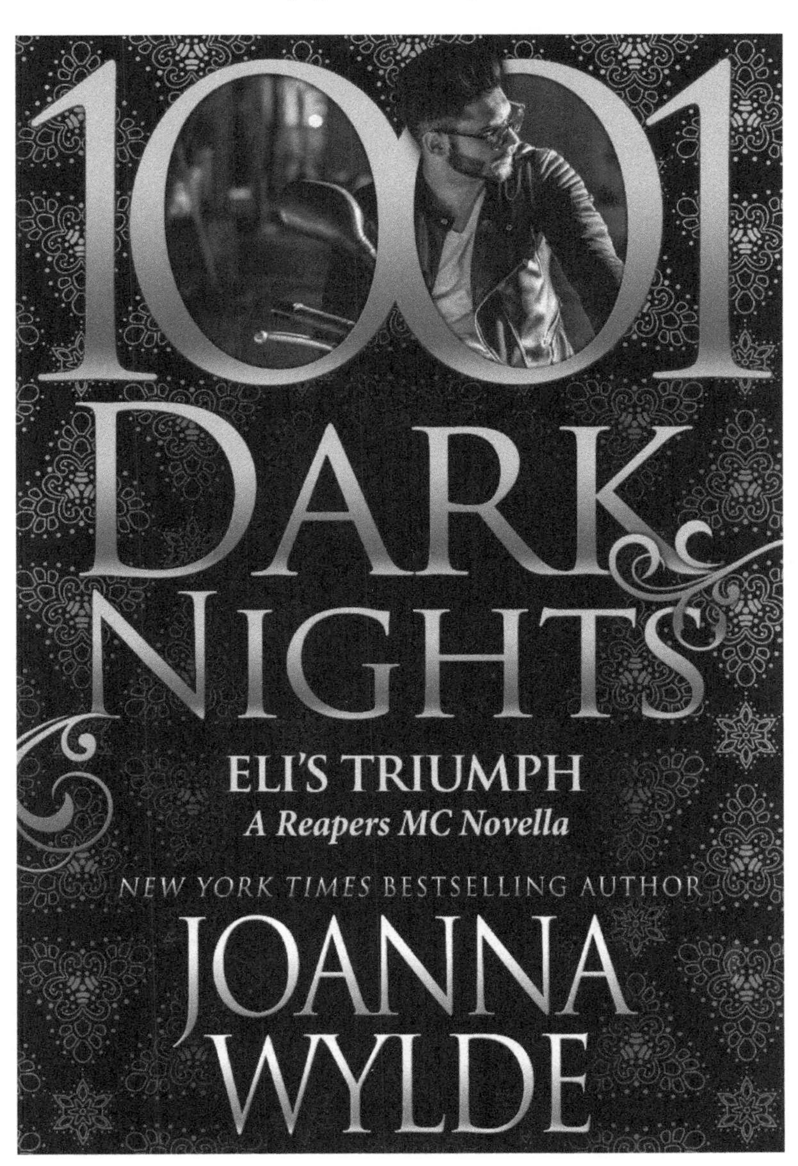

Dedication

For Liz Berry, Rebecca Zanetti, Margarita Coale, and Tina Gephart.

Acknowledgments from the Author

I'd like to thank Liz Berry and M.J. Rose for including me in 1001 Dark Nights, and for the grace and kindness they offered me during one of the most difficult years of my life. I'd also like to thank Kasi Alexander, Chelle Olson, Dylan Stockton and Kim Guidroz for the time and effort they put into producing this book. To say they went above and beyond is an understatement. It is appreciated.

Prologue

Hallies Falls
Washington State
24 years ago

~Peaches~

"Do you really think he can get away with it?" I asked, glancing toward Lemur. "I mean, I know he's evil enough…but I don't think Gus would let him, would he?"

The grubby little stuffed animal stared back at me, glass eyes cracked from hitting the floor too many times. His pink teacup sat on its saucer, untouched. He didn't say anything out loud, but I saw the answer in his face.

He didn't trust Eli King.

Neither did Eden, the doll sitting next to Lemur. She hadn't touched her tea, either, and who could blame her? Everything had been wrong since Eli moved in with us. Even our imaginary tea tasted wrong. Now it was nothing but water, and my special cakes were only chunks of bread.

My eyes slid toward the fourth place setting, set carefully on the old bandanna. The blue cup. That's where Gus was supposed to sit. It should be me, Lemur, Eden, and Gus.

Always.

But Gus was too busy to play with us today. He was working on his motorcycle, and he'd asked stupid Eli to help him. Sliding on my butt across the porch's battered boards, I peered through the railing to study the two of them.

They crouched in the driveway next to the bike—my giant, grumpy, snuggly Gus and a stinky boy who liked to think he was so much older than me, but he wasn't. Eli was only seven, and they were making him do first grade over again. Maybe he'd flunk this year, too. Then we'd be in the same class.

Gus poked at the engine with one of his tools. I couldn't see what kind because Eli was between me and him, which was pretty much where he always was.

Between me and Gus.

And if Lemur was right, Eli was doing it on purpose. Eden agreed… Sometimes, Lemur was wrong, but Eden? Eden was almost always right, and the two of them together had never been wrong before. There was only enough space for one kid in this house, and Eli was ruthless.

He'd already taken over half my bedroom.

My eyes narrowed as I considered his messy brown hair, hanging too long across the back of his neck. Maybe I could Superglue it to the bed while he was sleeping.

"Eli, go grab me a beer," Gus said, his deep voice rumbling across the yard. His bike rumbled like that, too. It needed a tune-up because the motorcycle club was doing something *very important* later this week.

Fixing the bike was worth canceling the tea party. I was okay with that. But when Gus needed a helper, he should've called me. I was the one who should be running toward the kitchen door to fetch a bottle.

"I've got to get rid of him," I whispered softly, trying to think of something. There had to be a way to make Eli go away. "I wonder if he's scared of spiders?"

My toys didn't answer. Turning around, I looked at them, biting my lip. I could tell that Lemur had an idea, but Eden seemed to be shaking her head at me. Her eyes had opened wider than usual, and I realized she was afraid.

She thought Eli might hurt her and Lemur.

My tummy flipped, and I felt sick.

I could see why Eden was afraid. Eli had already broken one of my teacups, and nobody but me knew that Eden and Lemur weren't just toys. They were *alive*. Not only living, but the best friends a girl could ever have.

Suddenly, this wasn't just about my room.

This was about protecting my best friends.

"Don't worry, I'll hide you," I told them, swallowing hard. "Before I do anything else, I'll hide you. And then I'll go find some spiders and put them in his bed. Or maybe a snake. I'll keep us safe from him. No matter what it takes, I'll get rid of Eli King. I promise."

Chapter One

Starkwood Saloon
Washington State
Present day

~Peaches~

"What do you think those bikers are talking about?" Megan asked, leaning next to me against the railing.

"Which ones?" I said, locking eyes with a man sitting across the room.

Eli King.

The only guy on Earth with the power to drive me absolutely crazy just by existing. Not the good kind of crazy, either. More of a plotting-vengeance-at-four-in-the-morning-because-you-can't-unhear-him-fucking-his-girlfriend-through-a-wall kind of crazy.

My nemesis sat enjoying a beer with three of the five Reapers who'd sauntered into the bar thirty minutes earlier. They'd taken over one of the far tables, settling in for the duration while the other two disappeared into the back with Gus.

Eli had abandoned his post to join them—apparently, club membership came before his job, which shouldn't have surprised me. His uncle always put the club first, too. That annoyed me, but what'd annoyed me more was the way Eli had asked for a beer when I took their order. Like I was his serving wench, and he wasn't the damned bartender who was supposed to be pouring those beers instead of drinking them.

Now, he leaned back in his chair, all relaxed and smug. Watching me. Probably pretending he was a king for real. *Maybe I should start a rumor that he needs to wear a plastic crown to get it up…*

Eli cocked a brow as I narrowed my eyes. Then he raised his bottle in salute as if to say, "*Hey, Peaches, having fun working while I sit on my ass drinking?*"

God, I loathed him. I hated his stupid long legs and his dumb arm muscles, and his hair. He'd gotten it cut, I realized. Had to have been that morning because it'd still been all shaggy last night. Definitely hadn't shaved, though. Just a hint of stubble around his chin… *Shit.*

Eli was being all sexy today, and that was the worst.

He lifted his bottle, flicking his tongue across his bottom lip right before taking a sip. I found my breath faltering because it reminded me of—

No. Not going there. *Never* going there. Didn't matter how attractive he was, didn't matter that Gus said he'd always seen us together. And it *really* didn't matter that Eli's ass looked absolutely fucking fantastic in a pair of faded jeans.

The man was a force of pure destruction, something I knew all too well, and the fact that he'd come back from prison even more pumped up and ripped than before, well…that was just God's sick joke on women everywhere. Under all those muscles, Eli was still the asshole who'd taken Lemur hostage when I was five.

The torment hadn't stopped there, either.

When I was sixteen, he'd beaten up my first boyfriend, Mark McDougal. Mark had dumped me after that. Said I wasn't worth getting an ass-kicking. Not even when I wore my black bikini. Just thinking about it made my jaw clench. *Ugh.*

I forced myself to take a nice, deep, refreshing yoga breath, repeating a peaceful mantra as I refused to notice how Eli's throat moved when he swallowed.

Inhale the goodness and love. Exhale the negativity and darkness.

He lowered the beer, still holding my eyes. Crap. He'd gotten into my head again, and he knew it. Not only that, he knew that I knew, which meant we weren't just catching each other's gaze across the room by accident. Nope. This was now the latest battle in our little war. My fingers tightened around the lemon I'd been slicing, sending juice squirting across the counter.

Yet another mess I'd have to clean up because of Gus's stupid nephew.

"The two guys in the office with Gus," Megan said, breaking through my thoughts. I hadn't even remembered she was standing next to me, let alone what we'd been talking about.

"What?" I asked, trying not to blink because Eli wasn't blinking.

"What do you think they're talking about?"

"Doesn't matter. You shouldn't be curious about them," I replied absently, my eyes starting to burn.

"Are you serious?" she asked, a hint of laughter in her voice. "That sounds a little dramatic."

I sighed. Megan had only been waiting tables at the Starkwood Saloon for a week. She didn't know the rules yet, so I'd have to educate her.

"They're part of the Reapers Motorcycle Club," I said. "And it's not a great idea to be asking questions about them. Doesn't matter what they're talking about because it's none of our business… Hey, does it seem like he's planning something to you? I don't trust that look on his face. That's the look he gets when he's up to something."

"Huh?"

"Eli," I said shortly. My eyes were seriously starting to hurt. Why wasn't he blinking? Was he even human? *Maybe he's half demon. Demons probably don't have to blink at all.*

"Eli?" she asked, sounding confused. "Why are we talking about Eli?"

"He's been watching me."

"Um, I think he's just drinking a beer," Megan said. "Maybe checking out your boobs a little, but that's nothing new."

Hmm… It couldn't possibly be that simple, but it did give me an idea. Maybe it was time to create a diversion. I shifted my shoulders, expanding my chest.

Disappointingly, his eyes stayed on mine.

"Someday I'm gonna own this bar, and firing his ass is the first thing I'll do."

Megan giggled. "That sounded sort of super-villain-ish. Do you have a lair? I wish I had a lair…"

I blinked, caught off guard. I hadn't realized that I'd said the words out loud. Eli smirked at me, gloating because he'd just won our little pissing contest. *Dammit!*

"I can't believe I wrote to him in prison," I told her, turning my back on the bikers. "Never should've been nice to him. He probably thinks that, deep down inside, we're friends or something. We're never going to be friends."

"Didn't he give you a ride home after work last night?" she asked, her voice light.

"Gus made him," I snapped.

"And did Gus make him hug you the other day?"

"He caught me and gave me a noogie. And it hurt, too. It's not a hug if it leaves bruises."

"He left bruises?" Megan asked, startled. *Shit.* I might be able to justify a rumor about him not being able to get it up, but telling her that he'd hurt me for real…yeah, that probably crossed a line.

"No," I admitted. "That was an exaggeration. But he's still pure evil, so don't fall for his shit. Or sleep with him. Every time a waitress sleeps with him, she ends up quitting without notice. Then I have to cover their shifts."

Megan nodded, looking a little uncomfortable. "Okay, then… Um, I think I'll go check the bathrooms. Make sure there's no ugly surprises before things start getting busy."

"Great idea," I told her, and she scuttled off. Then I reached for a washcloth because I had lemon juice to clean up. Then I'd have to go back over there and check on them. See if they wanted more… Eli would, I could already tell. Not because he was big on drinking, though.

He just wouldn't be able to resist an opportunity to order me around.

* * * *

~Eli~

"Looks like you gentlemen could use another round," Peaches said, her voice so sweet it hurt my teeth. She offered bright smiles to the brothers around the table. No smile for me, though.

Kinda surprising, actually.

Usually, the more pissed off she was, the sweeter her smiles got. Sweet and polite and so damned terrifying that I'd been afraid to sleep in the same room as her after Gus took me in. I liked to think that was because of the snakes she kept putting in my bed, but they weren't the only reason. Nope. The scariest part had been the way she'd glare at me through the darkness every night.

I spent a lot of time that first year wondering if Peaches would be strong enough to smother me with a pillow. You know, if I fell asleep before she did. Which never happened. Not once. Because I really didn't want to find out the answer.

At least I'd always held my own with the payback.

It'd probably been for the best when her mom and Gus broke up, all things considered. We might've killed each other for real if she hadn't moved out after second grade.

"I'd love another beer, gorgeous," Rollins said. He'd been the Bellingham sergeant-at-arms for more than a decade, and the man was one scary-ass motherfucker. But Peaches didn't seem too worried.

The girl had no sense of self-preservation.

I'd seen her go after a man my size with a bat during a bar fight just last month. It was shit like this that'd bothered me the most when I was locked up…knowing she was out in the world, unprotected, and there wasn't a damned thing I could do about it.

And Peaches needed protecting, no question. Instead of backing away from Rollins like a sensible woman, she giggled, then *accidentally* brushed against him as she leaned over to pick up his empty bottle. The move essentially flashed her tits for all the world to see, and I felt my smile stiffen. Fuckin' hated it when she did that.

Peaches knew this. That's why she did it.

Rollins shot me a look, then very deliberately checked her out. Mostly to piss me off—because he was an asshole—but also because he was a guy with a dick. And it was hard to blame him for appreciating a sight like that. The girl had an amazing rack. One I'd spent no small amount of time thinking about over the years.

High school had been hell for me and Gus both, although the reasons were different.

Peaches had started popping out of her shirts the summer before ninth grade. I could still remember my uncle telling me we needed to have a talk that August. He'd grabbed us a couple of beers, and we'd found a shady spot out back. Then he'd explained that it was my job to protect her from all the guys who'd be trying to get into her pants once they saw those new tits.

He'd also told me what'd happen if I touched her myself, starting with a casual comment about how many bodies were hidden out in the forest lands.

Bodies nobody would ever find.

Keeping her safe from the boys at school had been easy. Keeping my own hands off her was the hard part. Wasn't the only hard part, either. Most days, I'd jacked off two or three times thinking about that girl.

"I'd be thrilled to fetch you another drink," Peaches cooed at Rollins, all sunshine and flowers. "And it's good to see you again. How's Bella doing? I sure enjoyed meeting her last year."

Rollins' face softened. A chill touched my spine—the same one I'd felt in the darkness when Peaches and I had shared a room all those years ago. Guy like that shouldn't be so easy to manipulate, yet she'd just turned him from horny dick to whipped pussy with one question. "She's due any day now."

"I didn't know you had a baby on the way!" she squealed, and her eyes lit up. Jesus Christ, we were all fucked now. Peaches *loved* babies, and she never got tired of talking about them.

Some nights in prison, I'd have nightmares about another guy knocking her up. Other nights, I'd wake up shaking and covered in cold sweat because I'd flashed back to the time she'd suckered me into giving her a ride to a baby shower.

This was truly terrifying shit.

"I'm ready for another drink," I announced, cutting off the conversation before things got ugly.

Peaches turned on me, fury flashing in her eyes before she tamped it down. In an instant, her face was blank again. Still, it'd been enough to give away her new game.

She'd decided to give me the silent treatment.

"Draft this time," I added, wondering how long she'd be able to keep it up. Her smile reappeared, but I sensed the effort it took. Perfect. Time for another jab. "And try to pour it right so there's not too much head on it."

She stilled, her smile tightening. I could almost hear her arguing with herself. Would she stay quiet or go on the attack? Then her eyes narrowed.

Attack it was.

"Don't worry, I'd never give you head, Eli," she said sweetly.

Rollins snorted, and I blew her a kiss. Goddamn, but I loved pissing her off.

"Hey, Eli!" Gus called out across the room, his raspy voice disrupting the moment. He sounded older every day. Old and tired.

"Looks like they're ready for you," Rollins drawled, his laughter fading.

"Yup," I agreed, keeping it casual. Couldn't be one hundred percent sure what was about to happen, but I could make an educated guess.

If that guess was right, I'd spent half my life waiting for this moment.

Pushing back my chair, I stood, pausing to survey the room. The Starkwood Saloon hadn't changed much over the years, at least not on the surface. Menu had gotten better while I was gone, though, and profits were up. That was all thanks to Peaches.

It'd be a shame to fire her, but I'd do it if she couldn't show some respect once I was her boss. Still, I'd rather have her working under me. Or just under me in general. I swallowed… Yeah, this was gonna get complicated.

Gus slapped my back when I reached him, although I couldn't tell anything from his expression. Following his gaze, I realized he was watching Peaches as she collected the empties. Then she started walking toward the bar with her hips swinging. That's when it hit me again—the same feeling that'd made me break that teacup and steal that stuffed animal of hers all those years ago.

Got me every single fuckin' time.

"Hey, Peaches," I said, well aware I was playing with fire. Gorgeous, glorious fire. Totally worth the burn. She pretended she hadn't heard me, but she was listening. Time to push more buttons. "You know, you'd be a lot prettier if you smiled."

She didn't respond, but I saw her fingers whiten around the empty bottles. Satisfaction rolled through me, and my cock twitched. Then I pictured her glaring at me right before I bent her over the bar. That gave my cock a lot more than a twitch.

Yeah. Firing her would suck… And now I was thinking about sucking…

You gotta shut this shit down, I told myself firmly, which was just stupid. Shutting it down wasn't an option. Peaches Taylor had crawled under my skin when I was seven years old, and by now, I was addicted to the sensation. Sooner or later, I'd bend her over that bar for real.

Until then, I'd just have to get off by torturing her.

Seemed only fair, all things considered. I was a strong man. I'd had to fight for my club, and then fight to protect myself in prison. There weren't a lot of things on Earth that scared me…but every time I saw a snake, my heart about pounded right out of my chest. That's how much those fuckers freaked me out.

Peaches still owed me for those fucking snakes.

Chapter Two

~Eli~

Gage nodded as I walked into the office, pushing a battered folding chair toward me with his foot. He sat in one just like it, looking relaxed. That was a good sign. Rance had settled in behind Gus's desk, his face thoughtful.

"So, you know why we're here, right?" asked Gage, getting straight to the point. The question might've felt like a trap coming from someone else. But he was the president of my chapter of the Reapers MC, and I'd trust him with my life. *Had* trusted him with my life, actually. More than once.

"I'm thinking it's about the bar," I said, glancing toward Gus. The old man nodded, and a tension I hadn't even realized I'd been carrying lifted.

"Gus says he's ready to retire, and we need someone we can trust running the place," Gage continued.

That was an understatement. The Starkwood wasn't just a bar. It was a meeting place on some nights and a convenient alibi on others. Not to mention handy as hell for taking in dirty money and spitting it back out again, all shiny and clean. My new part to play wasn't a surprise, either. Gus had always planned on me taking over someday. I'd planned on it, too—until I got sent to prison.

The club had done their part, bringing in the best lawyer their money could buy. He'd ultimately gotten me out of prison on appeal, but that'd come down to luck. For all we'd known, I could've been stuck in that cell for the next two decades.

That's why they'd needed a backup plan—Peaches.

I knew Gus had talked to her last year about buying him out, and she was gonna be *pissed* when she learned that I was taking her place. Again.

"I'll give you a good deal," Gus told me, clearing his throat. "But it has to be reasonable, or it'll look suspicious."

"The money is covered," I reminded him. "Haven't touched it since I got out."

"Obviously, the club will throw in some resources, too," Rance added. "Just be aware that if you do this, there's no going back."

Somehow, I managed not to laugh out loud at that one. Wasn't a good idea to laugh at a club president—not unless he was joking on purpose. "All due respect, I already served five years for the club. Running a bar is nothing compared to that."

"And we appreciate it," Gage said. "We all know what you did. You were tested, and you didn't fail. We'll get the papers drawn up. Thanks for coming over, Rance."

"Anytime," the Bellingham president grunted. "And, Eli, I wasn't trying to question your commitment. Gage is right. We all know what you did for us. You know you've always got our support if you need it."

"Appreciated," I told him, savoring the moment. This was mine, now. All mine. Savage triumph hit as the full reality started to sink in. Today, the Starkwood Saloon was finally mine. Sure, I'd be working in a partnership with the Reapers, but I'd never expected anything else. Hell, I'd grown up in the club.

We all stood and slapped backs like it was any other day. Then Gage and Rance stepped out, leaving Gus and me alone in the office. I looked around the grubby room. It still held the same battered desk that'd been there when I was a child, although the old couch had been replaced at some point.

First time I'd ever gotten laid was on that couch.

"You could've given me a heads-up," I said finally, after a long pause. Gus shrugged, and I noticed that his shoulders seemed narrower. Less bulky. My uncle was getting old.

"Wasn't a done deal until today. There's a process for things like this. Gotta follow protocol."

I considered that, realizing he was right. And we still had one more step in that protocol. Not an official move, but an important one. Shit. Just thinking about it was enough to kill my mood.

"So…you gonna give her the news or should I do it?"

Gus sighed heavily. "My decision, my job to tell her. But I'm not ashamed to admit that I'm nervous. She might just torch the place."

The point was valid.

"Yeah, we should probably hide the matches."

"Peaches won't need matches," Gus said slowly, raising a hand to rub his temple. "She'll shoot fire straight out of her eyes. Her mom could do it, too. Never piss off a Taylor woman, Eli. They'll make you pay for the rest of your life."

"Too late."

Gus grunted, then nodded. "Can't argue with that. Do me a favor. If she kills me, make sure they never figure out what happened. It should look like an accident, not a murder. Understand? She's the closest thing I've got to a daughter." He shook his head slowly. "You know, if you'd claimed her ass when you got out, this wouldn't be such a big fucking deal."

"Have you *met* Peaches?" I asked, raising a brow. "It needs to be her idea. Otherwise, it's not happening."

A faint, bittersweet smile spread across my uncle's face. "Yeah, you're right about that. Her mom was the same way... I fucked that shit up, and I've regretted it every day since. Don't make the same mistake, you got me? She'll never forgive you."

"Oh, I'm aware. She still hasn't forgiven me for locking her in that closet. I was only twelve, for fuck's sake."

"You left her in there overnight."

"At least there wasn't a snake in there."

"Tell yourself whatever you have to, son," he replied, shaking his head. "Now, I'd best get this over with. Send her in, will you? Oh, and I was serious about covering things up if she murders me."

"I know. I'll go round up some bleach and a tarp while you tell her the news."

* * * *

~Peaches~

"Excuse me?" I asked, the words sharp and precise.

Gus wore the same calm, steady expression he always wore. Normal. Like he hadn't just smashed my world to pieces with one sentence.

"You heard me, sweetheart."

"No…" I said slowly. "Because it *sounded* like you just told me that you're selling the bar to Eli. And that can't be right. Because *I'm* buying the bar. We talked about it two years ago, remember? We even ran the numbers. We're supposed to do a contract for deed at the end of the year. That's only six months from now, Gus."

"Eli has cash," he said flatly. "With you, I'd have to carry a contract. I'll be dead before you pay it off, baby. He made the offer, and I accepted. The deal is done."

"What?" I asked, stunned. "Eli has *cash?* That's crazy. He doesn't even have his own apartment! He doesn't have a job history—nothing. There's no way."

"His dad died while he was in prison," Gus replied.

"He's never even met the guy. You're the one who raised him."

"True," Gus said. "The man was shit, no question. But he got killed by a drunk driver, and the driver's insurance offered a settlement. Eli was the only heir. It came in a lump sum, and it's been sitting in the bank ever since. That's a much better deal for me than a contract for deed."

"But we had a *deal,"* I insisted. "Eli has no clue how to run this place. He's only been back a few months, and half the time, he's fucking off with your club brothers. He spent the whole afternoon drinking instead of working!"

"Peaches, honey—"

"Don't *honey* me, Gus," I snapped, a wave of fury welling up deep within my chest. "You *promised* me this place. Said you could count on me to run it right. Or did I hallucinate all those conversations?"

"I can count on Eli to run it right, too," Gus said, holding my gaze. Funny how he managed to keep eye contact. You'd think it'd be logistically impossible, what with the giant-ass knife he'd just stabbed into my back. "You're damned good at your job, Peaches. I'm proud of everything you've accomplished here. But Eli is my blood, and he's part of my club. I know you don't want to hear this, but the only reason I talked to you about taking over was because I thought he was gone. He was always my first choice. Even if it wasn't for the cash."

His words made me see red. Literally. Flashes of crimson danced at the edges of my vision, and the air in the room seemed too thick for me to inhale at all, let alone catch my breath.

Motherfucking Eli King had done it again.

First, he'd stolen half my bedroom.

Then he'd stolen Gus.

Now, he was stealing the Starkwood right out from under me, and I could tell from the expression on my boss's face that he'd been telling the truth—this really had been his plan all along. Turning away from Gus, I ran my fingers through my hair, trying to think. *How could he do this to me?*

I wanted to kill Gus. No. I wanted to kill *Eli*. I wanted to kill him dead and then stomp on his body and set it on fire. Because no matter what I did, it would never be enough.

Eli *always* won.

"I'd like a few minutes alone," I said, forcing my voice to stay steady and even, despite the fact that I could feel screams of rage fighting to escape. I heard the creak of Gus's chair as he stood, and the sound of his feet as he came to stand behind me. He probably had that look on his face—the same one he always wore when I was sad. Soft and kind, as if he wanted to wrap me in his arms and protect me and keep me safe forever.

I'd trusted that look when I was a little girl. Believed it when I was a teenager, too, even after I'd learned the truth about why my mom had left him. And I'd trusted it two years ago when he'd first talked to me about buying the bar.

God, I was such an idiot.

"Gus just wasn't the man I wanted him to be." My mom's words echoed through my head. *"My only mistake was thinking I could change him, Peaches."*

Why the hell hadn't I listened to her?

"Doesn't feel right, leaving you like this."

"I don't really care how you feel, Gus," I said, refusing to look at him. Instead, I fixed my gaze on the signed poster from Daytona Bike Week that I'd given him for Christmas a couple of years ago. Finding it hadn't been easy. I'd had to hunt down the artist, a guy who worked at Harley Davidson.

"I'll always be here for you, baby girl."

His voice held pain, and a part of me wanted to push down the anger. Wanted to wrap my arms around him and tell him it was okay. Just like I'd said it was okay when he canceled my tea party to work on his bike. Or all the times he'd asked me to help close the bar, even when I'd worked doubles all week. I'd never told him no. I loved him too much. Loved him and the fucking Starkwood.

My fury exploded, and I spun on him.

"Get out."

Gus took a step back, and his eyes widened. He seemed almost afraid. Good. He *should* be frightened, because he'd just fucked up. Fucked up big time. Things would never be the same between us again, because Mom had been right about him.

I'd be damned if I'd give him another chance to hurt me.

He opened his mouth, but I raised my hand, holding it in front of his face like a stop sign.

"Get *out!*" I said, my voice rising. "Get the fuck out of here, you lying bastard!"

I stepped forward into his space, backing him toward the hallway with the force of my raw anger. His feet had barely cleared the threshold before I slammed the door in his face. I slid home the oversized barrel bolt with a satisfying thud, then turned to look at the poster again.

Rip it down, the rage hissed. *Slice it to pieces. He doesn't deserve it.*

It was a solid idea, and I knew exactly how to do it, too. Stalking around the desk, I reached up and under the flat surface, fingers feeling for the survival knife Gus had kept hidden there for as long as I could remember. That would be in addition to the gun he'd taped up along the inner right side, and the baseball bat leaning against the battered file cabinet.

It only took a few seconds to find the knife, and one more to pop the snap holding it in the scabbard. The blade slipped free, ten inches of steel alloy that'd be more than enough to shred the pathetic reminder of how much of myself I'd given to Gus's bar.

No.

It was *Eli's* bar now.

I raised a finger to test the blade, mesmerized as a tiny bead of blood welled up from a cut so clean that I hardly registered the pain. The sight fed the rage burning deep within, and I thought about Eli's smug face as he taunted me.

"You know, you'd be a lot prettier if you smiled."

Oh, I could give him a smile. A truly lovely one. Right across his smug throat. Gus thought Eli should have the bar? Fine, Eli could have the fucking bar. Eli could have everything.

Good luck trying to enjoy it once I'm done with you, motherfucker.

Chapter Three

~Eli~

I prowled through the bar, unable to focus.

Gage, Rance, and the rest of my club brothers had cleared out by the time I left Gus's office. Apparently, their business here was done, and socializing wasn't on the agenda. Probably looking to avoid any drama.

Hard to blame them.

The night that Glory—Peaches' mom—had walked in on Gus fucking one of the waitresses in the storeroom was something of a club legend. To say that she'd raised hell was a bit of an understatement… Only luck had saved the Starkwood from burning down.

Hopefully, history wouldn't be repeating itself.

The thought carried me down the hallway, and I found myself outside the office door. It couldn't have been more than ten minutes since Peaches and Gus had started talking, but it felt like hours. Nervous energy filled my body, pulling me in fifty different directions at once. Part of me wanted to go tell the staff who was in charge now.

Stake my claim and make it official.

Another part wanted to celebrate. Maybe get drunk. Getting laid would probably do some good, too. At the same time, I wanted to go through the books, start wrapping my head around the totality of the business. Gus would help with the transition, of course, and I'd grown up watching him. I knew the basics. Still, there was a big difference between being the boss's nephew and being the boss.

Oh, and there'd be a metric fuck ton of legal paperwork to deal with, too.

Logistics. Money transfers.

Title companies were a thing, although I wasn't quite sure what they did. Would I need one of those?

I had no fucking clue about stuff like this. As of this morning, I'd owned a motorcycle, three towels, a laundry basket of clothes, my leathers, a helmet, and my club colors. Oh, and that stuffed animal. Going from that to owning property and a business would be a hell of an adjustment.

This was going to take time. Time and hard work.

Celebrating probably shouldn't be my highest priority.

Leaning back against the wall, I crossed my arms over my chest as I waited. There was a storm building in Gus's office. I could all but smell Peaches' anger and betrayal, and I actually felt a twinge of guilt.

No. Fuck that shit.

I'd earned this bar, paid for it with five long years in prison, holding my tongue and taking the punishment for a crime that wasn't mine. Gus owed me for that alone. The fact that he'd get a cash payout was just a bonus at this point.

No reason for me to feel guilty. And that was the truth.

Still, I could see how much this sucked for Peaches. She'd put in time, too. Time and good faith. Riling her up was a blast, but I'd never wanted her hurt. Not for real. I cared about the girl. Cared about her a lot.

Too much.

Gus had been weak. I loved my uncle, but he'd fucked this one up big time. She deserved better from him—and from me. I should be in there with them. Decision made, I reached for the door.

"Get *out!* Get the fuck out of here, you lying bastard!"

The door burst open, and Gus stumbled out, walking backward. I caught his arm and steadied him as the slab slammed shut again. I heard the heavy bolt sliding shut, locking us out. My uncle looked at me, then sighed.

"Actually went better than I expected."

"Glad I don't have to deal with hiding a body."

"Not yet," he replied, then sighed again. "She's not a happy camper. Probably should've warned her that our plans might change once you got out."

"Why didn't you? Would've been a lot easier on her."

"Guess I didn't want her turning on me," my uncle admitted, surprising me with his honesty. "I knew she'd hate me for it. God, but I miss her mom. Saw her in town a couple weeks ago. It's been twenty years, and Glory still won't even look at me."

Raw pain filled his eyes. I cleared my throat, uncomfortable. Fuck. I didn't like this. Didn't like my girl hurting, and didn't like having to see my uncle like this.

Didn't like knowing I was part of it.

A loud thump came from behind the door, breaking the moment. There was a crash, and then some kind of tearing noise. Shit.

Some women pouted when they got upset.

Others cried.

Peaches had always skipped that part, moving straight to revenge. Another crash. This one so hard that the door rattled. I pictured her all pissed off in there, those glorious tits of hers straining against the front of her low-cut black Starkwood Saloon shirt. My cock twitched. Christ, she was hot when she got angry.

Her cheeks would be flushed, and she'd run her fingers through that wild, dark hair of hers in frustration.

Total sex hair.

Now my dick was getting hard, thinking about grabbing onto the strands, pulling her head back while I fucked her from behind.

I am such an asshole. The only woman I really cared about—hell, probably loved on whatever level I was capable of feeling such things—had just lost her dream.

A decent guy wouldn't be turned on right now.

Unfortunately, my sense of decency had died in prison, leaving behind a man who got off on the idea of sparring with Peaches. The door shook again, followed by a wordless scream of rage.

"Maybe I should—?"

"No," I said, cutting Gus off. "I'll handle this. You go out to the bar. Cover damage control. I'll take care of Peaches."

"I know that look on your face, boy," he said, warning clear in his voice. "You don't get to—"

"All due respect, Gus, but we're not in high school anymore. This is my business, not yours."

My uncle's eyes widened, and for a moment, I thought he might challenge me. Then he looked away, nodding slowly.

"Guess you're right," he said.

Another crash rattled the door as he walked away, and I settled in to wait. Sooner or later, she'd run out of shit to break in there. I wasn't stupid enough to think that'd be enough to exhaust her rage, so I'd best be ready.

In the distance, I heard Gus's loud voice announcing that everyone needed to head outside for a break.

The door rattled again, then it burst open.

Peaches stepped out, and the first thing I saw was the way her eyes seemed to shoot pure fire.

Just like her mother's.

The second thing was the giant fucking survival knife gripped tightly in her right hand. A sane man might've taken that as a bad sign, but I'd left my sanity behind me, right next to my decency.

This wasn't a threat. This was an opportunity.

Someone had to take her down, and as her new boss, that definitely qualified as my job. Only responsible thing to do, really… Couldn't let the customers see her like this.

If I got lucky, I'd get to wrestle with her a bit in the process.

"Still think I'd be prettier if I smiled?" she asked, the words intense and full of hate.

"Yeah," I replied, licking my lips. A wave of heat surged down my spine, and I felt my hips shift restlessly as my cock throbbed. "But pretty is boring. I like you better when you're pissed off. Makes me want to push you down over that desk and fuck you."

* * * *

~Peaches~

"You always find a way to make it worse, don't you?" I asked, fingers tightening around the knife's grip.

Eli nodded, wearing the same sly, taunting smirk he'd worn when he'd held his BB gun to Lemur's head all those years ago.

"You sure you want it to go down like this?" he asked, eyes flicking toward the knife. "That's a very grown-up toy, and you're not a very big girl. Hardly big enough to hold it."

Fucking.

Bastard.

He wouldn't stop until I snapped, of course. He got off on poking at me, and I knew it…but for once, I didn't care. I'd stepped out of that office fully intending to slit his throat. This just confirmed the decision.

And once I finished with him? Well, then I'd go after Gus. Because fuck them. Fuck both of them and their stupid club.

Eli just stood there, gloating. Waiting for me to bitch him out? I didn't bother. Shifting my feet for balance, I lowered the knife between us, then took a steadying breath. The blade was heavy, but I was strong from years of hauling big serving trays over my head.

I lunged.

He reacted instantly—Eli had always been fast—his hand flashing out to catch my arm, jerking it high over my head as he stepped into my space. But this wasn't our first fight, or even our first fight with a knife. I'd nearly taken his eye out at a second-grade picnic. I *knew* how he moved, and I knew how to use it to my advantage. The knife was just the bait. I ignored the pain of his fingers squeezing my wrist and brought my knee up toward his crotch with every ounce of strength I possessed.

It was random luck that saved his balls. He chose that exact moment to twist my arm down and around. That sent me lurching to the side, my knee smashing into his thigh instead of his nuts. Eli's eyes narrowed, and the smirk disappeared.

Good. About time he remembered to take me seriously.

His grip on my wrist tightened, squeezing the bones together until they screamed in pain. I kept hold of the knife. He could break my wrist for all I cared.

Taking advantage of his distraction, I jabbed the fingers of my left hand toward the little hollow at the base of his throat. He managed to partially deflect that, too, loosening his grip on my knife hand in the process. I tried to jerk it free, my other hand dodging his as he tried to catch it. The man might be fast, but I was faster. Fast and determined.

This time, I went for his nipple.

I twisted it hard through his shirt, savoring the vivid red flush that came over his face. Eli's nipples were sensitive as hell, always had been. It'd been a go-to for me all through elementary school. I hadn't tried it since we were adults, but some things never changed.

Then he caught my wrist, wrenching my grip loose from the

nipple in a move that must've been excruciating—I wouldn't let him go easily. That's where I had the advantage, I realized. Eli wouldn't hurt me. I knew it on some deep level. Instinctively.

He had both my hands now.

That should've been enough to stop me, but I was just getting started. I bucked against him, then threw my weight backward. He followed me, pushing me through the office door.

"Stop fighting," he grunted. I answered with a headbutt, which would've been a lot more effective if he wasn't so fucking tall. Instead of knocking him on his ass movie-style, I mostly whacked the hell out of my forehead on his chin. "Jesus, Peaches. You're gonna hurt yourself."

I tried to knee him again. He blocked it with his leg, using my arms to push me away just enough to transfer my wrists to one hand. That left the knife fairly close to his stomach. I could stab him, I realized. Throw my body into his as hard as I could. If I did, that knife would slice right through him.

Well, more through his side than anything, but the theory was the same. I took a breath, then hesitated.

Did I really want to do that?

An instant passed, and then it was too late. Using his free hand, he wrenched at my fingers. The knife fell to the floor, and he kicked it under the desk. Still holding both wrists in one hand, he wrapped the other arm around me, turning us both as he pushed my body toward the door.

At first, I thought he meant to march me down the hallway, presumably to gloat about how he'd beaten me. He caught the door instead, closing it with a crash. Then he shoved me against it, catching my hands with his again, pinning my wrists up and over my head. His big frame pushed into mine, trapping me, making it very clear that a five-foot-four-inch woman was a hell of a lot shorter than a man taller than six feet.

Eli had *seriously* worked out in prison.

I'd noticed how much he bulked up. Not that I liked noticing it, but I'd definitely noticed it. Now I felt it. Felt it in ways that reminded me that this wasn't the first time he'd pinned me down.

Hadn't been able to get the last time out of my mind, either, no matter how hard I tried to erase that particular memory.

"You need to settle the fuck down," he said, his eyes dark and hard, his gaze boring into mine. But his hips pushed against me when he said it, and I felt the length of something against my stomach.

At least part of him wasn't pissed off.

"Or what? You already won, asshole," I said, glaring up at him. My chest pushed against his as I tried to catch my breath. God. This sucked, because I wanted him. Wanted him in ways that just weren't right, because nobody should fantasize about fucking their mortal enemy. All I could think about was him sliding into me, though.

Deep inside, I clenched, feeling empty.

Then I caught his scent.

Shampoo. Not a man's shampoo, either. That was a woman's shampoo, which meant he'd spent the night with someone and then used her shower this morning, I realized.

God, what an asshole… The poor girl probably had no clue that he would never bother to call her. Odds were that he already had someone else lined up for tonight, and now here he was, grinding on me. Would I leave my scent on him, or would the next in line think that shampoo told the whole story?

It was a good reminder. Eli didn't even pretend to be decent. He never had.

"I *hate* you," I said, putting every bit of my rage and bitterness into my voice. His hips angled closer, and his cock pushed into me.

The place between my legs tightened, and my breasts felt full. A trickle of sensation wound its way along my spine. God must hate me because Eli had always made me feel this way. I'd fantasize about him at night, then hate him during the day. Because no matter how much I fantasized, he never paid attention.

I could hate him or fight with him all I wanted, but the problem was, any time we touched, he made me weak. Suddenly, I didn't want to kill him anymore.

I wanted to slide my arms around his neck…and then jump up, wrapping my legs around his waist. I'd grind against him until his dick hurt. Need burned inside of me. I recognized it and hated myself for it because nobody but Eli seemed to work me up like this.

It wasn't that I hadn't had sex. I'd slept with several guys through the years. But no matter who I fucked, they never quite got to me the way Eli did.

And they sure as hell couldn't satisfy me.

Although he'd satisfied me that night… The thought was enough to light a fire inside, and I blinked, trying to ignore it. Eli gave a low laugh. His hips rolled against my belly, and that hard length got bigger.

"You know you want it," he said, the words soft and knowing. Need wrenched its way through me. He was right. I totally wanted it.

But I'd die before giving him the satisfaction of admitting it.

"You had your chance," I whispered. His hips rolled again. God. He was too tall. His dick was centered on my stomach, and because of that, he wasn't touching me where I needed to be touched.

Evil, I reminded myself. A flash of Lemur's tiny stuffed animal face filled my vision, and I felt new resolve. It didn't matter how sexy Eli was, or how many dreams I'd had about his cock slamming home into me.

This was the same person who'd kidnapped Lemur.

Then he'd *murdered* him, caring so little that he hadn't even bothered to notice where he'd thrown the innocent little creature's body.

I'd sworn a vow that day, one that I'd nearly broken five years ago.

I wouldn't be breaking that promise today.

Eli transferred my wrists to one hand again then dropped his free palm down to my face, cupping one cheek as his thumb brushed gently across my lips. Back and forth, the scrape of callused skin across softness called to me. My nipples hurt, and I found my hips rocking forward involuntarily.

Hungry…seeking.

"You want it," he said again, his eyes catching and holding mine. "I do, too. I jerked off a thousand times in prison, picturing you under me. I'd lie awake at night, hand squeezing my cock hard enough to hurt, wondering what it'd feel like to sink into your pussy. This thing between us, Peaches, it's real. It's been real for a long time. We need to make peace."

His voice was so soothing…

My eyes fluttered shut as his thumb probed my lips. I hesitated, then opened my mouth, sucking his digit inside. Then I rubbed the bottom of it with my tongue, pretending I was sucking on something else.

Eli groaned, then shifted, lowering himself before sort of scooping up and into me with his hips. The new position had to be uncomfortable as hell, but it left his cock right where it was supposed to be.

"Some nights, I'd think about that time you stole my car," he continued, his voice near hypnotic. "I remember the look on your face when I finally caught up to you. Jesus. You were so proud of yourself. I couldn't decide whether to strangle you or fuck you over the hood."

His thumb pushed in farther. I didn't protest, I just sucked it in deeper.

"You used to piss me off so much."

My teeth nipped his thumb, and he groaned. I'd heard that sound before…the night he'd gotten arrested. That's the noise he'd made when I unzipped his pants then slid my hand inside to discover how ready he was for me.

The skin covering his dick had been tight.

Painfully so. Tight and hard and ready to thrust deep inside of me, just like his fingers had been inside of me as we kissed.

You could let him do that right now… His thumb pulled back, then thrust into my mouth again. Deeper this time. One of my legs shifted to the side, my knee sliding up and along his thigh. Eli shuddered against me, hips bucking into mine.

I tugged at my arms, and he let them go.

"I'm going to kiss you," he murmured, pulling his thumb free. Then I felt his breath on my lips.

Opening my eyes just a little, I reached up, tangling my fingers in his hair. Then his mouth came down over mine. I latched on to his bottom lip with my teeth and bit Eli King as hard as I could.

For Lemur.

He gave a strangled shout and jerked back his head. That was a bad move on his part, because I was still firmly attached. One of my hands gripped his hair as the other slid down between us.

Just like I had that night.

But this time, I didn't reach for his cock.

Nope. This time, it was all about the balls. Catching them wasn't easy—the denim of his jeans protected them—but I managed to get enough of a grip that he stilled as I tightened my fingers.

"Jesus," he tried to say, but the word was all garbled. My teeth still held him, and the faint taste of blood filled my mouth. I took a moment to secure my grasp on his nuts, giving them a squeeze for good measure. Then I let his lip go, tugging back on his hair, studying his face.

Eli might be bigger, heavier, and better at fighting than me, but I was meaner.

"Do not think for one minute that I'm stupid enough to fall for your shit," I said.

"I could kill you," he answered, frustration and anger warring for control on his face. *Nice.* "Don't you get it, Peaches? You may think you're all tough, but you're just a little thing. You can't beat me like this."

"You sure about that?" I asked, twisting my fingers. It had to be killing him, but he didn't blink.

"Yeah," he said. "I'm sure."

In an instant, he'd somehow shoved his arm between us, then twisted around. I flew toward the floor and would've hit it, except he caught me, literally hoisting me over his shoulder like a firefighter.

"Let me go, you fucking bastard!" I shrieked, trying to figure out how I'd gone from literally having him by the balls to…*this.* I started hitting his back and kicking, then tried to lift my entire body up.

That got me a smack on the ass, which I did *not* find amusing.

Eli took three steps, then flopped me down onto the couch. A second later, he was on top of me, thrusting his knee between mine. My arms were splayed out above my head, held down firmly by his hands. His hips pinned mine. I saw a little trickle of blood coming from his lip. My tongue darted out, and I tasted copper on mine.

We settled into glaring at each other, trying to catch our breaths. Then he spoke.

"You are a fucking bitch, Peaches Taylor."

"You better believe it," I replied, narrowing my eyes. "You think you've won—"

"I *have* won."

"But I'll find a way to make your life a living hell," I continued, ignoring his declaration. Eli snorted.

"You've been making my life hell since I was seven years old. That has to change if you want to keep working here."

"What makes you think I'd work for you?" I snapped.

"You love it," he snapped back. "And you're good at it," he added, clearly reluctant to admit the truth.

But he was right. I really *was* good at running the bar. Way better than Gus had ever been. We had a whole new class of customers. Dancing on the weekends… I'd changed the entire model, and it showed.

"Damned right, I'm good at it. That's why I should be buying the bar right now. Not you."

"So we both know that you're good at managing the place," he continued, ignoring my other statement. "And we both know that I've been gone a long time. Gus can help me during the transition, but if I really want this place to succeed, I need you here. I want you to manage the place. Officially. You're already doing all the work. Might as well have the title and authority."

My jaw dropped. "Do you seriously think that you can just sweet-talk me—?"

"Shut the fuck up, Peaches!" he snapped. It startled both of us. I was the one who blew up. Not him.

"Just shut the fuck up," he repeated. "For once. Listen to me, okay?"

"So you can feed me some line of bullshit about *needing* me?" I asked, suddenly tired. "You don't need me, Eli. You've never needed me. All you need is your fucking club."

"What's that supposed to mean?"

I closed my eyes, wishing I'd been smart enough to walk out when Gus told me the news. That was my big flaw, I realized. I didn't know when to let go. Never had… "It doesn't matter."

"The fuck it doesn't," he said, giving my hands a jerk. His hips ground into mine, and I felt my legs spreading for him, even as I hated him. "Tell me what you meant."

Fuck it.

"None of you let me talk to the cops after they arrested you," I said. "I was *there,* Eli. With you. I don't know who really killed that guy, but it wasn't you. You had an alibi. *You were with me.* Hell, you were almost *in* me."

His cock hardened as I said the words, and without thinking, I circled my pelvis into his. We were both thinking about that night now, and it hurt. "After all those years of fighting, that night we were *together.* And then you let them take you away. I could've saved you from that, but you wouldn't let me. Why?"

My jeans were soft, and I felt every seam and bump inside his as he slowly rocked against me. He didn't say anything for long seconds, and I felt the waves of need building in me even as my frustration grew.

"I couldn't," he finally replied. "I just couldn't, okay?"

"Why not?" I asked, knowing I was giving myself away, and not caring. I'd spent the last five years wondering why a man would *choose* prison… A man with an alibi. Someone who'd been all but fucking me while the crime was committed.

The silence grew painful as we stared at each other, my eyes pleading with his for answers.

"I can't tell you," he whispered.

That's what he'd said then, too.

"Let me go."

"No."

"Let. Me. Go," I said again, my voice harder. "I see how it is… I give up. You hear that? I. Give. Up. You win, Eli. You get the bar. You get to keep your secrets. But you don't get to fuck me, and you don't get to serve me bullshit and expect me to thank you with a smile. Let me up. I'm leaving."

He didn't move, and we lay there for a moment—him hard between my legs. Me, pinned beneath him. We were near each other like always, I realized. But we'd never really *be* together. Then he spoke, and his words shocked me.

"I don't want you to leave."

"Let me up," I whispered again, refusing to listen. To wonder why he'd say something like that. It didn't matter. Whatever game he was playing, *it didn't matter.*

Eli suddenly rolled to the side, then reached down to offer me his hand. I ignored it, sitting up, trying to think. He shook his head, then sat down next to me.

"I'll give you two weeks' notice," I said after another long pause. "You don't deserve it, but I've put way too much work into this bar to just walk off and let everything fall apart. Gus hasn't been running things for the past few years. I have."

"I know," Eli replied, his voice serious. "Gus knows, too."

Hearing the words hurt. More than I expected.

"Am I supposed to be thankful that he noticed?"

"Look, I know you're angry at him—"

"No, I'm angry at you."

"But he loves you. He's always loved you."

"Like he loved my mom?" I asked, turning to look at Eli directly. His eyes softened. We sat there for a moment, just staring at each other, and then the ridiculousness of the situation hit me.

"This is crazy," I said, glancing around and taking in the office. I'd shredded the poster. The chairs had been knocked over, and I'd smashed the keyboard into the wall.

Eli snorted.

"Your mom would've set the place on fire."

"My mom *did* set the place on fire," I replied, feeling a little smirk stealing across my mouth. "I feel like I failed her. I didn't even make it out of the hallway."

"The customers do a pretty good job of tearing up the bar itself," Eli said casually. "You're more of a specialist. Although I appreciate the fact that you didn't kill the computer. I don't know how good the backup system is."

I glanced over at it, thinking of all the hours I'd put in working on it. "It's set to automatically back up to the cloud. I do the books. Did you know that? Gus hasn't worked on them in years. You're fucked, Eli."

My smirk turned to a full-on smile at the thought.

"I know," Eli admitted, and he smiled, too. "Jesus, you're never boring. Don't leave, Peaches. Manage the bar. I'll pay you more. We can make this work."

"How much more?" I asked, allowing myself to consider it. Could I work for him? I wasn't sure…

"I don't know," he admitted. "I haven't seen the books. I don't even know how much you're getting paid now. You'll have to tell me."

I thought about it, glancing up at what remained of the poster. It'd taken months to find, but less than a minute to destroy it. Not that I regretted it. Gus deserved it. He really had fucked me over…just like he'd fucked over my mom. But I still needed a job, and Eli would be offering me a very nice salary, I decided. A very nice one, indeed.

Otherwise, he could figure out the passwords on his own, because Gus sure as hell didn't know them. Idiots. Both of them were idiots.

"I'll give it a month," I told him thoughtfully. "But don't fuck with me, Eli. I'm serious. Or next time, I really will slit your throat."

"I believe you," he replied, and it almost sounded like he did. I'd have to retrieve that survival knife before he remembered it. Hide it somewhere good. "I'm just glad you didn't have one of those knives when we were kids."

I considered the thought of my five-year-old self with a ten-inch steel blade, then nodded slowly.

"Yeah, you're probably right about that. I had more of a temper back then."

Eli coughed, then looked away. I could tell he wanted to say something. I waited, but he kept his mouth shut.

Wow.

Maybe he'd gotten a little smarter in prison. I still hated the bastard, but I could take his money. For a while, at least. Hard to know with an old building, though. So many things could go wrong. Maybe there'd be a fire, after all.

We'd just have to wait and see.

Chapter Four

Thirteen years ago

~Eli~

"So, I heard there's a party at the clubhouse this weekend," said Holly. She smiled up at me, twirling a strand of hair around her finger. My eyes slid down, noting just how perfectly her tits filled out the front of her spaghetti strap tank top.

Technically, those weren't allowed—too much of a distraction. I could appreciate a good distraction as much as the next guy, but seeing Peaches wearing one earlier today had been enough to convince me that maybe the school should enforce that rule.

Being a helpful kind of guy, I'd pointed that out to Peaches. Fortunately, her arms were a lot shorter than mine. Made it easy to just hold her back when she tried to punch me.

"You're too young for a club party," I told Holly, which was kind of unfair. We were the same age. But I wasn't like other high school seniors. I'd been born old, and the club was in my blood. The guys would eat Holly alive.

She took a step closer, the move almost predatory. Then a wave of her perfume hit me. Heavy and musky, and not in the good kind of way. I flashed back to the last time I'd fucked her.

That shit was potent, and it didn't wash off.

"You sure about that?" she asked, raising a hand and placing it on my chest. Then her eyelashes started flapping. The move was supposed to be sexy, but it came off more like a butterfly having a seizure.

"Not gonna happen," I said, reaching up and gently pushing away her hand. Then I turned toward my locker. We still had a few minutes to make it to class, but the conversation was over.

Holly didn't take the cue to leave.

"What do you think Mark sees in her?" she asked, sounding annoyed.

"Who?" I asked, then realized I'd fucked up. I knew damned well who she was talking about. Peaches and Mark McDougal had been dating for a month. Quarterback and cheerleader—the perfect cliché. They made out in the hall and sat together at lunch. It was cute and adorable and complete bullshit.

Mark was fucking at least two other girls on the side.

"Peaches Taylor," Holly said. "I know she's hot as hell, but she's not gonna fuck him. She's still a virgin."

"Why do you care?" I asked, keeping my tone casual. I'd been wondering if Mark had gotten to her yet. Fucker. "Nothing to do with us."

Holly laughed. "This school is too small for you to get away with that, Eli. You're hung up on her."

I turned back to her, frowning.

"My uncle was kinda her stepdad for a while. He likes me to keep an eye out for her. That's all."

Holly raised a brow, calling silent bullshit. "You're not going to invite me to that party no matter what I say, right?"

"Nope."

She rolled her eyes.

"Okay, then will you at least mention me to Bryce? I heard he's single again."

"You don't want to hook up with Bryce."

"Not your decision to make," she countered. It was a good point, but Bryce was thirty years old. Not only that, he had four kids by four different women. Holly and I had never been anything more than casual, but I had enough respect for her to think she could do better. "And I know it's none of my business, but if you turn around right now, you'll see what Mark's about to do to the girl you don't care about."

Keeping it casual, I grabbed my bag and then turned around,

taking in the hallway full of students doing everything but studying. Part of me noted Jenny Woelfel and her pack of mean girls huddled off to the right, sharpening their knives.

On the left was a clump of cheerleaders and football players. Peaches and Mark were with them. Mark stepped into Peaches' space, herding her back toward the wall of lockers, using his bulk to surround her.

He might not've fucked her yet, but he would soon.

I swallowed, reminding myself that she was sixteen now. It wasn't my place to step in, regardless of what Gus said.

"Wanna tell me again that you're not hung up on her?" Holly asked, her tone light and mocking. I didn't bother denying it this time. Jesus Christ, but I hated the way Peaches looked at him. Of all the guys she could choose, why *him?*

Mark McDougal was a piece of shit.

A spoiled, entitled asshole who'd never had to work. Never suffered or been alone.

Never had to fight for a goddamned thing.

His dad was a lawyer. Sleazy as hell, and a bully, too. Fucker sued anyone and everyone, draining their pockets until they settled with him just to make it end. He'd even gone after one of my club brothers over a fifty-dollar oil change at his garage.

Now, Mark was leaning down into Peaches, one of his hands rubbing up and down her arm as he whispered something to her.

She flushed, all pretty and nervous and giggly. Clueless. She was nothing more than a trophy for him. A pretty, popular toy to fuck for a while until he got bored or left for college.

Sure, I wanted to fuck Peaches, too. But I also wanted good things for her. Well, mostly good things. I wanted to do a couple of bad things…

Mark's head tilted, and I watched as his lips covered hers. The kiss started off soft, but within seconds, their bodies were pressed together all the way. Then the hand that'd been tracing her arm reached down to find her ass, gripping one cheek tightly. If she'd been wearing anything but jeans, his fingers would be buried in her ass. Whatever hatred I'd felt before doubled. Tripled.

I didn't just hate the fucker, I realized. I wanted to *end* him.

Someone gave a wolf whistle, and Peaches froze. Then her hands pushed at Mark, almost frantic as she realized what a show they'd been putting on. For an instant, the asshole ignored her attempt to get away.

Please, God, give me this one. Let me kill him.

I'd just stepped toward them when Mark pulled away. Peaches' cheeks were still flushed and red, but this time, she looked embarrassed.

Christ, she must have it bad. She'd forgotten where they were, and if Mark had any doubt about how easy it'd be to take her before, he wouldn't now. Just then, the asshole glanced in my direction. Our eyes met, and he gave me a slow smile.

Fucker reached down and grabbed his sack, deliberately adjusting himself.

Holly hadn't been wrong. The school was too damned small. Mark knew I wanted Peaches. I'd warned more than one guy off of her this past year.

"What'd you do to piss him off—?" Holly said, but I didn't catch the rest. I was already striding toward Mark, hands fisted with angry tension. Someone needed to teach that pissant a lesson about respect.

That's when Peaches stepped in front of me, pushing a hand against my chest.

"Stop," she snapped, and the softness on her face was gone. This wasn't Peaches, the girl who'd just gotten embarrassed by kissing in the hallway.

Nope, this was my old enemy. The tough, strong girl who'd put snakes in my bed.

Instinct kicked in.

"What's the matter?" I asked, taunting her. "Afraid your boyfriend can't take me? Or is it that he isn't enough? I wasn't planning on fucking you with my mouth for an audience…but if you're wondering how it's done right, I could help you out."

Her eyes flashed, and the hand on my chest pulled back to slap me. I caught it, blocking her easily enough.

"Go to hell, Eli," she hissed. "This is my life. You don't get a vote."

"That's where you're wrong," I said, savoring the anger on her face. Mark stepped up behind her and put a possessive hand on her shoulder.

I was bigger than he was. Tougher, too. I knew it, and he knew it, but if we got into a fight here, I'd be the one hauled out by the cops.

"Careful," I said, catching and holding Mark's gaze. Peaches might stand between us, but she was short enough for us to stare each other down. "She's club property, you know?"

"Shut the fuck up, Eli!" Peaches said.

"This isn't one of your little games," Mark added, sounding bored. "I'm not scared of you, King. You bikers may think you run things around here, but you're just a bunch of tweakers and losers."

Peaches stilled, and I felt storm clouds gathering. Then she jerked her arm free of mine and turned on Mark.

"Gus is like my dad," she snarled. Good girl. Her mom and Gus might've broken up, but she still found her way out to our place at least one night a week. Peaches and Gus were family.

Mark had just fucked up. Big time.

"I didn't mean it like—" he tried to say, but she cut him off with a wave of her hand. I smiled as the bell rang. All around us, students seemed torn between heading to class and watching the show.

"Most bikers are really great people," she continued. "And Gus doesn't use drugs. Don't go saying shit about people unless you actually know what you're talking about."

With that, she shoved Mark out of her way. Every step she took radiated anger as she snagged a backpack leaning against one of the lockers. She slung it over her shoulder with one hand and raised the other to flip us off over her head as she joined the stream of kids heading to class.

Within seconds, the hall cleared out, leaving Mark and me still facing each other. We'd be late unless we got moving, but I had an advantage over him in this particular situation. He cared about his grades. Me? Not so much.

"You hurt that girl, and they'll never find your body," I said casually, offering him my best smile. "Consider yourself warned."

Mark swallowed, and I almost laughed. He might act tough, but the fucker was a coward once the witnesses were gone.

"She doesn't belong to you," he said, his voice wavering. My smile got bigger.

"Nope, but she belongs to Gus," I replied, casually cracking my knuckles. "Don't think of me as a guy you go to school with. Think of me as Gus's eyes and ears. And fists."

Mark's mouth opened, then closed again.

Like a goldfish.

I couldn't help myself, I started laughing. My work might be done for now, but I couldn't help but catch him with my shoulder hard enough to knock him off balance as I walked away.

Mark started cussing, scrambling to stay upright. I didn't bother turning around to see if he'd fallen. I was too busy enjoying the moment.

Football practice was ugly that afternoon.

I wasn't really the football type, but I was big and fast. Had been a starter on offense *and* defense since junior year, although given how small the school was, it sounded more impressive than it actually was.

Coach had been in a bad mood, and it was contagious. First, he'd bitched us out for lack of team unity, then he'd divided us into two teams to scrimmage. Things got dark when Mark's friends decided to put all their energy into tackling me instead of going for the ball.

Things got even darker when I sacked Mark's ass on the next play.

Coach really lost his shit then, and we spent the rest of the afternoon running the bleachers. Fucking brutal. By the time we hit the locker room, I was ready to kill someone. Grabbing my bag, I cut between rows of lockers toward the door.

That's when I heard Mark's voice on the other side.

"Think I'll fuck her in the ass while I'm at it," he said, and he sounded just as angry as I felt. I stilled, something deep inside of me going cold and dark. One of his friends laughed, but it sounded nervous.

"Dude, are you sure about this?" another guy asked. It sounded like Troy, but I wasn't sure. "She's into you. It's gonna be easy. Why take the risk?"

"It's not a risk," Mark answered. "She won't even remember it if I do it right. And if she does, it'll be her word against mine. Not like anyone will believe her. She might be pretty and popular, but she comes from trash."

She comes from trash.

Fuck.

Me.

Time seemed to slow because I could see the whole thing playing out in my head. Peaches might be into Mark, but she was still a virgin—not necessarily a sure thing. And now he had something to prove.

A detached section of my brain noted that I should talk to the club president after I finished with Mark. The asshole apparently had roofies, and he'd gotten them from someone—someone that didn't belong to us.

The club wasn't a big fan of freelancers setting up shop in Hallies Falls.

And I wasn't a big fan of Mark fucking Peaches in the ass, either.

He was still talking, but I tuned him out, considering my next step carefully. Didn't really matter what the details were at this point. I knew everything I needed to know about Mark and his plans.

The only open question now was one of control. Realistically, would I be able to control myself enough not to kill him?

It was a serious question.

If I jumped him in the parking lot, there'd be witnesses. That was bad because I might find myself arrested. Or suspended. That'd complicate my life considerably.

On the other hand, if there were witnesses, I'd *have* to control myself, and there'd only be so much time before the cops arrived, which put a natural limit on the damage I could inflict.

"Can a girl on roofies give a blowjob?" one of the guys asked, and I had my answer.

Better to get arrested for assault than murder. And if I ever caught Mark McDougal alone, I'd definitely kill him. I'd take him down in the parking lot. That'd send a message to every guy in the high school, too.

Peaches Taylor might not come from money, but she had people.

People who'd stand up for her.

She'd probably hate me for doing it, but that was nothing new. She'd always hated me. Wasn't like I had much to lose.

Wasn't like she'd believe me if I just tried to warn her off, either. Hell, if I told her the sky was blue, she'd insist it was green just to spite me.

Decision made, I started toward the door again, making for the parking lot. Mark still needed to shower, which meant I had some time to kill. Might as well use it productively. That fancy car his daddy'd given him was real shiny. Too shiny. A few scratches would do it some good…

Maybe I'd write a little message with my keys. That way, all the girls would know what to expect from him on a date. Hell, it was practically a public service.

Just the thought made me smile. Pulling out my cell phone, I hit the call button. Gus answered on the third ring.

"What's going on?" he asked, gruff as always.

"Probably gonna need some bail money," I told him. "And a lawyer."

Gus sighed, the same one he gave when he realized he needed to swap out a keg. "All right, then. I'll call the club. This about Peaches?"

"You don't wanna know the details," I replied, tilting my head to the side so I could crack my neck. "I'll take care of this one. No reason both of us should get locked up tonight."

Chapter Five

Present day
Two weeks after getting the news about the bar

~Peaches~

"So, I ran the numbers," I said, handing my mom a can of Diet Coke. Then I climbed up onto the couch and crossed my legs, leaning against the arm.

"What numbers?"

The question came from James. He walked casually across the living room, coming to a stop next to my mom. His hand settled on her shoulder. I scowled because he wasn't supposed to be part of this conversation. The fact that he'd married my mom didn't make him part of my family.

"I was just calculating how many pairs of used panties I have to sell online before I have enough money to buy the Starkwood," I said, my voice sweet.

James raised a brow.

"And?" he asked. I frowned.

"And, what?"

"How many would you have to sell?" he elaborated, his face solemn. Holy shit. Did he think I was serious? For the thousandth time, I wondered how my crazy, wild, fun-loving mom had gone from Gus to a guy like this.

An accountant.

Well, a former accountant. He'd gotten into land development and real estate years ago, but spreadsheets were his first love.

"About fifteen thousand," I told him. "But I hear you can order them in bulk for discounts."

"Please tell me you just made that number up," my mom said.

"Nope," I admitted, wishing she was right. "I researched it. You can get about twenty-five bucks a pair on a fetish site…and you can do upgrades. Like, if I don't wipe—"

"I'll give you twenty-five dollars not to finish that sentence," Mom said, shuddering. James absently rubbed her shoulder, his expression thoughtful.

He *always* looked thoughtful.

I wondered if the expression ever changed. Like, say someone was going down on him, would he still look so…thoughtful? I pictured it and then realized that my mom would be the one doing the going down. And now *I* was the one shuddering in horror.

"So, you'd need three hundred and seventy-five thousand dollars to buy the bar?" James asked. "Based on gross, of course. You'd probably have to sell closer to twenty thousand pairs, given shipping and overhead. I don't know what the Starkwood's cash flow is, but three seventy-five seems low to me. Does it include the building, too?"

I studied James for a moment, trying to decide if he slept in a bed, or if Mom just shut him into a pod at night to recharge. Mom took a drink, sighing. She knew what I was thinking. We'd had this discussion before. But no matter how many times she tried to tell me that James was the man for her, I couldn't see it.

It wasn't that he was ugly. The guy was okay to look at. But there was no life in him. He was more of a robot than anything else…

I realized the automaton was waiting for an answer.

"It includes the building, the land," I told him. "All of it. At least, that's what Gus said would work when we talked about it. I don't have the income to qualify for a loan, but Gus said he'd carry the contract. Eli can give him cash, though."

"Hmm…"

"It doesn't matter, baby," Mom chimed in. "You don't want to buy that place anyway. Trust me on that. There's a lot more to running the Starkwood than you think."

"I've been managing it unofficially for years," I pointed out. "Still am. Although I haven't gotten my raise yet. Not until the papers are signed. Eli promised me more money than Gus is willing to pay."

"That's not fair," James said.

"Wow, thank you for pointing that out," I snapped. God, he annoyed me. I understood that Mom had left Gus for a reason, but seriously…this guy? "But there's a part of me that's kind of glad it's not finalized yet. Something could happen. The sale could still fall through."

"It sounds like it's a done deal," Mom said. "Doesn't matter if the papers are signed. The decision has been made. I'm not surprised, either. Like I said, there's a lot going on there. The Reapers will want Eli in charge. Wouldn't matter how much you offered Gus."

I opened my mouth to argue with her, then closed it again. Could she be right?

Gus had given me the bad news right after he finished meeting with two club presidents. I hadn't really questioned that because I *never* questioned what the club was doing. That was how I'd been raised.

Suddenly, it seemed painfully obvious.

Gus wasn't the only one involved in this decision. The Reapers must have something to do with it, too. Mom widened her eyes at me as if she knew what I was thinking and gave me a don't-say-it look. I shot a quick glance at James. He'd pulled out his phone, apparently fascinated by whatever was on it.

Fucking robot.

"Mom, you think you can help me in the kitchen?" I asked pointedly. She nodded, gently nudging James to the side so she could stand up. He hardly seemed to register the movement.

We passed from the living room through the large, formal dining room that'd always seemed too big to me, and then moved into a kitchen so perfect it could've been in a magazine.

The house was beautiful, but it had no soul.

Just like its robot master…

I leaned back against one of the countertops, ready for some answers.

"Why are you so against me buying the bar?"

"I've never wanted you to buy the bar," she said, clearly confused. "I've told you that all along. Since you were ten years old."

"Yeah, but you never told me *why*. And tonight, it sounded like you knew something. Something about the Reapers."

Mom took a deep breath, clearly considering her answer carefully.

"Seeing as I shared a bed with Gus for many years, it's safe to say I know a great deal," she finally said. "I know you care about him. You trusted him, and you counted on him. But ultimately, Gus couldn't be the man *either* of us needed. He failed both of us. That's the reality you've never wanted to hear."

The words hit me with physical pain. My eyes started to burn, and I knew they had to be getting red. Mom sighed, and I could see her eyes getting red, too. Absently, she raised her hand, taking a drink from the can of pop she'd brought with her from the living room.

"Why did you marry James?" I asked softly. "Were you just looking for someone who'd be the opposite of Gus?"

Mom's eyes went wide, and she choked. Her shoulders started shaking.

"Mom?" I asked, concerned. She made another choking sound, holding up her hand as her lips pressed tightly closed. Now, her whole face was turning red. I needed to help her, but I had no clue what was wrong.

A drip of Coke escaped her lips, running down her chin. She wiped at it, still shaking.

That's when I figured it out. Mom wasn't choking. She was *laughing*. Laughing with her mouth full of pop, trying not to spray it across the room.

Not the reaction I'd expected.

Her eyes caught mine, dancing as she held her fingers to her lips. I felt my own giggle starting. Apparently, that made it worse because she made sort of a smothered squealing sound, then turned away, stumbling toward the sink.

My giggles turned into full-on laughter as she sprayed out her drink, gasping for breath. Then we were both laughing. I still wasn't quite sure what was so funny, but it didn't matter.

It'd been too long since we laughed together.

"I looked up the property parcel and ran some more numbers," James announced, wandering in from the dining room. *What the fuck?* For some reason, that seemed even funnier to me, and a fresh burst of laughter exploded.

Mom gasped for breath, wiping her mouth with the dish towel that'd been hanging next to the sink.

"Would those be the panty sales numbers?" Mom asked, which

set me off again. James looked between us and gave a deep sigh.

"No, those would be property values on the Starkwood Saloon," he said. "It's very good. The price Gus offered you, that is."

"James, stop right there," Mom said, her voice sharp. Ouch. Clearly, we were done laughing. "It doesn't *matter* what the price is. Eli is buying the bar. Peaches can't afford it."

"Of course, the price matters," James replied, seeming almost confused. Mom and I froze, sharing a look. I waited for him to explain. He didn't.

"Why does it matter?" I finally asked.

"Because that's a very lowball offer," James said, giving his phone another glance. "It's worth nearly that much just in the land. If he'll sell it to you for that price, you need to buy it. No question."

"Are you fucking kidding me?" Mom burst out.

"No, I'm not 'fucking kidding' you, sweetheart," James said, and he sounded funny. Not the usual, boring robot voice… No, this was almost flirtatious.

My stomach turned.

That was weird. He didn't flirt. He didn't tease, and he didn't play games. James was a *robot.*

"Peaches, I'll back you," he continued. "In fact, I'll even give you some room to negotiate. You can go as high as four hundred thousand. We can hammer out the details later, but if they haven't signed papers, now is the time to move. You should call Gus right now."

"No," Mom said, her eyes darting between us. "James, we've talked about this. You know why I don't want her there."

"I know why you left," he said, his tone gentle and very *not*-robotic. "And I know that you don't want her at the Starkwood. But she's already there, and has been for years… If Eli takes over, he's making her the manager. She loves the place, and she's not going to leave anytime soon. So, the real question isn't whether Peaches is going to stay at the Starkwood, it's whether she'll be working for herself or for someone else."

I stared at him, trying to figure out what the hell had just happened. Clearly, James had paid a lot more attention to my life than I ever realized. Not only that, I knew he was smart. He had money, too. Money he'd made in real estate.

Hell, that's why most people thought Mom had married him.

"Thank you," I finally managed to say, still stunned. "But, why?"

James raised a brow. "Because it's a good deal, Peaches. That's how I've always worked. I watch, and I wait. That way, I'm ready when a really good opportunity crosses my path. That's how I got your mother, you know. Took me three years to convince her to go out with me, but when she finally said yes, I was ready."

"He was," Mom said, smiling at him. "That was the most romantic date I've ever been on. He thought of everything…"

James set his phone on the counter, then caught my mom's hand, pulling her toward him. She reached up to cup his cheek, even as he leaned down to give her a soft, sweet kiss. Then their mouths opened, and shit got real.

Jesus Christ.

Mom and James were making out like horny teenagers, right in the middle of the kitchen. The whole damned world had gone crazy, clearly. I looked away, uncomfortable. There was a wet, smacking sound, followed by a soft moan.

"Um, you need to stop now," I said, shifting my feet awkwardly. The smacking noises continued. Turning my head, I stole a peek at them. Holy shit, was James' hand reaching for Mom's butt?

"Stop!" I said, horrified. "I can't do this. I can't watch you guys make out in the kitchen. What the hell is wrong with you, Mom? I'm your *child.*"

She pulled away from James just slightly. "You're nearly thirty, baby. I know this may shock you, but I'm not dead. I still like to have sex, and this is my husband. It's allowed."

James wrapped an arm around her, tucking her into his side. She sighed happily, and I threw up a little in the back of my throat.

"You're disgusting."

"We're in love," James replied, the words sounding incredibly weird and wrong in his robot voice.

Mom laughed at the look on my face. "You know how you asked me earlier if I married James because he's not like Gus?"

"Mom!" I hissed, wondering what the hell she was thinking, saying that in front of him. She laughed again, and this time, the sound was deeper.

Sensual.

"I married him because, deep down inside, he's the man I need him to be," she whispered, and I realized that James was right.

They were in love.

My wild-ass, crazy mom was in love with an accountant who'd told me once that he didn't like motorcycles. Because they were too dangerous.

"Go talk to Gus," James told me, giving Mom another squeeze. "Make the deal. We'll figure out the details tomorrow. It'll be fair."

"Um, yeah…" I said, backing slowly away from them. I couldn't process this right now. *That's okay. You don't need to understand what just happened to take advantage of it. Just leave the house before they start making out again.*

"Peaches?" Mom said, catching my attention. She'd wrapped both of her arms around James again, resting her head on his chest. "There's another reason I married him, you know. The thing is, he's really good in the sack. I've always had a high sex drive, you know."

I turned and ran out of the room.

Chapter Six

~Peaches~

"Kinda desperate, coming here on your night off," Eli said as I walked up to the bar. "Usually, girls just text me when they want a booty call." His lips quirked up in a smirk.

"Go to hell," I replied absently. Where was Gus? The place was mostly empty, just a few of the Reapers hanging out in one of the corner booths. Megan was wiping down tables, and Eli was the only one behind the bar. I frowned, boosting myself up onto one of the bar stools. "Oh, and can I have a rum and Coke?"

Eli leaned forward on his elbows. "Too late. I already did last call for the night."

"It's hardly past eleven," I said, surprised.

"Slow night." He shrugged. "Decided to close early."

"I've been trying to convince Gus that we should close earlier when it's like this for the last three years."

Eli's mouth quirked up, radiating smugness.

"Gus isn't in charge anymore."

My stomach dropped. "Does that mean you signed the papers today? I thought they weren't ready yet."

Eli raised an eyebrow, but he didn't give me a direct answer. Instead, he grabbed a couple of shot glasses and set them out between us. Then he grabbed a bottle of Crown Royal from the shelf behind the bar.

"Eli, did you sign the papers?" I asked again, feeling nervous. He filled the shot glasses. This was starting to look like a celebration, which didn't make sense.

They weren't supposed to finalize things until next week.

"Got them today," he said, and I heard the triumph in his voice. That fucking bastard… It wasn't enough for him to take the bar from me. Nope. Now, he wanted me to *celebrate* with him. This was about him winning. Again. "Already looked everything over. We'll sign them tomorrow morning at the title company. Grab your drink, Peaches. It's time for us to make a new start."

Eli caught my eye, raising his glass in a toast.

I briefly considered throwing the shot in his face because I'd be damned if I would concede defeat. If the papers hadn't been signed yet, I still had a chance to make my offer. Eli didn't need to know that, though. So, I gave him a strained smile and forced myself to give his glass a token tap. Together, we downed the shots.

He reached for the bottle and started pouring again.

"Are you trying to get me drunk?" I asked, wondering if he had a deeper game. "Because I stole bottles of this shit all the time in high school. It'll take more than two shots."

"Not true," he said. "You always went for the crappy vodka. Easier to water down. Cover the crime."

He had me. I'd totally done that.

"You liked it mixed with Dr. Pepper," he added, lifting his glass again and grinning at me over the top of it.

"How the hell do you remember that?" I asked, startled. Eli held my gaze, and for once, he wasn't challenging me. He looked almost…friendly. Not luring-me-into-a-false-sense-of-security-so-he-could-destroy-me friendly, either.

Friendly for real.

It freaked me out.

"I'm not trying to get you drunk," he said. "I'm just feeling good about things. It's been frustrating, waiting to take over. I'm ready to have it settled. I know you're not happy about how things turned out—"

"Understatement."

"I get it," he continued. "The situation wasn't fair. But we have a chance to start things over again. Do it right. Both of us love this place. You've been working here for seven years. And starting tomorrow, you'll be the manager. Do you really want to be at each other's throats for the next ten years? Don't you ever get tired of fighting?"

I didn't know what I'd expected him to say, but that wasn't it. I grabbed the shot, downing it quickly. The first one hadn't done much, but this one set my head spinning.

Or maybe that was just the sound of Eli being reasonable.

"Let me ask you this," I said carefully. "If I'd won, would you be willing to celebrate with me?"

Eli didn't pretend not to understand.

"Yes, I would," he said. "But this wasn't about winning."

I raised a brow.

"Peaches, do you really think I want to take your dream away from you?" he asked. "I didn't plan for you to get hurt, but Gus promised me this bar a long time before he ever talked to you about it. I have dreams, too."

"What you mostly have is money," I said, feeling my frustration and anger rise. "Money you didn't even earn, for the record. I've spent the last seven years busting ass, and we both know I've been managing it for a long time. And don't tell me this was your dream. Nobody *made* you go to prison, Eli. We both know you didn't kill that guy. I was your fucking *alibi.* And yet, for some reason, *you chose prison* over staying with us—"

Horrified, I snapped my mouth shut, wondering where the hell that'd come from. Eli studied me, one of the little muscles in his jaw tensing.

Then his gaze flicked toward something behind me before he caught my eyes again.

"Let's talk in the office."

Sliding off the stool, I turned and saw that Gus had just walked through the door. Gage was with him, along with more club members.

Eli rounded the bar, catching my arm.

"Office," he repeated, tugging at me. I took a moment to consider. I'd come to see Gus, not Eli. But this many club brothers all together, right when the bar was closing…that struck me as odd.

"Are the Reapers having a meeting tonight?"

"Doesn't matter," he said. "We need to finish this conversation. Privately."

Gus caught my eye and offered a casual wave before turning back to Gage. A couple of the prospects started sliding tables together.

"You're done for the night," Eli said, and I blinked, confused. I thought he wanted to talk some more.

"Don't you need someone to serve the bikers?" Megan said. I hadn't even noticed her walking up to us. I swayed a little, realizing that those shots were hitting me a little harder than they should have…

I hadn't eaten dinner. Come to think of it, I hadn't eaten lunch, either.

"I think Gus and I can handle drinks for the club," Eli told her. "Peaches is here if we need help."

"What makes you think I'm willing to help?" I said, tugging at my arm. His fingers tightened, and he pulled me toward the office.

"You don't need to help," he said as we walked down the hall. "I was just getting rid of her. Now, let's finish that talk."

He opened the door, then pushed me toward the couch. Part of me wanted to argue with him, just out of habit. But I also wanted to hear what he had to say. So, I sat down, crossing my arms over my chest. Eli settled next to me, right in the middle of the sofa. Typical. He had a whole damned piece of furniture to sit on, but he had to take the spot right next to me. Making himself comfortable, he leaned back and turned toward me.

"You know what the club is," he said. "Right?"

"I know all about the club," I replied, wondering where he was going with this. "I grew up with the club. I lived in Gus's house before you, remember?"

"Jesus, why do you always have to bring that up?" he asked, clearly frustrated. "I was a little kid. I needed a place to live, and that room was big enough for both of us. Where was I supposed to sleep? The kitchen? Your bedroom was where they put me. I did what I was told."

"Did they tell you to kidnap Lemur?"

He blew out his breath in exasperation. "I was ten years old, Peaches. I'm sorry I took your stuffed animal. I've apologized about a thousand times now, but I don't have a fucking time machine. I can't fix it."

"You cut off his tail and kept it as a *trophy,*" I hissed.

Eli looked away. "That was shitty. Ten-year-olds do shitty things."

"You hung it on your rearview mirror in high school."

He shifted. Clearly, the guilt had gotten to him. I paused to savor the moment.

"Eighteen-year-olds do shitty things, too," he admitted. "And if I remember correctly, you stole that car. Smashed one of the fenders."

"It was a rescue operation," I pointed out. "I had to retrieve Lemur's remains and give him a dignified burial. The car was just collateral damage, something that never would've happened if you hadn't desecrated his corpse."

Eli closed his eyes for a moment, taking a deep breath. Then he opened them again.

"You know that the Reapers are more than just a bunch of guys who like to ride motorcycles together, right?"

"Everyone knows that."

"Yeah, but you grew up with it," he continued. "When we say we're brothers, those aren't just words... And part of that brotherhood is watching each other's backs. That's how this thing works."

"Were you watching someone's back when you went to prison for a crime you didn't commit?"

"Do you really expect me to answer that?" he asked. "Didn't we just cover this? You *know* how things are with the club. And you know we don't talk about this shit. What the hell do you want from me?"

"I want answers!" I said, my voice rising. "You call them your brothers. Brothers *love* each other, asshole. When you love someone, you don't let them throw away their lives in a prison cell!"

"That's not what happened."

"Then what *did* happen?" I demanded, shifting sideways on the couch, facing him. "Because I remember that night. We were drunk—which is the only reason I started kissing you, by the way—and you were nowhere near where that guy died. Why did you leave that night, Eli? And how the hell did you end up under arrest for something you couldn't possibly have done?"

He opened his mouth to answer, but I cut him off.

"Don't you *dare* feed me any more bullshit. I know *exactly* who and what the Reapers are—and what they're not. They didn't order you to take the fall for someone. You made that choice. You say you want us to be friends. That we should work together? Prove it. Give me an explanation."

The words hung between us, along with a thousand memories. Eli's eyes darkened, his expression intense as he caught my shoulders, pulling me toward him.

"Peaches, if there was any way to tell you, I would," he said, holding my gaze.

"You're a liar," I whispered. "You don't care about this bar, and you don't care about me."

"That's not true."

We stared at each other for long seconds, at an impasse. Then he shook his head slowly, muttering, "Fuck it."

Suddenly, his mouth was on mine, and I felt his hand sliding into my hair, gripping it tightly as his tongue thrust into my mouth. Sensations exploded through me—need and desire and just a hint of triumph. Because whatever it was that we'd felt for each other all those years ago, I hadn't imagined it.

We'd been frantic that night, ripping at each other's clothes, years of sexual tension driving us into a frenzy. This time, Eli's kiss was different. Not the crazed, sloppy mouth-fucking he'd given me at that party. This was deep and hungry.

As if he were starved for my taste.

The office door opened.

"It's time for the meet—oh, shit…"

I jerked away from Eli to find Gus standing in the doorway. He wore a strange expression. Not upset or angry, exactly. I'd have said he was pleased if he didn't look so uncomfortable.

"Give us a few?" Eli asked, his voice husky.

"Yeah," the old man said, glancing back down the hall. "You got ten minutes. People still need drinks, and I'll take my time pouring them. Join us after you put her in her car. She shouldn't be here tonight."

Gus shut the door, leaving Eli and me sitting next to each other. I felt stunned. Almost raw. I'd come here to make Gus an offer on the bar. Not to do…this.

"I don't suppose you want to pick up where we left off for another eight minutes or so?" Eli asked, trying to lighten the mood. I reached up and touched his face.

Remembering.

"You hurt me," I said after a long pause, forcing myself to drop my defenses. "You really hurt me, Eli. And setting whatever was between us aside, I could've *saved* your ass. You wouldn't let me, and you still won't tell me why. How can you not see how fucked-up that is?"

He swallowed.

"Yes, I did," he replied, and his voice was more serious than I'd ever heard it. "It was a shitty thing to do to you. Not to mention, stupid as hell. I'd give anything to go back to that night and change things. Wasn't like I planned it, Peaches. Nobody ever thought it would go that far."

His eyes were dark. Haunted, even. He was telling the truth.

"So, now what?" I asked.

"That's up to you," he said. "We can keep fighting. Try to run the bar together. Probably go crazy until you end up slitting my throat for real. Either that, or I'll lose my shit and fire you. Regardless, it'll get ugly."

"And what's the alternative?" I asked. "Let me guess. I walk away from the Starkwood?"

He gave a short, dark laugh.

"Yeah, like that's gonna happen."

Fair enough.

"We could try making peace," he said. "For real. Neither of us has to give up on our dreams if we work together. It doesn't matter whose name is on the deed, Peaches. We can be partners."

For an instant, something melted inside of me. If we were partners, then I wouldn't have to be on guard all the time. He drove me crazy, but it always left me feeling more alive.

What would it be like to truly work together?

Wait.

"It doesn't matter whose name is on the deed?" I asked, forcing myself to think things through.

"Not really," Eli said, catching my hand. Tingles danced across my skin where he touched me. I forced myself to ignore them.

"So why does it have to be *your* name?" I continued, keeping my tone casual. Eli raised a brow. "If it doesn't matter, I mean?"

"Um, because I have the money to buy it?" he said.

"How much?"

"How much, what?" he asked, and I caught the first hint of suspicion in his eyes.

"How much money did you get from your dad's settlement?" I asked, pulling away from him. "And how much is Gus charging you?"

Eli frowned. "Where are you going with this?"

"Let's just say, for the sake of argument, that I have enough money to buy the bar from Gus," I said slowly. "Do you think he'd sell it to me? If I could beat your price, I mean? Seeing as it doesn't really matter whose name is on the deed…"

Eli studied me.

"You've got money from somewhere, don't you?"

I took a deep breath, hoping I wasn't ruining everything. Eli was right. We couldn't go back and undo what'd happened in the past. But if we could make peace now… I thought about that kiss again, and how good it'd felt to be open with him.

"Yeah," I said slowly. "I've got money. I'm going to make Gus a cash offer. You say you want to be partners. Prove it. Tell me what you're paying him, and I'll tell you if I can beat it."

Chapter Seven

~Peaches~

Eli didn't answer. He looked away from me, then sighed and shook his head.

"I knew it," I told him. "You're so full of shit, Eli King."

"It's more complicated than that."

"No, it's not. Tell me what you're paying, and I'll see if I can beat it. Put up or shut up."

He wouldn't look at me. "You don't want to do this."

"You don't get to decide what I want," I said. "I'm twenty-nine years old, but you and Gus still treat me like I'm a child."

"That's not true."

"He just told you to *put me in my car*," I said, feeling my temper rise. I reached out and caught his chin, forcing him to look me in the eye. "I was sitting right here. Next to you. But when he wanted *me* to do something, he told you to do it. Like I'm your dog or something. It's getting a little bit old. Let me make my own fucking choices for once."

Eli blinked, clearly trying to figure out what the hell to say. Finally, he settled on, "You're not a dog."

"I *know* I'm not a dog. So, answer the fucking question."

"Three hundred and twenty-five thousand dollars," he said. "That's the settlement. It earned a little more sitting in the bank. I'm paying him three hundred and forty thousand for the land, the building, and the business."

"That's lower than he told me."

"Well, he was planning to carry the contract for you," Eli said. "This is cash."

"I can pay more than that," I told him. I studied his face, waiting for him to react. I expected anger—like I'd felt when I thought he'd won—or maybe frustration.

What I saw instead was worse. Much, much worse. Sadness, and maybe even a hint of…pity?

No. No fucking way.

"Peaches, he's not going to sell to you. It's about more than money."

The words were physically painful to hear. Another gut punch, almost as bad as when Gus had pulled the rug out from under me the first time.

"Why not?" I demanded.

"You know why."

"It can't be that special," I said, feeling almost anguished.

"What?" he asked, confused.

"Your *penis*. What the hell is it about having a penis that makes you more qualified to own this place than I am? Because as far as I can tell, that's the biggest difference between us."

Eli opened his mouth, then closed it again, seeming at a loss. Someone knocked on the door.

"Gus says it's time."

Eli blew out his breath in frustration, then ran his fingers through his hair. That made him look sexier, of course.

Almost like God was giving me the middle finger.

"Go," I snapped, pushing myself up and off the couch. "Go have your fucking meeting. Just don't think I'm taking your word for it. If Gus wants to turn down my money, he can do it in person. Oh, and I'll put myself in my car, so you don't need to worry about that."

"It's safer if I walk you out," Eli said.

To my horror, I felt tears welling in my eyes. Not only that, my nose felt runny. I grabbed the bottom of my shirt and pulled it up so I could wipe, flashing Eli in the process.

"Oh, fuck off," I said, hating myself for crying. Crying always made me feel weak. "You've seen my boobs before. I'm going to take a few minutes before I leave. Calm down. I don't want anyone to see me like this, okay? You owe me that much. I'll just sneak out the back when I'm ready."

"All right," he said, clearly reluctant to leave.

"Don't worry," I said. "I won't tell Gus you let me off the leash or make a mess in here. I'm a good dog that way."

"Peaches—"

"Shut the fuck up, Eli. Just shut the fuck up and leave me alone."

* * * *

~Eli~

I couldn't focus for shit on what Gage was trying to tell us.

I kept thinking about Peaches, and how much better she'd tasted than I remembered. Fucking hell… The night we'd almost had together, it'd been amazing. As the years passed, though, there were times when I doubted my memories. Kissing a girl couldn't feel that good. Not in real life.

Except it did with her.

Peaches and I had always had chemistry. It was probably what kept us at each other's throats. Although I could think of better uses for her throat. Christ, just the thought was enough to set me off. My jeans tightened, and I shifted uncomfortably in my seat.

Gus tried to catch my eye from across the table, but I ignored him, just like I'd ignored the seat he'd saved for me. I was still processing what Peaches had told me about the money. Well, trying to process it. Hard to think when all your blood kept pooling in your crotch.

I needed to get that girl into bed.

Soon.

Fighting with her was fun, but it wasn't enough. We needed to fuck. Repeatedly. And that couldn't happen until we resolved this whole situation.

Gus wouldn't sell the bar to her, no matter what she offered. I knew that for a fact, and it had fuck-all to do with her being a girl. He owed me in ways she couldn't begin to understand.

But even if he wanted to take the deal, the club would shoot him down. Her point about not having a dick was valid on that front… The Reapers might respect her—they'd never have settled on her as a compromise after I'd gotten locked up, otherwise—but she'd never be one of them. They'd take my side, even if Gus didn't.

"Eli?"

I looked up to find everyone staring at me. Shit. Gage must've asked a question, and I hadn't even noticed.

"Sorry," I told him. "Can you repeat that?"

"I was curious about the paperwork," he said. "Gus says you'll be signing things tomorrow. Anything I need to know?"

Well, shit. That was one hell of a loaded question. I glanced at Gus. I loved him, but he'd really cocked up this time.

"Yeah, I'd say there's a complication," I said. "Big one, actually."

"What's that?" Gage said, clearly surprised.

"Peaches Taylor is going to make Gus a cash offer tomorrow," I told them. "She says she can outbid me."

Silence fell across the table.

"There's no way," Gus said after a long pause. "She doesn't have any money. She doesn't have any credit, either."

"I suppose she could be lying," I replied, shrugging. "But I can't think of any reason she would. And since she doesn't have her own money, that means there's another party in the mix. Gotta be her stepdad."

Suddenly, everyone got really quiet.

James Carrington wasn't Gus's favorite person. Not that he'd have been okay with anyone who married Peaches' mom, but Carrington also happened to own the property next to Gus's house. There'd been a disagreement over an easement about ten years back.

I sat back, waiting for Gus's reaction. Surprisingly, he didn't blow up.

"Doesn't matter," he said. "We already made a deal."

"Don't you think Carrington will find it strange, considering he's offering more money?"

"We'll say it's part of your inheritance," Gus countered. "You're my only heir. It's a family deal."

"I think we should run it by the club lawyers," Gage said thoughtfully. "Carrington has a lot of connections, and the guy's like a fucking bloodhound when it comes to money. Tinker sits on the hospital board with him. She says he drives everyone crazy. Because if something looks even a little bit off to him, he'll spend hours tracking it down. We don't want that kind of attention."

"I've kept the books clean," Gus protested. "There's nothing for them to find. We should just sign the papers first thing in the morning. Then it'll be too late for her to make an offer. Problem solved."

Jesus. He was doing it again.

"You should talk to her," I said bluntly. "We wouldn't be in this mess if you'd communicated with her in the first place. I know you don't like it when she gets upset, but this is ridiculous. Grow a pair and own your shit."

Dead silence fell across the room. Conflict was nothing new among brothers, but Gus was essentially my dad. I'd never publicly questioned him before.

"Not your decision, Eli," Gus finally said. I'd expected anger, but the words came out sounding almost weak. "And there's no shit to own. I'm under no obligation to hear her out."

"I'm under no obligation to sign the fucking papers tomorrow morning."

"Is this really club business?" Gage asked, looking between us. "Or is it personal? Because it sounds personal."

"It's personal," Gus said. "Eli and I can talk after the meeting."

"It's not personal," I countered, starting to feel angry. "The club has a stake in the Starkwood. When you decided to sell to me, you got club approval first. I'm assuming that means you talked to them about carrying a contract for Peaches, too."

"He did," Gage confirmed.

"She does the bookkeeping," I told Gage. "At least, she does the books we show the IRS. When you agreed to sell to her—something nobody bothered talking to me about until after the fact, by the way—you were planning to bring her into the loop, right?"

"Moot point," Gus said. I ignored him.

"So, you were willing to trust her as a business associate," I continued. "She's been a friend of the club her entire life. If her stepdad is going to cause trouble, wouldn't it make more sense to meet with her? Maybe give her an explanation? I know you're afraid of pissing her off, Gus, but she loves you. She wouldn't set you up. Carrington won't get suspicious if he thinks she's the one who changed her mind. So, change her mind. Problem solved."

"I'm not afraid of anything," Gus snapped.

"My bad," I said, raising my palms. "I can't imagine why I'd think you were… What time did you want to sign those papers again?"

Someone snorted with laughter, quickly turning it into a cough.

"Peaches doesn't need an explanation," Gus said, sounding more defensive with every word. "You made your point, Eli. I fucked up by not telling her that things had changed. That was a mistake. But beyond that, she's just an employee. It doesn't matter what she thinks."

"She thinks you treat her like a dog."

He gave me a confused look. "A dog?"

"A *dog,*" I said. "And I can see why. You're treating her like a pet, not a person. She's worked here for seven years. You made a deal with her to take over, and then you jerked it out from under her, saying you needed cash. She got cash. Now, you're trying to hide instead of talking to her. It's like kindergarten."

"Eli…" Gage said, his tone warning me.

"All due respect, Gus, but have you considered that it's my ass on the line once the papers are signed? Peaches may love you, but she hates me. If you burn her again, I'll have to let her go. Is that really what you want?"

Gus looked stunned. "You'd fire her?"

"No," I said, hoping I wasn't making a huge mistake. But I couldn't forget the pain on her face. She'd said that I hurt her. And I had. But it'd been Gus hurting her, too.

He needed to be part of the solution.

"I won't be able to fire her," I told him. "Because I'm not buying the bar. Not unless you hear her out. You need to listen to her, and then you need to explain why you're selling to me in a way that satisfies her. Then I'll sign."

Gus's face flushed, and I heard a few mutters.

"He can't share club business," Gage said. "You know better than that, Eli."

"Then I guess Gus can't retire yet after all," I said, leaning back in my chair. "Gonna be a real bitch, running this place without me *or* Peaches. Good luck with that."

"I took you in when you had *nothing,"* Gus said, his voice rising.

"And I went to prison for a crime *you* committed." Everyone went silent. The words were true, but I'd never spoken them out loud before. I'd be lying if I said it wasn't a relief. But then I took a deep breath and focused on the only father I'd ever known. "I love you, Gus, and I appreciate everything you've done for me. But I already gave you five years. This time, you need to clean up your own mess."

Chapter Eight

Six years ago

~Peaches~

"You know," I said, speaking very slowly so the words wouldn't slur. "I think I like the *drinking* alcohol better than I like serving it."

McKayla nodded, her face serious.

"Way better," she replied, handing me her liquor bottle. "And that's not the only thing we've been doing wrong."

I took a deep swig. Tequila. Wasn't sure how much I'd had, but it was enough that it didn't burn going down anymore.

"Doing what wrong?" I asked.

"Working," she said, swaying to the side. I caught her arm so she wouldn't fall over. Not that it'd hurt her much. We were already sitting on the floor for reasons that'd made sense to me in the moment.

"We should stop *working* here," McKayla continued. "And start *drinking* here. You know, instead of working. I just think that'd be better. Can I have the bottle again?"

I frowned, considering the idea as I handed over the tequila. Challenging, with all the party noise. The buzzing in my head didn't help either. Every time I caught a thought, it tried to wiggle away.

"Drinking does seem way better than working," I agreed. "But we also need money to *buy* the drinks. So, if we stop working here, we'll probably have to work somewhere else. Otherwise, we'll run out of money."

"Oh," she said, her smile fading. She fell silent. I took the opportunity to survey the room—well, as much of it as I could see from the floor—pleased with how many people had shown up. All the Reapers, of course. Not just the locals, but quite a few from other chapters. Most of our friendly regulars, too.

The only one I hadn't seen yet was the birthday boy. Gus.

McKayla grabbed my arm, shaking it.

"What?" I asked.

"I've got the best idea! We don't need our own money to buy drinks. We just need someone to buy them. Anyone, really. So, why couldn't we just sleep with men to get alcohol? That's way more efficient than working."

"Tough call," I said slowly. "Because that sounds a little like prostitution."

"Nope. Prostitutes earn money. We wouldn't be earning money, just booze. And we'd keep it classy, too. No well drinks."

"Hard to argue with logic like that…"

"I know, right?" she said, giggling. McKayla was many things. Sweet and cute. Friendly.

Ultimately not much brighter than a chicken, though.

"So, assuming we decide to do this—and that's a big *if*—then who do you want to sleep with first?"

"Eli," she said with a little too much enthusiasm. "I'd really like to fuck Eli. But only once you're done with him. I follow the code."

I scrunched my nose at her. "I'm not interested in Eli. He smells like dirty feet."

"Yeah, I don't believe that," she said, reaching for the bottle again. "If you weren't interested, you wouldn't hang out with him so much."

"I hang out at Gus's house, which is where Eli happens to live," I corrected her. "Between that and work, I see him a lot. Doesn't mean I like it."

"Does that mean I can have him?" she asked, perking up.

I frowned. For some reason, I didn't care for that idea. *Don't think about it. Thinking is almost always a bad thing.*

"Okay, whatever," I said. "Just be sure to use like, six condoms. Because he's probably got all kinds of cooties."

McKayla gave a high-pitched squeal.

"You're amazing, Peaches. I love you!" she said gleefully, raising the bottle for a drink. But instead of swallowing, she lowered it, glee replaced by grief. "Oh, this is the worst. How could something so terrible happen in such a beautiful moment?"

"What?"

She tilted the bottle upside down between us. Nothing came out.

"The tequila disappeared."

"How did *that* happen?"

"Someone must've grabbed it while I was distracted. Then they drank all of if before putting it back in my hand, all without me ever noticing..."

I pictured Indiana Jones swapping out a bag of sand for treasure, and a snorting laugh escaped. McKayla shot me a dirty look. "Don't make fun of me. It could've happened."

"Yeah. Definitely the most likely explanation."

She sniffed. "Doesn't matter what happened to the booze. We need to focus on what's actually important—finding another bottle. Fast. Otherwise, we're at risk of sobering up. That's not okay."

"Once again, very hard to argue with your logic."

"Exactly," she said, nodding slowly. "Let's go get more tequila."

Standing up turned out to be a lot harder than I'd expected. My left leg had fallen asleep, and I'd been sitting on something sticky. Not only that, but by the time I completed the process, I couldn't quite remember why I'd needed to get up in the first place.

Fortunately, the music was good, and people were starting to dance. Not only that, I loved dancing. Always had. And now there was a dance floor right in front of me when I needed it most.

Clearly, God wanted me to go shake my ass for a while.

Who was I to argue with *God?*

An hour later, Gus still hadn't arrived.

The party was fantastic—even without the birthday boy—and I was having a blast. I'd danced with all kinds of people. Well, mostly women, but some of the younger guys, too. It seemed like half the state knew Gus, and they'd all shown up to party with him.

This included at least forty members of the Reapers Motorcycle Club, plus their old ladies. They'd come roaring into town earlier that day in groups, meeting up at the state park campground before forming a convoy to the Starkwood. Others had joined in behind them, and now there had to be at least a hundred motorcycles parked outside.

My ears were still ringing from the noise they'd made when they pulled into the lot. Or maybe they were ringing from the music. It was slowing down now, and people had started coupling up on the dance floor.

Seemed like a sign to me—time to rehydrate. Only water, though. I'd worked up a sweat. Winding my way through the crowd, I made for the bar.

That's when I spotted Eli.

He sat on one of the stools, surveying the party as if we existed for his entertainment. To his right sat Tinker, and just past her was her man, Gage. I'd always liked both of them. My appreciation for McKayla was fading, though. She'd squeezed herself into the space between the stools to Eli's left, resting her hand on his chest possessively.

Did it bother me? Absolutely not…although I couldn't see them together for more than a night.

Eli needed someone smarter than McKayla.

Someone who could keep him in line.

None of my business, really, but I still needed water, and the best spot for flagging down the bartender was probably that gap between Eli and Gage's old lady.

"Do you mind?" I asked Tinker, choosing not to acknowledge Eli's presence.

"Not at all," she said with a big smile, scooting over. "It's a great party, Peaches. You did a good job planning it."

Eli shifted, and his elbow caught me. Returning Tinker's smile with one of my own, I elbowed him back.

"Thanks," I said. "Although I didn't actually do very much. Gus planned most of it himself. Said what he really wanted was to see the rest of us having fun. Although I did pick up the cake earlier today."

Eli jostled me again, and I nearly fell into Tinker. Asshole.

"I'm getting some water," I told her. "Do you want anything?"

"I'm good," she said, raising her beer. Using my shoulder, I shoved Eli as I leaned into the bar, waving down the bartender, Ethan. I didn't know him very well yet—he was new to the Starkwood—but he'd been doing an okay job so far.

"Hey! Can I get some water?"

He nodded, and I turned around again, catching Eli with my shoulder another time. He looked at me, then leaned in toward my ear.

"You trying to cock-block me?" he asked, jerking his head toward McKayla.

"Oh, I didn't even notice you sitting there, Eli," I said brightly. "And McKayla's with you! Hi, McKayla!"

I gave her a little finger wave, and she finger-waved back, giggling. Then she stopped waving, and her hand dropped down to his stomach.

My eyes followed, noting how the faded jeans couldn't quite hide his package. Easy to see, with his legs spread wide like that. Then her hand slipped lower, sliding down his hip to rest against his inner thigh.

Ewww.

"Got your water, Peaches!" Ethan said, his voice pitched loud enough to carry over the chaotic noise of the party. I turned back to him, thankful for the distraction.

The water tasted good. Almost unnaturally so. Guess I hadn't realized how thirsty I'd gotten. Enough to chug the whole thing in one gulp.

I set the glass down to discover that Eli had swiveled the stool to face me. McKayla had disappeared. *Must be smarter than I gave her credit for…*

"Don't blame me just because she ditched you," I said. "She probably heard that you're a murderer. Nobody likes a murderer."

That's when I noticed Ethan standing in front of us. I think he'd been reaching for my empty water glass, but now he seemed frozen. Horrified, even. Well, fuck. If he couldn't roll with a joke like that, he'd never make it at the Starkwood.

"She's talking about a stuffed animal," Eli told him. "It was when we were kids. She's obsessed with it. I've told her to seek professional help, but she's too proud. Sad, really."

Ethan nodded, although the move was hesitant. Fair enough. Eli was a big guy with a tough reputation. Throw in the fact that he was a Reaper, and I could see why Ethan might be nervous.

"Eli's right," I said, catching Ethan's eye. "I was teasing him about something that happened when we were kids. He's just a big softie inside. Like a marshmallow, only less flammable."

I nudged him with my shoulder playfully. He bumped me back—just a little harder—and then I slammed my shoulder into him, all the while holding Ethan's gaze and smiling.

"So, where the hell is Gus?" Eli asked. "I thought he was supposed to be here by now."

"Hell if I know," I said, shrugging. "He'll get here when he gets here. Think I'm gonna dance some more. If you're very lucky, I'll let you dance with me."

"No dancing. McKayla's out there, and I'm afraid she'll jump me or something. I'd rather avoid that, all things considered."

"I thought you were into her," I said, thinking about her hand on his thigh. That might've been her idea, but he hadn't seemed unhappy about the situation. "You said I was cock-blocking."

"That was before I smelled her breath," he said, winking at me. "Or maybe I just wanted to piss you off. Either way, she's not my type."

"And what would your type be?" I asked, curious. He'd always fucked around, but as far as I knew, he'd never had a serious girlfriend.

"I like 'em with a little more spirit," he said, catching and holding my eye. "McKayla'd be fun for about ten minutes. Then I'd get bored."

"Really?" I asked, raising a brow. "Because I heard that you only need five. Seven, max."

He laughed, and I caught Ethan eyeing us again. I leaned into Eli.

"I'm not so sure about the new bartender," I said, pitching my tone low. "Seems like he spooks easily. Might not be tough enough for a place like this…"

"He wants to fuck you. And he doesn't like me because he knows he doesn't have a chance while I'm around."

Now I laughed. "Yeah, right. Like I'd ever fuck you."

"You'd fuck me before you fucked him," he said, his voice dry. I had to agree. Ethan was skinny. Stringy, almost. Bad skin, and hair that never looked particularly clean.

"You won't think I'm hitting on you if I agree, will you?"

"Nope. I can always tell when you're hitting me because it hurts, and then I wake up with bruises the next day. Let's go shoot darts."

Catching my hand, Eli pushed off the stool and pulled me through the crowd toward the back hallway. Gus's office was on the right. The storeroom was to the left.

I'd always seen it as a magical wonderland of pretty bottles and kegs to climb on, complete with a fort we'd built out of liquor boxes.

The finishing touch had been a dart board that we'd stolen from the main bar. Most of the time, we'd been pretty good about throwing the darts at the target instead of at each other.

Well, maybe not *most* of the time, but at least half…

Astoundingly, neither of us had ever gotten hurt during those epic battles for storeroom supremacy. Okay, so I'd stabbed him in the butt once. But it'd been an accident. Mostly.

Eli pulled a set of keys out of his pocket and unlocked the door. I reached for the light switch. He caught my hand.

"No, let's play in the dark. Like when we were kids."

"I'd sort of forgotten about that," I whispered, stepping into the room. We'd always kept the lights off. It made it harder for the adults to track us.

Now, I was one of those adults, and the storeroom had long since lost its magic. The bottles weren't treasures, and our fort had been broken down and recycled. But I knew for a fact that the dart board and darts were still here. So was the old wingback chair where I'd sat and read so many books. As my eyes adjusted, I saw the faint light shining through the two high-set windows on the far side of the room.

I couldn't remember the last time we'd actually played here. It'd been a long time. The darts and the board were still here, though.

Eli reached to the top of the shelf and grabbed an old shoe box. He opened it and pulled out a dart, handing it to me.

"What are we playing for?" I asked, stepping up to the silver duct tape that marked our line on the floor. Raising my hand, I sighted carefully on the bullseye. This was going to be a tough game, I realized. There was just enough light to see the target clearly, but not quite enough to see it well…

Oh. And I was still fairly drunk.

That probably wasn't going to help.

Eli hadn't answered the question, so I decided to ignore him and focus on my game instead. I took a deep breath, pulled back my hand just the slightest, and—

"How about a kiss?" he asked, his voice loud in my ear. The dart flew off to the left, bouncing off the concrete wall next to the target with a clang.

Sabotaging motherfucker.

"That one shouldn't count," I protested.

"Of course, it counts," Eli said. He used one of his big arms to sweep me to the side. Now, it was his turn to step up to the line.

"You know the rules," he said, radiating smugness.

"The only rule is that we don't tell on each other," I said, trying to glare at him. Hard to glare when all you wanted to do was laugh, though. "Everything else is fair game."

"There's your answer," he replied, shooting me a grin. He raised his hand to throw. On a wild impulse, I jumped at him, wrapping my arms around his neck and smashing my mouth into his.

Eli swayed, dropping the dart as he wrapped his arms around me. I ducked down, sliding out from under him, laughing. I staggered backward, nearly tripping over the chair in the process.

"What the fuck, Peaches?"

This struck me as incredibly funny, which made me laugh even harder. So hard that I couldn't breathe, let alone speak.

"I wish… I wish you could see the look…on your face," I finally managed to gasp out, although it took a few tries. "And my dart is closer to the target than yours is. That means I'm first."

"Never gonna happen," he said, and while the words were angry, his tone was teasing. Eli was having a good time, I realized. Both of us were. "That doesn't count as a throw. Nice try, but your timing was off."

I raised a finger, wagging it at him while making little tch-tch-tch noises. "The dart was in your hand. You raised your hand to throw, and then you released the dart into the air. That's a throw."

"No," he said. "You attacked me. Without provocation, I might add—" I snorted. "I dropped the dart as a direct result of that attack. That's a foul. Doesn't count."

"Only if you're following some set of rules," I pointed out. "I'd like to remind you that our only rule is that we don't tell on each other. Here's the good news, I wasn't planning to tell everyone about your shitty throw. But it definitely counts."

He narrowed his eyes. "Okay. You can go first."

I grabbed another dart, then stepped back to the line. Obviously, Eli was planning retaliation. I tried to watch him, but he moved behind me.

The back of my neck prickled like I was being stalked by a tiger.

"Don't worry," he said as I tried to aim.

"About you? Never."

Except I was worried. Because I could feel him back there.

Lurking. Waiting to pounce. *Just focus on the target. He's playing mind games with you.*

Taking a deep breath, I tried to concentrate. The bass from the party was a dim thump in the distance. Occasionally, a laugh or a shout could be heard.

The only thing I couldn't hear was Eli. Those big feet of his were like skis. No way could he move without making some noise, right? Except Eli was very sneaky…

Spinning around, I found him leaning against one of the shelves, a good six feet away. This time, he wagged his finger at me.

"Paranoia is a sign of a guilty conscience," he said, offering a shit-eating grin. I took a minute to consider throwing the dart at him. It'd be satisfying, no question. But he was trying to get a rise out of me. I didn't want to reward that kind of behavior.

I turned toward the board again, raised my hand, and then screamed as Eli's arms came around me from behind. One landed near my waist while the other crossed my chest, immobilizing my arms in the process.

"Bastard!" I shrieked, trying to sound outraged. But he'd lifted me, and now we were spinning around. I couldn't remember the last time someone had spun me around like that. I'd forgotten how much fun it was.

It felt like an hour but was probably only a minute or so before he stumbled. We lurched backward and almost crashed into the shelf. Somehow, he managed to fall back into the chair. I landed on top of him, laughing so hard that my ribs hurt.

Or maybe that was just from his arms squeezing me.

Eli's grip loosened, his hands dropping to rest loosely on my waist. I relaxed into his bulk, strangely comfortable.

"Your hair is smothering me," he said, catching my wrists and putting them together so he could hold them in one hand. Then he reached up and caught my hair, trying to finger-comb it to the side.

"Sorry," I told him, attempting to lean forward. He let go for an instant. Then his hands were under my armpits as he lifted me like a rag doll, draping me across his lap. His left arm wound around my back. My legs draped over the arm of the old chair as his right hand reached up and slid into my hair.

He pulled my mouth to his, and a world of sensation exploded through me.

I'd thought about kissing Eli in the past. The man was sexy as hell—you'd have to be blind not to notice. Blind, deaf, and without a sense of smell, more accurately. Every time I'd imagined those kisses, they'd been terrifying because Eli was intense. He never did anything halfway, and I suspected his kisses would overwhelm me.

Instead, his lips somehow managed to be soft while still demanding enough to leave no question as to who was in charge in the moment. His tongue slid into my mouth before I even fully realized what was happening. I was too busy squirming, aching, almost desperate from the sudden surge of need.

Feeling his tongue plunge deep, all I could think about was that I needed more of him inside of me. For once, I didn't feel like I had to fight or question what was happening. I just opened to him, drawing him in, wrapping my arms around his neck and pulling him closer.

His head slanted, kissing harder now. I felt something hard under my butt and knew it had to be him. I shimmied my hips, savoring the way it made him shudder. He pulled away for an instant, and our eyes met.

"Jesus, but that feels good," he said in a strained voice.

"Let's not drag Jesus into this, okay?" I whispered, then lifted my head, trying to catch his lips again. I didn't even notice that he'd dropped his hand to my waist until he tugged my shirt free from my jeans. I expected him to go for my breasts. Instead, he found the back of my pants, sliding his hand under the waistband and plunging deep to grab the cheek of my ass with big fingers.

He stilled, studying my face.

"You have no idea how many times I've thought about doing this," he said. He lowered his mouth for another kiss, brushing his lips across mine. It was lovely, but I needed more. He was kissing me like we were making love.

I wanted him to fuck my mouth.

Catching his bottom lip with my teeth, I bit down. Not hard enough to break the skin, but close. He groaned, and his hand clenched on my ass. Then he grabbed my hair with his free hand, twisting it around his fingers before jerking my head to him, holding me still.

My entire body clenched, liquid and hot and ready to take him.

If he can do this with one little kiss, what else can he do?

I clenched at the thought, spirals of desire zipping along my spine.

I had to find a way to straddle him. Rub against him. Fuck him. I ached for it, squirming against the cock prodding my ass, needing more, and needing it *now*. He groaned, and I couldn't tell if it was pain or pleasure. It didn't matter. All that mattered was getting him inside of me.

"Don't move," he muttered, pulling back on my hair for emphasis.

That should've pissed me off, yet somehow it just turned me on even more. Swiveling my hips, I tried to grind down on him. His hips bucked up almost instantly, and he moaned.

At least I wasn't the only one who'd gone into heat out of nowhere.

Nobody could be expected to sit still when they ached like this.

Still holding his mouth with mine, I rolled to my right, directly into his body. My legs swung down, one on either side of his strong thigh. I slid my hips back, experimenting with the new position.

Oh, that was… Really good. *Holy-fucking-shit* good.

We kissed like that for long seconds, me grinding against his thigh, him holding me by the hair with one hand. The other squeezed my ass, pulling my hips forward into him with every stroke.

It wasn't enough. I wanted all of him between my legs.

Eli must've been feeling the same way because he let go of my hair and pulled his hand out of my jeans. Before I could figure out what he meant to do, he'd wrapped his hands around my thighs from the outside. Then he stood up, lifting me as if I weighed nothing.

I shrieked, wrapping my arms tightly around his neck.

Hitching me upward, he pulled me into his body, sending my legs splaying to either side. I hissed as his cock found just the right place between my legs. Then he sat back on the chair, bringing me with him, and it all made sense.

Now, I straddled him, my legs spread wide, one hanging off each side of the chair, draped over the arms. He caught my hair again. I expected him to give me another of those devastating kisses. Instead, he pulled back, tilting my head to give him better access to my neck.

His other hand slid back down into my jeans. His fingers were still spread wide, but this time, his thumb landed deep, pressing between my cheeks.

I froze, uncertain.

"Nothing happens unless you want it to happen," he said, kissing my neck gently. He tightened the hand on my ass, pulling my hips into his, slowly guiding me back and forth along the length of his shaft.

Hunger pulsed through me…hunger and the realization that he was serious. Nothing would happen unless I wanted it to.

What we were doing right then was damned good. Near perfect. Wonderful and exactly what I wanted. But it wasn't enough. Grabbing the sides of the chair for leverage, I swiveled my hips into his, feeling the bulge of his cock in a whole new way.

Bet it would feel even better without all these clothes in the way.

"You say nothing happens unless I want it to happen." I tugged against the hair he still held. He let it go instantly. I lowered my mouth, giving him another kiss. "Pretty sure I want you to fuck me right here in the Starkwood Saloon storeroom."

His eyes darkened. I realized his lips looked unusually good. *Probably from me biting them…oops.*

"You're drunk," he said, lifting his hips to give me a better angle.

"I'm not that drunk anymore," I replied, even if it wasn't entirely true. I was definitely drunk. And thank God for it. Because there was no other way I'd have relaxed enough to kiss Eli King, let alone have sex with him.

And I really, really wanted to have sex with him.

"You sure?" he asked. He wanted it as badly as I did. I could tell. There was something so surreal and sweet about the thought of Eli caring enough to double-check.

Grinding down, I shuddered, wishing like hell I'd worn a skirt. Then I could just lift up enough for him to undo his fly, and…

"Yeah, I'm sure," I said, my voice husky.

Both hands caught my ass again, giving me just a hint of warning before he stood up. My legs wrapped tightly around his waist without bothering to ask for permission. I'd always known he was strong, but I hadn't even begun to imagine all the fun a person could have with that kind of strength.

He could fuck me up against a wall, then carry me into the bedroom over his shoulder, toss me on the bed, then fuck me again.

I'd never been so turned on in my life.

"Where?" he asked, looking around the room. "We could go to the office."

"People would see us," I said, laughing. "You can fuck me right here, on the floor. I don't care."

"It's dirty."

"You are such a girl," I said, still giggling. "You afraid your knees might get dirty? It may not be the most romantic of spots, but it's not like we're dating. And I know you've fucked quite a few women in here over the years, so don't even try to pretend you haven't. Either you lay me down on that floor and fuck me, or I'm going out to that party and finding someone who will. Your choice."

Eli's eyes flashed, and I knew it was all over.

"Let me down," I told him. He lowered me, sliding me down every inch of his body until my feet found the floor. Instead of stopping, I lowered gracefully into a kneeling position, catching the end of his shirt and lifting it just enough to kiss his stomach.

His entire body shuddered.

My hands found the fly of his jeans. I cupped my fingers around his erection through the fabric, squeezing it tight. Then I looked up at him, offering a teasing smile.

"No fucking way," he said, shaking his head slowly. "I can't believe I'm saying this, but don't even consider giving me head. You wrap that mouth around me, and I'll last all of five minutes."

"Yeah, I thought ten minutes was a bit optimistic," I said, blowing him a kiss. Then I reached down and caught my shirt, pulling it up and over my head.

The look on his face when he saw my bra was more than enough to justify what I'd paid for it. But when I reached for my pants, that's when things got good. He stilled, standing over me almost mesmerized as I slowly popped the button on my fly, then lowered the zipper. The fabric sagged, clinging to my hips. I gave a little shimmy, which was enough to drop them a couple of inches lower…

"Shit," Eli muttered, ripping open his own jeans. He grabbed his cock, fisting it as I very slowly, very deliberately slid my fingers down the midline of my body.

When I reached my panties, I dipped them under, finding my clit with my middle digit. I gave it a quick rub, my breath catching, and then pushed my hand down farther, my finger sliding through my cleft.

"Nice and wet," I told him.

Eli shoved down his jeans, then dropped to his knees in front of me. First, he kissed me, cupping the back of my neck with one hand while the other wrapped tightly around my waist. He started lowering me to the floor, then paused.

"Hold on," he said. Leaning back on his heels, he caught the bottom edge of his shirt, pulling it up and over his head. Shaking it out flat, he spread it on the floor next to us. "Better. Now lay down."

I took a second to kiss him one more time, then lowered myself to the shirt. Something felt really bizarre, and I realized that this was the first time I'd ever done anything Eli had asked me to do without fighting with him first.

His hands found my jeans, and I lifted my hips so he could pull them off, along with my underwear. Then they were gone, and he was crawling up and over my body until our eyes met.

"You sure you know what you're doing?" he asked.

"Most guys don't ask this many questions when a girl tells them to fuck her."

"Yeah, well those guys probably weren't raised in a house where they had to worry about finding snakes in their beds."

The words sounded angry, but the tone was teasing. Resting his weight on his left arm, Eli reached down between us with his right, finding my clit right away. I gasped, and my hips rocked toward him.

The tip of his cock brushed against me.

"You have no idea how long I've been waiting for this," Eli whispered. My hips curled toward him, and—

The storeroom door flew open, banging into the wall.

"Eli! Where the fuck are you? We got a situation."

"Don't you dare answer," I told him, somehow whispering and shouting at the same time. I twisted my hips up and into him a second time, and his dick slid into me about half an inch. *Goddamnit.*

"Eli, there's big fucking trouble. It's Gus."

That sounded like Gage. Shit. Normally, he'd just send a prospect if he had a message. There must be something seriously wrong happening with Gus. My stomach gave an anxious little flip.

"What's wrong with Gus?" I asked, nudging at Eli to let me up. He rolled off me, and I started feeling around for my clothes. Suddenly, the lights came on, blinding me.

"Turn off the fucking light!" Eli shouted.

"Eli? Is that you?"

"Yes, it's Eli. And Peaches," I said, trying not to let my tone waver. I pulled on my pants, trying not to think about how many people would figure out that we'd… Eli made a growling noise, and a muscle in his jaw started twitching. "We'll be out in a minute."

"Move fast," Gage said. "It's serious, Eli. I need your ass at Gus's house in the next ten minutes. Pipes is waiting in the parking lot. Leave your bike here. I got a feeling we'll need you on Gus's before this is over."

"Fuck!" Eli said, slamming the flat of his palm against the floor.

Someone was feeling grumpy about his blue balls.

"Breaking your hand isn't going to help Gus."

"No, but it might protect him," he said. "Because unless this little emergency of his involves him dying, I'll be tempted to finish the job. Then I'll have to deal with the body. That'll be a real bitch if one of my hands is broken."

"What a…heartwarming thought."

"Yeah, I'm all heart."

"I'm coming with you," I said. "If he's dying, I want to say goodbye."

"Gus is way too mean to die," Eli told me. "Lots of people have come after him through the years. Note that they're gone, and he isn't."

"I'm serious. I'm coming with you."

Eli stopped and turned toward me. His hands moved to my shoulders, giving them a gentle squeeze as his eyes caught mine. "This situation is club business, Peaches. I can't bring you with me just because you're my girlfriend. That's not how my world works."

I ignored his use of the word *girlfriend* and the hope that it gave me. "Sometimes I think your world is bullshit."

"Yeah, sometimes I think my world is bullshit, too," he said. "But it's the only one I got, so I'm gonna make the most of it."

Chapter Nine

Present Day

~Peaches~

"I went to prison for a crime you committed," Eli said, his voice ringing through the Starkwood. "I love you, Gus, and I appreciate everything you've done for me. But I already gave you five years. This time, you need to clean up your own mess."

Holy.

Fucking.

Shit.

For an instant, I thought I'd heard Eli wrong. What he'd just said couldn't be true. No way. Except Gus had been late to his own birthday party. I'd seen him come through the back door with Pipes, right about the time Eli was getting arrested for murder.

Eli couldn't have gotten to the house until after the killing, I reminded myself. And the murder had definitely taken place. Somebody had offed the guy. So why hadn't I suspected Gus before now?

Probably because you didn't want to.

Eli's announcement was essentially a live grenade, tossed into the middle of the meeting. Now, everyone was arguing. I couldn't hear much in the way of details, but at least a few of them sounded pissed because they'd been left out of the loop.

Good to know. Probably meant that the Reapers MC hadn't been behind this particular shitshow.

I didn't hear Gus say anything in his defense, and I had no way of seeing his reaction. Couldn't see much of anything because the only place to hide was behind the long wooden bar itself. If I'd planned to spy on them ahead of time, I might've been able to come up with something more comfortable. Maybe built myself the roadhouse equivalent of a duck blind. But it'd never occurred to me to spy on a meeting before.

Ever.

I'd learned from a young age that when the Reapers were talking, it was time to disappear. Let the men do their thing and stay out of the way. That hadn't been a winning strategy for me.

Hadn't worked out so great for Eli, either.

If I'd gotten in the way a little more, maybe Eli wouldn't have gone to prison. I couldn't blame Gus for all of—

Wait.

Where the fuck did *that* crazy thought come from?

Of course, it wasn't my fault. The real villain here was clearly Gus, with a possible assist from the Reapers. My heart hurt to think about it. I wanted to find an excuse for him, but Eli had been sentenced to *twenty years* in the state penitentiary.

How could Gus even look him in the eye?

Eli was innocent. I knew that for a fact, and apparently, so had Gus. And, yeah… It was great that the Reapers had hired a fancy lawyer to appeal the conviction, but Gus still owed Eli five years of his life.

Damned right, he should have to clean up his own mess.

At least now I understood why Gus was selling low to Eli. Hell, he should be *giving* him the Starkwood.

The tone of the meeting had changed from argument to shouting match, but I didn't care anymore. I'd heard everything I needed to know. Now, it was time to get my ass out of there, before someone noticed me. I didn't think I needed to be afraid of the Reapers, but I'd never dreamt that Gus would let Eli go to prison for him either.

Mom had been right—Gus wasn't the man that either of us needed him to be. The thought twisted my heart in terrible ways, but I couldn't deny the reality.

No. You can't think about this right now. You need to focus on getting out and getting safe. Figure out your emotions later.

Right. Grief couldn't hurt me if I refused to feel it.

Thankful for the noise, I slipped out from behind the bar and headed down the hallway, moving quickly. Past the office, past the storage room. Through the back door and out into the parking lot. I made it the whole way in complete silence. Then my car beeped when I unlocked it, shattering the stillness outside.

Stupid noise almost gave me a heart attack. There was usually at least one prospect stationed out front during meetings like this, to keep watch over the motorcycles. I kept expecting him to come running around the building, possibly with guns blazing.

Nobody seemed to notice, though. Lucky for me, in addition to the regular parking lot, Gus had worked some sort of deal with the national forest, and we'd gotten permission to use one of their gravel lots for employee parking.

It made for a long walk in, but tonight, I was thankful for the distance. They'd have to be watching exactly the right spot to see me pulling out. I kept my headlights off until I made it around the big bend in the highway, though. Just in case.

I didn't plan on driving to Gus's house.

Okay, so I'd planned to go there originally, but only so I could make him a cash offer. Given what I'd just heard at the bar, that seemed fairly pointless.

Not to mention wrong.

Eli had literally done time for Gus. I'd probably have to shank the old man myself if he backed out. Not that I thought Eli was a great guy or something, but he was better than some. Most, really.

If you love him so much, why don't you marry him?

Good God. Now my own subconscious was making fun of me. If I had to put up with a voice in my head telling me what to do, at the very least, it should be male, with a sexy Irish accent… Maybe Jonathan Rhys Meyers, although I'd settle for Colin Farrell if I had to.

Thankfully, the gravel country road leading to Gus's house was right ahead. Less than five minutes later, I'd parked my car and made my way around the back of the old farmhouse, to the kitchen door, finding it open.

This wasn't a surprise because it'd never been locked the entire time I'd known Gus. Same with the barn, and the shop—something that had come up during Eli's appeal. Gus had claimed that not only did he leave his place open, but that he didn't have the keys to lock it even if he wanted to.

Anyone could've taken his pickup that night.

That's what he'd told me, at least. And I'd believed him.

Stepping into the narrow galley kitchen brought back a thousand memories. Me and Mom, baking cookies. Me and Gus, microwaving marshmallow Peeps. There were even memories of Eli and me. Most of them involved chasing each other with knives.

"How the hell did we never get seriously injured?" I said, feeling almost wistful.

This was crazy. As an adult, I could see that my idealized fantasy had never existed. Yet for some reason, I was still sad about losing it.

And I'd lost another huge chunk of it today, in Gus.

Opening the fridge, I found a can of Dr. Pepper, which made me smile. Gus was an idiot who'd cheated on my mom and sent Eli to prison in his place. Yet for some reason, he always had Dr. Pepper waiting in the fridge.

How could he remember to buy me pop, yet conveniently forget all about my mom whenever he'd fucked someone else?

Eli wouldn't do that. Or would he? No, he wouldn't. He was better than that.

Taking a large plastic tumbler out of the cupboard, I filled it with ice from the little plastic trays Gus still used because he didn't trust ice makers. He had one at the bar, of course. Said that's how he knew they couldn't be trusted, which had always amused me.

I refilled the ice trays with fresh water, then grabbed my pop and the cup before passing into the dining room. At least, that's what my mom had always called it. In reality, there was just one big room across the front of the house, divided into two sections—one for eating, one for watching TV. For years, any time I came to visit, Eli would have to sleep out in the "living room."

Walking over to the sideboard, I opened one of the doors and pulled out a bottle of vodka. I was old enough now that I didn't have to worry about how full it was. I still enjoyed the occasional drink, but I wasn't much of a partier anymore.

Not after Eli had gotten arrested.

A part of me had always wondered if he'd refused to let me talk to the cops because I'd been drinking that night. They might not have trusted a drunk girl with club connections.

I'd spent years wondering *what if*. Whenever I'd asked Eli about it, he'd always changed the subject.

Now, I knew the truth. None of it had anything to do with me.

Popping the tab on the Dr. Pepper, I filled the tumbler about halfway full, then topped it off generously with the vodka. Then I turned to face the room, raising the glass high for a toast.

"To the snakes!"

"What the fuck is it about snakes that turns you on so much?" asked Eli, who seemed to appear out of nowhere. "If it's a fetish thing, I'd prefer that you keep it out of the bar."

"Holy shit!" I yelled, so startled that I dropped the cup, sending pop and vodka splashing across the scratched wooden floor.

"Funny how you can carry entire trays of drinks over your head, but that one plastic cup is just too hard for you to handle when you're here."

"It's warped from the dishwasher. Kind of like you," I snapped, then realized what a rude thing that was to say. Apparently, I'd told myself that he was the enemy for so long that I'd programmed my body to keep up the hate, even when I wasn't feeling it.

"Sorry," I said. "Let's try this again. You said something about this cup, and how hard it is for me to handle. I just realized you're playing that game with me, aren't you?"

"What game?" Eli asked, pretending that he didn't know exactly what I was talking about.

"The one where we trick each other into saying things that can be used against us."

"Yeah, I think I remember that one," he said, offering me a lazy smile. "But I'm not playing it tonight. If something sounds bad to you, that's because you have a dirty mind."

"So, you're telling me that you can't see how me saying I can always handle hard—" I stopped talking, wondering if there was anything in the kitchen suitable to bash in his skull when I swung it around by its handle.

He burst out laughing. I flipped him off, trying not to smile. Or worse, start laughing with him, because…the thought seemed to hang there, right in front of me, waiting for me to own it. I swallowed. This was going to change everything.

Eli isn't my enemy. Eli is one of my best friends. I've always been able to trust him with my secrets, even when keeping them gets him in trouble.

And he's always been able to trust me.

"Tell me about the night you got arrested," I said, letting the game go.

He gave me a wary look. "You already know everything you need to know."

"Bullshit," I insisted. "Tell me the real story."

"No," he said, and his voice softened. "Peaches, it would hurt you, and there's nothing good that can come from it. It's time to let it go."

"Why?" I said, stepping over the river of Dr. Pepper and vodka. "You afraid it'll be too hard for me to handle? I can't believe I fell for that. Probably because it doesn't even sound dirty anymore. I can't decide if the culture has changed that much, or if we were just exceptionally sheltered children."

I took another step toward him, and then another, closing the distance.

"You were sheltered," he said, catching and holding my gaze. "Me, not so much. Gus took me in because my mom was into meth. I don't remember the worst of it. Your mom always said that was my brain protecting my heart. Because some things shouldn't be remembered."

"I'm sorry," I said, reaching my hand out to him. He took it, his big fingers wrapping around my smaller ones, strong and warm.

Eli snorted, breaking the moment. "You were sorry that you had to share your bedroom."

"I was *five*. Every five-year-old on Earth has anger management issues they're working through. By definition."

"And have you finally worked through yours?" he asked, the question playful but very real at the same time.

"Not all of them," I admitted, walking toward the big, comfy couch in the living room. I'd started sleeping down here once they'd taken Eli away. For some reason, stealing his bed hadn't felt right. "I still need to hear about what happened that night. When you got arrested."

"Why?" he asked. "Talking about it won't change anything."

I let his hand go, settling back into the center of the brown sectional. It didn't match the rest of the house on about a thousand different levels, but it was comfy, and I loved sleeping on it.

Eli sat next to me, stretching out on the long section that extended into the center of the room. It was more of a bed than a couch.

"One last chance, Eli," I said. He reached over, catching my hand. Something wild gleamed in his eyes as he tugged me toward him. I started to scoot in his direction when I realized that he was using sex as a diversion.

"No fucking way," I said, pulling my hand back. I wanted to glare at him, but it took just about everything I had not to crawl into his lap. "I want to hear it from you. All of it."

His gaze sharpened. "What time did you leave the bar tonight?"

I considered pretending that I didn't know what he was talking about. That's what I'd done when I *borrowed* his car my junior year. He hadn't fallen for it then. No point in playing games. Not now.

"The last thing I heard was you telling Gus to clean up his own mess."

Eli leaned back against the cushions, propping up his feet as he studied the ceiling.

"Then you heard the part that matters," he said. "What else do you want to know?"

"Everything. But I understand that some things aren't supposed to be talked about. I can respect that."

He rolled his head to look at me, raising a brow.

"Okay, so I can sort of respect it a little bit…" I amended. "And I know Gus needs to tell the story for himself."

"Very true," he said.

"You know, I worshiped him when I was a little girl. I knew he wasn't my real dad, but it felt like he was. Then you came along, and he didn't have time for me anymore. Somehow, I convinced myself that there was only room for one child in this house. I had to get rid of you."

"You may have mentioned that a few times when we were kids," he pointed out, his voice dry. "I think the most memorable time was that day at the pond. You threw popcorn out into the water and told me that was the only food I was allowed to eat."

"I was horrible," I admitted. "I know I was horrible. I shouldn't have treated you that way, but I was only five."

"C'mere," he said and held his hand out to me. I took it, letting him pull me over for real this time. He rolled up on his side, creating enough space for me to lie on my back, bringing us face-to-face.

It felt horribly intimate. I wasn't just looking at him. I was smelling him and feeling the heat of his body.

My hands lay folded across my stomach. He tangled his fingers with mine, softly rubbing his thumb across the tiny strip of bare skin that'd been exposed when my shirt rode up.

"Better," he said. "So, let's get this out of the way. I know you were a kid. I was a kid. Neither of us had any control, and both of us were scared that Gus would love the other one more. The big difference was that you had your mom on your side, no matter what. I didn't have anyone but Gus. That's why he chose me, Peaches. And if he hadn't done that, I'd probably be dead by now."

"Yeah, I realize that now," I told him. "But I couldn't see it back then."

"In fairness, I couldn't see it either. I was used to living one meal to the next, hoping we'd land in a safe place for the night."

I tried to imagine that, but I couldn't. Mom wasn't perfect, but she'd always been totally on top of the whole food/shelter/clothing thing.

Even when I started kindergart—

A sudden realization hit me, and I swallowed. Eli had lowered his head, bringing our faces closer.

"Eli, I have another question," I said slowly. "Why did you get held back in the first grade?"

"Because I'd never been to school before. Didn't even know the alphabet."

"Did…?" I paused, licking my lips. That caught his attention, which was probably a good thing given what I needed to ask him. "Did I make fun of you because you couldn't read?"

He pulled his hand free of mine, then slowly moved it up my center. It came to rest right below my collarbone.

"You made fun of me every single fucking day for two years," he said, the words slow and even.

If I could've rolled into a ball and ceased to exist, that would've been the moment.

"I don't think sorry quite cuts it," I said after a long pause. "I really was the worst."

Eli nodded his head, moving just a little bit closer. If I raised my head even an inch, I'd be kissing him.

"How come you don't hate me?"

"Well, I'm older than you," he said, sounding way too damn smug. "More mature. I like to think of you as this silly little butterfly that dances all sum—"

I crushed my mouth to his because after what he'd just said about me making fun of him, telling him to shut the fuck up was probably a bad move.

But listening to that butterfly shit wasn't a real option, either.

Fortunately, Eli didn't seem overly invested in continuing the conversation. Instead, he shifted his body and slanted his mouth down across mine, taking control.

There was a new power in him, I realized. One that had nothing to do with all that muscle he'd built while he was serving time. This strength was all mental, and I had a feeling it'd grown out of his need to survive.

My higher mind appreciated that and admired him for it. But in my gut, what I noticed first was how much that strength attracted me. I'd spent years thinking about what it might feel like, should I ever find myself under him again. Not that I'd have admitted that to anyone, including myself…but anytime he was in a room, I found myself fighting with him.

Fucked up? Yes.

Especially since memories were fickle creatures. Nobody felt as good as Eli had felt that night we'd almost had sex. My intellect understood this. My subconscious? Not so much. At one point, I'd read a book about retraining the brain, and decided to try writing letters to myself, explaining all the reasons that Fantasy Eli had nothing to do with Reality Eli.

Now, I found myself under him again, with my hands roaming his body as my legs begged to wrap around him. Time to face a hard truth—this was way, *way* better than I remembered.

The chemistry between us had always crackled. It was there when we kissed, taking charge in the same way it did when we fought. There was no denying it, either. Every time his lips brushed mine, desire scorched through me. Like wildfire.

But power and chemistry weren't the only things for me to appreciate.

Eli had always been a large guy with a big frame, and he'd had more than enough muscle the night they'd taken him away. Still, he'd gotten bigger while locked up. Not ginormous and bloated.

Just very solid.

It took a special kind of guy to pull off muscles like that without intimidating a girl, I realized. Eli could hold me down and do whatever the hell he wanted with me, but I'd never worried about that with him.

Probably because, deep down inside, I knew he cared about me as a person and not just getting in my pants.

He'd continued the weightlifting once he got back. Though now, he liked to mix his workouts up a bit more, just because he could. So far, he'd gone snowboarding, rafting, hiking… Fucking quite a bit, too. Or so I'd heard. Not that I'd listen to gossip like that deliberately, but sometimes people just said things in public, and it wasn't like I could turn off my ears.

Eli ended the kiss, pulling away as I gave his lip a lingering suck. Then he caught my chin, forcing me to meet his gaze head-on. His eyes were intense. Almost *too* intense.

He was hungry, I realized. And not the kind of hungry you could fix with chicken nuggets.

"Five years," he said, shifting his left leg so that it slid down between mine, spreading my legs wide beneath him. "I sat in that fucking prison cell for five years, and there wasn't a single day that I didn't regret leaving you. Not just leaving the party or getting myself wrapped up in something so much bigger than I could possibly understand at that age, but leaving you. I missed the hell out of that mouth of yours."

"How come you missed me?" I said, the words painful but honest. "I bullied you. Constantly. I couldn't see it through an adult's perspective before. Now I can, and I'm not okay with what I did to you."

Eli pushed his thigh deep between my legs, then started rubbing it back and forth against me. It felt incredible, yet it wasn't quite enough to be satisfying. Just unspeakably distracting. I squirmed beneath him, searching for a spot with just a bit more friction. Eli let out a low laugh, and I realized this wasn't just sex for him.

It was a sensual kind of revenge.

He could torture me for hours like this, bringing me closer to the edge or holding me back, depending on his whims. I tried pushing up and into him with my hips. I just needed a little more—

"So, you want to know why I don't hate you," Eli said, his voice low and husky. I waited, but he took his time, brushing his lips against my cheek. Fuck. I was supposed to be listening to him and owning everything I'd done wrong.

"Okay," I said, trying to focus. It wasn't easy. Every time his thigh drifted over my clit, I sort of lost track of who I was for a moment.

"Hallies Falls is a small town," he said. He'd started kissing softly along my jawline at the same time, which wasn't particularly helpful. Although I hadn't gotten the impression that being helpful was his goal.

"Yeah, I'm fairly sure we all know how small it is," I said, wondering where he was going with this.

"So, when I got here, everyone knew why Gus had taken me in," he said, shifting his hand to my breast. His fingers splayed wide and wrapped around it, giving me a gentle squeeze. "The shit my mom got into was all over the news. I was supposed to be a victim, whether I felt like one or not. The kids at school had to pretend we were friends, even when we hated each other. And all the teachers were so busy feeling sorry for me that none of them bothered to teach me. I was young, but I wasn't stupid. None of them gave a shit about me."

"Wait," I said, not wanting to challenge him, but what he said didn't add up. "You'd already been to first grade when you moved in with Gus. I remember because you were two years older than me, but only one year ahead. They held you back."

"That didn't actually happen," Eli said, pausing to trace my ear lobe with his tongue. "Someone told me to lie about it. Said it would make me fit in better than admitting I'd never been to school. They were wrong."

He gave my ear a sharp nip with his teeth, and I sighed. Couldn't quite decide if that counted as pain or pleasure. Maybe something in the middle.

"So, suddenly, I was in this weird little town where I didn't know anyone. Not even my own uncle. And no matter what I did, everyone treated me like I was weak—"

My snort of laughter cut him off, and he let my boob go long enough to attack my side with a vicious tickle. I screamed, arching under him and begging for mercy. He laughed but let his hand go back to my breast while kissing the side of my neck at the same time. That sent a fresh wave of tingles rushing through me. My hips lifted, my right leg bending and falling to the side.

"So, like I said, they all thought I was some kind of victim, and they treated me that way. Drove me fucking crazy," Eli murmured. "Because I was strong. I'd kept myself and my mom alive. For *years*. And then suddenly I was supposed to turn into a kid again. It was bullshit. All of it. But there was one person who saw through it. You. I was your enemy, and you were out to get me because you knew I was dangerous. Not only that, you saw that being younger was an advantage you could use. Anytime you wanted to, you could've screamed for help, and we both knew people would've taken your word over mine. But you never did."

"Of course not," I said, feeling slightly offended. "That was our only rule. Remember?"

Eli lifted his head, studying my face carefully. I had no idea what he was trying to see—maybe some trace of the little girl I'd been?

"That was the rule, all right. And you never broke it. Not once. That's how I knew I could trust you."

"You trusted me too much," I told him. His fingers let my breast go, only to find it again after sliding his hand up and under my shirt. "I still wish I'd broken it, at least that once. I should've talked to the cops."

"You're really not going to let that go, are you?" he asked, shifting his pelvis so the hard ridge in his jeans could rub back and forth across my hip bone.

"No," I said, determined. Eli started grinding against me, slowly swiveling his hips. Shit. I couldn't think when he did that. Simply wasn't possible. "Let's compromise. We can talk about it after. I don't know how long I can take this. At some point, you're gonna have to fuck me. Sooner rather than later, please."

"I love it when you're all horny," he told me, his voice registering slightly lower than before. At least I wasn't the only one slowly going crazy. "It used to be that I'd get frustrated when I looked back on those years. I needed to learn how to *read*, for fuck's sake. I didn't have time to be a victim. But now, it's our games that I think about the most. They were the only part of my life that made sense."

"Those were fights," I reminded him gently. His fingers found my nipple, holding it lightly. "I never played with you. You broke my teacup."

"Peaches, those were definitely games," he said, and I saw the laughter in his eyes. "My mom and me, we lived on the streets. Sometimes, we'd find an apartment somewhere, but one thing was always the same. There were always predators. Some of them tried to kill us, but a few of them went out of their way to give me the skills I needed to survive in that world. Do you really think that a little girl with a pink foam princess sword could've won against me? I fought other kids for food while our moms got high together."

I shivered, trying to imagine what that might've felt like, but I couldn't. The idea that a child had to fight for food…that was beyond my comprehension. And I'd known he and his mom had been homeless, but that hadn't really meant anything to me back then. To me, *suffering* meant sharing my bedroom. He was right, I'd been naïve as hell.

Too naïve to pity him.

I swallowed, wanting to cry or apologize or *do* something. *Anything.* Except refusing to pity him was the one thing I'd gotten right as a kid. I'd be damned if I'd go weak and fuck it up now, just because I could finally understand the truth.

"What about Lemur?" I asked, trying to lighten the mood. "Was taking him one of those games, too?"

"No." Eli grinned, lifting his hips to reposition himself slightly. "That was something else. That was about the fucking snakes you kept putting in my bed."

I took advantage of his repositioning to slide my hand down between us. Eli was hard as granite, and I felt every inch of his thick, heavy length, despite the fabric separating us.

My fingers tightened around him, and he groaned. Perfect. I wanted to guide the conversation away from the snakes. Talking about them wouldn't end well, for either of us.

"I've never forgotten how much I wanted you that night," I told him softly. "Or how amazing it felt when you touched me."

"I've never forgotten, either," Eli replied. "The good news is that tonight, we're gonna give that another shot. And this time, I don't give a flying fuck if Gus is literally on fire. I'm not leaving you."

Chapter Ten

~Peaches~

Eli's mouth caught mine for another kiss, but this one was different. Deeper. Hungrier. Almost desperate in its intensity. I didn't even notice when his hand drifted down toward my jeans, or when he opened them. The kiss consumed me completely, right up to the instant his finger found my most sensitive spot.

I froze, mesmerized as the digit circled my clit, sending little shockwaves of raw sensation radiating out from my center. At first, there was nothing but perfect pleasure. He'd found exactly the right spot, and now he was utterly focused on working it, every movement slow and steady. Tension started to build within me, along with fresh need.

This was great, but I needed more.

"Faster," I whispered, letting my head fall back. Eli gave a low laugh, but he didn't change what he was doing.

I squirmed, starting to feel frantic. But instead of giving me what I desperately wanted, he pulled away from my clit entirely.

"Eli—" I started to protest, but before I could say more, he plunged his finger all the way into me, hitting my g-spot on the first try. My back arched, and I made a noise halfway between a groan and a scream because whatever he was doing…it worked for me.

Holy hell, it worked.

I'd wanted him to go faster, and now he was. Fast and hard, his fingers plunging just like his dick likely wanted to do. I knew this because my hand was between us, holding him so that every time he moved, I felt just how much he wanted to fuck me.

"I want to see you come first," Eli whispered. As if I had a choice about the sensations ripping through me. That terrible tension was swirling and building with every stroke, and my heart was starting to race.

"That's a great idea," I gasped. I felt like I should remember something, but every time I started to form a coherent thought, that finger of his hit my g-spot again.

Probably something about getting him off, I realized.

Except he'd said he wanted to see *me* get off, which sounded more and more awesome by the second. His hand found a slightly different angle, somehow discovering a way to slide across my clit each and every time. I liked this development.

I liked it a *lot.*

I liked it so much that when he did it again, my toes curled so hard that it hurt, and I started to pant. I was close—really close—and I could feel my orgasm, hovering just out of reach, calling to me. The sound of my heart beating fast filled my ears as every muscle in my body tightened and…*holy shit, was that his thumb touching my—?*

I convulsed once, and then a second time, waves of release smashing through the coiled tension, rocking me in a series of little shocks that left me blinking.

Eli's hand was suddenly on my stomach, rubbing it gently as the last tremors settled. I looked up at him, and he gave me a crooked smile.

"Hell of a bite you got there," he said softly.

"What?"

"You bit my shoulder. Like a vampire. It was hot, but it also kind of hurt."

My eyes focused slowly, and then I saw it. A set of bite marks that were already starting to bruise, right in line with my mouth. I swallowed, trying to remember how that'd happened, and coming up blank.

"I'm sorry?" I said, hoping that was right. Eli's hand slid up, then caught my hair, fisting it as he jerked my head back.

"You're gonna have to make that up to me," he whispered. I tried to answer, but then he kissed me. If the last one had been hungry, this one was starving. He went deep, filling my mouth as he lifted his hips, his hand fumbling with his fly.

I wanted to help, but I couldn't see anything. Suddenly, his jeans were open, and I felt the hard, sleek length of him brush my hand. Then he was settling between my legs, the head of his cock poised at my opening.

Raising his head, Eli pulled away from the kiss. I found myself wanting more and trying to catch him. He caught one of my hands, threading his fingers with mine as he pressed the back of my hand down beside my head.

Then he paused, looking down at me. I couldn't read his expression. In that moment, Eli King was every bit as strange and dangerous as he'd been when I first met him, and he was holding me down.

He could do anything to me, I realized.

Anything at all.

It should've scared me, but instead, it turned me on.

"What's the matter?" I asked. "Are you scared that I'll bite you again?"

Eli slowly shook his head.

"No, you don't scare me."

"Maybe not," I whispered. "But I know what does. You better fuck me right now, or I swear to God, I will fill this whole damned room with snakes while you sleep."

"You are ridiculously fucking crazy," he said. "And now you're mine."

He thrust into me as he said it, filling me so completely that I forgot how to breathe. Then he pulled back and did it again, moving faster with each stroke. Over and over again, he hit that spot inside exactly right, somehow sliding over my clit just enough to qualify as an art form as he did.

This time, I didn't feel a slow build of coiled tension.

I didn't have that luxury.

It was like my wires had gotten crossed, and my body wasn't sure what to do, so I wrapped my legs tightly around his waist and just held on for the ride. I could feel him inside me, pulsing and growing, and I knew he wouldn't last long.

That was okay. I wasn't going to last much longer, either.

I'd just finished the thought when the climax hit, slamming into me as I screamed, convulsing around Eli. It was too much for him. His hips surged into mine one last time, and he jerked as he filled me.

I didn't know how long we stayed like that.

Long enough that I'd stopped shuddering, and my heart rate slowed. We found each other's gazes again, and I watched as a slow change came over his features.

He looked different. Happy.

Smiling.

"So, did you make it ten minutes?" I finally asked. "Because I forgot to hit the stopwatch."

"Don't talk," he said, leaning down to kiss the side of my neck. "I don't want you to ruin it."

Outraged, my hands attacked his sides, and he started laughing. That set me off even more, and then he was tickling me while I tried to attack him with my nails. Then his head hit the wall, and I pressed my attack, rolling him over to climb on top of him.

Not long afterward, I discovered something quite wonderful about Eli King. Apparently, he really was a five-minute man, because that's all it took for him to recover.

Directly after that, I learned something else.

He could keep going for more than ten minutes. Significantly more. So much more, that between the night ending and the next morning beginning, we realized that we absolutely needed to get something to eat.

That's how I found myself on the back of Eli's bike as he tore through the darkness, feeling wild and free in a way I'd never experienced before.

Eventually, Eli pulled off to climb a hill overlooking the valley. There, we sat and ate some snacks we'd gotten at a gas station, laughing and telling stories all the while, refusing to think about anything more than us, right there in that moment. That's when I learned the best thing of all about Eli King.

Seemed he'd always had a fantasy about getting me off while sitting on his Harley, wearing nothing but his belt and a sprinkle of powdered sugar.

I didn't just have a hot biker going down on me in the moonlight that evening.

I had a hot biker going down on me in the moonlight *while I ate mini donuts coated in powdered sugar.*

Life simply did not get any better than that.

The roar of a different motorcycle woke me up early the next morning, just as the sun started to rise.

That'd be Gus, finally coming home from a night of whatever it was he did after the bar closed. I knew this because that'd been his habit ever since I was a little girl. Not every day, but definitely two or three times a week.

I'd loved those mornings.

Mom would still be sleeping, so those were my special times with Gus. He was always in a great mood, too. He'd announce that he wanted waffles, but that he couldn't make them without a helper.

It was my job to watch the waffle iron for when the light turned off so they didn't get burned. Sometimes, I got distracted and missed it. That never bothered Gus, though. He'd just give me a hug and insist that he liked them best when they were extra crispy.

Then we'd sit down and eat together while he told me stories and let me use as much syrup as I wanted. We always finished by putting together a breakfast tray for Mom. Gus had to carry it upstairs, but he'd let me take it into the room to give to her.

Mom loved getting breakfast in bed, sometimes so much that she cried. Tears of happiness, she'd told me, because she had the world's best daughter. Those mornings were some of my favorite childhood memories, pure and beautiful and precious.

Mom's reaction hadn't been tears of happiness, though. I'd figured that out years later once I learned the real reason she left him. The real reason he came home late all those mornings and was in such a good mood.

Eli's arm tightened around my waist, reminding me that I wasn't a little girl anymore. His body spooned mine, our legs tangled together in a delicious echo of what'd happened last night. His solid bulk was comforting, and the gentle rise and fall of his chest reassured me that all was good.

Safe.

Funny how that worked. There wasn't another person on Earth with the power to piss me off like Eli could. Yet when shit got real, we stood together.

Always.

We kept each other's secrets, and while I loved torturing him, I was protective, too. Watching his court case had been like a slow-motion car crash, and his refusal to take my help cut me. Deeply. I'd hated him for it.

I'd also written to him in prison and sent care packages.

Downstairs, the kitchen door thudded as it closed, reminding me that I had unfinished business with Gus. He'd used Eli to save his own ass, something Eli seemed willing to leave in the past.

Very Christian of him, but I was feeling less saintly about the situation.

Eli shifted, rolling onto his back. Moving carefully, I started untangling myself. I hated to leave him, even for a minute. This still felt like some kind of crazy dream that might evaporate if I wasn't careful, but putting things off with Gus would only make it harder in the long run.

I padded to the door, instinctively avoiding the board that creaked. The bedding rustled. I glanced back and saw that Eli had rolled into the warm spot I'd left behind.

His eyes were still closed, and his lips had parted just a bit. He looked so young and innocent…almost sweet. He wasn't innocent, of course. Eli had suffered more as a small child than most people did their entire lives. He'd survived, though. Survived and then sacrificed himself to protect the only family he had left.

Downstairs, I found Gus mixing the waffle batter, whistling a little song to himself. The sound was happy. Cheerful.

"Morning, Peaches," he said, like nothing had changed last night. I suppose that, in his mind, it hadn't. He had no clue that I knew what'd really happened. "Coffee is started. There are fresh strawberries in the fridge if you want some with breakfast."

Walking over to the coffee maker, I pulled out two mugs, filling one for myself and one for Gus. He sprayed the waffle iron, carefully spooning the batter onto the griddle.

"Doesn't look like you slept on the couch last night," he said. "Suppose that means you and Eli—"

"I overheard your meeting at the Starkwood last night," I said, cutting him off. He didn't respond for a moment, just stared down at the waffle iron. "It's time for you to tell me the truth."

He turned to me, his face serious. "Peaches, it's complicated—"

"Is it? Because it seems pretty simple to me. You threw Eli under the bus to save your own ass. You fucked me over, too, but that's kinda minor in comparison. You say it's complicated. Great. You can take as much time as you want to explain it. But I'm not leaving without answers."

"You don't know what you're asking," he said.

"I know Eli won't buy the bar until this talk is over," I countered. "I'm not five years old anymore, okay? I'm an adult. Enough of one to manage your bar for you. So, talk to me."

Pushing off the counter, I held a mug out to him. He took it, and for the first time in my life, I saw his hand shaking. Like an old man's hand, the skin like parchment.

"Let's sit down for this," he said, turning off the waffle iron. I followed him out of the kitchen to the table. We sat down, and I took a sip of my coffee, waiting for him to say something. He didn't, and the silence grew more and more uncomfortable. Finally, he spoke.

"You aren't going to make this easy for me, are you?"

"That's a matter of perspective," I said quietly. "Eli spent five years in prison, covering your ass. Pretty sure this conversation won't take nearly that long."

He swallowed. "I'm afraid you'll never forgive me."

"That's a valid concern," I said quietly. "I can't see myself forgiving you. At least not anytime soon based on what I know right now."

"You never pull your punches, do you?"

"Either you tell her, or I will," Eli said, startling both Gus and me. I looked over at him. He'd pulled on his jeans to come downstairs, but nothing else. His chest was bare, and his hair screamed "*sex*." I imagined mine did too. Just seeing him made me feel stronger. Safer. Like the two of us could take on the world. He came to stand next to me, resting a hand on my shoulder.

"Okay," Gus said, and I heard the resignation in his voice. "So, it was my birthday party that night. Everyone was down at the Starkwood. I'd spent my afternoon trying to figure out some paperwork. Had a few drinks along the way. Probably a few more than I realized. And, yeah, I know I shouldn't drink and drive. If it makes you feel any better, I haven't since that night."

He paused, taking another sip of coffee.

"So, my doorbell rang. It was Mia Eirwood, carrying her baby. Her husband, Kevin, locked them out of the house. No diaper bag, no cell phone. Nothing. That guy…" Gus shook his head. "That guy was human garbage. And Mia was a sweet little thing. Busted ass working to pay all their bills, all the while Kevin was fucking around on her. He was cooking meth out there, too. Someone needed to do something about him."

"You don't get to be the hero in this story," I said, my voice cold. Gus gave a bark of laughter.

"Oh, I'm aware," he said. "And if I'd been sober, it would have played out different. But that baby was all red from crying, and there was this bruise just starting to form on Mia's neck. I just kept thinking that the next time, he might kill her. Or that lab of his might blow up. Touch off a fire that'd destroy all our homes. Something bad was gonna happen sooner or later. Figured it'd be best if I made him go away. So, I did. I gave her one of those disposable cell phones and told her to call Gage. Said he'd take care of her. Make sure she had protection. That kind of thing."

"Did she know what you were planning?" I asked, remembering the gossip. People had whispered that she'd been sleeping with Eli. That they'd plotted the murder together. But there hadn't been any evidence, and Eli's plea bargain had specifically stipulated that he'd acted alone.

Last I heard, she'd moved to California.

"Naw, she was just a kid," Gus said. "Clueless. So, I grabbed my gun and took the pickup over to his place. Figured I'd kill him and then stash the body somewhere before hitting the party."

Gus's voice was so casual as he talked about stashing a body. Scary casual, as if he were talking about a bag of recyclables. Not a person. Eli's hand tightened on my shoulder, reminding me that I wasn't alone.

"I already told you I was drunk," Gus continued. His eyes were fixed on the wall across from him. Maybe a part of him had to pretend that he was alone to say these things out loud.

"Wasn't thinking it through, obviously. Everything went just fine until I ran the truck off the road. Hit my head pretty good in the process, which didn't help. Couldn't get the truck out of the ditch, so I called Gage. He got Eli and sent him and Pipes to deal with it. It's hard to remember the exact order of everything."

"Gus was drunk," Eli said flatly. "And he definitely had a concussion. We used Pipes' big diesel to pull the truck out of the ditch.

I sent Pipes and Gus back to the party—wanted to establish at least a partial alibi—and then I drove the pickup back to the house. Parked it in the shed. The plan was for me to ride Gus's Harley back to the bar. I'd just pulled out of the driveway when a sheriff's deputy pulled me over."

"I was an idiot," Gus said quietly. "About everything. And sloppy. Didn't even notice an extra car in the Eirwood's driveway. There was someone inside the house besides just Kevin. Whoever it was saw the whole thing. Apparently, they ransacked the house afterward. About an hour later, someone made an anonymous call to the cops to report what'd happened. You probably remember that part from the appeal."

"I do remember it," I said quietly. "Because the sheriff's deputy had no reason to pull Eli over. He just assumed he was involved because he's a biker."

"Exactly," said Eli. "But we didn't know that until a lot later."

"People are too damned prejudiced," Gus muttered. I shot him a dirty look.

"You actually committed this particular crime, Gus," I reminded him. "And then Eli went to prison for it. Not you."

Eli straightened and then stepped around the table to sit down facing me. I reached my hand out toward him, and he took it.

"I made a choice," Eli said quietly. "Washington has a three strikes law, and Gus already had two. They'd have put him away for life. Worst case, we knew I'd still be eligible for parole."

"The lawyers said the appeal was strong," Gus added defensively. "The deputy claimed that he'd stopped Eli based on that 911 call, but they couldn't produce a witness or a recording. Sure as shit didn't have a warrant. I knew we'd get Eli out eventually."

"And what about the Reapers?" I asked. "What did they think?"

"It doesn't matter," Eli told me. "None of it. I'm out of prison, and it's all over. They never tied Gus to the crime at all."

"Gage said it was bullshit," Gus said, his voice haunted. "They wanted to fight it all the way. Eli was more worried about protecting me than he was about himself. He figured that if your alibi accounted for him, then they'd start looking at me. You were part of it, too."

That caught me off guard. "What?"

"Gus is talking out of his ass," Eli said, shooting him a nasty look.

"He didn't want you to lose me," Gus said, ignoring Eli. "He'd already watched you lose me once. Didn't want to see it again. So, he took the bullet and pleaded out. Lawyers helped him with that part…the whole thing was a setup, 'cause they were already planning the appeal."

I couldn't breathe, trying to comprehend what Gus had just told me.

"Eli?" I finally asked, still trying to wrap my head around it. "Is that true?"

He shrugged, glaring at Gus. "It was a small factor. Not the only, though. So, don't get too full of yourself. If it makes you feel better, I had plenty of time to think things over while I was locked up. I should've fought from the beginning and let it play out naturally. For what it's worth, Gus didn't talk to me before offering to sell you the bar. He already knew my feelings on the subject. I was totally against it, and I still am. It's too fucking dangerous."

"So, it's too dangerous for me but okay for you?"

"I'm a member of the club," Eli said. "I took on that risk when I joined. You're a civilian."

"But why should *either* of us have to be at risk?" I demanded. "Why can't one of us just buy the Starkwood and run it? No Reapers, no danger, just good food and cold beer!"

"Because the Reapers own half the business," Gus said quietly.

That threw me.

"No, they don't," I said. "You do. James looked up the property values and the liquor license and… Oh, shit. You mean they own it secretly. Like the Mafia or something?"

"I inherited the bar," Gus said. "You knew that. Well, I didn't get it free and clear. It came with a lot of debt. Eventually, I wanted to buy a house, but I couldn't get a loan from a bank. So, I asked the Reapers if they'd be willing to buy a stake in the business. They said yes. There aren't any records, of course, but Eli has known about it for years."

"So you're saying the Reapers Motorcycle Club owns half the bar you wanted me to buy from you," I said slowly. "Were you planning to tell me this before or after I signed the papers?"

"I'd have told you before," Gus said. His eyes had reddened, the surface shiny with tears. For an instant, I felt sorry for him. Then I remembered all the times my mom had cried when I brought a tray of waffles to her in bed.

I wanted to believe that he'd have been honest with me before it was too late.

"You're an incredibly selfish person," I said, pushing my chair back as I stood. "I don't even know what to say to you. Other people aren't just tissues to be used and thrown away when they get inconvenient, Gus. I can't believe I used to wish you were my dad."

Turning my back on him, I walked toward the stairs, trying to think. Obviously, I couldn't buy the bar. But Eli shouldn't buy it, either. I knew the club was into illegal stuff. I wasn't a total idiot. But what Gus had described…that was serious shit. They had to be laundering money or something.

The thought stopped me in my tracks.

I'd been doing the Starkwood books for two years. Obviously, not the real books, but I'd seen enough that it'd been confusing at times. Now, everything made so much more sense. This was horrible. But it might also be an opportunity.

"Eli, can I talk to you upstairs?"

* * * *

~Eli~

I wasn't quite sure what to expect when I followed Peaches upstairs.

I'd seen her angry plenty of times throughout the years. Hell, she was mad around me more often than not, usually because I provoked her, which was definitely my second favorite way to spend time with her.

I'd never seen Peaches like this, though.

She wasn't screaming or throwing things. There was no fire in her eyes. If anything, she seemed to be concentrating really hard. Like she had an idea, which was a turn of events that rarely ended well for me. My dick gave an optimistic twitch as she sat down on the bed. The room still smelled like sex, for fuck's sake, but I had no illusions.

Whatever she wanted to talk about didn't involve me getting laid. So, when she leaned back against the wall, looking toward the door, I leaned back next to her.

"So this whole time, you were only going to buy half the bar," she said slowly. "And you always knew that was the deal."

"Yup. I've known it since I turned eighteen. The Reapers have been silent partners since before we were born."

"And you're okay with that?" she asked, turning to look at me.

"It is what it is," I said. "You're not stupid. You know the Reapers are into all kinds of things. Gus and I are both part of that. I chose this life, and I'm at peace with what it means."

"And the Reapers had nothing to do with you serving time? They didn't ask you to do that?"

"No, they didn't," I said. "This wasn't about the club at all. They paid for my lawyer—we have a fund for that—and they bought a pig to roast at the party when I got out. But shooting that guy? That was Gus, all by himself. He called us for help, and we answered because that's what we do."

"He may not always be right, but he's always your brother…" she said, the words trailing off. I nodded, and we both fell silent again. Her hand slipped down, catching mine. I raised it to my mouth, kissing her fingers.

"So, I have this thought," Peaches said, breaking the silence.

"I'm listening."

"What if we bought the bar together?" she asked. "If we put our money together, we'd have enough to buy all of them out. Last night, you said you wanted to be partners with me. That it didn't matter whose name was on the deed. I thought you were full of shit, but that's the kind of partnership the Reapers have with Gus already, isn't it?"

"Well, that wasn't exactly what I was thinking," I admitted.

Peaches laughed.

"You were thinking more about me putting in my time and energy there the same way I would if I owned a stake. You'd let me make decisions, and we'd be like partners, except your name would be on the deed, and you'd have the power to fire me."

"When you put it like that, it sounds bad," I admitted. She offered me her sweetest smile, and suddenly, all I could think about were those lips of hers wrapped around my cock.

"It *is* bad," she said. "But I have a different idea. One that could work for both of us. What if I buy out Gus, and you buy out the Reapers? That way, you're the silent partner, and unlike me, you'd actually have the force to assert your rights if I decided to cheat you."

I stilled, almost startled by how obvious it was.

"Do you think we could do it?" I asked her. "Let's assume that the financing works, and the Reapers are on board—and I'm thinking I could make that happen—do you really think you and I could be equal partners in something like that? Without killing each other?"

"Have we killed each other yet?" she asked, her voice softening. She tugged her hand free from mine and then dropped it to my inner thigh, rubbing it back and forth. My dick took notice, and I felt my balls clench. Then her fingers drifted up, cupping me and fondling me through my jeans.

"You came close last night," I said, trying to follow the conversation. Hard to concentrate, given what she was doing. Peaches touched her lips to mine, just the hint of a teasing kiss. Then she pulled away.

"You're my best friend, Eli. I'm attracted to you, and I definitely like having sex with you. I've spent hundreds—maybe thousands—of hours thinking up new ways to make your life a living hell, yet you still go out of your way to run into me. You like being with me as much as I like being with you."

"I'd rather be in you," I said. In a flash, she jerked her hand away from my dick to punch my shoulder. She hit hard, too. Not hard enough to hurt me for real, but she wasn't playing around, either.

"God, you're an asshole. I'm trying to have a serious talk here!"

"You know, it turns me on when you're mad enough to call me names," I said, which was true. Her eyes had reclaimed their sparkle, and her cheeks were flushed.

"You're like a two-year-old."

"And yet you keep coming back for more," I pointed out. "That's what you just said, right?"

Peaches opened her mouth to argue, then snapped it shut again. She closed her eyes and took a deep breath. When she opened them again, her face was serious.

"Are you going to buy the bar with me or not?"

It was a great question. A complicated one, too. Not because I didn't think we could work together. I *knew* we could work together. But there was more at stake here than the business.

"Question for you," I said, catching her hand again. "We've known each other for most of our lives. If we buy the bar together, we're stuck with each other. Maybe not forever, but for a long time."

"I know."

"I can't run a business with you and watch you fuck some other guy, let alone marry him or carry his babies. I've always known you'll settle down someday, and I'm not lying when I say I wish you the best in life. But once you marry someone else, I don't want to be trapped in a business partnership with you. That's my definition of hell."

Her eyes widened, and she swallowed. "So, what's your question?"

I paused, the words on the tip of my tongue. Once I said them out loud, everything would change. Either she'd be with me or she wouldn't.

Fuck it.

"If we're going to buy the Starkwood together, we should get married."

"Eli—"

"Hear me out, first, okay? I just think that—"

"Eli—"

"Just listen to me. Then—"

"Eli, I'm trying to—"

"Christ, Peaches. Just give me—"

"Shut the fuck up!" she burst out, and I could hear the laughter in her voice. "I keep trying to say yes, but you're so in love with the sound of your own damned voice that you can't even—"

My hand caught the back of her head, ending the argument with a kiss. Her arms came around me, pulling me down over her body as she collapsed backward onto the bed.

Time seemed to freeze in that instant, marking the spot where my life transitioned from before to after. Was this really happening?

"Hey!" Peaches said, snapping her fingers at me. "Pay attention."

"What?"

"I asked if you were serious about me carrying babies," she said. "But you were zoned out or something. Which isn't exactly flattering, considering we're in the middle of something physical here."

"Um, probably," I told her. "I mean, I'd like to have kids someday."

"That's good," she said, biting her lip. "Because we didn't use any condoms last night, and I just realized that I forgot to refill my prescription this month."

I blinked, growing very still. "So, you could be pregnant…?"

"Theoretically," she said. "I mean, people have sex all the time without getting knocked up. But it's nice to know you wouldn't be upset. At the very least, it seemed like something I should mention before we have sex again. Because that's the direction this is heading, right?"

"Yeah, that was the plan," I said. "Are you okay with it?"

Her eyes turned thoughtful, and then she started to nod slowly. "I think I am. We should do this, Eli."

"What? Fuck? Buy the bar? Get married?"

"All of it. I want to do all of it."

"Can we start with the fucking?" I asked.

"I think that can be arranged."

Epilogue

One year later

~Peaches~

"Okay, you can look now," Mom said. "What do you think?"

I opened my eyes, gasping at my reflection in the half-circle of mirrors strategically surrounding my little platform. I still looked like me, of course—same dark hair, although it'd gotten thicker. Same face, complete with a random zit on the chin. Same waistline I'd had when Eli and I had finally admitted how we felt about each other.

Hadn't seen *that* for a while.

Kinda nice to realize it still existed, even if it took a corset to coax it out.

My boobs were another story. They'd always been generous, and they'd gotten more so with a side of backache once the babies arrived. I'd come to accept this new reality, even if I wasn't totally comfortable with it. Usually, I just threw on a big T-shirt and called it good.

This dress was a hell of a lot more tailored than a T-shirt, though. I took a deep breath—well, as deep as I could—watching first with awe and then something closer to fear as my chest expanded upward and outward from the dress, yet somehow didn't break free in an explosion of overpriced fabric.

"Do you have any idea how much money you could make stripping right now?" Megan asked.

"Not enough to cover daycare for twins," I told her, turning to the side to study my profile. Holy shit, was that really me in the mirror? Nipped-in tummy, massive rack. Hips that flared out just the right amount, all draped in a classic white mermaid dress so perfect a princess could've worn it.

"Do you see that?" I asked. "Or am I hallucinating?"

"See what?" Mom asked.

"My waist," I said, feeling almost giddy.

"Of course, I can see your waist," she said. "Don't tell me you aren't happy with your figure, Peaches, because you look amazing. I know you're frustrated that you haven't lost all the weight yet. But that's not realistic. Women are *supposed* to have some extra while they're nursing. It took a million years of evolution to create those curves of yours, and you should be proud of them."

I laughed, shaking my head.

"I'm not upset," I told her. "I'm just excited to see it again. When the salesperson brought that corset into the changing room, I thought she was crazy. I'm a believer now."

"Foundation garments are critical," said the sales associate, smiling at me.

"What about her boobs?" asked Randi, one of my friends. We'd grown up together, but we'd only gotten really close over the last couple of years. "I think it's amazing they haven't popped out yet, but that fabric looks really delicate. Are you sure it'll hold?"

"This is where strategic taping comes in," the associate said, her voice confident. "It may look like her décolletage is insecure, but she could jump on a trampoline if she wanted to. We take these things very seriously."

I gave a little hop, watching as my girls flew up and then came in for a safe landing.

"We'll take it," Mom announced. "All of it. And throw in some extra tape, too."

"It's too much," I said, shaking my head. "Things are tight enough already financially, and we're still getting hospital bills. It's really gorgeous, but I can't justify it. What about that other one? The one on sale?"

Megan and Randi exchanged dark looks, and the sales associate literally flinched—a response reflected back to me in all six mirrors.

"James and I will be paying for the dress," Mom said.

"Mom—"

"He said if you argued, I should threaten to tell you what we did in bed last night. And then again this morning. I don't want to give out any spoilers, but it involved a new kind of lube. Originally developed at NASA, according to James. You can use it for anything, but I really like it for—"

My vision narrowed, turning black around the edges as I swayed. The sales lady and Randi each caught one of my arms, easing me down.

"Are you all right?" Randi asked. I shook my head.

"No," I said, shuddering.

"Still want to argue about who's paying for the dress?" Mom asked.

I looked up at her, wondering how such a sweet-looking woman could be so sadistic.

"Thank you very much for your generous gift."

Two hours later, I walked through the door of the Starkwood Saloon in full wedding hair and makeup. It was only a test run, but seeing my sleep-deprived eyes without black circles was almost as good as discovering I still had a waist.

Several of our regulars were already there for the afternoon, all of them asking about the wedding plans as I passed through. I answered as quickly as possible, eager to see my babies. The office door stood open a few inches, which meant they weren't asleep. They weren't crying, either. Things must've gone well.

"Eli, you won't believe—" The words died as I stepped into the room. "I didn't realize Gus was here."

Eli sat on the couch, cradling Lynette as he gave her a bottle. Next to him was Gus, holding my son, Augie. Gus looked up at me, his face full of wonder.

"I can't believe how tiny they are," he said. "You did a hell of a job, Peaches."

"I thought you were still in Mexico," I said slowly. "You should've let us know you'd be in town."

"So you could avoid me?" he asked. I considered lying, but decided the truth was better.

"Yes."

I shot a dirty look at Eli, which he pretended not to notice. We'd have words about this little ambush later.

"Gus needs to talk to you about something."

"I'm not sure we have anything to talk about."

"I'm pretty sure you do," Eli said, leaning forward a little to balance himself before standing up from the couch. "Lynette and I are gonna go check on the bar."

He gave me a quick kiss on the cheek as he brushed past, which I allowed because I looked particularly good at the moment. Best for him to be fully aware of what he was missing when he didn't get laid tonight.

I closed the door, then walked over to the couch. Gus looked old, especially next to the baby. I wanted to rip Augie out of his arms, but my boy was asleep. Eli and I had a second rule now—never wake a sleeping baby. And it came with built-in consequences.

"You had something you wanted to say?" I asked.

The old man nodded.

"I love you," he said.

"Great," I told him. "Glad we clarified that. You can leave now."

"I'm sorry I wasn't a better man," he added. "I'm really proud of you, Peaches."

Silence fell between us, broken only by a tiny baby snore.

"You know I love you, too," I told Gus.

"You always have. I took that for granted for a long time. I won't do that ever again."

His words pulled at my heart, reminding me of how much faith I'd put in him. How much I'd been willing to overlook. A part of me wanted to fall into his arms and cry because he'd always been my safe place.

"I had you on a hell of a pedestal," I admitted. "I should've seen it earlier."

"That I'm a selfish bastard?" he asked, quirking his mouth.

"Something like that."

"I can't go back and change things, baby girl," he said quietly. "But I'd sure like the chance to prove I'm a changed man now."

"Actions speak louder than words," I said. Augie snorted, stirring in Gus's arms. We both watched as little hand stretched open, then relaxed again as he drifted back to sleep.

"I understand," Gus said. "I know it won't happen overnight. But sooner or later—if you give me a chance—it'll happen. You'll see that I've changed."

"Did you have anything else you wanted to talk about?" I said, suddenly uncomfortable. "I'm sure you have things to do. Wouldn't want to keep you."

"I have a present for you," he said, nodding toward a large manila envelope sitting on the desk. "You and the babies. Go ahead and open it. Eli already knows about it."

"Nice of you guys to wait for me…"

"I needed to run it by him," Gus explained. "Make sure he understood."

I shot him a look, then picked up the envelope. A sheaf of papers slid out, and I skimmed the one on top. Letterhead from a lawyer's office. Was I reading it wrong? Because it looked like…

"It's the house," Gus said. "I'm giving it to you."

I blinked. "You're giving me and Eli the house?"

"No," he said. "I'm giving *you* the house. I'm hoping you and Eli will decide to live there, but that's your decision to make. Not mine."

"Why?" I asked, stunned. "This isn't about money, Gus. You can't buy me off with a house. I can't accept this."

"Don't accept it for yourself. Accept it for your babies. You can sell it someday, maybe pay for their college."

"I have absolutely no clue what to say," I admitted. "This feels wrong. Weird. What the fuck, Gus?"

"I want you to have it because I made a promise to your mother," he said. "When she left me."

"What was that?"

"That if she let me stay in your life, I'd never hurt you. And then I broke that promise. Like you said, actions speak louder than words. I can't give her the security or peace of mind that I took from her all those years ago. But I can give it to you, and her grandchildren. This is my apology."

My eyes watered, and I blinked furiously, trying not to cry. "Fuck you, Gus. I can't believe I'm falling for your shit again."

"So you'll take the house?"

I reached for a tissue from the box on the desk, blotting my eyes carefully, then nodded.

"I'll take it. But I'm still pissed at you for a lot of reasons. Including fucking up my makeup when I finally look decent for the first time in months."

A slow smile spread across his face, and Gus looked ten years younger. "Thank you, baby."

"Don't read too much into it," I snapped. "I'm not asking you to walk me down the aisle."

"I know."

The door opened.

"All good in here?" Eli asked, pitching his voice low as he stepped inside. "Lynette fell asleep."

"Not yet," I replied. "But it will be. Kids will have to share a bedroom, though. Sooner or later, we'll have to tell them we did the same thing. Could get weird."

"Shit," said Gus. "I hadn't thought of that."

"It'll be fine," Eli told me. "We'll just need to make sure they're both scared of snakes. Mutually assured destruction."

"Is that how it works?" I asked.

"It's always worked for us," he replied. "Hey, Gus?"

"Yeah?"

"Why don't you take Augie for a little walk so I can have some alone time—well, partial alone time—with his mama."

"Too soon," I told him. "I'm still pissed at you for setting up an ambush."

Eli gave me a look. "Seriously?"

I decided to let him off the hook. "No, I'm not pissed at you. But I'm not ready to let him take Augie for walks around the bar yet, either."

"That's good with me," Gus said, clearing his throat. "Because I think this kid needs to be changed. That's a little outside my area of expertise."

"I got it," Eli said.

"I can do it," I told him. "You watched him all afternoon."

"Yeah, but he might spray you and ruin your makeup. That'll put you in a bad mood, which could fuck up my plan to get laid tonight."

"So you think you're getting laid tonight?" I asked, catching a strand of my hair, then twisting it around my finger.

"Pretty sure of it," Eli said.

"Why's that?"

"Because I have something you want."

"I'm still in the room," Gus said. "Just in case you've forgotten."

"Shut up, Gus," I said, watching as Eli carefully set Lynette down in her little bassinet. He walked over to the battered old file cabinet that'd been in the office for years, opened the bottom drawer, and pulled out a brown paper bag. It looked old, and I could see dust in the creases.

"I meant to give you this years ago," Eli said. "But I kept putting it off, and then I forgot about it. When Gus talked to me about giving you the house, it came back to me."

"I had no clue it was in his closet," Gus said, clearing his throat. "He only told me this morning."

I frowned as Eli handed me the bag. The paper was stiff, but after a few seconds, I managed to open it. What was that? It almost looked like...

"No way," I said, pulling out a little stuffed animal. He looked exactly the same…well, mostly the same, anyway. Probably better not to think about his tail. "It's Lemur. I thought you buried him out in the woods!"

"I know," Eli said, clearing his throat. "I always planned to give him back. I really did. The tail, too. That was supposed to be a joke, but then you freaked out, and I realized how bad I fucked up."

"Why didn't you just tell me?" I asked. "I missed him so much, Eli."

He shrugged. "Maybe holding onto him was an excuse."

"To do what? Fight with me?"

"Fighting was better than nothing," Eli said. "In a weird way, Lemur tied us together. Except we've got kids now, and we're getting married. Pretty sure I can fight with you anytime I want at this point."

I hugged Lemur close, closing my eyes to savor the feel of his tiny body in my arms. It wasn't the same, though. He smelled weird. And his fur wasn't as soft as I remembered. Nowhere near as soft as Lynette's and Augie's hair.

"I'll take him now," Eli said to Gus. I opened my eyes to watch them—the two most important men in my life, carefully transferring my son from one set of hands to the next, and something inside me shifted.

It took a second to realize what it was.

My anger.

It was gone.

Gus had been right. He'd said it would happen, and it had. I'd forgiven him. It didn't change what'd happened in the past, and I had no clue how things would be in the future. But for the first time since I was five years old, everything was right again.

I gave Lemur another hug, then set him down on the couch. Lynette had started to wake up, and she needed me a lot more than Lemur did. Someday, she'd be big enough to have tea parties on the porch, I realized.

My porch.

I couldn't wait.

* * * *

Also from 1001 Dark Nights and Joanna Wylde, discover Shade's Lady and Rome's Chance.

About Joanna Wylde

Joanna Wylde started her writing career in journalism, working in two daily newspapers as both a reporter and editor. Her career has included many different jobs, from managing a homeless shelter to running her own freelance writing business, where she took on projects ranging from fundraising to ghostwriting for academics. During 2012 she got her first Kindle reader as a gift and discovered the indie writing revolution taking place online. Not long afterward she started cutting back her client list to work on Reaper's Property, her breakout book. It was published in January 2013, marking the beginning of a new career writing fiction.

Joanna lives in the mountains of northern Idaho with her family.

Also from Joanna Wylde

Reaper's Property
Reaper's Legacy
Devil's Game
Silver Bastard
Reaper's Fall
Reaper's Fire
Reapers and Bastards
Shade's Lady
Rome's Chance

Discover More Joanna Wylde

Shade's Lady: A Reapers MC Novella
By Joanna Wylde

Looking back, none of this would've happened if I hadn't dropped my phone in the toilet. I mean, I could've walked away from him if I'd had it with me.

Or maybe not.

Maybe it was all over the first time he saw me, and he would've found another way. Probably—if there's one thing I've learned, it's that Shade always gets what he wants, and apparently he wanted me.

Right from the first.

* * * *

Rome's Chance: A Reapers MC Novella
By Joanna Wylde

Rome McGuire knew he was in trouble the first time he saw her.

She was sweet and pretty and just about perfect in every way. She was also too young and innocent for the Reapers Motorcycle Club. He did the right thing and walked away.

The second time, he couldn't resist tasting her.

Gorgeous and smart, fun and full of wonder, she jumped on his bike and would've followed him anywhere. Still, she deserved a shot at happiness somewhere bigger and better than a town like Hallies Falls. Walking away wasn't so easy that time, but her family needed her and he had a job to do.

When she came around a third time, he'd had enough. Randi Whittaker had been given two chances to escape, and now it was time for Rome to take his.

This time, the only way Randi would be leaving Hallies Falls was on the back of Rome's bike.

Take the Bride
A Knight Brothers Novella
By Carly Phillips

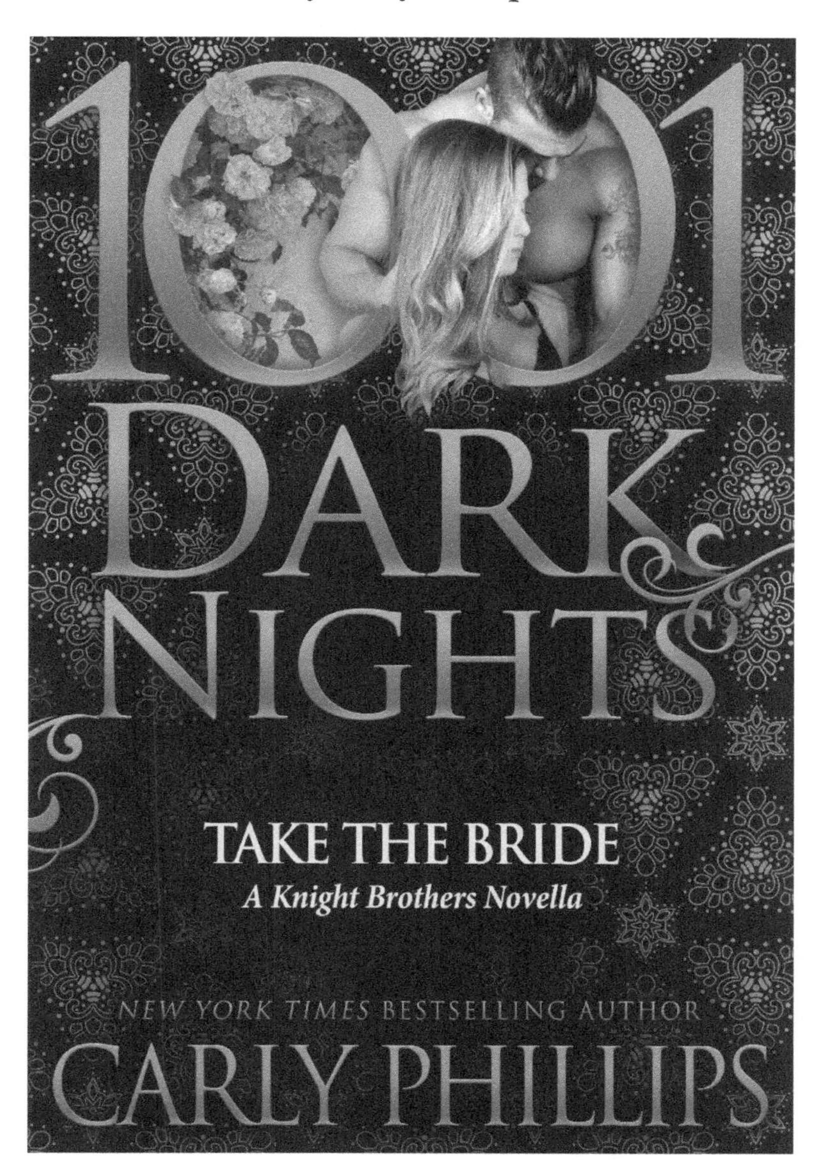

Acknowledgments from the Author

Thank you Liz Berry and MJ Rose for making a dream come true. I'm thrilled to be part of the 1,001 Dark Nights family. It's truly an honor to be among such amazing talent and company. I'm so grateful!

Chapter One

A cellist played Vivaldi's "The Four Seasons" as Sierra Knight's bridesmaids, her maid of honor, and the flower girl made their way down the aisle in a large church located in the Upper East Side of Manhattan.

Sierra couldn't see the procession but she'd been at the rehearsal, and she knew what was happening in the sanctuary of the church. From behind closed doors, where she stood with her oldest brother, Ethan, the deep strains of the string instrument reverberated around her, her heart beating hard and fast in her chest.

She smoothed a hand down her fit-and-flair style wedding gown with lace and beading that she'd loved the moment she'd slid it on. The cathedral-length veil in tulle was matched by the long train flowing behind her. She'd never felt more beautiful… or more nervous.

"Are you sure this is what you want?" Ethan asked, obviously reading her nerves as he put a hand on her trembling arm. "The car's out front, the engine's running," he said, half joking, but she heard the serious note in his voice.

As her oldest brother, he was the father figure she'd always needed since their own parent never lived up to the role. Although Alexander Knight was sitting in one of the pews up front with wife number four, he wasn't the man Sierra wanted walking her down the aisle. He hadn't earned that honor nor had he seemed insulted that he hadn't been asked to play the traditional role.

She thought about Ethan's question, swallowed hard, and nodded.

"Jason is a great guy," she said, meaning every word.

She'd been with Jason Armstrong, a lawyer, for over a year and she knew him well. They'd met through friends and begun dating soon after. He had a calming presence and he catered to her every desire. He was a kind, decent man.

"I know I'll have a good life with him," she reassured her brother, glancing at his strong jaw, which he'd set as he narrowed his gaze.

"I married a woman I thought I knew," Ethan said, digging into his own pain to make sure Sierra was okay. "Mandy wasn't who I believed she was. I just want you to be sure you want to marry him."

Ethan had recently lost his wife to an accidental drug overdose, then gone on to find out she'd been having an affair and stealing from the family company to subsidize her drug addiction. He was not only grieving, he was coming to terms with the betrayal.

But his words now were coming from an honest and good place, one of love. "Don't get me wrong," he continued. "I like Jason. We all do," he said, referring to her two other brothers, Parker and Sebastian. "But are you passionately in love with him?"

She did her best not to blush at the question asked by her brother. He pushed the point, forcing Sierra to wonder if Ethan saw something in her relationship she hadn't wanted to acknowledge.

But she shook her head, ignoring the sudden burning behind her eyes. "Not everyone gets passion, Ethan. It's fine," she said softly. "I'll be fine." So why did she have a case of anxiety? Why was her chest weighty and heavy?

The music transitioned from Vivaldi to the more traditional "Here Comes the Bride," and Sierra drew a steadying breath.

It was time.

The heavy wooden doors were opened, and beyond her veil, she faced the room full of family and friends who stood as one, the sounds of them shifting positions echoing in the large room.

With Ethan by her side, she began the long walk down the aisle, taking her time as she'd been instructed at rehearsal. She looked at the familiar faces around her, some of whom she worked with at Knight Time Technology, where she was head of the Social Media Division, some who were extended family, others friends from high school and college.

As she approached the front rows, her gaze landed on the one man she shouldn't think about today.

Ryder Hammond.

Her brother Sebastian's best friend.

Her high school boyfriend.

Her first love.

She swallowed over the sudden lump in her throat, unable not to compare his rugged good looks to the man waiting for her at the end of the aisle. Jason, lean and handsome in his tuxedo, his blond hair neatly trimmed, his face perfectly shaved, his gaze patiently on hers.

Then there was Ryder. His jet-black hair was too long to be considered neat, but it suited his sexy features, as did the stubble he hadn't shaved on his face. His suit jacket fit him perfectly, accentuating muscles he'd achieved by working in construction when, at this point in his career, he could sit behind a desk if he chose. He liked to build with his hands. Hands she was intimately familiar with, and at the thought, her nipples tightened beneath her dress.

His green eyes locked on hers, a wave of what looked like longing flashing in his gaze. She could once read every emotion on his face, but she didn't know now whether it was her mind conjuring what she wanted to see or whether desire was, in fact, what he was thinking and feeling now. They both knew that a big wedding had once been their dream. Or at least it had been the fantasy she'd woven for them both and he'd let her.

A small tremor rippled through her at the thought, the memory of them lying under the big tree in her backyard as she detailed her idea of a perfect day. Sierra and Ryder, she'd thought, had been meant to be. Until he'd broken up with her and ripped her heart to shreds at the same time.

Ethan paused at the slight shudder that overtook her. "Are you sure?" he whispered, so low only she could hear.

"I have to be," she replied just as softly.

With a half shake of his head, he continued their path to Jason. The man she was marrying.

Another few steps and Ethan paused at the end of the aisle, lifted her veil, and kissed her cheek. "Be happy," he whispered. "I love you."

And then he handed her off to her groom.

She met Jason's gaze and took his hand, smiling, her nerves settling down as they took their places. He was solid and secure, everything she needed and wanted in her life. Her father had given her a revolving door of so-called mother figures who wanted nothing to do with her as she grew up. He hadn't had any more time for her than they had. And so she'd dreamed of marrying one man and living the happily ever after that had eluded her father after her mom passed away.

She pushed useless thoughts of the past aside. She had no reason to question her decision to marry Jason, who offered her exactly what she craved. It had just been last-minute jitters that had hit her before, Ryder merely a reminder of adolescent daydreams.

Her thoughts were normal for any bride, she thought, as the priest began to speak. Jason held her hand and she looked into his eyes, the ceremony going on as planned, as the words were spoken around them.

"If anyone can show just cause why this couple cannot lawfully be joined together in matrimony, let them speak now or forever hold their peace."

Sierra's gaze shot to the priest in annoyance. She'd specifically asked for that line to be omitted, along with anything else that was sexist, such as her obeying her groom.

She blew out a harsh breath, realizing the priest was still waiting, glancing around the room.

It was as if an invisible pull had her looking away from Jason, turning, her gaze locking with Ryder's.

What happened next occurred in slow motion.

"I do," Ryder said, rising to his feet.

He did not just say that, she thought, panic setting in, her stare still joined with his.

"What the hell?" Jason asked, sounding pissed off.

"Sir?" the priest asked, clearly taken off guard. After all, how many times did an actual objection occur except on TV?

"I object," Ryder said, loud and clear.

People pointed and whispered.

"Fuck," Sebastian said from his place beside her brothers and Matthew, Jason's best man.

Suddenly chaos erupted around them. Ryder started forward at the same time Jason lunged toward him. His best man grabbed him, holding him back from going after Ryder, whose sister, Skye, one of Sierra's bridesmaids, ran for her brother.

"Calm down," she heard Matthew say.

Sebastian, she noted, went directly for Ryder, stopping him from getting near her as he spoke to him. Sebastian's wife, Ashley, came up beside him.

"Honey, are you okay?" Maggie, her bridesmaid and wedding planner, grasped her hand.

She turned to her friend, who looked beautiful in the deep purple dress Sierra had chosen. "I don't know," she said. And she didn't.

What had Ryder been thinking, objecting at her wedding?

"Oh, shit. Lena's diving into the flowers!" Rayna, her maid of honor and best friend since high school, cried, causing Maggie to leave Sierra's side and help their friend run for the little girl, who, unattended, was pulling petals from the floral arrangements.

"Someone call an ambulance! Candy's feeling faint!" Sierra's father's voice boomed through the church.

A glance told Sierra that her stepmother, an attention-seeking whore who'd worn white to the wedding, something Sierra knew because they'd stopped by the bridal room to see her, was fanning herself and causing her own scene.

"Go," Sierra said to Joy, her final bridesmaid, who was standing around wringing her hands. "Call 911 for my dad."

Sierra looked to Ryder again, who was deep in conversation with Sebastian, Parker, and Ethan, who, if Ryder was lucky, wouldn't beat him to a pulp for humiliating her this way. Suddenly he glanced up and met her gaze, those green eyes looking into her soul. He'd once known her better than anyone.

She'd even dreamed of walking down the aisle to him, and her stomach twisted with an unexpected pang of regret. She stared into his handsome face, his eyes never leaving hers, and a shock of longing slid through her.

Shaken, she tore her gaze from his and headed directly for Jason, stopping in front of him.

His face was red from anger, his best man still had a hand on his shoulder, and his sister was standing beside him.

"What's going on?" Ethan came to her side and faced Jason, wrapping an arm around Sierra.

"Jason, we can continue where we left off," she said, meeting his gaze.

His face contorted with hurt. "Seriously? Do you think I didn't notice you looking at him when you were walking down the aisle to me?" he yelled, outraged, startling Sierra with his outburst.

"Wait, what?" He was angry with her?

Her brother's supportive hold on her tightened.

"The priest asked if anyone objected, and you turned around and fucking looked at him." She'd never seen Jason this furious.

But, oh God, she had turned and looked at Ryder. But she hadn't wanted to end the ceremony. Yes, she'd thought about Ryder briefly as she'd walked down the aisle. She'd had a moment when she remembered the past, but she'd headed toward her future. Toward him.

Ryder showed up just then, facing Jason.

"It's him." Jason pointed, shoving his finger into Ryder's chest. "It's always been fucking him. At every family function, always around. You wanted him to interrupt the wedding," he said, accusing her of being at fault.

Ryder appeared about to grab Jason's finger when Sebastian pulled him back. "Don't," her brother muttered.

Sierra blinked, tears in her eyes. This couldn't be happening. Her life was falling apart and she had no way to stop it.

* * * *

Oh, shit. What the fuck did I just do?

Ryder Hammond stared into the eyes of his best friend, who appeared ready to murder him. Next to Sebastian were his two brothers, looking equally furious, and Ryder knew he was in deep shit.

Had he really just objected at Sierra's wedding?

He began to sweat beneath his suit. But he'd done it, the words had spilled forth, and now he had to dissect why. Ignoring the swearing men beside him, Ryder thought about the moment the big wooden double doors had opened and he'd seen Sierra in her wedding gown.

Her long light brown hair tumbled over her shoulders in perfect curls, her curves showing in her fitted dress, her cleavage just appropriately peeking out from the dipped neckline. Her gorgeous face had glowed as she walked down the aisle to another man.

He'd come today because, as a close family friend, he'd been invited. Because he thought he'd made his peace with the way things had ended between them. And for closure. Once she was married, she'd be lost to him forever. And that was the thought that had run through his head at the moment the priest asked if anyone objected.

He hadn't planned to open his mouth.

He hadn't meant to ruin her wedding.

He had intended to watch her be given away to another man and, dammit, be okay with it.

But he wasn't.

So here they were.

He glanced at her brothers, Sebastian, his closest friend, and Parker, because Ethan had gone after his sister. "I have to talk to her."

"No fucking way," Sebastian said, one palm on his chest, blocking him from moving forward.

"If I knew you'd planned this shit, I never would have let you in the door," said Parker.

Ryder held up both hands. "It wasn't planned. The words just came out of my mouth. But now that I said them, I need to speak with your sister." He shoved past the brothers and headed directly for Sierra, who stood talking to the man she was supposed to marry.

His gaze locked with hers but Jason wasn't having it.

"It's him." He pointed, shoving his finger into Ryder's chest. "It's always been fucking him. At every family function, always around." Jason turned to Sierra. "You wanted him to interrupt the wedding." He was clearly furious.

Ryder would be fucking livid if the situation had been reversed, and he had a moment's pity for the man, already opting not to grab his finger and break it when Sebastian pulled him back.

He didn't need Sebastian's muttered word, "Don't," to tell him to behave.

"I'm out of here," Jason, the groom, muttered.

"What?" Sierra cried, stricken, and the sound went straight to Ryder's gut.

"You don't want to marry me or this whole mess would have ended up differently," Jason said, turning and storming out, his best man and sister rushing after him.

Tears streamed down Sierra's face as she glared at Ryder. "How could you?"

"Come on," Sebastian said, his hand on Ryder's shoulder. "Let's go somewhere and talk."

Ryder shook his head, determined to talk to Sierra.

"Don't do this unless your intentions are fucking good," Sebastian muttered.

Ryder glanced at Sierra, who looked distraught and upset, causing his stomach to churn with the knowledge that he'd caused her pain. That had never been his intent, if he'd had any intention at all.

But he shook his head. He wasn't finished here. "I need to talk to you," he said, glancing only at her.

"You don't have to say anything to him." Ethan had his arm around her, holding her upright.

Her eyes were narrowed, her lips pursed. He remembered that look, one that would often end up with them in a heated kiss or resulting in hot and heavy angry sex. She was pissed as hell. But she wasn't storming away.

He extended his hand toward her, needing the moment alone.

Sierra stared at him and he looked back, their gazes locked in a way only they could understand.

"Five minutes," she muttered.

Glaring, she ignored his outstretched hand and stormed past him, her gown with the long train trailing behind her as she headed for the dressing room.

Despite her anger, she was willing to talk, which told him one thing.

There was still something between them.

Something, he could work with, he thought, and followed her out.

The moment he joined her in the small room, Sierra spun to glare at him. "How could you do this to me?" she asked, face flushed, eyes wide and glassy, makeup stains on her cheeks. She was beautiful despite her tears.

He shoved his hands into his front pants pockets. Meeting her gaze, he opted for the truth. "It wasn't planned."

"Oh, that makes it better," she muttered. "You ruined my wedding on a whim."

He ran a hand over his face, knowing that despite the blurted-out objection, the feelings behind it were real. "The priest's words were a wakeup call," he said.

She blinked at his comment. "For who?" she asked. "You made your choice years ago and it wasn't me."

He winced at the reminder of all he'd thrown away, no matter that he'd made the decision for all the right reasons. But he didn't have time to dwell on the past now.

She turned to head back inside the church and panic struck him. He knew if she walked away, it would be for the last time.

"Sierra, wait."

She glanced over her shoulder and he knew he had mere seconds to convince her not to leave.

"Do you really want to go back into that room with all the chaos and insanity waiting for you?" he asked. "Your stepmother is splayed out on the floor, moaning and waiting for paramedics to tell her she's fine. The flower girl is having a meltdown. Your brothers are plotting to kill me, and you have a room full of people in there who expected a wedding."

She shuddered at the reminders. "Then I want to go home."

He raised an eyebrow. "Where your bags are packed and your things are in boxes so you can move in with the same groom who just abandoned you instead of fighting for you?"

Tears filled her eyes as she met his gaze. "I hate you."

His chest squeezed at her blurted-out words. "No, you don't, but I understand why you want to think you do."

She glared at him. "So what are you suggesting?"

"Let me get you out of here. Give everyone a chance to calm down and think. Let cooler heads prevail."

She glanced toward the sanctuary, where the sounds of chaos still carried to them.

"Come on." He held out a hand, and this time she placed her palm in his, the warmth and electrical connection between them instantaneous despite the wary expression on her face and the emotional walls between them.

Before her brothers could burst into the room, he led her outside and toward his car, helping her climb in and tucking her dress inside before shutting the door.

He had her where he wanted her. He just didn't know what he was going to do next.

* * * *

With no destination in mind, Ryder drove them over the George Washington Bridge and out of New York City. Beside him, Sierra sat, her dress fluffed around her, staring out the window, not saying a word.

Except to hand her his phone and tell her to text her brothers and let them know she was okay, he left her alone, hoping she wasn't stewing and building up a case of righteous anger against him. He wanted the chance later for them to really talk.

He was surprised when, after about half an hour, she fell asleep, leaving him to his own thoughts and self-recriminations, and he had many, not all revolving around his actions at the wedding.

He glanced over, taking in her delicate profile, noticing the freckles on her nose, remembering how he'd pretend to count them, one by one. He swallowed a groan, not wanting to wake her up, but asking himself, how the hell had they gotten to this point?

He gripped the wheel tighter, the past coming back to him. As Sebastian's best friend, he'd been around the Knight house all the time when they were growing up. Two years apart, he couldn't help but notice as Sierra matured into a gorgeous woman. He'd been attracted to her and knew better than to screw around when it came to his best friend's sister, but when they finally did get together, it was in a relationship.

And her brothers, knowing him as they did, had actually approved of them as a couple. They'd trusted Ryder to do right by her. Crazily enough, knowing that had played into the decisions he'd made.

Although his family wasn't as wealthy as Sebastian's, his dad had done well until a market crash hit and his business took a dive. He should have gone away to school, but his dad had had a heart attack before he could leave and Ryder had stayed home to help run the family business with his older brother, Andrew. His father had developed a weak heart, resulting in many hospital trips over the years, and Ryder had never regretted his decision.

At his older sibling's urging, Ryder had gone to school at night, earning his undergraduate and master's degrees, but during the day, he'd worked overseeing the day-to-day construction side of the business while his brother handled the office management part of the company.

And during the summer before Sierra's senior year, they'd first gotten together. As the school year began, she'd applied to college, always planning to go to school away from home. Even before they'd been a couple, she'd talked about how eager she'd been to finally get away and have independence without three older brothers watching over her. But their romance had taken a turn neither had expected, getting hot and heavy quickly.

He'd fallen hard and fast for the girl with the beautiful face and the big heart. They'd both lost their moms at a young age, hers to cancer, his to a freak car accident, and they'd had that loss in common. Because her family had money, which included having a housekeeper and a cook, there was always food left over after dinner. And she'd insisted on bringing meals to his dad when he came home from one of his frequent hospital trips.

Before Ryder knew it, they'd found themselves making plans for the future. She'd detailed the wedding of her dreams and he hadn't freaked that she wanted to spend the rest of her life with him. He'd wanted the same thing. There'd been something deep and meaningful between them from the beginning that had only grown over time.

Except that Sierra had started to talk about staying home and attending a local college instead of going away and being exposed to all the things she'd wanted before they'd gotten together—college, independence, life, and yes, dammit, other guys. She needed to experience more before she committed to him. She needed to be certain of what she wanted, and as a senior in high school, she couldn't possibly know what was best for her.

Ryder never wanted her to resent him for holding her back, so he'd broken up with her so she could live her original dreams, crushing his own heart in the process.

Knowing he'd lost her for good, he'd gone on with his life, and though that had included being with other women, none had ever come close to making him feel what she had. Over the years, he'd watched her date other men, knowing he'd lost his chance, that she still harbored anger and resentment despite putting up with him for Sebastian's sake. When she'd ended up engaged, he'd known it really was over for them. No someday in their future. Until he'd opened his mouth at the wedding.

He glanced up, realizing he'd been driving for over an hour. He was on Route 80 in New Jersey, signs for the Delaware Water Gap and the Poconos ahead of him.

Shit.

He glanced over to the passenger side of the car. Sierra was still asleep. She was going to fucking kill him when she realized where they'd ended up, but what the hell.

He only had one chance to win her back, and he couldn't do it in the city with her surrounded by her brothers and friends. Instead he was headed another thirty minutes away to a mountain resort that he was pretty sure was the cheesiest honeymoon capital of the northeast. A place that advertised heart-shaped bathtubs and themed rooms.

A place where they could be alone.

Chapter Two

Sierra woke up as the car turned off, the motor coming to a stop. She shook her head and looked around at the unfamiliar surroundings. Trees were visible outside the windows, and a glittering sign said *Paradise Cove*, and beneath it, *A Couples Only Poconos Resort.*

"You have got to be kidding me!" She glanced at Ryder in disbelief. "What the hell are we doing in the Poconos?" She'd obviously fallen asleep for a good two hours, the shock of the day along with the glass of champagne she'd had prior to the non-wedding catching up with her.

He treated her to his most charming grin. "You always said you wanted to honeymoon here. That it was romantic."

"I was seventeen!" she yelled at him. "I didn't know any better. And we aren't on our honeymoon." She glanced down at her white wedding gown, not missing the irony of the situation but in no mood to find it funny.

She and Jason were supposed to be on their way to St. Lucia tomorrow morning. Instead she was in the honeymoon capital of Pennsylvania. Her stomach cramped at the reminder of all she'd left behind earlier today. Although she'd texted Sebastian from Ryder's phone, she hoped her brothers weren't too worried about her. She'd left her own phone in the bridal room and couldn't know whether Jason had tried to reach her or not. But her brothers knew she was with Ryder, and if Jason wanted her, he certainly could contact them and find out how to talk to her.

Instead she was in the Poconos with her ex. She looked at the man who'd driven her over one hundred miles from home and waited for an explanation.

He placed an arm behind her seat, turning to face her. "By the time I realized how far I'd driven, we were half an hour from here. I couldn't think of anywhere else to crash. And I wasn't about to turn around and drive another two hours home."

She frowned at him. "So now what? You expect me to stay here with you?"

"Would it really be so bad?" he asked, his voice gentling. "I understand you're angry with me, but we're here. It's late. Let's just go inside and see if we can get a room."

The very idea of it was crazy. Nothing good could come of her being alone with Ryder now, and she really shouldn't have left with him. But it was too late to take her actions back now.

She blew out a resigned breath. "Fine. But I hope they have a gift shop," she muttered, needing a change of clothes because nothing about this trip had been thought through.

She climbed out of the car and Ryder helped her gather the train and fold it up so she could hold it over one arm. Then together, they walked into the main area of the resort and headed to the reception desk.

"I assume you have a reservation?" the woman behind the counter asked, her gaze traveling over Ryder in his suit, Sierra in her white gown.

"Umm, no. But we'd like a room for a couple of days," Ryder said with a smile.

"One night," Sierra countered.

He frowned at her and the girl behind the desk looked confused. She typed something into the computer and glanced up at them. "Our honeymoon suite is booked and we only have suites, not rooms, but I'm sure you'll love what's available. All of our suites have round king-size beds beneath celestial ceilings, log-burning fireplaces, and heart-shaped tubs or champagne-glass-shaped whirlpool spas."

Sierra felt her mouth drop open at the description. It was everything she'd seen in commercials as a young, love-struck girl dreaming of romance.

"I don't think–"

"We'll take one," he said, cutting her off.

The clerk looked back and forth between them, a definite furrow between her eyebrows. "We can only offer you two nights. I'm sorry but we're booked after that."

Before she could utter another word, Ryder slid his credit card across the counter. "We'll stay both nights. And the airline lost our luggage, so do you think you could hook us up with the basics?" he asked.

She was grateful he was thinking of everything, even if she was still annoyed with him. Besides, she was beyond uncomfortable in the wedding gown, and Sierra hoped the woman could help them.

The clerk's gaze softened at the mention of missing suitcases. "That's awful and frustrating. I'll send up toiletries and amenities," the woman said. "There are bathrobes in the rooms, and the gift shop and stores open tomorrow morning. You'll be able to pick up more things to wear then."

"Thank you," Sierra said, appreciating the woman's kindness.

"We're grateful for anything you can do," Ryder said.

He slipped a tip across the counter and the clerk glanced down and grinned at him. "Thank you. I'll call housekeeping right now. In the meantime, here are your key cards. Breakfast and dinner are included. A continental breakfast is served in the room tomorrow. I'll even throw in some parts of our honeymoon package," she whispered to Ryder, making Sierra wonder how much money he'd given her.

No matter the amount, she had no intention of making use of their specialty package, she thought, exhaustion seeping into her bones despite her long nap. The day had been overwhelming and was definitely catching up with her.

She unwittingly sagged against him, and his arm immediately came out, wrapping around her, holding her for the first time in forever. It took all her willpower not to lean her head against him and let him take over.

"Come on, sweetheart. You look dead on your feet," Ryder said, and taking her by surprise, he swept her into his arms.

Just like a real bride.

Although she wanted to argue, she was just beginning to realize how much her feet ached from the high-heeled designer shoes she'd worn. Keeping her mouth shut and letting him hold her had nothing to do with how much she liked the feel of his strong arms wrapped around her. Or the notion of being carried across the threshold of their romantic suite.

Once more, she pushed the thought of what should have been happening tonight aside. It didn't matter whether or not Jason would have carried her over the threshold or let her walk across on her own. He'd abandoned her, she thought, and to her surprise, tears stung her eyes.

Despite being prepared, when they walked inside, the over-the-top décor took her by surprise. The room was red and white, from the bedding on the circular mattress to the drapes hanging over the windows and the red lacquer dressers and night tables.

Across the room she saw the bathtub reachable by a set of stairs. "Oh my God."

"Welcome to the Champagne Tower Suite," Ryder said, lowering her carefully to her feet.

"That's obscene," she muttered.

"Or sexy," he whispered in her ear.

She trembled, nipples puckering, and she stepped aside, annoyed with her body's reaction to him. Feet cramping, she immediately kicked off her heels and pushed them to the corner of the room.

She didn't know how she was going to survive the romance of this place with Ryder staying in the same room with her. Yes, it was cheesy, but there was something romantic about it if she let her imagination run away with her, and surrounded by the color of hearts and flowers, which sat on the table, it was hard not to. Especially since she used to fantasize about honeymooning here with him.

"Are you hungry?" he asked, drawing her attention.

She glanced over her shoulder. "I don't know if I'm more hungry or tired. I'm afraid I'll fall asleep before we even get room service delivered."

His gaze softened. "Let's just put in for an early breakfast."

"Sounds good." She glanced at the bed, realizing they were obviously going to be sharing that cozy mattress. She also knew she couldn't sleep in a heavy terrycloth robe, which meant she was climbing into that bed in her bra and panties. She blushed at the thought.

"Your cheeks are pink. What's going through your mind?" he asked.

She pulled her bottom lip between her teeth. "I have nothing to sleep in."

His gaze darkened. "You can wear my shirt."

She shook her head. She wasn't about to cuddle up and be surrounded by his masculine scent. It was going to be hard enough to sleep beside him.

"I can't sleep when I feel confined," she said, using a legitimate and acceptable excuse that wouldn't embarrass her. She normally got in bed wearing a short silk camisole that she barely felt on her skin. "I'll make do. Can you help me get out of this dress?"

He walked up behind her and she was immediately aware of him, the warmth of his body as he came close. "Lift your hair," he said in a gruff voice.

She raised the heavy strands and pulled them over her shoulder, then felt his big hands come to the tiny buttons that began midway down her back. He struggled with the size of them, muttering as he worked, his breath warm as he leaned closer for a better look.

His scent was familiar and arousing, her imagination running away as his hands touched the buttons the way they'd once danced over her skin. Her entire body felt like it was on fire, awareness sizzling through her veins. Need pulsing inside her. Her thong panties were damp, her nipples hard, desire a living, breathing thing inside her . . .

In all her time with Jason, she'd never experienced passion like she had with Ryder, and the fact that just his nearness had her hyperaware of him put her on alert to the fact that her feelings for him hadn't dissipated in the time they'd been apart.

"There. Finished."

Ryder stepped back and she nearly sagged with relief. She'd come so close to turning around and plastering herself against him, reliving a past that she'd never quite gotten over.

It had been one thing for her to acknowledge to her brother that she didn't share a passionate love with Jason, but to experience the difference now with Ryder was disconcerting. Just a few touches from Ryder made her truly realize exactly how much she'd been willing to give up in her marriage.

And on that thought… "I'm going to the bathroom and I'd like to climb into the bed without you watching."

He frowned. "I just unbuttoned your dress lower than your ass. Besides, what I haven't seen just now, I've seen before," he reminded her.

"Not lately you haven't." She stormed into the bathroom and

slammed the door behind her, frustrated with herself for feeling anything for him at all.

Before she could even let the dress slide off her shoulders, a knock sounded on the bathroom door. "What?" she called out.

"Housekeeping brought some toiletries," he said.

"Thanks," she said, accepting the Paradise-Cove-labeled bag through the door and then shutting it quickly, luckily not catching his hand as she did.

A little while later, she'd brushed her teeth, washed her face, and cleaned up after the long day. After hanging her dress on the hook behind the door, she stepped back into the room to find he was already in bed. His bare chest peeked out from beneath the red satin comforter as he waited for her to join him, tanned and muscular and more appealing than she wanted him to be.

Those strong arms had once held her tight, given her comfort, and caused her arousal. She wished what she felt was only sexual, but this was the man she'd loved and had dreamed of spending the rest of her life with in a way much different than the plans she'd made with Jason.

After the breakup, she'd spent years seeing him with Sebastian, blocking out her feelings for him, and ignoring the pang of regret that inevitably came with him being near. She hadn't been the one to end things, and despite being hurt by his actions, her feelings hadn't turned off as easily as she'd wanted them to. Viewing him in that luxurious bed now was like a punch in the stomach, creating a yearning she'd tried to push away a long time ago.

"Shut your eyes," she bit out, knowing she was being childish, but she didn't care. She wasn't ready to parade in front of him in the see-through bra and panties she'd bought to wear beneath her wedding gown, for her wedding night. With another man.

She shuddered at the thought, wondering why she hadn't spent more time mourning Jason's loss than she had thinking about being in a honeymoon suite with her first love. Ryder had ruined her wedding and the future she'd had planned… and yet she'd left the church with him willingly. She didn't like herself very much right now.

"Come on," Ryder said, placing his hand over his eyes. "They're closed." He'd shut off the overhead lights in the room, leaving the lamp on by the nightstand.

Having no choice but to trust him not to peek, she walked out and came to the bed, sliding into the satin sheets. She pulled the comforter up around her and sighed. "I'm good."

He lowered his arm and met her gaze, his expression contrite. "It's going to be okay," he said, although he couldn't know any such thing.

"So now you can read the future?"

"I wish," he muttered. "No. I just have faith. For now, though, can we just get some sleep?"

"Yeah." She knew they'd have plenty of time to talk tomorrow, although she wasn't looking forward to a rehash of the past or the present. But maybe for both of their sakes, they needed to resolve their issues and her anger over the end of the relationship once and for all. So that she could figure out what she really wanted for her future, though she was beginning to suspect that it wasn't with Jason, a man who'd so easily walked away from her at the first sign of trouble.

Turning on her side away from him, she punched the pillows and curled into the soft sheets. She was exhausted from the events of the day, which should be running through her head. The loss of the future she'd planned, the things at home waiting for her, presents to return, apologies to be made, boxes to unpack. But those things weren't first and foremost on her mind.

Because when she breathed in deep, she smelled the musky scent of the man beside her. And whether it was her imagination or not, she imagined she could feel the warmth of him beside her. Her body was well aware of his presence, and her heart banged loudly in her chest, anxiety clawing at her, not because of what she'd lost but because of the possible reasons Ryder had objected at her wedding.

Like it or not, he was back in her life. She didn't know what she'd be doing with him… and that was the real cause of the apprehension keeping her awake. Not the man shifting beside her, also unable to sleep.

* * * *

Ryder woke up to Sierra wrapped around him, her mostly naked body plastered to his, his cock hard, morning wood making itself known. It'd taken him forever to fall asleep last night. He was too aware of the woman curled away from him, trying her best to stick to her side of the bed. So he was shocked now that her head was in the crook of his arm, her hands on his chest, her knee hiked up over his legs.

When he heard a knock on the door, he assumed it was room service bringing breakfast. He slid out from beneath her, and though she shifted and moaned, winding herself around the pillow instead of him, she didn't wake up.

The waiter set up their continental breakfast on the table before accepting a tip and leaving him alone. He took in the double coffee cups, the muffins and croissants and other baked goods, and headed back to see if Sleeping Beauty was awake.

He stepped over to the bed and eased himself down onto the mattress. The round shape was disconcerting. He settled back against the pillows, and no sooner had he relaxed than Sierra rolled back, positioning herself against him once more. They hadn't slept in the same bed in the past. She'd been a senior in high school and her spending the night wasn't an option. But when they'd lie outside in her backyard, this was the position she'd take.

Wrapping an arm around her, he closed his eyes and breathed in her sweet scent, different now but no less alluring. She appealed to him on many levels beyond sexual. Her sharp mind, her normally sweet personality, although he understood why she wasn't treating him to that part of her now. She loved family the way he did, wanted similar things out of their future. He knew because she'd laid it all out for him once upon a time.

And he'd thrown it all away. For good reasons, but it didn't make him feel any better or change their situation now.

He must have fallen back to sleep, and when he woke up, they were wound around each other still.

Sierra's eyes opened wide and she attempted to pull away but he held on tight. "Don't."

With a resigned sigh, she laid her head against his chest. "What are we doing?" she asked him, voice calmer than yesterday.

She was obviously more relaxed and accepting of their situation than she'd been.

"We are exploring our options. Seeing what's still between us."

"We are?"

"You tell me." He was putting out feelers, testing where she was when it came to him.

She swallowed hard, her throat moving against his skin. "I don't know, Ryder. You can't just interrupt my wedding and now say we're going to see what's still between us."

At her unwillingness to fall in line with the plans he wanted, his heart kicked harder in his chest. "Tell me something."

"Hmm?"

"I know I ruined your big day." There was no getting past that. "But did I… I mean, were you really in love with him?"

It was a stupid question. On the one hand, she'd been in a wedding dress, ready to commit her life to the other man. On the other, she had gotten into the car with him, so Ryder held his breath for her answer.

"I was going to marry Jason."

She pushed herself up and away from him, and he didn't pull her back.

Yet.

"Yes, but what was between you? Were you in love?" he asked again, needing answers. He couldn't keep her here just because he needed to see if there was a second chance for them. Not if she'd truly been in love with someone else.

She blew out a long breath. "Right before the doors opened, Ethan asked me if I was sure." Not meeting his gaze, she said, "It gave me pause and I… I had second thoughts."

She lifted her face to him and tears shimmered in her pretty blue eyes. "It's not that I didn't love Jason. We were compatible. He offered me everything I wanted in my life."

"Security and a future aren't enough to base a lifetime on." He named the minimal things she would want in order to marry someone because he knew her that well. He had. He still did.

She sniffed. "Yes, well, it seemed enough at the time. I do love him," she said, her words a knife to Ryder's chest.

"But you aren't in love with him."

"How do you know that?" she asked, some of the fire from last night back in her tone.

He rolled his shoulders. "Easy. Because when he walked out on you, you let him go." He debated his next words, then decided it wasn't the time to hold anything back. "When I broke up with you, you didn't let me go as easily." He shuddered at the memories of a time that had nearly killed him. "But you stood in a wedding dress and you let Jason walk out the door."

She blinked and the tears she'd been holding back rolled down her cheeks. He swept one away with his finger.

"I was in shock."

"Maybe. You also got in the car with me. Was that because you were in shock?"

She glared at him but it didn't last long.

He didn't want to push her further. He already had his answer about her second thoughts.

It was all he needed for now.

* * * *

Before Sierra could reply to Ryder's comment, her stomach grumbled loudly and she groaned at the sound. "I'm starving."

His lips curved in a smile. "Well, it's a good thing breakfast is already here." After swinging his legs over the side of the mattress, he walked to the table and returned with a tray full of food, placing it down on the bed.

She pulled her gaze away from his tight ass in his boxer briefs, clenching her teeth at the intimacy he was clearly already comfortable with. She wasn't. Instead she pulled the covers up higher, covering her breasts and her bra.

"I can't promise the coffee is still hot, but there's enough pastries and muffins in here to quiet the beast," he said with a laugh.

She glared at his joke about her noisy stomach, then turned to focus on the food he placed on the bed before climbing back into his side.

Picking which kind of muffin she wanted was a welcome, easy decision. Because as she ate—a blueberry muffin and then a scone, making up for not eating much at all yesterday—she was tortured by facts that were hard to admit to.

She'd rolled into Ryder in her sleep. She'd willingly turned to him in a way she'd never gone to Jason—they'd slept on separate sides of the bed, coming together to have sex when they were due, not out of some sense of innate need that couldn't be contained.

When she looked back on yesterday, walking down the aisle after Ethan had asked if Jason was the man she really wanted, she hadn't been sure. And when push came to shove, instead of fighting for her, Jason had stormed out, leaving her to Ryder. The guy who hadn't let her marry another man.

That told her where she stood with her groom now. Not that they didn't need to talk and have a rational conversation, if such a thing were possible. But she knew they were over. How could they be anything but? The truth hurt along with the loss of the future she'd clearly seen laid out for herself.

She glanced at Ryder as he watched her quietly. He'd always known when to talk and when to stay silent, reading her mind in ways Jason never had. She rubbed her eyes, wondering now why she'd thought settling emotionally or physically was enough for her. She ripped a piece of croissant off the end of the roll and shoved it into her mouth. No more carbs, she thought, finally feeling full.

She studied him through lowered lashes, knowing that they hadn't yet had the much-needed conversation about their past. Given that she wasn't ready to go home and face the ramifications of a canceled wedding, they had time before they dug that deep.

But they were here together now. "You're crazy," she muttered.

He grinned. "Can't say I haven't thought the same thing myself after yesterday. But in that moment, I couldn't stand by and lose you forever." He rose to his feet, picked up the tray, and put it back on the table, returning to her side of the bed and sitting down beside her.

He grasped her hand, holding her palm in his. "I always considered you mine, even after I let you go. I just didn't let myself go there again."

She saw the truth swirling in the green depths of his eyes, and she was forced to ask the question she'd wanted to put off, the one that had always haunted her. "Why didn't you come to me sooner?"

He shook his head, letting her know it was obviously something he'd thought about before. "Because I'd made my decision to let you go so you could pursue your dreams and live the life you'd planned."

She tilted her head to the side, wondering if she'd heard him wrong. "But I planned my life with you." A life, a future, she'd seen it all in vivid color in her mind… until he'd shattered her dreams.

"But before me you'd wanted to go away to college," he reminded her. "To have time to explore without your brothers always there, and you deserved to have those things. Not to make a choice at seventeen years old that would bind you to me for the rest of your life. I didn't want you to end up resenting me." He glanced at their intertwined hands, then up at her face.

She opened her mouth but he cut her off, placing his finger over her lips. "I know you wouldn't have agreed with me. That's why I made the choice for you," he said.

"You had no right to decide for me." She swallowed over the lump in her throat, a combination of pain and anger, unable to believe that while she'd always thought he'd ended things because he no longer loved her, he'd been looking out for her in his own misguided way. "What about after? Why didn't you come to me after I came back from school?"

He groaned, the sound resigned. "I broke your heart. I devastated you and I didn't think you'd give me another chance. You were dating and I thought you needed to do that, too. Then you met Jason and suddenly things were serious." His thumb brushed over the top of her hand as he paused, deep in thought.

"I told myself it was what I wanted for you, to move on and be happy. I had my feelings for you bottled up so tight I never let myself go there emotionally. But then you walked down that aisle and I really saw you. And realized all I was losing. So when the minister asked if anyone objected, I didn't think, I reacted." He met her gaze, and in that moment, he was the same boy she'd fallen in love with. "I followed my heart and I can't tell you I regret it. I only regret that you were hurt in the process."

She shook her head, the truth as difficult to hear as it was for her to process. "Like I said, Ryder, you're crazy."

"Crazy for you," he said, leaning forward and sealing his lips over hers.

He caught her off guard, but the heat and warmth of his mouth were familiar and surprisingly welcome. His lips moved over hers, his tongue darting inside as he licked, sucked, and devoured her in a way no man but him ever had. His kiss turned hotter, one that stated his intention to possess and stake his claim.

There was no other way to explain it and nothing she could do but grasp his shoulders and hold on for the ride while enjoying every second. He pushed her against the pillows so he could deepen their connection, and her heart pounded against her chest, desire for this man consuming her and forcing her to come to painful conclusions.

Losing Jason had been difficult. Embarrassing. Painful, even. But losing Ryder when she was younger had hurt even more. She'd always wondered what could have been. What could she have done to change the outcome of their relationship? What could their future have been if things had been different?

She never thought she'd have the chance to find out, but here they were. She lifted her hands to his hair and curled her fingers into the long strands, holding him to her, kissing him back as thoroughly and as deeply as he kissed her, until he lifted his head, breathing heavily.

"We're good together, Sierra. And we owe it to ourselves to explore it further. I want to be the man to give you everything you want and need and dream of." He met her gaze. "But it's up to you. In the meantime, I need a cold shower," he muttered before turning and walking away.

Leaving her to decide what happened next.

A few seconds later, the sound of the water turning on and running echoed through the pipes in the room. He was in the bathroom naked, droplets cascading over his well-honed body, soap making his muscles slick and wet.

She laid her head against the pillows and groaned in frustration. She could lie here debating what to do for the next two days she had in this hotel suite, a respite from the insanity and chaos that awaited her at home, or she could do what her body told her it wanted. What her heart had wanted since the day he'd ended things between them.

He'd hurt her once, walked away without warning. What was to prevent him from doing the same thing again? She couldn't ever let herself forget that.

But she'd thought she'd moved on from him enough to marry another man. Clearly, she'd been wrong. Closure was important and she needed to know if her memories were just that or if he was going to forever ruin her for another man and a real future.

If that was the case, God help her.

She might not know what she wanted from life right now, but it had become crystal clear that it wasn't Jason. But she also knew that just because Ryder had stopped her from being with another man didn't mean he automatically fit into the space Jason had left behind.

With that warning firmly in mind, she contemplated exploring this thing between them and putting it to rest once and for all.

Chapter Three

Lifting the covers off her body, Sierra stood and unhooked her bra, dropping it to the floor, followed by her underwear. Then she drew her courage around her and headed for the bathroom, pushing the door open and stepping into the steam-filled room, her heart racing wildly in her chest at what she was about to do.

Ryder's face was upturned to the water, and she took a second to admire the width of his chest, the hard muscles in his arms, and the way he braced his strong legs, his cock hard and standing upright. He obviously wanted her as much as she wanted him.

Desire didn't scare her. It was the notion of falling hard for him all over again that frightened her. But she'd made her decision. She'd be brave and see where things stood, and right here, right now, she wanted Ryder.

Needed him.

Without waiting for him to notice her, she opened the shower door and stepped in. His eyes opened and flared but he didn't hesitate. He pulled her against him, the hard ridge of his erection nudging against her belly.

She gasped at the feel of him, at the desire that spread through her and lit up her body, as his mouth descended on hers.

Water slid over her but she didn't care, not when he was devouring her, his tongue delving deep into the back of her mouth, tasting her everywhere as it tangled with hers. With a moan, she wrapped her arms around his neck and gave in to the yearning that was consuming her.

In the past, their time together was often rushed, hidden from adults, stolen moments when they could be together. Today they had all the time in the world or at least as long as the water remained hot, she thought, holding back a laugh.

He gripped her head and tilted her neck, giving him deeper access to her mouth, his lips gliding over hers, back and forth, and she pushed against him, rubbing her aching breasts over his chest.

"God, I missed this. I missed you." His huskily spoken words sent a shiver through her along with a hint of hope that she ruthlessly squashed.

"Tell me," he said, nipping on her bottom lip.

"What?"

"That this isn't just revenge sex. Angry sex. Tell me you want me, too."

Dammit, he was going to dig into her emotions and there was no way to stop it. Because she couldn't deny the truth, and maybe she didn't want to anyway. She'd been denying her feelings for Ryder for way too long, and it was time that she was honest with herself, as well as with him.

"I'm not here because I'm angry or pissed or because I want to get back at Jason for walking away from me. I missed you, too," she admitted.

And she had.

So much it hurt.

"Then take off the bracelet," he said on a growl.

She blinked, looking down at her right wrist, which held a bracelet that Jason had bought her with their initials intertwined. He'd given it to her when their relationship had gotten serious, and she'd been wearing it for so long it had become a part of her. She'd forgotten she still had it on, and she said a silent prayer of thanks Jason's best man had been holding on to her engagement ring along with the wedding band. Ryder's reaction to that wouldn't have been good.

Although she'd made no decisions about her life, she knew things were over with Jason or she wouldn't be here now, with Ryder. She unhooked the bracelet, stepped out of the shower, and put it on the counter, returning to Ryder.

"Done," she said.

With a groan, he slid his hands down her neck and over her breasts, cupping the mounds. She closed her eyes as he plumped her flesh, then pinched her nipples as he pulled, the mix of pain and pleasure shooting straight to her core.

She'd been young when they were together last, and sex had been hot and frenzied so as not to get caught by an adult or so she could rush home for curfew.

She hadn't been his first, though he'd been hers. Another reason she'd fallen so hard so fast for him. He'd been patient and sweet that initial time. But they'd both been inexperienced despite the burning passion between them.

Now he was a man in charge, one who knew how to arouse a woman, and he was taking care of her with an expert touch. He slid his hands through the soap on the shelf, rubbing both palms together before turning his attention back to her breasts, soaping them up while playing with her nipples, alternately pinching then soothing the sting.

Her legs trembled, need pulsing in her core. As if he knew she needed him now, he dropped to his knees, pressing his mouth to her stomach in a reverent kiss.

"Oh God." Just the sight of him kneeling before her had moisture settling between her thighs and her damn heart swelling in her chest.

He glanced up at her, then slid his mouth lower, over her pubic bone and to her bare sex. The anticipation was killing her, made more intense when he slicked his hands up her legs until they settled at her thighs, her body on edge as she waited for whatever he planned next.

He licked over her sex and she leaned back, her head hitting the wall.

"I'd forgotten how good you taste," he said, following that erotic comment up with another teasing glide of his tongue. "I'm going to rectify that," he murmured, then began to eat at her like a starving man devouring his last meal.

She had nothing to hold on to as he slid his tongue over her lips, nipping and licking over and over before thrusting it into her body. She whimpered at the slick invasion, shocked when he began to circle her clit with one thumb.

Her fingers curled into his hair as he worked her into a frenzy, her orgasm building fast as she came with a cry, her body not her own as waves of pleasure overtook her.

Coming back to herself, she realized he'd stood up and she looked into his satisfied expression. "Pleased with yourself?" she asked.

"Quite," he said with a grin.

Glancing down, she saw his cock hard and erect, in need of attention. She reached between them, wrapping her hand around his velvety thickness.

He grasped her wrist and pulled her off. "I'm not coming unless I'm inside you."

She moaned her frustration. "Why don't the same rules apply to us both?" she asked as he slipped his fingers between her lower lips once more.

To her surprise, her hips bucked greedily, as they sought out harder contact, more friction.

He chuckled at her clearly mixed message. "Because I'm in charge, sweetheart."

And as his finger pinched her clit, she couldn't bring herself to argue the point.

"This pussy's mine, baby. Nobody else's," he said as he slid one finger inside her, then another.

"Oh God."

"Am I right? Nobody's ever worked you up like this?" he asked, not mentioning anyone else by name, but Sierra knew he was staking his claim. And why.

And as he hooked his finger, gliding the pad over her G-spot, she felt as if he owned her. Her legs trembled, her body shaking as a need to climax built inside her. He knew just where to touch her and how. He rubbed over the spot inside her while holding her upright with one hand around her waist.

"Tell me or else." He stopped all movement, gliding his fingers out of her body.

"It's yours. Only you can get me this hot. Now don't stop," she implored him, and he immediately reinserted both fingers into her body, pressing, gliding in and out, taking her higher.

Before she knew it, she was coming, the waves of rapture rushing through her and consuming her whole. As she returned to herself, he was kissing her, rubbing his cock against her.

She moaned, arching into him, needing to feel him inside her.

"We need to talk," he said, meeting her gaze. "I don't have any condoms. It's not like I came prepared for this. And I've never not used one."

She looked into his familiar green eyes, and in this, she trusted him. "I'm on the pill. And I've never had sex without one."

"I swear to you, neither have I."

She reached for his shoulders, but he grasped her hips and spun her around. "Hands on the wall."

He was a different man than the boy she used to sleep with, she thought, enjoying everything he did to her body. Without hesitation, she braced her hands against the tile, her ass out.

He eased her legs apart and slid his fingers over her, slicking her own juices around her body. Then his thick cock grazed her entrance. She gasped at the size of him, closing her eyes and groaning at the delicious invasion. He shoved in deep, his back covering hers as he paused for a long while.

"What's wrong?" she asked when he paused and waited.

His lips grazed her neck, licking, nibbling, and kissing her. "I'm just savoring the moment," he said in a deep voice, made rough by emotion.

Her heart cracked at the admission, the words meaning something deep in her heart. The heart she'd sworn to protect.

And then he started to move again and she wasn't thinking about anything except maintaining her hold on the wall and the way he filled her up, thick and hard. With his grip on her waist, he pounded into her, taking everything and giving back at the same time.

"Ryder, Ryder, Ryder," she chanted in time to his thrusts. "I'm so close."

"Damn, my name on your lips sounds like heaven," he muttered. "Wait for me," he said, followed by increasingly faster shifts of his hips.

She held on, whimpering, until he groaned. "Now, sweetheart."

She gasped, released everything she'd been holding back, and screamed as she came, feeling him swell and pulse inside her as he climaxed along with her.

Her legs shook and she wasn't even aware when he turned her around and eased her down on the stone seat in the shower. The water had cooled and he moved quickly, soaping up his hands and rinsing them both off.

She was a boneless mess as he cleaned them both up, shut off the shower, and wrapped her in a fluffy white towel.

He dried her off, then slid the hotel robe around her body. By then she was able to help get herself together. He dried himself quickly and picked her up in his arms, striding back to the bed. He stripped her of the robe, and they crawled back under the covers, where she proceeded to crash hard.

* * * *

Ryder couldn't fall back to sleep. Not after what had just happened in the shower with Sierra. He wanted a second chance. Not because the sex was spectacular, which it was, but because this woman was the very best part of him.

As much as he, his father and brother, had been a tight-knit family after his mother died when Ryder had been thirteen, it had taken being with Sierra to fill that missing piece and make him whole.

After he'd ended things, he'd more than missed her but he'd had to let her go. He'd had no choice but to move on with his life, and sure, there had been other women, but he'd already had the best and none after had been her. None lived up to her memory, so he'd never gotten close with anyone else, never considered a future with any other female.

As he'd told her, he hadn't let himself think about going back to her, but now that he thought about it, maybe a part of him had been holding on to the past, hoping for another chance with her. Something had kept him from moving on completely.

She, on the other hand, had had no choice but to believe they were over for good. He'd given her no reason to think they could have anything ever again. She'd been so hurt, she'd avoided him when his relationship with her brother brought them together. She'd had boyfriends who came and went. And then she'd found Jason, a good man, but she hadn't been in love with him. Something inside Ryder's chest had loosened when he'd heard that, learned she'd had second thoughts.

He might have objected as a spur-of-the-moment decision, the fear of losing her forever suddenly stark and clear. But when they'd been in the car, his understanding had crystallized, along with his determination to see if what they had was still real.

By this morning, he knew what he wanted.

And when she'd joined him in the shower? A purely primal need to claim her had overtaken him. He'd never experienced a moment like that with a woman ever before in his life.

He didn't think that just because he'd explained himself, she'd fall into his arms and they could go forward together. She was sweet and sensitive and he'd bruised her heart. He'd also proven himself to be unreliable when it came to his staying power. Which left him in the unenviable position of having to win her all over again.

Because he had every intention of keeping her, this time for good.

* * * *

Since Ryder was the only one with pants and a shirt to put on, he went to the shops downstairs and bought everything he could think of that they might need. Most of the clothing included resort logos, which he didn't think Sierra would be too fond of but he found amusing.

The weather in Pennsylvania was warm for this time of year, so he picked out tank tops, T-shirts, shorts, and sweat pants for later on when the sun went down. He added bathing suits, knowing Sierra was going to strangle him for his choice for her. He shrugged. Next time she could go shopping for them, he thought wryly. He even found resort-themed flip-flops so they didn't have to wear their dress shoes. All in all, he was pretty impressed with himself.

While in the lobby, he looked into the resort's offerings for things to do while they were in the Poconos. The hotel and its neighboring resort events were booked thanks to it being the end of May and the beginning of the late spring-early summer season. But there was a small bay trip that had been booked by a couple who had apparently had an argument and abruptly canceled their reservation.

Ryder was able to order a picnic basket filled with lunch and Prosecco, a golf cart that he could use to drive them to their destination, and thanks to the fact that the water rides were open and full, they might even find time and space to be alone.

He was walking back to the room when his cell rang. He pulled it out of his pocket and glanced at the screen, hitting answer.

"Sebastian." He wasn't shocked to hear from Sierra's brother.

The man might be Ryder's best friend, but his first concern was always going to be his sister. As it should be, Ryder thought. He had no doubt Sebastian was making the call because he was the closest to Ryder, but Ethan and Parker were probably right there, breathing down his neck, waiting for answers.

"Hey, man. Everything okay?" Sebastian asked.

"Everything's fine. Sierra's okay," Ryder said, reassuring his friend. He stopped by a tree outside and spoke quietly and in private.

"Is she? Because she was supposed to be married and on her way to her honeymoon right now."

He glanced up at the blue sky. "She left with me willingly. I didn't kidnap her or anything. We're… working through things." Ryder blew out a breath, knowing he had to tread carefully.

His personal relationship and what he did with Sierra was none of her brothers' business, even if her well-being was.

"Can I talk to her?" Sebastian asked.

"I'm not in the room right now, but I'll let her know you called, and if she wants to get in touch, she will."

A few beats passed before Sebastian spoke again. "You hurt her badly once. I know you had your reasons and I was torn by what you did, but I understood it. But if you aren't in this for keeps, Ryder, bring her the hell home now."

"I'm in it deep." He just wasn't sure whether or not she was. "Have you heard from Jason?" He forced out the name because he needed to know if the man had had a change of heart, wanting to find and talk to his almost-bride.

"No."

Ryder heard the anger in that one word, and though the news came as a relief to him, he knew it was going to hurt Sierra to know the man hadn't come after her. Unless she asked, he had no intention of telling her and rubbing salt in an open wound. One Ryder, himself, had created.

"I didn't handle it well but I know what I'm doing," he said to his friend. He was trying to win the girl.

"I hope so," Sebastian said. "I'll talk to you soon."

"Yeah." He disconnected the call and Ryder shoved his phone back into his pocket, pushing away thoughts of Sierra's groom.

He clearly had no place in her life.

But Ryder wasn't ready to think about what the future held for them. After coming together in the shower, they'd silently agreed to drop the heavy conversation and just enjoy the time they had here. He could tell from her change in mood and how she'd relaxed that she wasn't dwelling on yesterday, the wedding, or anything they'd discussed about the past.

The time would come when they'd have to deal with leaving here and whatever the future held. But while he had the chance, he had every intention of finding his way back into her heart.

He arrived back at the room, bags in hand, to find Sierra sitting with the hotel robe wrapped around her, thumbing through a resort magazine.

She glanced up as he walked in the door, excitement in her expression as she eyed the packages. "What did you get?" she asked, tossing the magazine onto the other side of the bed.

"A lot of clothing with Paradise Cove logos on it." He tossed the white plastic bags onto the mattress. "But the good news is, we have plans for today. A picnic on a small bay near a lake."

She raised her eyebrows at that. "And what are we wearing there?"

"Bathing suits."

She narrowed her gaze. "Oh, really? And how did you know my size for that?"

"Guesswork based on how you fill my hands," he muttered. "It'll be fine. We should be alone. Let's just get changed." He opened one bag, then another, pulling out his shorts so he could change.

Knowing he was in for it when she saw her bathing suit, he grabbed his clothes and headed for the bathroom, closing the door as she yelled.

"I'm not leaving the room in this!"

He winced. Manning up, he returned to face her. "Come on, it's not that bad."

"It's nonexistent, that's what it is!" She held up the tiny red bikini for him to see. Not that he'd been able to get the idea of her wearing it out of his mind since he'd seen the suit on the mannequin in the store.

He couldn't help the grin lifting the edges of his mouth. "Wear it for me?"

Her gaze softened at the request. "Here in the room, yes." She pointed to the spa tub. "Not out in public."

"When we use that tub, you're going to be naked," he told her. This time those blue eyes of hers darkened with need. "Come on. Just change into it and let's enjoy the day." He used his best cajoling tone.

Frowning at him, she snatched up the suit and stormed past him into the bathroom.

He chuckled, calling out, "You might need help with some of the ties!"

She cursed at him from behind the door.

A few minutes later, he'd changed into the shorts and slipped on his shirt just as she walked out of the bathroom in the bathing suit he'd chosen.

He nearly swallowed his tongue at the gorgeous sight. Despite her concerns, the top of the suit had a ruffle over her breasts but her ample cleavage was evident above the edging. She held the sides together with her arms, the strings dangling in the back. And the bottom was a sleek triangle that left little to the imagination and had his mouth watering.

"Turn around and I'll help you." He made a pivoting motion with his finger.

"No." Her eyes flashed icy fire at him.

"You're going with it untied?"

She shook her head. "I'm not going."

He bit the inside of his cheek. "Turn. Around."

"Fine!" She spun one hundred and eighty degrees, giving him a look at her sleek back… and the globes of her ass.

His cock throbbed inside his shorts. He'd be lucky if they made it out of this room. "You look edible," he murmured, cupping his hand over one cheek and squeezing the bare skin.

She sucked in a startled breath. "You can't really expect me to go out in this."

"I can." He reached for the strings and tied the back of the suit into a tight bow. "And I do. You look amazing and the girl at the desk promised me we'd be alone. They're fully booked at a concert on the pier. It'll be fine." He leaned in close and pressed a kiss to the flesh between her neck and shoulder.

A full-body tremor shook her frame. "Ryder," she said in a husky voice.

"Sierra. Come on a picnic with me. You won't be disappointed. I promise."

* * * *

Thank goodness Ryder had bought a tank top dress for her to wear over the bathing suit. Red, in the resort colors, with the white Paradise Cove logo above her breast. Sierra didn't care because her ass cheeks were now covered.

She walked beside him and he took her hand. She couldn't help but notice how good her hand felt in his bigger one. How right. She pushed those thoughts aside and focused on where they were heading. They approached the far side of the resort, where he gave his name and a golf cart was waiting for them.

The man in charge handed him a resort map and indicated where their destination was by drawing a circle with a magic marker. "Basically follow this path until you reach the bay," the older gentleman said.

"Thank you." Ryder tipped him before helping Sierra into the passenger side of the cart.

He walked around, joining her, and soon they were off.

The sun beat down overhead, but the covered cart protected her skin. And when she'd packed a bag for the day, she saw that Ryder had bought them sunscreen, too. She'd noticed a picnic basket and ice bucket in the back of the cart, and she had a feeling he'd thought of everything for this little trip.

She glanced at his profile, his face covered in sexy scruff, a Paradise Cove baseball cap backwards on his head. His facial features were relaxed as he maneuvered the cart with one hand.

Considering all they'd been through in the last twenty-four hours, it was amazing they were here. Together. She couldn't say she didn't want to be here, and that scared her.

"Looks like this is it," he said, pulling the cart up to the edge of the path and parking it.

She'd been lost in studying his handsome face, she thought, as she turned to look at the scenery in front of her. Sun danced over the water. The sky was clear, the temperature warm. It was a beautiful day, and she was glad he'd dragged her kicking and screaming here. She knew they couldn't go into the lake. Although it was hot today, the temperature hadn't been consistently warm enough for the water to be comfortable for a dip.

Together they carried supplies from the back of the cart to a place on the shore. They spread out a large blanket, put the picnic basket on it along with a cooler that, it turned out, contained Prosecco on ice.

Then they settled down on the blanket. She opened the basket and began taking out the assortment of food the resort had supplied. Everything from sandwiches to cheese and crackers, strawberries dipped in chocolate, and the wine.

"Sebastian called me earlier," Ryder said, as he opened the bottle and poured the liquid into plastic cups.

He handed her one and she took a long, bubbly sip. "I know what he wanted. What did you tell him?"

Ryder glanced at her. "That you were fine. And here of your own free will."

Her lips curved into a smile. "Poor Sebastian. He must feel like he's in the middle of something he doesn't understand."

Ryder shook his head. "He's not in the middle. He's all Team Sierra. If I hurt you again, he'll kick my ass and not think twice."

"He's a good big brother. But he's also your friend. You know that. Even after you broke up with me, you two stayed close." As she spoke, the truth dawned on her. "Sebastian knew why you ended things, didn't he? And he let me cry over you, knowing your feelings for me hadn't changed?" she asked, her voice rising. "That's not Team Sierra all the way."

He took a large gulp of the drink, too. "Yes, it was. He wanted you to go away to school because it's what you always said you wanted. He didn't want you to have any regrets in your life, either. He was torn but he thought he was protecting you."

She shook her head in frustration. "Why the hell don't the men in my life think I can make decisions for myself?"

"You were too young to know what was best. And honestly, we can't go back and change the past, so we have no choice but to live with it and move forward. Like we had started to. Can we do that?" He lifted his hat off his head, adjusted it, and slid it back on again.

She drew a deep breath, knowing he was right. "I'm trying."

But there was a huge issue of the trust that had been destroyed in his making decisions for her and behind her back at the same time. His willingness to hurt her to give her what he thought she needed. That frightened her.

"That's all I can ask," he said, sounding and looking relieved.

Another question ran through her mind. "Did he say if Jason reached out?" She hated bringing him between her and Ryder, but she had to know.

Ryder shook his head. "He hasn't heard from him. None of your brothers have." He set his jaw, then said, "I'm sorry."

"You didn't stop him from trying to talk to me." Or from picking up where they'd left off in the ceremony, which she had asked him to do.

As much as she hated to admit it, Jason had done her a favor by walking out. She'd been settling, and by extension, so had he. As angry and hurt as she was, a part of her was coming to understand the way things had played out yesterday. Not that she wanted to dwell on it now. She'd promised herself these two days of respite and she planned to take them.

She breathed in deeply, then exhaled in an attempt to let the negative energy go.

"Take off your dress and let's relax in the sun."

She rolled her eyes. "You're pretty focused on seeing me in that bikini."

He pulled off his shirt and tossed it on the edge of the blanket, drawing her gaze to his tanned, well-muscled chest. "You look pretty focused, too."

She couldn't help it. She laughed as he broke the lingering tension.

Although they weren't totally alone—a few couples were far away on their own spots around the lake—she knew nobody was paying attention to what she and Ryder were doing, too wrapped up in each other to pay attention to anyone else.

She shifted to her knees, lifting the dress, easing it off her head, and placing it on top of his tee.

He patted his lap. "Lie down and let's chill."

Scooting forward, aware of her skimpy suit, she positioned herself until she could place her head in his lap and stretch the rest of her body out on the blanket. She inhaled and took in his now familiar scent, the heat of the sun feeling good against her skin, and she sighed with pleasure.

"Remember when we used to do this under the big tree in your yard?" he asked, looking down at her.

She nodded. "It was hard to find places where we could be alone. Even there I was never sure one of my brothers wasn't looking out a window, watching."

He laughed. "I'm glad I just have an older brother. No sisters to worry about."

"How is Andrew?" she asked.

"Still a workaholic. Still looking for a woman able to tolerate him."

His lips lifted in a grin and she knew he was kidding. He'd always been able to joke about his stuffy older sibling. But they both knew it was thanks to Andrew that Ryder hadn't just stayed home to work at his father's business but had gotten his degrees.

"And your dad?" she asked.

"Retirement is good for him. Good for his heart. So is Elsa, his next-door neighbor in Florida, where he moved. They're together without living together."

She smiled. "Cute. I'm glad everyone is well in your family."

"What about you?" he asked. "I know how your brothers are, of course, but how are you? How's work? Are you happy?"

Her job as the head of the Social Media Division for Knight Time Technology made her happy. "I love the work. I appreciate being able to contribute to the family business by doing something I not only love but I'm good at. It's fulfilling. And I have a good staff and friends. So my work life is great. Personally, family-wise, it's been tough."

"Ethan," he said and she nodded.

"It was hard, him losing his wife that way. And when Sebastian and Ashley went to San Francisco to figure out some company issues, they ended up asking me to do some digging—and I'm the one who found out Mandy had been cheating on Ethan." Her heart squeezed hard in her chest.

She hated that her brother was so unhappy. As the unofficial head of the family, he took care of everyone else, and he deserved more from life than he'd gotten so far.

Ryder squeezed her bare shoulder in support. "Ethan's tough. He'll come out on the other side."

"Eventually, I hope," she murmured, as she relaxed into his lap.

Ryder reached over and picked up a strawberry, its bottom covered in chocolate. "Hungry?" he asked.

"For chocolate? Always."

He grinned and held the small piece of fruit over her mouth so she could take a bite. "Mmm," she said as the mixed sweet and sour flavor exploded on her tongue.

"Does it taste good?"

"Mmm-hmm."

He dipped his finger into the wineglass and ran it over her lips. She slid her tongue out and licked her mouth, catching his fingertip, too. She sucked the liquid off him, watching above her as his gaze darkened with unmistakable need. And beneath her head, his erection swelled and thickened. She felt the arousal in her own body, her breasts suddenly heavy, a slick pulsing between her thighs.

She wasn't surprised when he tossed his hat and leaned his head down, his lips pressing hard against hers.

Chapter Four

Ryder kissed her, not caring about their awkward angle, taking in her sweet taste and wanting more. He needed to touch her, so he cupped his hand around her neck, then glided his fingers over her collarbone, feeling her delicate body beneath his hands. With a groan, he continued his exploration, dipping his fingers along the neckline of her bathing suit top, the pads grazing the swell of her breasts.

She shivered and her nipples puckered into tight buds, making his mouth water. He shifted her so she was lying on her side instead of straight out in front of him, giving him easier access to slide his hand where he wanted. And what he wanted was to touch every inch of her he could on his path down to her pussy.

He moved his hand, ignoring her breasts, another destination in mind. He splayed his hand across her stomach and she moaned, obviously enjoying it.

Mine, he thought.

Not wanting to freak her out completely, he kept the feeling to himself. When he'd gone to the church yesterday, he'd had no idea he'd be here with her today, trying to cement his place in her life. But with his hand possessively on her belly, he had a vision of her pregnant with his child. He swayed, suddenly dizzy, in shock at the course his thoughts had taken. But with everything inside him, it felt right.

She felt right, not just to the touch but to the emotions swirling inside him.

"Ryder?" she murmured. "Is everything okay?"

He glanced down at her, taking in the freckles on her nose, and grinned. "Couldn't be better. I just like the feel of you beneath my hand."

"Mmm," she said, closing her eyes. "I like it, too."

He shifted his stare to his tanned hand against her paler stomach and swallowed back a groan.

With her pleasure as his sole focus, he slipped his fingers beneath her bathing suit and she jumped in surprise.

"Shh. Let me play." Her sex was bare, which turned him the fuck on. He ran his fingers over her pubic bone and lower still, finding her pussy wet for him.

Her eyes flew open, her gaze coming to his, a hazy sheen covering the blue, as desire took hold. "We're outside," she said in a husky voice.

"And at a couples resort and nobody is anywhere near us," he reassured her.

Using two fingers, he slid her juices over her sex, keeping his touch away from where she needed him most. He teased her, arousing her until her hips were rotating in circles, gyrating, low moans coming from deep in her throat.

"Ryder, make me come." She begged him, both in words and with her body's reaction to his fingers, which dipped and played around and around.

Still not touching her clit, he slid one finger inside her and she gasped as he filled her. "Feel good, sweetheart?"

"Oh God. Good but not enough to get me over." She arched her back in silent supplication.

He wiggled her bottoms lower on her thighs so he could pump his finger in and out of her body, her inner walls clasping him in tight, wet heat. His dick was so hard he thought he might come from giving her an orgasm alone.

As he worked her with his finger, he finally gave her what she needed, circling his thumb over the tiny, hard nub that was practically begging for his attention. And if they weren't outside, as she'd pointed out, he'd lift her hips to his face and suck on her until she came. Saving that for later, when they were alone in bed, he pressed hard against her clit, his finger shifting inside her, pressing on her spongy inner walls.

She stiffened at the sudden pressure and began rocking against his hand. "Oh, oh, God, Ryder, I'm coming."

He didn't stop, keeping up both movements as she flew, his gaze on her beautiful face the entire time.

And as she climaxed, her body shook, trembled, grasping his finger, the sight a gorgeous one to behold.

She collapsed onto the blanket, her breath shallow, a fine sheen of sweat glistening on her skin.

"I died and went to heaven," she muttered, pushing herself to a sitting position and glancing directly at his lap, where his cock was hard and evident against his bathing suit shorts.

"What about you?"

"Nothing we can do about it out here. Talk to me about something else. Anything else to distract me."

"Umm–" She obviously searched for something to discuss, but she didn't tear her stare from his erection.

"And stop looking at my cock," he told her. "Or we are going to give those people on the far side of the lake a show."

Her eyes opened wide and she leaned over, opened the picnic basket, and took out food. "Let's eat," she said, her cheeks flushed as she handed him what looked like a chicken sandwich.

He shook his head and laughed. "Can't say I'm hungry for food but yeah. Let's eat."

They chowed down on the contents of the basket, Ryder discovering he was starving after all. Sierra talked about her job, how she was thinking of expanding her social media services to companies beyond Knight Time Technology because she had the time. She even discussed opening her own business so she could work part time from home.

They talked about how his father's business had grown since he'd retired. Ryder and his brother, Andrew, had grown the construction business, expanding into luxury homes. The kind of home he'd like them to live in together one day.

He found himself thinking about the future and things they'd once talked about a long time ago.

"Do you still want a dog?" he asked.

"I do. But working from the office and living in an apartment makes getting one difficult. And besides, I don't want a smaller one. No matter how cute, I'm afraid they'll be loud and yappy."

He grinned. Yet another thing they were on the same page about. He'd love nothing more than a big-ass dog like a Newfoundland or a

St. Bernard hanging around the house he'd already built and lived in alone.

Assuming he got the girl.

"What about you?" she asked. "Still want a huge dog?"

"I do." He met her gaze, his voice serious as he said, "I want it all. The family, kids, dog, wife, house… everything we dreamed of."

Her eyes opened wide and a visible tremor shook her. "It's getting late. We should get back," she murmured and started to pack up their picnic.

He told himself not to be discouraged by her reaction, that she had a lot going on her mind and more going on in her personal life that had to be dealt with than he did.

Ryder didn't believe in love at first sight, and in no way was that what they'd experienced. They'd built a relationship, piece by piece, despite the fact that they'd been young and inexperienced in life and love. He was close to her siblings, they shared a love of family, and had wanted the same things out of life. He'd loved everything about her, from her generous personality to the way she'd naturally given him what he needed emotionally, making it easy to return the same.

He'd loved her then. He loved her now and he didn't want to lose her again.

With a muttered curse at the way she'd closed down emotionally, he loaded the golf cart up again.

They drove back to the resort and returned the items. He took heart in the fact that she let him hold her hand as they walked back to their room, and when they stepped inside, he was surprised by what awaited them.

The suite had been cleaned and the shades pulled down. Fake candles were lit around the living room and along the stairs leading up to the hot tub. A champagne bucket sat by a large cheese-and-cracker platter on the table. Rose petals lined the floor leading to the bedroom, where white washcloth swans had been created and sat, intertwined, on the red bed.

"Wow, this is incredible," Sierra said, happiness in her tone as she glanced around. "And the hot tub looks inviting," she murmured.

"Does it?" he asked, imagining them inside it.

"It does." With a twinkle in her gaze, she pulled her dress off and immediately removed her bathing suit. Next, she slid off her flip-flops. Then she turned and walked toward the stairs, giving him an amazing view of her from behind.

He adjusted himself, squeezing his cock tight in warning to behave. It wasn't time. Yet.

Glancing over her shoulder, she crooked her finger at him. "Aren't you going to join me?"

She didn't have to ask twice. He dropped his shorts, removed his shirt, kicked off his flip-flops, and followed her up.

When he joined her in the hot tub, she was playful and eager, kissing him as she grasped his shoulders and lowered herself onto his eager cock.

Whatever was going on with her emotions, sexually she was all in, and they spent the rest of the late afternoon together in the Jacuzzi and the later part of the evening and night enjoying the luxuries provided by the hotel.

The only drawback to the entire day was the emotional separation he knew was between them. He wished he was privy to what she was thinking, where her head was when it came to them and the future.

But she was keeping her feelings close, and his gut told him it wasn't the right time to ask.

* * * *

Sierra woke up the next morning to an orgasm building inside her that wasn't a dream. One thing she'd learned about Ryder as a man, he was a generous lover, always giving to her, not caring if he received in return. Of course, she always tried, but he was demanding, wanting to come inside "his" pussy, as he'd declared her private parts last night.

He loved oral sex, which in turn had, in two short days, taught her to love oral. He hadn't yet let himself finish in her mouth, but he thoroughly enjoyed what she did to him before he slammed inside her and made her come so hard she saw stars.

No one could say they weren't sexually compatible, she thought, as his mouth worked on her now. She arched her back, and unable not to, she ground herself against him as his tongue slid in and out of her sex, his teeth alternately grazing her clit.

Her climax, when it hit, was as explosive as usual with Ryder, sending her soaring. And when she came back down to earth, it was to the sight of him rubbing his mouth on her thigh with a grin.

"Good morning, sweetheart."

"Good morning." She smiled back, but neither the incredible orgasm nor his easy, sexy smile could prevent the unwelcome anxiety that balled in the pit of her stomach. Because it was the morning of their second day.

The end of their retreat.

Time to return to reality and everything that waited for her. She had to face the people she'd left behind when she'd willingly run away from her wedding with the man who wasn't her groom.

"Talk to me," Ryder said as he slid up beside her and pulled her into his arms. "I saw the minute your mind turned back on."

She rubbed her eyes, which had stupid tears forming. "It's time to go home."

"It is." His jaw pulled tight. "But that doesn't have to mean the end of us." He threaded their fingers together in a show of unity she wasn't sure she could reciprocate. "I understand that just two days ago you were engaged to another man." He paused, then said, "But he let you go."

"He did. But that doesn't mean I'm–"

"I love you, Sierra."

The words she hadn't heard in years seemed to echo around her. Words she'd come to believe were a lie because, if he'd loved her, he wouldn't have left her.

"I have always loved you," Ryder went on, not waiting for her to reply. "I just shoved the feelings away so you could go on with your life. The time wasn't right then but it can be now."

She glanced at their entwined hands. "Do you have any idea how much you hurt me back then?"

His silence told her that he did. Or at least, now he knew.

"You took all my hopes and dreams and crushed them because you decided you knew what was best for me. That just because I once wanted to go away to college, I couldn't change my mind. You didn't trust in me, the things I told you I wanted, the hopes and dreams I spun for us… You let them all go."

"I–"

"I'm not finished," she said, staring at the blank television screen across from the bed, not looking at him as she let all the feelings of the past spill forth. "You let me think you didn't love me anymore, and I know you dated other women after me. Of course you did." The pain of that sliced through her as if it were fresh and new.

"None were you," he said so low she had to lean close to hear.

So close she smelled his natural scent and wanted to burrow into his embrace. But she couldn't because that would be cowardly.

Dealing with her life, then being alone were both brave and necessary. "I need to go home, Ryder. I need to talk to Jason. We need closure."

"I don't like it," he muttered.

She didn't laugh at his petulant tone. "You don't have to. That's just the way it is. And I need time to think." About them, she thought, letting the words go unsaid.

"I said I don't like it but I didn't say I don't understand it." He sat up, jarring her because she'd been leaning against him.

The next thing she knew, she was on her back on the mattress and he was looming over her, his hands on either side of her shoulders, his big body warm and tempting above her. Those beautiful green eyes stared into hers, and she saw the truth in their depths. He loved her now. And she was very much afraid she loved him, too.

But she wasn't ready. Just because she was suddenly single didn't mean she could make decisions about another relationship or commitments to a man who'd once pushed her away.

"Ryder–"

He shook his head. "No more talking. I'm going to take you home and give you what you say you need. But I'm going to give you one last thing to remember me by before you go," he said before his lips descended on hers.

Her hands came to his head, sifting through the silken strands, holding him tight as he kissed her. Wanting him with every fiber of her being.

Unlike many of their moments together here, this wasn't the frenzied, hot and heavy sex she'd gotten used to. The kind with the fire that burned out of control. This was slow and sensual. As if he wanted her to feel every glide of his lips, every stroke of his tongue, and memorize the sensations.

She knew she'd never forget. He was gentle as he made love to her mouth, slowly relearning all the spots inside that were made just for him. He kissed her like that for what felt like hours, reminding her of the times when they were younger. When they knew they couldn't go further but they could kiss and make out and he could grind himself against her, and it was hotter than the sexual act itself.

His thick erection slid over and over her sex, gliding against her clit, rocking her ever so slowly to orgasm. She'd forgotten what these kinds of make-out sessions were like. The sweet intensity. The deep kisses. Hands moving everywhere. And hips rotating over and over until the heavy waves came at her almost out of nowhere, then consumed her.

"Oh God, coming, coming, I'm coming," she whispered on a ragged moan, the hard press of his cock thrusting against her sex.

Only when she'd succumbed to her last tremble did Ryder speak. "Eyes on me, sweetheart."

She hadn't realized she'd closed them. Forcing her heavy lids open, she met his gaze.

Desire flashed in the depths of his eyes. "I want you to know who's making love to you," he said as he notched himself at her entrance, then slowly, deliberately thrust in deep.

Her eyes opened wider as he took her completely, filling her up, both her body and her heart. Damn him, she thought, tears threatening. She didn't want to cry at how good they were together. She couldn't do that and leave.

But she was going to leave him. She had to figure things out alone.

"Stop thinking." Arms braced on either side of her shoulders, he raised his hips, and she shuddered, aware of every inch of his velvety length as he pulled out of her, then shoved back in. "Feel us, Sierra."

She couldn't do anything but feel as he thrust in and out, over and over. But before she could even start to build toward a climax, he stopped and pushed himself to a sitting position, taking him with her.

"What are you doing?"

"Making you feel."

And then they were rocking together, face to face, eye to eye as he hit her clit with every roll of his hips against hers. It was sweet and emotional, the waves building as he made love to her, slowly and deliberately taking them both up and over.

And when she came, his hands were in her hair, pulling her into him, sealing his lips over hers as the pulsing of his erection and the low, satisfied groan told her he came, too.

They came together.

* * * *

The ride home was silent. Ryder left Sierra alone with her thoughts, knowing his words had already come from the heart and his actions had left her with no lingering doubt about how he felt. He loved her. He wanted to spend the rest of his life with her.

But she'd made her feelings clear, too. She needed time. So they had packed their wedding clothes and extra resort wear, pulling things together and using extra laundry bags from the hotel to put their resort clothing in. He'd tossed everything into the trunk and off they went.

He drove her to the apartment building where she and her brothers resided. The place itself was owned by Knight Time Technology and all the siblings lived in separate apartments in the building. Sebastian with his wife, Ashley, Ethan, alone now that Mandy was gone, and Parker.

Sierra, he knew, had packed her things to officially move in with Jason after they returned from their honeymoon. She was going home to big boxes and everything unsettled.

He hated it.

He wanted to be there to make things easier for her, but she'd insisted that she was going home alone. That they weren't returning as a couple.

Fine.

He could accept what she wanted for now, but that didn't mean he was leaving her to deal with the shit storm he'd caused and she'd left behind.

For tonight, he walked her up to her door, making sure she got home safely, and kissed her good night—a long, lingering, sizzling kiss that hopefully would keep her tossing and turning all night long.

Then he went home alone to think.

And to plan.

* * * *

Sierra stared at the taped-up boxes that filled her living room and wanted to cry at the sight. When she'd packed them up, she'd been excited to start her new life. Now she had to undo it all.

Sunlight streamed through the window in the living room, casting a glow directly on the wrapped packages, the gifts from the wedding. Her stomach churned at the sight. Obviously her brothers had decided this was the best place to leave them. Somehow she'd have to return them all. Make sure everyone who'd given her a gift got a refund.

She ran a hand over her eyes, wishing she had her Keurig, but that was packed in a box, along with her coffee pods, sugar, and cups. What she needed was a Starbucks run before tackling anything here, including letting her brothers know she was home.

She grabbed her purse and started for the door when she heard a knock. Oh, no. Ryder must have spoken to Sebastian already, and instead of going to work, he was here to…

What? Lecture her? Hug her?

She swung the door open wide, speaking as she did. "Sebastian, I was going to call— Ryder. What are you doing here?"

He stood at her door wearing a pair of aviator glasses that looked sexy on his face, a backwards ball cap that reminded her of their day on the lake at the Poconos, and food. But she hadn't expected to see him again… well, not until she was ready.

"I come bearing sustenance." He held out a Starbucks bag. "Venti vanilla latte with three extra pumps of syrup and a pumpkin loaf." He dangled the bag as a peace offering.

She narrowed her gaze. "How do you know my order?" Or at least the order she would use on a day she was feeling particularly down.

He shrugged. "I asked your brother."

So he had spoken to Sebastian, which meant she was going to have company times three… four if you counted Ashley, very soon. She hadn't even called her own friends yet, unsure of how to explain what she'd done. It was going to be easier to rationalize why Ryder had interrupted the ceremony than why she'd left with him, she thought, cheeks burning.

Ryder cleared his throat. "Can I come in?"

She stepped aside so he could enter and shut the door behind him, accepting the coffee and bag with the treat. She stepped toward the kitchen and put everything down on the counter.

She turned, realizing he'd followed closely behind. He looked better than she did, his faded jeans and black shirt giving him a sexy appearance, while she wore a clean pair of sweats from the Poconos resort and a T-shirt with a logo on it.

She needed to find the boxes with her clothing. "Why are you here?" she asked again.

"Because you have a lot to do and I want to help you do it." He spread one arm, gesturing to the other room, where the boxes were piled. "After all, it's my fault." He had the good grace to look embarrassed.

She blew out a breath, knowing his coming here was a sweet, thoughtful gesture. "But didn't I say I needed time?" she asked, trying to be gentle but knowing she had to stand firm.

He folded his arms across his chest, his muscles showing beneath his T-shirt. "I didn't say I was going to kiss you. Or fuck you. Or make slow, passionate love to you—although that's all on the table if you just give me the okay."

Now her cheeks were flaming, she thought, as she spun away. "If you want to help me, then thank you." She wasn't going to look a gift horse in the mouth. Besides, he was right. It was his fault she was in this situation. "All my furniture is still here. I need to cancel the movers for next week," she muttered. "But we can open boxes and start putting things away… Oh, damn."

"What's wrong?" he asked.

"The scissors are packed. I have no way to open the boxes."

He frowned. "Tell you what. I'll run to the store and buy scissors so we can get started. You make whatever phone calls you need to make."

"I don't have my phone yet."

Ryder lifted his cap and reset it on his head. "Sebastian said he'd come down this morning, so I'm guessing he'll bring it."

Her eyes opened wide. "Can you be gone when he shows up? It's going to be hard enough to talk to him without you here!"

He shook his head. "I'll go get the scissors. But get used to having me around helping you. That's nonnegotiable," he said, and with a grin, he turned and walked out, leaving her flustered, flabbergasted, and pissed.

She didn't need his help. He'd caused this mess! But it really was nice of him to acknowledge it and want to fix it. *Because he has an agenda! He wants you and this is his way of getting an in!*

She really needed to stop arguing with herself, she mused, as the doorbell rang.

"Sebastian." This time when she opened the door, it was to her brother.

Times three.

Chapter Five

No sooner had Sierra opened the door than her brothers barged in, one right after the other without waiting to be asked or even saying hello to her first.

"Come in, why don't you," she muttered to herself.

"Jesus Christ, Sierra. I was so fucking worried about you," Ethan said, pulling her into his arms, and her brief flare of frustration with him eased.

She wrapped her arms around his waist and laid her head on his chest as she had many times when she was a little girl and things in her life had gone wrong. He'd always been there for her and she knew he always would be. They all would. For all their overprotective ways, they were wonderful big brothers and she loved them.

"I'm fine," she assured him. Taking a step back, she spun around, a forced smile on her face. "See?"

Sebastian shook his head at her antics.

"You gave us a scare when we came into the room and you were gone," Parker said. "With Ryder."

"He didn't kidnap me," she said, defending Ryder. "I went willingly. And I checked in. I let Sebastian know I was okay."

"Doesn't mean we didn't worry," Sebastian said, holding out her phone, and she took it gratefully.

"Don't you three have to be at work?" she asked, taking in their dress. They all wore suits meant for the office. Now that they saw she was fine, maybe they'd go without forcing her to talk about things.

Ethan scowled. "Now listen to me, young lady," he said in the tone he'd used when she was a naughty teenager. "Do you really think you're getting off that easy?"

She rolled her eyes, but before she could say anything, Sebastian did. "Lay off, Ethan. She's an adult. She can make her own decisions."

She blew out a relieved breath, glad she had at least one brother on her side. Parker, as usual, said nothing, just watched carefully as things went on around him. Neutral, hence his nickname in the family, Switzerland, she mused. Which also came from his past as an almost-Olympic skier before a career-ending injury prevented him from fulfilling his dream.

"Now tell us what decisions you've made." Sebastian folded his arms across his chest and pinned her with his steady gaze.

"Seriously?" She'd thought he understood her best in this situation, that he was going to give her space. Apparently not. "Listen, guys. I love you and I know you love me. But I didn't walk into that church planning to run away with Ryder. I don't know what I want! Or what I'm even ready for now."

Their gazes softened.

"Do you love him?" Ethan asked. There was no question he was talking about Ryder and not her former groom.

She blew out a long breath, then strode to the window and looked out over Manhattan. With the crowded buildings and the people down below rushing along the sidewalks, it was such a big difference from the wide-open spaces and trees in the Poconos.

Did she love Ryder?

There were different kinds of love, she knew now. She'd loved being with Jason. She enjoyed his company, they had wanted the same things out of life, and she knew he'd give her the family of her own that she wanted.

But Ryder filled her soul. It might be a cheesy movie phrase but he completed her. He was her other half, and she didn't need to dig deep to explain to herself why. It was a fact of life, like breathing.

"I love him," she admitted, saying the words out loud for the first time in forever.

Parker came up behind her and wrapped an arm around her. "Trust yourself," he said, kissing her on the cheek.

"I do. But can I trust him again?" she asked quietly.

Could she believe in Ryder to give her the security she desperately needed? Could she trust him not to get something crazy into his head and make a decision for her that would leave her gutted again?

"You're adults now," Sebastian said. "I told him not to go there with you if he wasn't all in. So for what it's worth, I trust him."

She swallowed the lump in her throat.

"Let me put it to you this way." She turned at the sound of Ethan's voice. "If I were walking you down the aisle to Ryder, I wouldn't stop and ask if you were sure. And I wouldn't worry deep down that you weren't getting every last thing you needed from the man you loved."

Parker stepped forward, taking her hand. "I agree with them, sis. He's a good guy. And it's clear as hell he loves you."

She looked at Sebastian, Ryder's best friend. He knew him better than anyone here.

Her youngest brother nodded his head. "He'll do right by you this time. I know he was trying to do right by you last time… and so was I. I'm sorry I didn't tell you I knew why he ended things. We both thought we knew what was best, and we should have let you make your own decision about what you wanted in life."

She blinked and a tear ran down her face.

"Ryder learned his lesson," he said in a gruff voice. "He loves you and he won't leave you again."

For some reason, hearing it from her brother was something she'd desperately needed. Ryder might have promised the same things, but Sebastian's trust in him took care of the final worry she had.

Was it crazy to contemplate jumping from almost marrying one man straight into the arms of another? Completely insane, she thought. But how could she risk losing him again for the sake of taking time she didn't need?

"I love you guys," she said to her brothers. "And I'm sorry I made you worry."

"Love you, too," they all muttered in their rough, brotherly way.

"What are you going to do?" Ethan asked.

She ran her tongue over her dry lips. "Well, I'm going to find the box marked *clothing* and dig out something normal to wear." She glanced down at the red Paradise Cove sweats she had on. "And then I'm going to go see Jason, talk to him, and return his bracelet."

She had the bracelet sitting on her nightstand. She'd unpacked it first thing, not wanting to misplace it.

"Want me to go with you?" Sebastian offered.

"Any of us?" Ethan asked.

Parker just nodded his agreement.

"No." She rubbed her hands together nervously. "I have to face this on my own. Jason stormed out without talking to me. Is that love? Was he having second thoughts of his own and Ryder just gave him an excuse to walk away?" She gave voice to the questions that she hadn't let herself deal with during her weekend away. "Or was he just embarrassed by the fact that I did turn around to look at Ryder instead of staring at my groom?"

Ethan met her gaze, a warm smile lifting his lips. "When did you grow up on me?" he asked with a chuckle.

Given everything going on in his life lately, she liked hearing the slightest laugh from him.

"I don't know when, but I'm certain it's thanks to you that I'm able to handle this. All of you. You've always been there for me. But now it's time for me to stand on my own two feet."

And that meant facing the man she had been supposed to marry.

* * * *

Sierra approached Jason's secretary, a woman she not only knew well but who had been at their aborted wedding. Hoping her cheeks weren't as red as they felt, she stopped at the desk.

They'd agreed she'd come to see him at the office. She wondered if it was because he had work to do or because it was less personal to have this conversation here.

"Hi, Claire."

"Sierra. Hi," the other woman said softly, no judgment in her expression. "Mr. Armstrong is expecting you. You can go right in."

Nerves fluttered again in her belly. "Thank you." She stepped around the desk and approached his door. She knocked once and stepped in at the "Come in" she'd received in response.

Jason sat at his desk, standing as she entered the room. He did well and his office décor reflected as much, with a large mahogany desk, a plush leather chair with wood-grain accents, and large paintings of the ocean on the wall beside his diplomas.

"Hi." She clutched her purse tightly in her hand.

"Hi."

Awkwardness surrounded them, so she forced herself to step forward and sit in one of the client chairs across from his desk. Taking her cue, he strode around the desk and seated himself in the chair beside her.

She took in the lines around his bloodshot eyes. "You look tired."

"Didn't sleep much this weekend."

She managed a nod, her throat too full to speak.

"I did a lot of thinking," he said.

"Me, too."

He raised an eyebrow at that and she blushed, glancing away. She didn't want to discuss her time with Ryder with her ex.

"Look, I just want you to know, I had no way of knowing Ryder was going to interrupt the wedding that way."

He cleared his throat. "I don't blame you for that."

But he obviously blamed her for other things, she thought. And maybe rightly so. "I'm sorry I looked at Ryder when I went down the aisle. I didn't mean to. I was taking in everyone and my gaze landed on him."

"And when the preacher asked if anyone objected? Are you sorry for turning to him then?"

She blinked and did her best not to flinch at his harsh tone. She needed to own her actions, to accept responsibility. "I didn't even realize that I had… but yes. Of course I'm sorry."

He shook his head. "Look, I promised myself I wasn't going to fight with you and I'm not. I just… It was embarrassing, Sierra. And it killed me that something inside me knew all along that you belonged to him. That's why I walked out. Not because of anything you did or didn't do that day. But because I was the odd man out at my own wedding. And I shouldn't have been."

Tears filled her eyes. "I showed up at the church wanting to marry you. But I think we can both admit now that it would have been a mistake. That maybe there were second thoughts neither one of us gave voice to before Ryder did it himself."

He drummed his fingers on the arms of the chair before speaking. "I hate this. When I had a chance to get over my anger and embarrassment, I was pissed at myself for walking away and not fighting for you when I had the chance. Maybe if I had, if I'd shown you that I–"

Before he could go on, she shook her head, not wanting him to put himself out there and embarrass himself more. Once Ryder had objected, he'd owned her.

She might not have known it at the time, might have been furious, angry, humiliated, and a million more adjectives she couldn't think of at the moment, but the biggest one was the one she hadn't known at the time.

Relieved.

She'd been relieved he'd spoken up and put a claim on her at last, because she'd never stopped loving him.

"I'm sorry," she said, forcing the words over the painful lump in her throat.

She opened her purse and pulled out the bracelet she'd put in a jewelry bag she'd found during her unpacking. Placing it in his hand, she curled his fingers around the beautiful jewelry she'd been proud to wear.

"Jesus," he muttered. "We can't try?"

"No," she whispered.

"You're with him."

She hoped to be. She hadn't left Ryder with any indication, positive or negative, about what she wanted for the future. She'd needed to come to him with a clear path to the future and an even clearer heart.

"I'm sorry," she said again. "I'll take care of canceling the movers, returning the gifts… anything else that comes up, just let me know." She pushed herself to a standing position and he rose to his feet. "I wish you all the best, Jason. And someday you'll find someone who deserves you."

She turned and walked out, her heart pounding like a drum, dizziness spinning around in her head. God, that was awful. She'd hated hurting him and he hadn't deserved what she put him through.

* * * *

Ryder sat in his favorite chair in his family room in the small house he'd bought and renovated for himself. The television was off, leaving him to his own thoughts… and they sucked.

He'd spent the afternoon helping Sierra unpack her things and put them away in her drawers and cabinets. When he'd suggested they order in Chinese for dinner, she'd turned to him with an unreadable expression on her face, and his stomach had cramped badly.

"I need to run an errand," she said from where she stood by an empty box in the bedroom.

"What kind of errand?"

She'd begun pulling clothing she'd just unpacked out of the drawers. "I, umm, I texted Jason earlier. I'm going over there to talk."

His stomach had plummeted to the floor at the news. He'd known she wanted to talk to the man face to face, but he hadn't thought she'd rush over there so soon.

"I have to give him his bracelet back," she said softly. "And we have unfinished business to discuss."

Knowing he'd had no choice, he'd nodded and left her to do what she needed to. Without pressure or influence from him.

So here he sat now, alone in the dark, nursing a beer and hating that he didn't know what was going on between them. As much as it pained him, Sierra had been about to marry the man. Could he be having regrets over walking out and want her back?

Fuck. He ran a hand through his hair.

He wanted her back, so he couldn't blame Jason if he was feeling the same way. And Ryder had no moral high ground to stand on. He'd dumped her when they were younger, devastating her in the process, leaving her unable to trust him, his words, or promises now.

His doorbell rang so he put the bottle on the side table and headed to answer it. Probably a neighbor, he thought. They were a friendly bunch around here, always stopping by for one reason or another.

He opened the door in time to see a car which had been parked in his driveway pull out and away. In front of him stood Sierra.

She wore a pair of tight black leggings, ballet flats, and a pink shirt molding to her curves. Her long hair fell over her shoulders in disarray, just the way he liked it. She looked good enough to eat.

He blinked. "Well, this is a surprise."

"A good one, I hope? Because I let the Uber driver leave."

He grinned. "Always good to see you, sweetheart." He just wondered what she wanted. She'd taken a car out of the city and to Long Island to visit him.

She pulled her bottom lip between her teeth, telling him she was nervous. "Sebastian gave me your address."

That's right. She'd never been to his place. Never had a reason before now, he thought. "Well, come in. It's small but I've renovated the whole house. Everything is new. I'd love for you to see it."

He was proud of his work in general, but he loved his home, with the high beam wood ceilings and hardwood floors. It also had enough land and room for additions to be put on, should the time come when he needed it. And God, he hoped he needed it soon.

"Did you take care of your errand?" He forced the word out as she entered the house and he shut the door behind her.

"I did." She faced him, her knuckles white, she was gripping her purse so hard. "That part of my life is over."

Relief swept through him. He didn't know what he'd expected, but if he were Jason, he wouldn't have let her go easily. He didn't want or need to know the details unless she offered them. What mattered to him was that she'd ended things for good with her ex and she was here now. With him.

"And then you came to me?" he asked, wondering what was going on in that enigmatic mind of hers.

"I did."

He blew out a harsh breath. "Sweetheart, you're going to have to give me more than two-word answers and explain where we stand."

She laughed nervously. "Right. Well, it's not that easy to just say it."

"I don't know why unless you're here to end things with me, too." Jesus, why the fuck had he even put that idea out there? "I told you what I wanted already. I want our dream. The one we talked about a long time ago." His heart threatened to explode out of his chest.

"The family, kids, dog, wife, house… everything we dreamed of," she said, repeating his words back to him.

"Yes. That."

"With me."

"And nobody else," he said, staring into her blue eyes.

She visibly swallowed hard. "And you won't ever make a decision for me that ends us. Not ever again."

He shook his head. "Not in this lifetime or however many more I have," he said, barely recognizing his gruff voice as he realized he was about to get everything he'd ever wanted or dreamed of. Everything that mattered to him, anyway.

"Okay. Good. Because I want the same things. The family, kids, dog, husband, house… everything we dreamed of… with you."

He didn't hesitate, pause, or think. He swung her into his arms and headed straight for the bedroom, laying her down on his California-king-size bed. For the wife, the kids, and the massive dog he wanted.

The things it appeared, now, he was going to get.

He came down beside her, pulling her into his arms. "Jesus, you know how to nearly drive a guy to insanity. I died a little inside, knowing you were with him."

She slid her hand over his cheek. "I needed to clear the way for us."

"When did you decide there would be an us?" Because as far as he knew, even earlier today, she was hesitant.

"My brothers came to see me when you went out to get scissors. We all talked. And they convinced me you weren't going anywhere this time. And in my heart, I know we're meant to be."

He let out the breath he'd been holding, probably since interrupting her wedding.

She was his.

All fucking his.

She leaned over and pressed her lips to his. With a groan, he came over her, his mouth sealed against hers. He slid his tongue into the depths, possessing her, devouring her, staking a claim that would last forever.

Stripping off their clothes while kissing and laughing wasn't easy but they managed, coming together again, skin against skin. He glided his hands up from her waist, his thumbs brushing the undersides of her breasts.

She moaned at the light touch and he dipped his head, pulling a nipple into his mouth. Her fingers came back to his hair, holding him to her as he licked, nipped, and laved at the distended peak before switching breasts and giving the same attention to the other side.

He lifted his head, looking into those eyes he loved, before raising himself up. He grasped his cock in one hand and slid it over her damp sex. She sucked in a shallow breath, and he did it again, gliding the head over her clit until she arched her hips, seeking harder, deeper contact.

He couldn't wait to be inside her and poised himself at her entrance. Their gazes held as he pushed into her. She locked her arms around his neck, her stare never leaving his, and as he thrust deep, he knew she was with him one hundred percent, finally giving him all of her.

"Mine," he said, groaning, taking her for the first time with total awareness of what they were to each other.

What they would be.

Forever.

* * * *

Later, when they were both sated, multiple times over, they lay entwined together. Sierra glanced up at the ceiling, noting the skylight above them for the first time.

"You didn't tell me your house was like the Paradise Cove suite," she said, laughing against his chest.

She hadn't yet seen the rest of the house, but the warmth of this room, the vaulted ceilings, the wood… She was in love.

"I didn't even think about it, to be honest. This one has a shade that works on a remote control. I can shut it at night so the sun doesn't wake me in the morning," he said.

"Oh, nice," she murmured. "So close it now so we don't get woken up at dawn," she said on a yawn.

"You're staying?"

She heard the hope in his voice and knew she'd have to work hard to convince him she was here and all in. "Are you kicking me out?" she asked, glancing up at him with a fake pout on her lips.

"Never," he said, reaching for the remote on the nightstand and shutting the shade.

The next morning, Sierra woke Ryder with her mouth around his hard-as-a-rock erection. She had no intention of being told no this time. She was going to take him all the way to the end. She sucked him down until he hit the back of her throat.

He groaned and began to pump his hips, back and forth, until she knew he was close. And if she hadn't sensed it, his tap on her head would have told her. She shook her head, then went about ignoring him until he came with a shout, spilling himself down her throat.

Satisfied now, she rose and slid up beside him, a grin on her face. "Good morning."

"I told you I like coming inside my pussy."

She shook her head, blushing and laughing at him. "It's better for you to get used to it now."

"Get used to what?" He pushed himself up in bed, his hair messed and sexy, just how she liked it.

"That you won't always get your way." She shrugged. "Just a warning. I've been too easy on you until now."

He tilted his head back and chuckled. "Okay, sweetheart. Consider me warned. So how did you sleep?"

"Amazingly good." The best sleep she'd had in forever, she thought, snuggling into him.

"So when are you moving in?" he asked.

"What?" She sat upright in bed.

"When are you moving in? I figured we should get started on our dreams right away."

Her heart began a rapid beat inside her chest at the idea. "Didn't I just pack and unpack?"

"And didn't I help you? So, when can we do it again?"

Did she really need to play games? To worry? To wait? When it was right, it was right. "How about we get back to work this week and start packing again this weekend?"

He shook his head. "How about we take the week off—since you'd already planned for that—and move you in right away?"

She met his gaze. The eagerness she saw there matched her own. "Okay," she said softly.

"Good. I love you, Sierra," he said, pressing a kiss against her lips.

"And I love you."

"So when can we go pick out our dog?"

She threw her head back and laughed. This man would not only keep her on her toes but he would make sure he satisfied every dream she'd ever had. And even those she wasn't aware of having.

Epilogue

Two years later

"Jilly, you can't ride the dog!" Sierra called out to her daughter from where she stood in the kitchen baking cookies for the family gathering they were hosting later today. Her brothers, Ryder's brother, and some of their friends were coming.

Named after Ryder's mom, Jillian, their daughter was an adorable mini-me to her mom and a headstrong child, to boot. And right now, she was attempting to climb onto the back of their St. Bernard, Wiley.

The dog was good-natured and only four years old. They'd found him at the shelter when he was approximately two. The original couple who'd had him hadn't anticipated the amount of work and food a dog of his size entailed. And since it would only get worse, Wiley had found his way to the shelter. And into their home.

Sierra had moved in that same week they'd gotten together and started up her home social media company, Knight Time Social, soon after. She'd then gone off birth control and he'd knocked her up immediately, he thought with a grin. She had an assistant she'd hired and the business was growing. He was so damned proud of her.

He walked up behind her and wrapped his arms around her waist, resting his chin on her shoulder. "Hey, sweetheart."

"Hey." She turned in his arms. "Are you here to steal cookie dough?"

"Nope. I'm here to steal a kiss," he said and brushed his mouth over hers, once, twice, before diving in for a real one. He slid his tongue past her lips and devoured her mouth, tasting a hint of chocolate, making him realize she'd been sneaking cookie dough herself.

"How are you?" she asked after he'd broken the kiss, only to come up for air.

"Good. You?" Because their family would be here soon.

"Good. Pregnant."

"Good. I'll make sure we have extra chairs in the family room for— Wait, what?" he asked, her unexpected words sinking in.

"I'm pregnant. Again," she said, her eyes lit up with happiness. "Your sperm are potent, Ryder Hammond. This time you bypassed my birth control."

He was stunned. Yeah, they wanted more kids, but no, they hadn't planned for another one so soon. Not that he was complaining, he thought.

With a whoop, he picked her up and spun her around, placing her down at the same time he felt a tug on his pants.

"Daddy, up!"

Grinning at Sierra, he bent down to pick up their daughter into his arms, then spun her the same way he'd done to her mother.

She giggled, the sound going straight to his heart. "Hey, baby. You're going to be a big sister!"

"Yay!" She clapped her hands happily.

He had no idea if she even understood what he meant. Snaking out an arm, he pulled Sierra in with them, causing Wiley to give a woof, obviously annoyed at being left out.

"Are we telling the family?" he asked.

"I say we keep it to ourselves for another month or two. Unless little mouth here slips up." She kissed Jilly on the nose and she swiped at the spot with her hand.

Ryder's heart swelled with happiness. There was a time he hadn't thought he'd have this—the family, the kids, the dog, the wife, and the bigger house.

"We're going to have to talk about expanding." He'd had plans drawn up for the future, but apparently that time was now.

"Okay."

"Okay." He kissed her and put his wriggling daughter down so she could run after Wiley.

He looked around, his heart full. He woke up every day grateful and glad he'd stood up and objected at Sierra's wedding, taking off with the bride.

Nobody said he wasn't determined when he went about achieving his dreams.

* * * *

Also from 1001 Dark Nights and Carly Phillips, discover Dare to Tease, Sexy Love, and His to Protect.

* * * *

Dare to Tease by Carly Phillips
A Dare Nation Novella
Coming March 23, 2021

New York Times and *USA Today* bestselling author Carly Phillips **returns to her sexy Dare world of rich billionaire sports heroes in her new DARE NATION SERIES!**

Brianne Prescott, publicist to the biggest athletes in the world, goes up against the one man she can't resist.

About Carly Phillips

Carly Phillips gives her readers Alphalicious heroes to swoon for and romance to set your heart on fire, and she loves everything about writing romance. She married her college sweetheart and lives in Purchase, NY along with her three crazy dogs: two wheaten terriers and a mutant Havanese, who are featured on her Facebook and Instagram. She has raised two incredible daughters who put up with having a mom as a romance author. Carly is the author of over fifty romances, and is a NY Times, Wall Street Journal, and USA Today Bestseller. She loves social media and interacting with her readers. Want to keep up with Carly? Sign up for her newsletter and receive TWO FREE books at www.carlyphillips.com.

Also from Carly Phillips

The Knight Brothers
Take Me Again
Take the Bride
Take Me Down
Dare Me Tonight

Rosewood Bay
Fearless
Breathe
Freed
Dream

Bodyguard Bad Boys
Rock Me
Tempt Me
His to Protect

Dare to Love Series
Dare to Love
Dare to Desire
Dare to Touch
Dare to Hold
Dare to Rock
Dare to Take

Dare NY Series (NY Dare Cousins)
Dare to Surrender
Dare to Submit
Dare to Seduce

Billionaire Bad Boys
Going Down Easy
Going Down Hard
Going Down Fast

Going In Deep

Hot Zone Series
Hot Stuff
Hot Number
Hot Item
Hot Property

Lucky Series
Lucky Charm
Lucky Streak
Lucky Break

Discover More Carly Phillips

Sexy Love
by Carly Phillips
A Sexy Series Novella

Learning curves have never been so off-limits.

Professor Shane Warden is on the verge of getting tenure. He never thought he'd see the day, after a false accusation from a student years ago that nearly destroyed his career, and decimated his ability to trust. But the moment he walks into class and lays eyes on the seductive blonde with legs that go on forever and lips he immediately wants to kiss, he knows he's in trouble.

This time for real.

Single mom Amber Davis is finally living her dream of going back to college. In the ten years since she dropped out to have a baby--and recover from his father's death--it's been the goal that always felt just out of reach. Until now. But one look at her hot, sexy professor, and Amber is head over heels in lust. It doesn't take long before their attraction blazes out of control.

Neither of them can afford a forbidden affair.

Yet it's the one thing they are powerless to stop.

It will only take one hint of a rumor to destroy everything they've worked so hard to achieve... and in this case the rumors are true.

* * * *

His to Protect: A Bodyguard Bad Boys/Masters and Mercenaries Novella
by Carly Phillips

Talia Shaw has spent her adult life working as a scientist for a big pharmaceutical company. She's focused on saving lives, not living life. When her lab is broken into and it's clear someone is after the top secret formula she's working on, she turns to the one man she can trust. The same irresistible man she turned away years earlier because she was too young and naive to believe a sexy guy like Shane Landon could want *her*.

Shane Landon's bodyguard work for McKay-Taggart is the one thing that brings him satisfaction in his life. Relationships come in second to the job. Always. Then little brainiac Talia Shaw shows up in his backyard, frightened and on the run, and his world is turned upside down. And not just because she's found him naked in his outdoor shower, either.

With Talia's life in danger, Shane has to get her out of town and to her eccentric, hermit mentor who has the final piece of the formula she's been working on, while keeping her safe from the men who are after her. Guarding Talia's body certainly isn't any hardship, but he never expects to fall hard and fast for his best friend's little sister and the only woman who's ever really gotten under his skin.

Take Me Down

Knight Brothers Book 3
By Carly Phillips

Next from Carly Phillips in the Knight Brothers series:

Opposites not only attract, they combust!

Parker Knight was going through the motions… and then he met her.

In sweet, sexy Emily Stevens and the rundown resort she runs with her father, Parker sees the chance to reclaim the life he once lost and take care of the first woman who makes him feel … everything. He wants her in a way he's never desired a woman before and yearns to sample the treats the sexy baker has to offer.

But Emily doesn't trust charming city guys, especially one who is going to leave when his time off is over. No matter how good he makes her feel, in bed or out.

Parker has his hands full, not only with a wary Emily but with someone who doesn't want the lodge to succeed, and if things keep getting worse, not even a Knight can save her.

Sign up for the 1001 Dark Nights Newsletter
and be entered to win a Tiffany Key necklace.

There's a contest every month!

Go to 1001DarkNights.com to subscribe.

As a bonus, all subscribers can download FIVE FREE exclusive books!

Discover 1001 Dark Nights Collection Seven

THE BISHOP by Skye Warren
A Tanglewood Novella

TAKEN WITH YOU by Carrie Ann Ryan
A Fractured Connections Novella

DRAGON LOST by Donna Grant
A Dark Kings Novella

SEXY LOVE by Carly Phillips
A Sexy Series Novella

PROVOKE by Rachel Van Dyken
A Seaside Pictures Novella

RAFE by Sawyer Bennett
An Arizona Vengeance Novella

THE NAUGHTY PRINCESS by Claire Contreras
A Sexy Royals Novella

THE GRAVEYARD SHIFT by Darynda Jones
A Charley Davidson Novella

CHARMED by Lexi Blake
A Masters and Mercenaries Novella

SACRIFICE OF DARKNESS by Alexandra Ivy
A Guardians of Eternity Novella

THE QUEEN by Jen Armentrout
A Wicked Novella

BEGIN AGAIN by Jennifer Probst
A Stay Novella

VIXEN by Rebecca Zanetti
A Dark Protectors/Rebels Novella

SLASH by Laurelin Paige
A Slay Series Novella

THE DEAD HEAT OF SUMMER by Heather Graham
A Krewe of Hunters Novella

WILD FIRE by Kristen Ashley
A Chaos Novella

MORE THAN PROTECT YOU by Shayla Black
A More Than Words Novella

LOVE SONG by Kylie Scott
A Stage Dive Novella

CHERISH ME by J. Kenner
A Stark Ever After Novella

SHINE WITH ME by Kristen Proby
A With Me in Seattle Novella

And new from Blue Box Press:

TEASE ME by J. Kenner
A Stark International Novel

FROM BLOOD AND ASH by Jennifer L. Armentrout
A Blood and Ash Novel

QUEEN MOVE by Kennedy Ryan

THE HOUSE OF LONG AGO by Steve Berry and MJ Rose
A Cassiopeia Vitt Adventure

THE BUTTERFLY ROOM by Lucinda Riley

A KINGDOM OF FLESH AND FIRE by Jennifer L. Armentrout
A Blood and Ash Novel

Discover 1001 Dark Nights

COLLECTION ONE
FOREVER WICKED by Shayla Black
CRIMSON TWILIGHT by Heather Graham
CAPTURED IN SURRENDER by Liliana Hart
SILENT BITE: A SCANGUARDS WEDDING by Tina Folsom
DUNGEON GAMES by Lexi Blake
AZAGOTH by Larissa Ione
NEED YOU NOW by Lisa Renee Jones
SHOW ME, BABY by Cherise Sinclair
ROPED IN by Lorelei James
TEMPTED BY MIDNIGHT by Lara Adrian
THE FLAME by Christopher Rice
CARESS OF DARKNESS by Julie Kenner

COLLECTION TWO
WICKED WOLF by Carrie Ann Ryan
WHEN IRISH EYES ARE HAUNTING by Heather Graham
EASY WITH YOU by Kristen Proby
MASTER OF FREEDOM by Cherise Sinclair
CARESS OF PLEASURE by Julie Kenner
ADORED by Lexi Blake
HADES by Larissa Ione
RAVAGED by Elisabeth Naughton
DREAM OF YOU by Jennifer L. Armentrout
STRIPPED DOWN by Lorelei James
RAGE/KILLIAN by Alexandra Ivy/Laura Wright
DRAGON KING by Donna Grant
PURE WICKED by Shayla Black
HARD AS STEEL by Laura Kaye
STROKE OF MIDNIGHT by Lara Adrian
ALL HALLOWS EVE by Heather Graham
KISS THE FLAME by Christopher Rice
DARING HER LOVE by Melissa Foster
TEASED by Rebecca Zanetti
THE PROMISE OF SURRENDER by Liliana Hart

COLLECTION THREE
HIDDEN INK by Carrie Ann Ryan
BLOOD ON THE BAYOU by Heather Graham
SEARCHING FOR MINE by Jennifer Probst
DANCE OF DESIRE by Christopher Rice
ROUGH RHYTHM by Tessa Bailey
DEVOTED by Lexi Blake
Z by Larissa Ione
FALLING UNDER YOU by Laurelin Paige
EASY FOR KEEPS by Kristen Proby
UNCHAINED by Elisabeth Naughton
HARD TO SERVE by Laura Kaye
DRAGON FEVER by Donna Grant
KAYDEN/SIMON by Alexandra Ivy/Laura Wright
STRUNG UP by Lorelei James
MIDNIGHT UNTAMED by Lara Adrian
TRICKED by Rebecca Zanetti
DIRTY WICKED by Shayla Black
THE ONLY ONE by Lauren Blakely
SWEET SURRENDER by Liliana Hart

COLLECTION FOUR
ROCK CHICK REAWAKENING by Kristen Ashley
ADORING INK by Carrie Ann Ryan
SWEET RIVALRY by K. Bromberg
SHADE'S LADY by Joanna Wylde
RAZR by Larissa Ione
ARRANGED by Lexi Blake
TANGLED by Rebecca Zanetti
HOLD ME by J. Kenner
SOMEHOW, SOME WAY by Jennifer Probst
TOO CLOSE TO CALL by Tessa Bailey
HUNTED by Elisabeth Naughton
EYES ON YOU by Laura Kaye
BLADE by Alexandra Ivy/Laura Wright
DRAGON BURN by Donna Grant
TRIPPED OUT by Lorelei James
STUD FINDER by Lauren Blakely
MIDNIGHT UNLEASHED by Lara Adrian

HALLOW BE THE HAUNT by Heather Graham
DIRTY FILTHY FIX by Laurelin Paige
THE BED MATE by Kendall Ryan
NIGHT GAMES by CD Reiss
NO RESERVATIONS by Kristen Proby
DAWN OF SURRENDER by Liliana Hart

COLLECTION FIVE
BLAZE ERUPTING by Rebecca Zanetti
ROUGH RIDE by Kristen Ashley
HAWKYN by Larissa Ione
RIDE DIRTY by Laura Kaye
ROME'S CHANCE by Joanna Wylde
THE MARRIAGE ARRANGEMENT by Jennifer Probst
SURRENDER by Elisabeth Naughton
INKED NIGHTS by Carrie Ann Ryan
ENVY by Rachel Van Dyken
PROTECTED by Lexi Blake
THE PRINCE by Jennifer L. Armentrout
PLEASE ME by J. Kenner
WOUND TIGHT by Lorelei James
STRONG by Kylie Scott
DRAGON NIGHT by Donna Grant
TEMPTING BROOKE by Kristen Proby
HAUNTED BE THE HOLIDAYS by Heather Graham
CONTROL by K. Bromberg
HUNKY HEARTBREAKER by Kendall Ryan
THE DARKEST CAPTIVE by Gena Showalter

COLLECTION SIX
DRAGON CLAIMED by Donna Grant
ASHES TO INK by Carrie Ann Ryan
ENSNARED by Elisabeth Naughton
EVERMORE by Corinne Michaels
VENGEANCE by Rebecca Zanetti
ELI'S TRIUMPH by Joanna Wylde
CIPHER by Larissa Ione
RESCUING MACIE by Susan Stoker
ENCHANTED by Lexi Blake

TAKE THE BRIDE by Carly Phillips
INDULGE ME by J. Kenner
THE KING by Jennifer L. Armentrout
QUIET MAN by Kristen Ashley
ABANDON by Rachel Van Dyken
THE OPEN DOOR by Laurelin Paige
CLOSER by Kylie Scott
SOMETHING JUST LIKE THIS by Jennifer Probst
BLOOD NIGHT by Heather Graham
TWIST OF FATE by Jill Shalvis
MORE THAN PLEASURE YOU by Shayla Black
WONDER WITH ME by Kristen Proby
THE DARKEST ASSASSIN by Gena Showalter

Discover Blue Box Press

TAME ME by J. Kenner
TEMPT ME by J. Kenner
DAMIEN by J. Kenner
TEASE ME by J. Kenner
REAPER by Larissa Ione
THE SURRENDER GATE by Christopher Rice
SERVICING THE TARGET by Cherise Sinclair

On behalf of 1001 Dark Nights,

Liz Berry, M.J. Rose, and Jillian Stein would like to thank ~

Steve Berry
Doug Scofield
Benjamin Stein
Kim Guidroz
Social Butterfly PR
Ashley Wells
Asha Hossain
Chris Graham
Chelle Olson
Kasi Alexander
Jessica Johns
Dylan Stockton
Richard Blake
and Simon Lipskar

CPSIA information can be obtained
at www.ICGtesting.com
Printed in the USA
LVHW091627020321
680381LV00001B/36